OF FRICTION

OF FRICTION

ALTERED EARTH SERIES
BOOK 1

S.J. LEE

PEW BOOKS

Of Friction is a work of fiction. Names, characters, places, and incidents are products of the author's imagination or are used fictitiously and are not to be construed as real. Any resemblance to actual events, locales, organizations, or persons, living or dead, is entirely coincidental.

OF FRICTION

Copyright © 2024 by S.J. Lee
Excerpt from *Of Abrasion* by S.J. Lee copyright © 2024 by S.J. Lee

All rights reserved.

This book contains an excerpt from the forthcoming book *Of Abrasion* by S.J. Lee. This excerpt has been set for this edition only and may not reflect the final content of the forthcoming edition.

Library of Congress Cataloging-in-Publication Data is available.

ISBN (paperback) 979-8-9892965-0-7
ISBN (ebook) 979-8-9892965-1-4

No part of this publication may be reproduced, stored or transmitted in any form or by any means, electronic, mechanical, photocopying, recording, scanning, or otherwise without written permission from the publisher. It is illegal to copy this book, post it to a website, or distribute it by any other means without permission.

Cover design by Jason Arias

*For me, mainly—
but also for those who are trying to figure out who they are,
no matter their chapter in life.*

CONTENTS

Preface	ix
The World	1
Prologue	5
PART I	
Mass	7
PART II	
Acceleration	119
PART III	
Force	289
Acknowledgments	375
Of Abrasion	379
Glossary	383
About the Author	387

PREFACE

I don't normally read the front matter of books. They've always just been that part—filler and obstacles to the actual content. So, if you're actually reading this now...I admire you because I know past-me would've flipped right by.

As said on the dedication page, this book is mainly for me. To explain that, I have to go to the beginning. But the beginning of what? The writing process or this book's universe? Let's start loosely with this...

I'm a fiction reader, mostly science fiction, which says something about myself, I guess. Growing up, when I wasn't reading or going about the usual motions, I was daydreaming. I think I was eleven or twelve years old when I started escaping into my own stories. Middle school was an awkward time, if not the *most* awkward. I built scenes, worlds, and characters in my head while I played songs on repeat on an old CD player that took two AA batteries. Long road trips with the family? Six people, sometimes more, squeezed into a minivan? No problem. I'd look out the window and immerse myself in weird worlds full of...angst. So much angst. Why, teenage me?

I created at least three different stories throughout the

years. *This* book's universe took root in college (that's more than a decade ago—terrifying). It started with a band of characters, which I keep and touch upon in the series, but as time and experiences shaped me, I built on what was originally a side character. Like my previous stories, I created scenes I'd play over and over in my head like a TV show when I was bored, when I couldn't sleep, or whenever I wanted to feel that lurch in my gut. Oh, angst. I don't know why I'm this way. Stop judging me.

So, after all this time, how did the writing process even start? Mind you, I don't really consider myself a writer. Even now after struggling through *this*, it's still difficult to accept the title (I love imposter syndrome and self-doubt). Sure, I wrote a bunch of stuff in grade school—short stories, poetry, comics, etc., but then I traded it for sports and other hobbies. I've tried recording this story several times before, but I was never happy with what I produced, and most of it was abandoned or ended up in the trash. Writing is hard. Writing sucks. Two out of ten: do not recommend. For those authors and writers out there who love doing this and *keep* at it, I have nothing but respect for your grit and masochism.

Let's just say this book was a culmination of everything. Coming back from a year-long assignment in Iraq and dealing with the culture shock and complete change of pace was a big factor. I associated burnout with productivity and then I hit a "third-life"[1] crisis of "what the hell am I doing?" I didn't want to retire and look back, thinking my job—which is pretty darn cool—was all I had to be proud of. It's a job. A part of me. But not necessarily the other way around. I wanted something tangible. Something to hold in my hand that I created and say, "Look. I did this."

The actual trigger for starting this was a godawful web series. Cringe central. The writing was absolutely terrible, but I finished the entire series. The damn movie, too. And maybe one or two fanfics. I'm too embarrassed to even say which web series—I'm that annoyed I enjoyed it. But that cringe-binge was the catalyst.

I can write better than this.

With a "fuck it" attitude, I vomited out a screenplay in nine days. It wasn't any good; I had never written a script before. And the last two scenes were the only parts I actually had in my head to start. Turns out that story bouncing around for years? That was mostly angst. Little did I know, I had to create an actual plot and devices. Frankly, most scenes playing in my head for the last fifteen-plus years are in the second book (**angst**), and I realized I had to do this part first to get there. Funny. More writing.

As I started revising the screenplay, I wasn't happy with the amount of story I could control. A movie or show becomes a movie or show, not only from the script, but through the actors, the direction, the production. And that...that was too much work.

So, here's the novel instead.

I hope you enjoy my pain. But even if you don't, that's okay[2]. Because after everything, this was really for me—an arduous and cathartic process to materialize something that has only been in my head until now.

That said, I strongly encourage you to find that "something" and do it, too. Just for yourself. Even if it drives you nuts, like this did me. Who knows, this novel might be your catalyst to say fuck it, *I can do better than this.*

---

1. I was told I can't have a mid-life crisis at age thirty-five, to which I responded, what if I die at seventy? The probability is there, but "third-life" is my compromise.
2. I lied. I seek and want approval just like every other weirdo in this world.

OF FRICTION

THE WORLD
AS IT IS

SCIENCE WAS RIGHT.

All the red flags were there, ignored by governments, brushed off by corporations, disregarded by billionaires whose philanthropic "save our green planet" efforts were a show, scams that their overpaid PR teams said would trend well, or help with taxes. When taxes still mattered.

But science was right, and the earth's temperature rose. Fires extinguished swaths of forests, entire species jetted past "endangered" to "extinct." Crops failed. Ice melted. All of it. Sea levels surged and drowned whatever remained of cities after the wars. Husks of skyscrapers served as tombstones, monuments to a taken-for-granted point in the timeline.

The average human could go about their normal life at an internal temperature of 98-degrees Fahrenheit (give or take). However, life was overwhelmingly *not* normal, and it wouldn't wait for the frail human body to adapt. There was really only so much a person could do.

By the time the same governments and greedy bastards realized that they also lived on the same green, now yellowing planet, it was too late for any actual reversal. So, ironically, they turned to science.

At first, that science was a potential gateway to life in the stars. But after so many failures, they only succeeded in creating an expedited armor of space debris which made it too dangerous—near impossible—to find a life for themselves on a nice, vacation home planet.

So, they turned to another science. "Make us better, help us survive," or something like it. The right amount of money and selfishness bought substantial advances in technologies and genetic engineering by the end of their suffocating lives. And this science, now in the hands of unethical old men, introduced a more resilient, adaptable, and evolved being.

The altered human race came into existence. These *Altered* could survive in this blue and tan world easily. It was a win for the test-tube babies, the new line of advanced people. Good for them.

Not so good for the governments, the rich dicks, and remaining humankind. No, the original humans were still stuck with their 98-degree (give or take) meat sacks. It was karma, except with extra-large "fuck yous" to everyone else who was still alive.

The bad news became worse news when the creations opined that humans, as they stood, were obsolete. The Altered outgrew their makers, shutting them out like a bonus middle finger to the remaining hominids.

The Altered were just *better*. And they knew it.

So the humans stayed human, and the Altered multiplied and prospered. Here began the new world where humans found themselves the minority, struggling yet surviving in a world their ancestors simultaneously destroyed and created.

On the bright side, humans finally came together (mostly), setting aside petty nationalism, race, religion, and other societal squabbles (mostly). A bigger, more accepted "us versus them" was left dangling, something to cling onto. Even as the earth began its own recovery over the years and decades, opposing sides and players would continue to rub against each other, waiting to see who would catch fire first.

PROLOGUE

SHE CALLED *after him as worry filled her chest. Her lungs had started to strain, and each beat of her heart pounded in her ears, echoing the question and individual words one after another.*

Where.

Was.

He.

She burst through crowded alley after alley, searching. He had been just in front of her. How did she lose him?

A shadow darted ahead.

There.

Dread filled her dry throat. It wasn't him. The figure was too small, but she recognized it—the mark, the target. But how?

She looked around the street, scanning for her brother. When she saw him only a minute before, he'd been trailing right behind the mark and gaining ground fast. She had lost them in the maze of narrow and winding alleys, but he would have caught up by now, called it in.

So why was their target there in front of her? Alone.

Where was he?

She pushed forward and picked up her feet, dodging people and obstacles in her way. She tapped her comm device and panted out her location. The others would catch up—her brother would catch up, wherever he was.

She kept her eyes drilled into the back of that dirty tunic and crashed through a busy intersection, into stalls and racks of textiles. Shrieks lifted and scattered as she barreled through.

Get out of the way!

She was so close.

The figure took a sharp turn into an alley, and she followed.

Dead end.

It was a lucky break for her.

Unlucky for the target. It was cornered. Trapped.

She heard a teammate, and then another behind her, their own footsteps slowing. Their short breaths were loud. Was he there with them? She resisted turning around to check, afraid the target would somehow vanish if she looked away.

Little eyes glinted out of the obscured shadows. Blinked. It was a young girl, not even a woman yet. A sliver of sunlight confirmed the mark on her neck, emblazoned into her skin.

A light flickered underneath the thin fabric on the girl's chest.

Her breath seized, and her chest tightened. She rocked back.

Get out.

Get out now.

And then she was backpedaling, turning, and running for her life. She searched for his familiar face as she tried to put enough distance between herself and the target. She kept running as she heard the hideous roar and the warm, heavy pressure nip behind her.

Where was he?

PART 1

MASS

1

THE MARINE

WHEN SAM RYAN WOKE UP, she was still upset.

Her dismantled rifle lay in front of her on the table, its individual pieces set out in a row like a work of carefully curated museum art. It was the second time she had stripped the weapon and brushed, oiled, and polished the parts inside and out with a ritualistic fervor. She must have fallen asleep before she could reassemble it.

Craning her neck from one side to the other, Sam stretched out her tight muscles. Something fell off her shoulders. A light blanket from the galley. She glared at the dark fabric where it hung partially over the cargo bay bench, threatening to cascade onto the riveted floor. A quick scan of her surroundings assured her she was alone. Her only company was the stacked boxes labeled "UMF" around her.

The United Military Federation. Sam was on her third contract with UMF, ten years in, coming on eleven. Her contract end date wasn't for another ninety-seven days, but she had submitted the renewal request after the last mission. It was an easy decision. Command would automatically approve it when her window came up in a week; she had no doubt about it. There would be no objections. Why would there be? She was good at what she did, one cog of a reputable recon duo. Her half-brother, Scott "Mute" Reckert, was the other half. No pun intended.

Her brother.

Sam was angry at her brother. He was willing to throw it all away. Worse. He was *going* to throw it all away.

She thought it was a joke at first. His sarcasm at its best. Scott was one of the most decorated marines of their outpost. He could have switched contracts and started a career track as an officer if he wanted. Not that he wanted it—both of them preferred to do the actual job. This job, together.

Her brother had over seventeen years on five contracts. If he completed two more, Command would provide him an acre of his own pensioned land. It was a generous plot, enough for a dwelling and a farm, and it'd be within a reasonable distance from Ursus, a spot outside Gould, the boring settlement he had grown up in. He'd be well-off at forty years old—retired from a steady career, able to live however he saw fit with his acre and pension. He wouldn't be wealthy like the upper class with their large flats in the nicer part of town, but he'd be comfortable.

Sam had seen his many drawings of a two-story house, a small farm, and a mundane life. They were designs of a future in the form of mindless doodles in the dirt while on missions, and on his tablet at his compound apartment while off missions.

His low, raspy words echoed in her head. "I'm out, Sammy."

I'm out.

She was confused. She didn't understand. They were a team. Over six years together, blood and sweat, thick and thin, covering each other and their unit. They had always been together. Twenty-three years she had been glued to his hip. She had been his shadow until one day, after years of hard work and practice, she was her own independent equal. Twenty-three years he had practically raised her, been her guardian, her brother, her best friend, her mentor.

It was obviously not going to be forever, but their time in UMF wasn't supposed to end this way. Or this soon. Sam figured they'd have at least six more years together before she had to wrap her mind around being on her own. She searched back in her memories for any indication, any warning signs she had missed. None. No, only just an hour before, when he cautiously took a seat next to her in the ship's frigid galley.

As his hands wrung and wrestled themselves in his lap, her concern grew. When he motioned, THIS IS MY LAST MISSION, a stone sunk in her gut. When he talked, she flinched, stunned.

Sam waited for the laugh, the punchline, but it never came. The realization set in. He wasn't joking, and she had already missed a lot of the quiet ambush spun by his hands. Her eyes watched his fingers twist and turn as they seemed to stutter their own speech, her brain not translating, still in shock. By the time she came to her senses, he said those two damning words.

I'm out.

I'm out.

I'm out.

It was the only sign and declaration just before his—*their* last mission together.

Of course, she took it personally.

Sam had sat up straight and asked him why.

He hesitated. Time slipped as his mouth and hands went still.

Sam demanded a reason, any reason. Something to help with her confusion.

But he closed her out.

She always told him everything. She thought he did, too. But not this. Apparently, now he kept secrets. Did she do something? Did he not trust her? Or worse, did he not respect her enough to look her in the eye and tell her why he was leaving the military? Leaving her?

Sam stormed out of the room before she lost her composure any further. He didn't even try to stop her. She spent the rest of the trip in the cargo hold, lividly working on her carbine as if she could transfer the cleaning motions to her own head, erasing "I'm out, I'm out, I'm out" like it was unwanted carbon that had built up in the weapon's chamber. Not that there had been anything to clean. She had already maintained her trusty rifle before the trip. But it was her thing. The familiar motions wrapped around her like a security blanket.

She was less, but still incensed when the announcement came over the ship intercom. *Thirty minutes to dock.* She had thirty minutes to push her feelings into a box and shove it to the back of her mind.

Sam Ryan was a marine—hell, a Special Operations Group marine—and a damn good one. The mission came first. She would deal with this betrayal later.

The mission always came first.

$$\oplus$$

The fast transport was like a dragonfly, skimming across the water's surface. As the ship slowed, nearing the expansive port of the sprawling city, it glided past the commercial freighters within the busy harbor into a gated section filled with similarly armored watercraft. A haggard metal sign with the faded words "RESTRICTED AREA: Authorized Personnel Only" clanged against the post from which it hung. As the propulsion system powered down with an elongated whisper, a metallic ramp extended from the ship's side and folded down, latching onto the docking platform.

Sam walked down onto the dock carrying a large assault pack and loose armor. A thin metallic cuff with a display rested snug against the lightly tanned skin of her left wrist. With her right hand, she adjusted the strap of a polished, short-barreled rifle slung over her shoulder. Her eye caught the corner of dark ink on the inside of her forearm: a tattooed circle around a white, fleshy scar line, splitting the shape down the middle.

A warm but refreshing breeze, a mix of ocean brine and the flat smells of civilization, lifted Sam's spirit. The morning sun embraced her face, and she shut her eyes, letting herself fold into the moment. Another draft swayed light blonde locks into her face despite the bun. Her hair disrupted the visor's hololens, and she secured the stray locks behind an ear. Her fingers brushed the edge of the device hooked around the back of her head, one tip extending to her left temporal bone and the other wrapping behind her ear, peeking out to the hinge of her jaw.

Sam slowly opened her eyes and squinted into the morning light, taking in the chattering dockhands, the large harbor, and beyond it, the glossy black of the ocean stretching to the thin horizon. She rolled her shoulders and neck to increase blood flow to her taut muscles. Overnight travel was always cramped, never relaxing enough for actual rest. The last couple of hours on this specific one hadn't helped.

Her stomach twisted and gurgled. Their last full meal had been before she and her brother boarded the ship. She had avoided the nutrition bars in the kitchen, no desire to chew through their dry texture. Coffee was also available on board, but its color reminded her of dehydrated piss. She drank what she could tolerate, solely as a languishing grasp at energy she knew she'd need for the day ahead. She should have slept more but couldn't, not after...

Behind her, a uniformed man with short golden-blond hair walked out of the cargo hold. His boots were heavy, each step reverberating against the ramp, each a grating blow to Sam's ears. Scott stopped briefly at the edge as if to say something.

In the long second that ensued, a debate swung in Sam's mind of whether or not to turn around, confront him, and demand answers. But in the end, paralysis chose for her. She ignored him. Her jaw clenched in anticipation of another slurry of words and motions to make her day worse.

But there was nothing.

He moved past her to the monotonous buildings at the end of the dock. The familiar scent of his apartment's indoor garden floated behind him like a specter.

Sam watched as her brother's knuckles whitened around the handle of his long rifle bag as if he was wringing the life from it. She scoffed at his back. *Good. Suffer.*

Her left eye twitched. She didn't mean it. Not really. They hadn't talked or looked at each other since their last conversation. Her chest tightened with irritation and guilt as she watched him amble away.

They were siblings. They had many disagreements before, but this one vexed Sam. She wasn't used to feeling this way, especially toward him. All their past arguments were trivial—many of them brought about by hunger or exhaustion—and quickly resolved.

She had a seed of doubt. Perhaps she had been too rash in her initial reaction. Perhaps she had missed something he had said before. It all came crashing down now.

She was sure about one thing—*she* was tired.

Sam tried to center herself, raising her left hand to pinch the bridge of her nose. She filled her lungs with the port air, which now had a stronger hint of metal and trash—something she hadn't detected before. She pushed out a slow, deep exhale, and the detached armor in her hand settled limply against her rig.

Sam nodded a greeting to a group of dock workers as they passed by, staring at her. She moved her hand from her face and softly tapped the tech behind her ear. The hololens disappeared, and she adjusted her effects as she hurried to catch up to her brother.

"You're worse when you're hungry," she said. Sam wasn't sure who she meant it for, her brother or herself. If Scott heard her, he didn't show it.

When she fell in step with him, they had passed through the military's port administration building in sustained silence. She stayed within an arm's reach and matched his casual pace despite his longer stride. An unsaid, unfamiliar distance hovered between them despite their proximity. But together, they moved forward into a compound of gray buildings.

This was the home of UMF Command, the military's center of operations, its pulsing human brain. Just past it, carved into the hills facing the ocean, the largest human population center on the recovering planet was an explosion of colors and structures, a clashing contrast to its stoic, gray neighbor. It was Station City, just outside UMF headquarters.

⏀

0816

The numbers illuminated on Sam's wrist display. She set her hand back down on the table with a light clink from the cuff as it tapped the metal surface—the fourth time she had checked her commcuff since sitting down. Her leg bounced like an agitated spring, ready to uncoil and launch. The breakfast surge had passed, and the main DFAC, the military's dining facility, was partially occupied, gradually emptying like a lazy falling tide. Their table in the back corner provided a reticent refuge and vantage point.

Across from her, Scott shoveled food into his mouth. His brows furrowed as he focused on satiating the hunger that came with a lengthy journey. Ursus Outpost was a long ride from the north in the expeditionary fast transport, and they had left at the teetering hour where late night met early morning. A fleck of paste sat on his unshaven jaw, and Sam resisted the urge to wipe it off with the thin excuse of a napkin in front of her.

She picked at her food. It was standard UMF pulp, this time with too little seasoning. In any other routine situation, she would have thought about how the military could still mess up basic culinary fundamentals when an abundance of salt was readily available, especially with water filtration farms from Ursus to Station City working at full capacity. She set her utensil down. The five large spoonfuls she had hoisted into her mouth had quelled her body's rumblings. That would suffice for now.

Really, she was more interested in ensuring they weren't late for their first meeting with their new, temporary team. It was her first assignment away from Ursus's area of responsibility, and she wanted to make a good impression. She was also admittedly distracted by the newness of everything around her. Though the uniforms and the DFAC's bustling operation were all familiar thanks to the standardized processes of UMF, it *was* still a new place for her. She had never been to Station City. Technically, she wasn't in the city but rather UMF Station, its own campus outside the proper metropolitan limits. It didn't matter. She hadn't been here before. Sam only traveled where the outpost or Command sent her, and those missions were often limited to the north and bordering areas where Altered and humans clashed.

Resisting the urge to look again at her commcuff, Sam turned her attention to the buzz of scattered conversations. She concentrated discreetly on a discussion from a neighboring table.

"—was chatting with Luna. She said her company is gonna cover City Center with District's SecTeam. Two-week detail 'til the summit is over."

"Damn. Lucky. We know where we're going yet?"

"Nah. Hope we get a good one. I wanna see the Royals."

"I want to see a praetorian!"

One marine scoffed. "Y'all are idiots. Fuck the Royals. Fuck the alties. It's all a sham."

"Still. Biggest thing that's happened in years."

"No way, don't care. You really think things gonna change? Plus, it's gonna fuck with my commute, man."

Someone laughed.

"Your own fault for…"

Sam tuned out the conversation. She had seen the trending posts on the network about the supposed talks with the Altered governing body: the Sovereign and his Royal Court. It was another effort for official peace, and Sam was skeptical. Humans and Altered had been in a tense standstill well before she had taken her first breath. During her time with the military, there had been no blatant moves between the two races, but that hadn't stopped UMF's involvement in counterterrorism on both sides. Or getting involved with human-human and human-Altered civil squabbles that local SecTeams couldn't handle. UMF was the only overarching force protecting all humankind, with little to no support from the multiple settlements that continued to attempt their independence from Station City's republic. Humans had a habit of violence and selfish actions, often to their own detriment.

Sam thought herself apathetic, or at least impartial, to the governing structures of her own kind. Her outpost, Ursus, and many nearby northern settlements aligned with Command and Station City. Her brother's hometown, Gould, had its council, which served the settlement's general matters. Not that she cared much. She lived and spent all her time at the outpost. She had little interest in politics and would only believe it—official peace between humans and Altered—when she saw it.

Sam turned her observation to the marines in their gray-colored uniforms, a lighter variation than the one she wore herself. Something was different with the military folk here; she couldn't quite put a solid finger on it. They all worked under the same core leadership, but the Station service people had a more…city feel. Though Sam had ensured her shirt and pants were tidy and as wrinkle-free as possible, the surrounding uniforms were just more pristine. She compared the others' neat hairstyles to her updo and was grateful she had adjusted her bun into a tighter knot high on the back of her head. Somehow, Station marines looked trendier. Stylish. Tight. It had to be a headquarters thing. Sticks up their asses.

She shook the quick judgment out of her head.

They were marines. Just like her.

Sam Ryan was a marine. She'd be a marine until the day she died. She knew nothing else, nor did she care much about anything else.

Despite her youth, she had been longer in the corps than most. Sam didn't see herself retiring after the usual seven contracts, even after a generous acre of land. What would she even do with a plot of property? Despite the inconsistent seasoning of food, despite the tedious bureaucracy, annual training refreshers, and the occasional hiccups in operations, she liked her job. She liked her life. UMF was where everything made sense to her. It was where she belonged.

She also had nowhere else to go. Her mother abandoned her as a newborn, and she didn't remember her father—he died when she was young, too young to remember a burglary gone wrong. Junkies. She despised them.

A year or so after she was left on the doorstep, her father had registered her as Ryan when the census people showed up. Not Ryan Reckert, like her brother. Just Ryan. She wasn't sure *why* Ryan. Maybe her father had been disappointed she wasn't another son and went with a middle-ground name. Or worse, her father hadn't cared at all.

Scott said little about him, even when she was younger. She learned not to ask after the first outburst, a rare sight for her quiet half-brother. Scott, eleven years old when she dropped into his life, had named her Sam, and called her Sammy when he was feeling particular.

Her brother had turned to the marines at sixteen, two years into university, two years shy of graduation and a future beyond the military. Sam never asked why. It was another unspoken topic she learned to leave alone. It didn't matter, because she was proud of him. He was a great marine, a recon specialist with a steady and consistent demeanor. He was the perfect fighter against all forms of opponents, be it Altered or human radical.

When her brother and his friends joined SOG, Special Operations Group, she aspired along with them. At sixteen, she earned her own diamond tab and joined them. For seven years, he was one arm; she was the other.

And now he was leaving her.

Sam stiffened, and her mouth pinched. She internally cursed her circuitous brain. She had been doing so well in distracting herself. Her leg bounced harder as she willed her focus back onto the marines in the dining room.

What was left of the breakfast crowd paid little attention to the duo in their dark charcoal uniforms, although she spotted a handful of marines glancing at their table from afar. Though she couldn't hear it, she recognized the words from the movement of their lips. Her callsign. Her brother's.

She fixed her shirt collar and thumbed the top point of the matte diamond pin. Then, Sam consciously stilled her leg and replaced it with the familiar and comforting scratch of her index fingernail on the right side of her thumb. It was a bad habit for as long as she could remember, but it helped calm her nerves.

She made a note to change into a lighter outfit later. Sam didn't enjoy sticking out, an occupational mentality already proving difficult seated across from the only other light blond in the room. It was made worse by also being the only two in the room to sport the latest visor, the light and sleek tech around their heads. Other marines had older, clunkier versions hooked over their ears or hanging off their necks. She could only do so much to fit in. It was a constant struggle.

A loud clatter startled Sam out of her thoughts. Scott's utensil rattled against his empty tray where he had dropped it.

She narrowed her eyes, and her upper lip curled. "Feel better now?"

The first words she had said directly to him in the last hours slipped out with biting venom. So much for putting emotions aside. Guilt punched her chest.

Scott mirrored her spite, mocking her, but an unsubtle, affable smirk followed behind. He brushed his short hair with a quick hand and leaned back into the stiff chair, arms stretching up and behind him. He stifled a yawn, and Sam resisted the contagious action.

She turned her wrist. The fifth time since they sat down.

0819

Her leg stuttered up and down. "What time do we need to be at Command again?" The words came out strained, but it was an attempt at normalcy.

Scott shrugged and returned Sam's irate stare.

She raised her hands to her chest, pressed each thumb and pointer finger's pads together, and flicked them out. USELESS.

He shrugged again and grinned.

She never understood how Scott could be so relaxed before operations. Never mind how okay he seemed with the current state of their relationship. Sam had never felt this distant from her brother.

A corner of anger slipped, aimed at him. "You're the worst," she grumbled and returned her gaze to the room, desperately trying to reel in her emotions.

Her brother grinned. He pointed at her, crossed his arms lazily in an "x" across his chest, and tapped his sternum with his finger. YOU LOVE ME.

She sneered with a pointed side-eye and snapped back, "Love is a strong word."

Scott recoiled, and Sam felt another sharp pull of regret as his face fell, playfulness gone.

Dammit.

She forced a small snort to backtrack. "I deal with you? I tolerate you?" she said. "Those might fit better."

Scott applied a stiff smile and folded his arms. He gnawed at his bottom lip and played with a thin chain around his neck as they sat in silence.

Time stretched and billowed, and Sam fought the urge to check her cuff display. This wasn't how she wanted to start their day, especially her first time in headquarters. It was supposed to be exciting. Fun. Happy. She definitely wasn't happy.

A deep voice shattered the bloated pause. A welcome rescue and interruption.

"Hello, Golden Twins."

A terrible rescue and interruption.

Sam and Scott turned to the tall, dark-haired man who had approached their table. He wore similar gray uniform pants like the other Station marines, but a fitted, black T-shirt hugged his torso instead of the usual button-up. Over his right breast, a black diamond—almost like a spearhead—was printed, barely visible. It was the same shape on the recon duo's collars, the unremarkable insignia of UMF's Special Operations Group.

The siblings looked at him. Frankly, it wasn't the first time they had heard this nickname. They were used to the slew of monikers, labels, and nicknames that humans, bored or amused, gravitated toward. Their physical appearance was no help for the lengthy list. Such was the life of two natural blonds in a world of predominantly mixed ethnicities. Their father was of the old blood, a small pocket of resistant people who didn't believe in the future's diverse melting pot. Petty racism was a cockroach, unkillable even in climate change and a fast-adjusting world.

The man winced, his face scrunched and wrinkled. "I am so sorry," he said. "That...was a description I was given by a *bad* source." He cursed something unknown, then held his hand out between the siblings. His face split into a grin, desperate to start anew. "I'm Yuri Gregov with Razor-Echo. You can call me Gregov. Greg. Greggo. Or Yuri. Most just call me Yuri."

Play nice. No judgments. Yet.

Sam gave him a tightlipped smile of acknowledgment and

took his hand. She'd stick with "Gregov." First names were too casual, too intimate.

She didn't know how, but Gregov's smile grew wider, and his large nose crinkled at the intersection of his heavy brows. "My lead sent me to meet you. Figured I might catch you both here after your travels. It's a long way from Ursus." He still clutched her hand, shaking it mindlessly.

She really wanted it back.

"Valkyrie," Sam offered. Having reached her limit, she pulled her hand free. She glanced at her brother, and his gray-blue eyes twinkled back at her.

Asshole.

Scott wiped his hands together, then leaned over the table. Sam caught a glimpse of the smooth, pink scar on his palm before Gregov's large hand enveloped it. Scott firmly shook with one pump and released his grip, pulling back into his seat.

Dick.

"That's Mute," Sam said instead.

Gregov looked between the two, happy as could be. "Good to meet you both." He then motioned to the plates. "Need more time?"

Sam looked down at her unfinished tray. The white blob was a blemish against the silver color. She winced. *Wasteful.* "Oh. No, we're ready to go," she said.

Gregov clicked his tongue and gave them an enthusiastic thumbs-up. The siblings picked up their trays and followed him to the facility exit across the room. He glanced over his shoulder. "Sorry to rush you. Our timetable seems to have moved up."

"No worries," Sam said politely. She found herself irked by the Station marine's chipper personality, though she knew she had no reason to be. *She* was off. But she breathed a little better when Gregov left them at the cleaning station and moved to the exit.

Out of earshot, she leaned back to her brother. "Twins? Is that still going around?"

Scott harrumphed.

"Come on. Do I actually look like you? There's no way I look like you." She turned and regarded his face intently to reassure herself. Sure, they shared a father, but they also had other genetic sources. Aside from their same hair color, maybe, just maybe, they had a similar nose and cheekbones. But that was it. She found another set of dark rings underneath his eyes that hadn't been there before. He looked tired, older than she remembered.

"You're too old," she blurted out.

Scott arched an eyebrow and signed back. You wish you looked like me.

Sam snorted.

I have all the pretty genes in this family.

She guffawed and shoved him to the side, rolling her eyes. "You are the fucking worst."

The emotional box from before was closed, stowed away in the depths of her mind. Sam was okay with that. Even if it was only temporary.

2

T IS FOR TEAM
(AND TEMPORARY)

TO MOST OF the Station City population and nearby towns, Command remained a bland feature, an unremarkable vital organ. They existed. For a minority, the military was just another useless appendix that would burst at any moment. To Sam, UMF was the shielding skin on the body of humankind, the only unifying defense for all the separate human settlements...or at least whatever was left on this side of the hemisphere and planet.

Sam was excited to be at the core of her livelihood, to finally experience the headquarters of her life and purpose. She was grateful she wouldn't be distracted by the city's attractions, not yet at least.

Though her brother didn't normally show grand emotions, she knew he was thrilled. He wanted to bring Sam around the city after the mission, whatever the mission was, and she had lapped up his uncanny enthusiasm. He had signed to her about the food, the markets, and the small museum of human history he visited before she joined SOG. She had smiled more in amusement at her brother's strange zest. She had all the time after the mission to be a tourist. For now, she was delighted to see UMF headquarters in person.

Gregov apologized to them for the long walk, then said something about the team's issued vehicle at the maintenance shop. Sam didn't mind. She happily took in every sight as they passed building after building. Small two- and four-seater vehicles, what the marines called rabbits due to their swift speed and maneuverable size, whizzed by on the roads, dodging pedestrians left and right.

She ignored the whispers from a group of young recruits who turned and gawked as they passed. Their guide didn't seem to notice as he chattered away about the different structures.

Gregov quieted when they came up to an annex in the corner of the large compound. The only indicator of the unassuming building's function was a metal plate above the access console to the right of an equally unassuming door. A diamond shape had been laser-cut into the smooth surface.

With a swipe of his cuff, Gregov led them inside. A small blast of cool air greeted Sam as the door closed behind them, and her skin prickled. They walked through a spotless corridor lined with unmarked doors—Sam counted twelve, six staggered on each side. Her right index finger picked the rough skin on her thumb as they moved beyond the halfway point. At the fifth door on the left, their guide palmed the panel, and it slid open with a soft *shhhhk*, like a blade being sheathed in its sterile scabbard.

This was Razor-Echo's team room.

Just inside the door, vertical lockers stood as a welcoming line along the back wall of an open layout. In the center of the room, a young woman stood with two other men, all dressed like Gregov—uniform pants and black T-shirts. The woman's black-brown hair was pulled into an ornate but neat bun, and she stood with her weight on one leg, arms crossed. She was shorter than Sam by several centimeters, but standing beside the two other men, she looked quite petite.

At the sound of the door, one man, a young, lean male straightened up, a head taller than the woman whose shoulder he had been leaning on. His darker, smooth complexion contrasted with the other muscled male across from him, who, leaning back against a chair, was still taller than the other two. The much larger marine had a rough shadow across his firm jaw and chin. Their conversation trailed off, and they turned to face the Ursus marines.

"Good morning," a low voice boomed from behind the group.

The two men and woman split to the side, allowing a stocky, square-jawed male in full uniform, gray shirt, and gray pants to approach the newcomers. After a loud pat on Gregov's tricep, the man stopped before Sam and Scott. He was slightly above her eye level.

"Vallen Krill." He produced a hand and shook both of theirs quickly and firmly. "I'm Echo team lead. We're really glad to have you here. Heard a lot about you two."

"Good things, I hope," Sam said.

"Of course, only the best." Krill beamed, and the smile reached his eyes. "Sorry to pull you in early. Command wants us to move a bit faster. Summit and all."

Sam nodded, grateful for the expedited timeline.

"I know you just arrived this morning, so I'm sorry to drop you right into it. I promise we'll give you a good tour after." The lead gestured them forward.

The other marines wrapped around and moved to the other side of the room, where metal chairs surrounded a table facing a holoscreen.

At the end, a woman with olive skin stood. Sam hadn't noticed her with the others blocking her view. The woman's brown hair was pulled into a loose braid draped over her right breast. She wore the same uniform pants and black T-shirt that fit extremely well on her slight, slender curves. She was intimidatingly beautiful.

The woman observed the siblings, and Sam's eyes connected with light-brown, upturned eyes. Something in her stomach fluttered, and she averted her gaze to the back of Krill's wavy dark-brown hair. She felt the brunette's eyes still on her, and she was embarrassed and confused at her body's sudden betrayal.

Sam was relieved when Krill turned and motioned toward the empty chairs. "Please," he said. And then a sharp, authoritative glance propelled the others to fill the seats.

Sam sat on the farther side, facing the door. Her brother pulled the chair to her left away from the table, and sat, immediately slouching.

The braided woman walked around and took the other seat next to Sam; a light scent of cinnamon fluttered into her nose. Sam tensed, straightening in her seat. She wondered if Station City had a more diverse selection of goods, including soaps and perfumes. Probably. The scent was pleasant.

Under the table, Sam scratched at her right thumb with a fingernail. She focused on Krill, who took his place at the head of the room and turned on the holoscreen.

Once everyone settled, Krill motioned at Sam and Scott with a loose hand. "As you all know, we have visitors on loan to us." He dipped his chin and extended an open palm. "Some of us know of you already, but…if you could be so kind?"

Sam lifted her left hand in a half wave at the others. "Valkyrie." She jerked her head to her left. "Mute."

Short and sweet.

A silence followed.

Maybe *too* short and sweet.

She looked into the air above the marines around the table, specifically avoiding the woman to her right. She didn't want to risk another blushing betrayal, especially not in front of people she didn't know.

Krill quirked his eyebrows, and Sam tightened her lips into a toothless smile. The skin on her thumb was beginning to grow raw.

"Right…" Krill said. "Thank you." He waved a hand to his side. "You've met Greg, er, Gregov, my second and comms." He then pointed to the petite woman in the next seat mirroring Sam's succinct introduction. "Kai—" he started, and then corrected himself. "I mean, Wester. Engineer."

Wester waved emphatically to Sam and Scott, and the corners of her dark-brown, almond eyes crinkled.

Krill continued down the side of the table. "That's Nasiri. Weapon—"

The young marine lifted a thin finger. "Nas. I go by Nas now."

"Really?" the broad-shouldered male to his left scoffed and rolled his hazel eyes. His arms folded across his barrel of a chest.

Wester also shook her head, lips pursed in amusement.

Nas shrugged. "What! Everyone else has short names. I'm just making it easy."

Krill shot his teammates a black look and continued. "*Nas*. Weapons and covering for Intel." He motioned at the grumpy muscular man. "And Fox. Also, weapons."

Fox tipped his head. He looked Sam up and down with a mischievous twinkle in his eyes, although his attention cut short at a glance from Scott.

Sam ignored it.

The team leader's hand jumped over the siblings to the last, unintroduced Echo member, the woman on Sam's right. "And finally, Tanner. MED."

The woman tapped her right temple with a long finger in a half-assed salute. Sam glanced at Tanner's face and then immediately moved her eyes past the few frivolous sun freckles, holding steadily on Krill. She wasn't ready for another round of whatever she had felt, an overflowing, intense…something.

"That's Echo." Krill clapped his hands and rubbed them together. He grinned at the two new additions to his team. "Welcome. We're thrilled to have you with us, even if it's only for one mission." He ran his fingers through his hair. "I guess we'll dive in. *Please* hold questions til the end." The last sentence was pointed to the other side of the table.

Krill turned back to the console and dimmed the room lights. A map popped onto the holoscreen and cast a soft blue glow around the space. "Everyone knows the Royals, their emissaries, and entourage will be in town with the summit this coming week. Command wants to make sure that nothing endangers those talks. That's priority."

"Are we—" Wester started but shut her mouth at a look from the lead.

"Sorry, Kai," he said, shaking his head. "Spartan-Seven and Bravo are pulling site security for the event along with several other units from Station. But we get to go on a trip. We're being sent to check out reports of increased COC activity along the border."

He motioned at the western ridge of the southern continent on the map, far from Station City. "Intel received some reports from the closest outpost. Little scrapes here and there, but we've been having incidents along the back shipping lanes as well—not sure if it's the same thing, though. Doesn't seem too crazy, but Command wants to confirm this won't bubble up into the summit and Station business."

Krill looked around the table. "Intel thinks the Children of Charon may be up to something. Basically, we're going out to check and make sure it doesn't endanger anything. If it does, put it down. Again, nothing too crazy."

"COCsuckers," Fox grumbled and rubbed the stubble along his chin and jaw.

Some others nodded in agreement.

"And the alties there?"

So much for holding questions until the end of the brief.

Krill seemed used to it. "Big Intel said a Legion garrison was set up in the last years just south of the settlements, so I'm sure there are several reasons why the COC is causing trouble."

"But we have an outpost there. Why don't they check in? They're closer," Nas said.

Krill sighed. He manipulated the screen and zoomed in on pre-highlighted points on the map. "I don't know, but we'll check in with the outpost, then visit the two big towns in the region. We relay whatever we find up the chain, and Command decides what to do next."

"Nice," Nas piped in. "I'm sick of protection."

Fox grunted. "Once a meat shield, always a meat shield."

"I wouldn't mind protection for the summit," Wester said, but she quickly refocused. "And the shipping lanes?"

Krill took a deep breath, then met the three offenders with a firm gaze. "Charlie's been tasked with that. It should be a relatively simple recon and monitor op. This is last minute, and Command's already tied up with the summit and other requests. Odisho and Erickson are being tasked to Bravo for the summit, and thanks to Ursus, Valkyrie and Mute are joining us. They've got more expertise with alties and COC than our units in any case."

Fox muttered, "In case shit hits the fan?"

Krill shot him a look. "You and your phrases...but yes."

As much as Sam hoped for no figurative shit hitting any metaphorical fans, part of her sought the adrenaline from things getting dicey. It was always a guilty pleasure when she saw action, where her lengthy experience and training clicked in automatically.

"It's a full day of travel to Temunco. The outpost is also the closest to the southernmost settlements, Matam and New Zapala." Krill pointed at a small dot on the continent's coast. The outpost sat on the edge of land, and a water line traced north of it, winding inland toward two other highlighted dots. "They're expecting us, and we have to confirm when we get there, but they'll probably provide prowlers and drivers to this point." The lead touched a cluster of dense contour lines east of the outpost. "From here, we'll have to hoof it to Matam."

"Convenient," Fox stated. "No roads?"

"There's a river, too. Why not that route?" Nas asked.

"Not sure. Terrain may be too rough for the prowlers *and* rabbits. River wasn't an option given. It probably has to do with the territory. I don't know the full details yet. Again, we'll find out more when we get there."

Krill looked over his team. "Hey, we've never been there before, and it'll be a tough trek, but we've been through worse, right? Just stay on your toes. When we go further south, it might get interesting... Doesn't help that the settlements don't look kindly on UMF." He paused, visibly raking his mind for something else. His face lit up. "Oh, and the last team who went there a while ago didn't run into wunbies, but Intel says there's been an uptick in sightings."

Wester perked up. "In the Andes? That's far from their usual stomping grounds, no?"

"In general," Krill said. "Apparently, they've been gaining some popularity with the alties in Arshangol."

Echo nodded around the table, Sam with them. Unlike her lack of interest in politics, she had been following any mention of the radical Altered group, self-named "The Promised," or what the general Altered population considered "Apostates." The marines enjoyed the moniker "wunbies" for the terrorist group, a term stemming from their supremacist mantra "one blood, one promise."

Although the Altered were elitist, the majority of the genetically-engineered race left humans alone most of the time, probably hoping they would die out on their own. Apostates, however, were violently supremacist and sought to actively guide humans to their demise. They brought their own kind's ire on themselves with their extreme loyalty to the last Altered Sovereign, whose reign sought to eliminate humankind. It didn't help that the Apostates lacked care and mindfulness about collateral damage, happy to abduct and torture any Altered they thought sympathized with humans.

All extremely subjective.

The one saving grace was that these Apostates didn't look to have any organization, mostly making network news with their sporadic lone-wolf murder sprees. Sam and Scott's last mission had been a long hunt for one of these radicals, a bomb-maker wreaking havoc on nearby towns.

"That's pretty much all I have right now, but we'll get a detailed brief once we're in Temunco. I'll update if I receive anything else in the meantime." Krill looked up. "*Now*, are there any questions?"

A hand peeked out above the tabletop across from Sam. "Why aren't we taking an airship?"

"Airships are reserved for the summit," Gregov replied. "Priorities."

"Got it." Wester popped her lips in acknowledgment.

"Even if not, the airships can't handle the turbulence over that topography. Too dangerous," Nas said.

"Anything else?" Krill asked.

No response.

"Great. We leave twelve hundred sharp from the docks. So that gives you..." He checked his commcuff. "Three hours. Get your gear and affairs in order if you haven't already." Krill stared pointedly at the woman sitting beside Sam. "Assigned ship and other details will go to your cuffs."

Scattered, soft noises of acknowledgment flitted around the table in return, and chairs scraped against the floor as Wester, Nas, and Fox stood up. Gregov turned to Krill, and they talked softly, their backs to the group.

Fox leaned over and offered Sam a hand. She took it and felt the hard calluses on his palm. His lips cracked into a smile, and she glimpsed a sliver of straight white teeth between. "Nice to finally meet *the* Valkyrie." He let go and glanced at her brother. "And you. I've heard you're an amazing shot. One of the best."

Scott shrugged.

Fox's eyes darted away, and he winked at the medic before he moved away to the lockers.

Before Sam could follow the man's attention to Tanner, Nas punched out a fist, which Sam and Scott amusedly returned with a bump.

"The name's Saif Nasiri. But Nas is easier." His eyes glistened.

"And you can call me Kai. No one calls me Wester," the engineer said next to him. "Nice to meet you, I look forward to working with both of you."

Sam nodded to the two marines. They both looked to be in their early twenties, no older than her.

Nas and Wester turned around to join Fox on the other side

of the room. They murmured together, probably about the mission. Gregov was now conversing with Tanner, and Sam couldn't make out their hushed words.

She looked around the room, unsure of what to do next. She and Scott were already packed and ready to go, having just come off the ship. Another three hours was going to be excruciating.

Before the discomfort settled, the lights re-engaged in the room. Krill raised his voice over the growing chatter. "Make sure requisitions are filled out right, please. If LOGS hounds me one more time—"

"He'll bunk you with Fox," Tanner said as she rose out of her seat.

Wester, Nas, and Gregov snickered while Fox lifted his middle finger to Tanner. She smirked and returned double middle fingers. Fox failed at hiding the grin forming at the corner of his mouth.

"I would never torture any of you like that," Krill said calmly, not bothering to look up from the console display.

Sam's anxiety resurfaced as Wester, Nas, and Fox left, jabbering away. The door slid shut behind them, throwing the room back into a quieter space. Sam watched as Tanner and Gregov moved to the kitchenette and chatted with each other. She quickly looked away as those light-brown eyes swept over her.

"Sorry. The briefs don't normally go like that." Krill shook his head. "Thanks for coming on such short notice. I really appreciate it. It's been such a cluster these past weeks."

He sighed, leaning against the table. "I take it you're both already good to go, having just arrived, but..." He trailed off as Gregov and Tanner moved toward the door. Krill raised his hand to catch their attention. "Greg, you free?"

His second-in-command shrugged and nodded.

"Great. Can you show these two around the base real quick? Help them with anything else they need. Maybe the armory?"

The tension in Sam's shoulders dissipated. *Good. Something to do.*

Gregov clicked his tongue. "Sure, boss."

Krill cringed. "Don't...call me..." He gritted his teeth and took a breath.

Sam noticed Tanner's grin widen. The medic shared a subtle hand slap with Gregov behind her back.

"Thank you," Krill said, "See you soon."

Echo's second winked and jerked his head to the door, beckoning Sam and Scott to join him. Sam rose, but she waited for her brother to move toward the door first. She glanced back at the team lead, nodded in acknowledgment, and followed Scott.

As she drew near the two waiting marines, her eyes met the medic's again. Sam willed herself to hold the connection longer this time, still uncertain about the strange effect the other woman had on her, but she was grateful as it broke in passing. Her cheeks warmed, but the door slid shut behind her before anyone could notice.

3

ADHESION

SAM WAS no connoisseur of vehicles, but even she had to admire the resplendent scout cruiser in front of her. The light-armor ship was built for speed, and parked at the dock now, its varnished body seemed to ache for motion. Sam's eyes were drawn to the bow where "UMF" was printed in dark, blocky print. There really was no need to label the ship. All militarized watercraft were UMF, even the ones that escorted commercial vessels in heavily disputed waters. But humans always prided themselves on ownership and unnecessary labels. The military was no exception.

Sam felt a nudge to her side. In the corner of her eye, she could make out crossed fingers waving in the air. READY?

She nodded, then cast a glance back at the compound and city just beyond. The siblings moved up the ramp carrying their gear plus an additional belt of disc grenades Sam had rapturously snagged from the SOG armory. They hung casually around her neck over her undone armor and kit.

"Valk! Mute!"

Gregov's voice carried out from the ship's belly. He waved them over to the open locker further inside. Nas was with him.

"You can store your gear here. Just find an empty locker. Weapons on the rack over there." Gregov pointed to a metal compartment that looked like a robot's ribs, a few rifles already lodged in its bones. "I'm heading to the bridge, but I'll see you guys in a bit. Galley's the second door on the left."

He threw a look over his shoulder at Nas and clicked his tongue. "I've got a lock on, don't bother going through my stuff."

Gregov clapped Scott on the back as he stepped around them and took the flight of stairs in the center of the hold. The steps led up to a catwalk and beyond that, a main passage on the top level, leading further into the ship.

As Echo's second left, Sam and Scott packed their items into the nearest compartments. Nas thumbed Gregov's locker, but with Sam watching, he turned away with a sly grin. Instead, he grabbed a small pack on the shared bench, opened the main pocket, and tilted it forward. His dark-brown eyes glimmered as individually wrapped bars shuffled to the lip of the bag.

"I snagged some chocolate from the DFAC," Nas said triumphantly. "They're not the best, a little too artificial for my taste, but hey, still better than nothing, right? I'll leave them in the kitchen. Help yourself." He clutched the bag to his chest and skipped away toward the upper deck.

Sam gave her brother a brisk, bemused smile, and Scott returned it, clamping his lips together in a thin line and shaking his head side to side. Their brief walking tour around the campus had been a welcome distraction. Sam was glad for the time it had spared her from her thoughts. If she ignored them long enough, they wouldn't affect her, right?

The weapons rack clicked as Scott locked in his gun. His marksman rifle's barrel stuck out at least a head higher than the next longest weapon: a stocky light machine gun.

Sam sat on the bench and lifted the belt of grenades over

her head. She was gentle, even though the discs, each inside their own chambers on the bandolier, were designed to withstand bumps and rough handling. This was upgraded technology, and she was delighted with her new tools.

In her periphery, she saw Scott turn to her. His lips parted slightly as if he had something to say at the tip of his tongue. Her jaw clenched. So much for ignorance. Were they going to do this now?

Nothing.

She felt his eyes study her, but she gazed down, noting and fixing the positions of the little lethal pucks. A greasy layer of hurt, guilt, and what felt like a hundred other conflicting emotions simmered within her. She smothered it, refusing to let any turmoil touch the surface. She could control herself.

"Go ahead. I'll catch up," Sam said. It was a dismissal to save herself. Or save *him* from herself.

Scott lingered, cautious, and Sam held her breath.

Without a word or motion, her brother walked away and left her alone. She let out a breath as his boots tapped against the metal steps. The terrible pang in her chest dissolved, but an invisible layer of grime still lingered inside.

Sam stowed the belt neatly into the locker on top of her gear and pulled her carbine rifle into her lap. Pre-mission routines would save her. She traced her fingers along the cool metal and then the three, small laser-etched letters on the side of the weapon. She removed the weighted magazine, checked the ammunition inside, and clicked it back into place. She then fit the butt stock into her shoulder, barrel-up in a modified high-ready position to look down her sights, tapping her visor against the rifle to engage her hololens. Satisfied with the sync, she rechecked the sights one more time, and disengaged.

"Nice gun."

The mellifluous voice startled her. She looked up.

Tanner was beside her, nimbly setting her equipment down on the bench. Sam suppressed a flinch. She was a recon specialist; she was usually more aware of her surroundings. She felt naked at that moment. Unprepared. She wasn't used to being crept up on.

"Thanks," Sam mumbled.

The feeling passed as she looked over her company. The other woman was older than her, but not by much. Sam detected that airy scent of sweet cinnamon again. She lowered her head, focusing intently on her rifle's sights as a flush warmed her cheeks.

Tanner stashed her pack into an open locker next to Sam's.

"Isn't it a little on the nose?"

Sam's forehead wrinkled, confused.

"Your callsign. Valkyrie," Tanner said, "unless that *is* your name…"

Sam shifted uncomfortably. She was given the nickname when she officially joined UMF. As the only blonde in her basic training class, and the youngest by a large margin, it *was* quite on the nose. Her classmates had given her the handle with spite and jealousy; in the early weeks of training, they spat it out with a heavy bitterness only pubescent youth knew. She learned to embrace it, and the name quickly lost its initial insult.

"I didn't choose it," Sam said flatly. She swallowed and added, "You can call me Ryan if you want." She felt vulnerable again. It was now the most she had spoken to someone other than her brother since they first arrived in Station.

"First or last name?"

Sam glanced back.

"Ryan. Is that your first or last name?"

"Oh. Last." Sam's leg bounced, and the coolness of her rifle rubbed harshly against the fabric of her pants. She didn't know if she should say more, didn't know why this woman made her so nervous, but she also didn't want her to leave.

Tanner didn't seem to mind. She offered a hand. "Tanner, last name. Miriam, first name."

Sam placed her weapon to the side, took the woman's hand, and gripped it firmly. It was pleasantly soft, and she felt a curl of warmth in the back of her mind.

Miriam.

She didn't know what she had been expecting and hadn't even been considering her new teammates' first names—it wasn't relevant. But now, as she repeated it in her head, she was glad to know it. The name suited the woman.

Miriam, the medic.

She followed the woman's eyes as they flicked down to her bare forearm, at her tattoo and scar. Sam pulled out of the connection and crossed her arms across her chest. "You're the medic."

Idiot. What a dumb thing to say.

The other woman looked back at her, her eyes bright and sharp. A grin grew on her face. "I've patched up here and there."

"She's also the reason we *have* to get patched up," a deep voice rang out from above.

Sam looked up at the catwalk.

Gregov peered down, bent over with his forearms resting on the wide banister. His mouth curved into a smile, an eyebrow cocked. How long had he been there?

Tanner—no, Miriam bared her teeth at him.

Before Miriam could retort, a harsh screech shot the marines' attention to the large bay door. In the middle of the frame, Wester sheepishly shrugged. With a short, final scrape, she wrestled two large bags over the ship's edge and continued to the open locker, dragging her items smoothly along the bay floor.

Gregov looked back down. "And all for what, a better look at a certain someone?"

Miriam threw her head back and shut her eyes tightly. "That was *one* time, Yuri. And it wasn't just about her. Please get your story straight."

He waved a hand at Wester as she joined the others. "Kai got a concussion!"

As if on cue, the engineer dropped her bags with solid smacks on the metallic ground. Wester beamed, and her hands splayed forward. "In all fairness, I was already pretty hammered," she admitted, then proceeded to nudge the abused parcels into a bottom locker with the side of her boot.

"And nothing a quick second in the MedJet couldn't fix," Miriam said. She caught Sam's eye and gave her a wink.

"Anyhow, I came to warn you," Gregov said, "Fox is trying to claim your chair. Get up here."

Whether that statement was true, it had the effect he was looking for. He walked off with a smirk as Miriam slammed her locker dramatically.

"That dickshit," she growled, although Sam knew she didn't mean it. The woman's eyes twinkled at her, and she felt that warmth in the back of her head again. "Come on. Put your baby away. I'll show you around."

Sam chuckled and moved to lock her rifle carefully away in the rack. Miriam wasn't wrong. That carbine was an extension of her arm and body.

Miriam waited patiently to the side for both Sam and Wester; once they were ready, they moved together up the stairs and further into the cruiser. Miriam cupped her hands over her mouth and shouted upward. "Fox! I will kill you if you touch my chair!"

Wester's eyes widened. "You should sanitize just in case."

⏀

The ship's interior galley was a divergence from its militant exterior. Colorful, comfortable chairs and odd, mismatched tables dotted the room. The pleasant essence of coffee beans lingered around the space. After a cursory tour of the cruiser, Sam was initially uncomfortable with the galley's strange aesthetic. However, the longer she sat, the more she enjoyed its personality. It was a soul buried inside the vehicle's monotonous skin, skeleton, and muscle. Sam felt like she had been transported to a different world and time.

Outside the small windows, the ocean stretched out as the ship coasted along effortlessly, indifferent to the swell. Sam sat in a faded chair in the center of the room, facing the two doors and kitchen just beyond another half wall. Her brother reclined in a chaise behind her. Sam already felt this trip to be markedly better than the one earlier.

She focused on her surroundings again. It was a strange space, but she felt an affinity with it—almost a reminder of a lost childhood. Some of her earliest memories were when she wasn't officially in UMF yet—not even the age of seven, sitting in team rooms quietly coloring or playing simulation games on her brother's or his friends' holopads. Scott and the others were still teenagers or had just breached their twenties. UMF outposts had always recruited kids from nearby settlements to shore up their numbers. It was a strong culture of indoctrinating young marines. Youth was plastic. Manageable. Malleable.

Staying at their flat in Gould, the nearby settlement, was never an option for Sam. Scott didn't allow it. He told her several times that she was safer at the outdoor range than in the empty suite he had inherited after their father's passing. Sam didn't know where she was born, but she was raised in Ursus, went to the standard school in a nearby encampment, and stayed with her brother, an exception, possibly even an experiment, made by UMF's leadership. She was always meant to be a marine.

A yawn escaped her mouth. A long trip plus a new city, new teammates, and then another lengthy leg would be rough. Her body still felt brittle from the morning travel.

"Coffee?" Miriam's honeyed voice snapped Sam to the present. Again, Sam hadn't noticed the woman's quiet arrival. Miriam held out a mug in one hand.

Sam took the offered vessel with both hands, careful not to spill its contents. She could feel the cup's warmth radiate into her skin, but it was nothing compared to the sensation of Miriam's fingers brushing hers in the exchange. Sam's gut flipped.

"Thank you," she mumbled.

Miriam waved her fingers as if it was nothing. "Elly brews it herself. Much better than the slush back in Station." She placed her cup onto the table and sat down in her chair, a green bucket seat mottled with faded orange dots. It was ugly. And loud.

Sam ducked her nose closer to the mug to hide her amusement. The steam from the elixir wafted upward, and an earthy fragrance swirled into her nose. She took a careful sip. It was *good*. Rich, yet bright.

The calm ambiance shattered as the galley door slid open. Nas and Wester entered, oblivious to the others in the room.

"—don't know why that'd be your choice of battery. You know the labs are working on new processes that outlast wind, even solar-powered capabilities!"

"So, it outperforms them, fine. But it's still *unethical*—"

Wester froze, sniffing the air. Her eyes widened, and her voice raised in pitch. "Is that what I think it is?"

Miriam elevated her cup over her head.

Wester locked onto the container. "Elly's?" she exclaimed.

Miriam pumped the cup upward again, careful not to spill its precious nectar.

"Oh, hell yes." Wester scurried into the kitchen around the corner, leaving Nas alone.

The interruption and her absence didn't seem to faze him. He raised his voice. "Okay, so maybe it's a little questionable where and how we get it, and I guess the labor issues, too, but come on, Kai, you have to admit that it's a pretty big deal..."

Sam took another slow sip from her mug, bemused.

"The potential of the battery and its elements is almost limitless. Why—"

"Saif Nasiri!" Wester reappeared around the corner with two cups in her hands. Light steam drifted up from them. "I. Don't. Care." She emphasized, as her eyes gleamed with excitement. "Coffee."

Nas's mouth stuttered, and his face furrowed as he weighed on his next actions. He lightened. "Did you get me some chocolate too?"

A drop of the dark liquid sloshed over the container's lip onto the young man's boot as Wester pressed one cup toward him and glared.

"Hey!" He deftly cradled the mug before she could smash it further into his chest.

Wester pushed past him, and the scowl on her face immediately dropped, turning into a wide smile that creased the corners of her eyes. Behind her, Nas flew around the kitchen wall.

Wester set the cup down on the table opposite Miriam and let herself fall into the chair to the left of Sam. Once comfortable, she grasped the drink again. After a large swallow of the liquid energy, her almond-shaped eyes closed, and her shoulders relaxed. Wester sighed. "This is the best part."

Sam had to admit the coffee and the galley's odd, yet cozy ambiance was a great start to this mission.

The mission.

Scott's last mission.

Sam's eye twitched as dark emotions crept into her mind again. She twisted in her chair to peek at her brother. His eyes were closed, and his hands rested comfortably on his chest and abdomen. He was listening; she was sure of it.

Perhaps the elixir energized her weary brain, but a realization dawned on her. Sam could still change his mind. Maybe Scott didn't have a good reason for leaving two contracts short of a pension. Maybe things had gone stale for him, and he just needed some rejuvenation, some new scenery, a new team. Renewal orders could still be assigned, and resignation requests rescinded.

But first, she needed a peace offering.

"Scott. Want some coffee?"

Without opening his eyes, her brother lifted one hand and waved in her direction. NO THANKS.

His loss. But Sam turned back around, reinvigorated. She could change his mind before they headed back to Ursus, probably even before returning to Station City. She had a new challenge, a personal mission. She was good at missions.

Sam's heart was much lighter when Nas emerged from the kitchen, a cup in one hand, a handful of candy bars in the other, and a nutrition bar hanging by its wrapper corner between his teeth. He sat next to Wester and dumped the candy onto the table in a pile. He tasted the coffee, then set it down to rip furiously into the foil of a chocolate bar.

Wester's face compressed as Nas took a giant bite. "We just ate," she groaned.

Nas scrunched his shoulders and finished the slab in another large chomp. "I'm hungry again," he said, out of the corner of his mouth.

Miriam lifted her right hand and hid her mouth from Nas across from her. She half-whispered to Sam, aware the others could hear, "He's our baby Echo. Just joined SOG and our team a few months ago."

Wester leaned over and ruffled Nas's thick dark-brown hair. He let her; she had clearly done this many times before. He tore into another bar, narrowing his eyes at Miriam and then the engineer.

Wester rubbed it in further. "And we love you, growing boy."

Nas covered his chocolate-filled mouth with the top of his fingers. Sam wondered if Wester had reprimanded him for manners before. "Shut up. You only joined right before me."

Sam's eyes widened. "Have either of you been on this kind of operation before?"

The three looked at her, and Nas's face fell.

Did she say that out loud? Had she been too frank? Condescending? Sam waved a hand, trying to take it back.

"Yes and no. This is their first outside of the Station area. Other than the summit preparation and one-offs, it's been pretty slow," Miriam said with a smile.

Sam exhaled.

"But Nas was with the anti-piracy regiment before," she continued.

"It was boring, though. I wanted to be with the infiltration team to find new alty tech instead."

"You'll have plenty of time to lead that group whenever you're done with SOG, *Baby Echo*." Wester's eyes crinkled.

"You're only nine months older than me, Kai."

"Sure, but I'm twenty-three. You're twenty-*two*. Plus, age and maturity are two different things." Wester poked a finger into Nas's rib and grinned.

He rolled his eyes, and Sam folded her lips into her mouth, suppressing a chuckle.

It surprised her. Perhaps she was cracking with exhaustion. Despite her hesitancy on their experience level, she had to admit this was conceivably the first group of marines she was at ease with. She loved her team in Ursus, but they were all older and had always felt more like Scott's friends.

Miriam suddenly leaned into her. The medic's face was a breath away from her cheek. Cinnamon.

"If they didn't look so different, you'd swear they're siblings."

Sam forced a laugh and rubbed her thumb up and down against the ceramic mug. The other woman pulled back, much to Sam's relief.

"How much older is he?" Miriam chucked her chin at Scott.

Sam glanced back. Her brother's chest rose and fell in a slumber-like rhythm. "Eleven years."

Miriam's eyes widened.

Sam wasn't surprised. Most people didn't expect that much of an age gap. Scott looked younger, although she always thought his gray-blue eyes gave it away. They carried a heavy weight, an experience of a much older person. The dark rings underneath his eyes were especially telling now.

"He's my half-brother. We shared a...father, but Scott raised me," she said with a sniff.

"He doesn't talk much," Nas blurted out. His face contorted and then he recoiled. "Oh. Shit. Is he...can he not..."

Sam chuckled in response. "No, he can. He just prefers not to."

Come to think of it, she couldn't recall a moment when her brother said more than a few direct sentences in a conversation. He had always preferred using his hands, signing his thoughts and humor, but even those were rather curt and straightforward. Their friends and colleagues back in Ursus had mentioned offhandedly how her brother was a chatterbox in standard school and uni. It must have been a life before Sam.

She dug her thumbnail into the bumpy keloid texture on her forearm but quickly tucked her left hand under her thigh when she noticed Miriam watching.

Wester flicked Nas's shoulder, and he recoiled. "You should take some pointers from Mute," she said.

Nas cackled mockingly, then leaned forward, motioning at his own ear. "Is that the newest visor? I didn't know they were ready for use yet."

Sam touched the tech around her head. "Hm. We're part of a test group I think, so it must be?"

"And you have the implant that goes with it?" Nas pointed at his eye.

Sam did. She recalled the sand-like feeling that lingered in her left eye for days after the procedure. She hardly noticed it now. It synced perfectly with the visor's hololens.

"Oh, I'm jealous. The capabilities...that's really new stuff. I think they reverse-engineered some alty tech," he sputtered. Nas pulled out an earpiece from his pants pocket. It was like Sam's visor but clunkier and attached to an extending base to fit around the user's head. He swirled the visor around his finger and scoffed. "We're still running the fourth generation. You'd think SOG is tip of the spear. How does an *outpost* get tech faster than Station? The tech lab is *in* the City."

"Not just any outpost. Ursus runs the most night ops."

Sam was grateful Miriam responded first—she didn't know the answer to Nas's question. UMF had offered her an option to make her better at her job and she took it. Sam personally thought Ursus ran *too* many night ops, but the new tech had made her and Scott's lives easier. Human vision could only process so much in the dark. The visors, specifically the later versions, could add a bit more to low-light vision and were significantly more comfortable and adaptable than the typical night-vision goggles. They were great for missions, quelling Children of Charon attacks, and any other human scuffles. But human tech was severely unmatched compared to genetically engineered vision when they were searching for or in combat with Apostates and Altered assailants. The Altered had a type of tapetum lucidum, a layer of eye tissue and membrane to see in the dark.

"Yeah...I guess it makes sense," Nas said. "But it'd be nice if Command gave us the option to upgrade." He pocketed his visor and slumped in his chair.

"I'm not upgrading," Wester said.

Nas turned, his manicured brows furrowing.

"What. I'm not! Hell no." Wester shifted in her seat and passed an apologetic look to Sam. "Look, I have the rest of this contract with yoomy, but I am out once that's done. That upgrade is too invasive. Even if I only had it for a short time... ugh, I don't even want to think about how they'd uninstall it."

Nas wiggled his head from one side to the next, and Sam shrugged. She had also considered what would happen when she needed to remove the implant, but she figured her pain tolerance and whatever drugs they pumped into her system would be worth the advantage.

To Sam's surprise, Miriam agreed with Wester. "Same, but maybe another contract for me. I'm not exactly in a rush to get back to that life." Miriam's lips pinched as she thought. "I think Yuri might be in the same boat."

"I mean, yeah, okay. But come on. New tech…" Nas trailed off.

Sam was shocked. None of the three were career marines, four if Miriam's statement was true about Gregov. They were SOG. It was difficult to get selected already. Why wouldn't they stay in UMF? Sure, the military had its bureaucratic moments and occasional bad eggs, but she had always thought SOG and general marine life were good. They had a decent package with credits, allowances, pension, authority, and status. Sam didn't consider herself very altruistic, but it was a bonus that their general aim and missions were actively helping advance humankind in this tense landscape. She owed so much to the military organization.

Maybe she had perceived Echo wrong.

"You're not staying with yoom—UMF?" she heard herself say out loud, interrupting the conversation that had turned to something about technological differences with the Altered—she wasn't sure. Sam was in her own head and had fallen behind in the discussion.

The others turned to her. Miriam raised an eyebrow, and Sam looked away, focusing on Wester instead.

"Well, no. I only joined after high-uni because it's good for the resume," the engineer explained.

Sam suppressed her astonishment again. Wester went to higher university. This meant she had only just joined UMF and recently earned her SOG black tab. It also meant that she probably came from the upper class. Sam felt a pang of insecurity, but she just as quickly nudged it away. Maybe Wester had been accepted into the elite cadre with her family's connections.

"I'd like to join City Center after," Wester said with a sigh. "If only I had been born or graduated a few years prior, I'd be in that summit with the Royals and emissaries." Her eyes brightened. "These talks, they're...monumental. We're talking about the possibility of peace, official trade, and open channels. Oh, it's really exciting."

"Sure, monumental, but boring. The real moves are in the tech and gen labs. That's where I'm going next," Nas said. "Or I'd love to. I've got to make more credits for the family first. We didn't *all* come from money." He jabbed the smaller woman in the arm and then pointed at Miriam.

Both rolled their eyes.

Sam quieted as she felt herself mentally distance from the Station marines. Were they really that different from her? Whatever comfort she had just found in the group withered as she became more conscious of their contrasting backgrounds, lives, and ambitions.

"Look, all I'm asking for is cooler missions. I mean, we *are* SOG. Aren't we supposed to be getting the better stuff?" Nas continued.

Wester rolled her eyes again. "We're on this mission, aren't we?"

"Sure."

"*And* you get to cover for Intel," Wester said.

"Why didn't Jace come again?"

"MED. Something about fit for duty with his...you know. Regardless, he got pulled into BigInt," Miriam said.

"I guess," Nas mumbled.

"It's the life of HQ, Baby Echo," Miriam said and shrugged. "Protection, keep the peace, and now and then, one of these ops."

"Maybe I can transfer to Ursus," Nas muttered.

Sam looked up at the mention of her home base.

Nas brightened and straightened in his chair, his eyes wide at Sam. "Can I see your stuff?"

Wester's head whipped to him, aghast. She flicked him again, much harder this time. "Nas! So inappropriate."

He blanched, more from confusion than pain. Nas's face fell, and he looked at Wester, his eyes heavy-lidded. He intoned in a flat voice, "I meant her gear. Shit, Kai."

Sam and Miriam laughed.

"Leave the Valkyrie be. Don't scare her away just yet," Miriam said. She gave Sam a kind look. "Let her enjoy her coffee."

Nas shrunk back in retreat. "Maybe later?"

Sam rubbed her eye and gave him a short, amicable nod. The young man was elated. She took another taste of her coffee and was happy about the change of topic. She decided she was too tired to make sense of the others' views of UMF service. Hold off on judgment for now.

The galley door slid open, and the group turned to the entrance. Krill entered the room; to his side was a short woman in a black jumpsuit. A casual touch to Krill's arm caused his face to break out in a glowing grin. His smile, however, dropped when he realized they had an audience. The pilot said something hushed to him and then walked into the kitchen.

Krill strolled over to the group. He avoided Miriam's hard stare, and instead, glanced at Scott in the back and then the others. "Elly made coffee?"

The woman Sam presumed to be Elly rejoined the galley and stopped behind Wester's chair. She handed Krill a mug and sipped her own cup. Her lips pressed together, and she sighed. "Hm. Not as good this time. Must've steeped it too long."

Ignoring Miriam's still unwavering gaze, Krill addressed Sam and gestured at the pilot to his side. "Valk, this is Elly, our pilot for this run. Elly, this is one half of our recon duo from Ursus, Val—"

"Ryan," Sam interrupted, then stumbled over her words.

"Sam. Or Valkyrie. Whichever." Callsigns, begone. She might as well join Echo's last name customs. Sam did hate sticking out.

She shook Elly's hand.

Nas grumbled, "I like Valkyrie…"

Elly patted Nas's shoulder and smiled at Sam. "Welcome. It's not often I have Ursus folk on my ship. Just this usual lot." She dug an elbow into Krill's side, and he grinned stupidly, his teeth white and square.

Miriam narrowed her eyes.

"I'll have my crew, Lev and Trick, pop by when they can. Lev's on the bridge with Yuri right now. Trick is…maybe in the hold?"

"Oh, we saw Lev with Fox earlier," Wester said, rolling her eyes. "He's trying to flirt with her. Again."

Elly laughed. "Oh, sweet Fox. Ambitious as ever." She winked at the medic. "But he's no Lady Tan."

Miriam raised her right brow in return and shook her head slowly. "Fox doesn't stand a chance. Lev will chew him up."

Wester and Nas nodded fervently.

Elly smiled again to the group and then, specifically, to Sam. "It's nice to meet you, Ryan Sam Valkyrie."

Sam winced internally. She felt silly now, giving her first name.

"Make yourself at home. We're making good time." She touched Krill's elbow.

Echo's lead glared around the table, letting his stare linger on Miriam. "Don't cause any trouble."

The two excused themselves and exited, heads close together, chatting away. Sam had a stitch of envy. The lead and pilot looked impeccable together. It was another feeling to be quickly swept away.

"They're totally back together," Nas said once the door closed.

Miriam nodded into her cup.

"What?!" Wester choked and spat up coffee at Nas. She set her cup on the table, but in her haste, it spilled more liquid onto the surface. She coughed several times and attempted to recover, her face now a bright shade of red.

Nas stood up to avoid more of the dark drink and rushed to the kitchen to clean up.

Wester chased after him, still flushed. "I'm sorry!"

The coffee on the table pooled toward Sam, and she pushed back her heavy chair, rotating her leg outward to avoid the inevitable drip. In her rushed movement, her limb brushed Miriam's.

Sam froze. The back of her skin electrified and tingled with the hasty contact.

"Sorry," she mumbled.

Miriam paid no mind. "Is Sam short for something?"

"Hm? No. I-I don't think so."

Miriam waited, but Sam provided nothing further. She was still disoriented. The other woman shifted in her fuzzy chair, bringing her mug to her lips.

"Interesting. First name Sam."

Hearing her name from Miriam's lips sent a warm shiver down Sam's spine.

Φ

The time flew by.

Sam had meant to sleep on the trip but was too stimulated —she wanted to know more about her teammates. Normally, she would have thought to retain a degree of separation, to stay objective and professional. It was a temporary assignment, and she knew they'd go their separate ways after this mission, but she found Echo and their dynamics with each other fascinating, if not deeply entertaining. Despite their differences—and there were quite a few—everything was new and refreshing.

This is what she had learned so far:

Miriam Tanner was best friends with Yuri Gregov. The two had grown up together and were practically neighbors. Both were good friends with Vallen Krill from their recruitment basic class before they joined SOG. Krill had been the obvious next team lead since the previous one had taken a contract with higher command.

Kai Wester and Saif "Nas" Nasiri were joined at the hip, prone to arguing about jellyfish farms, water filtration, technological advances, political affairs, and everything in between. Nas was the most recent addition to Echo, and he was a gearhead, quick to excite over any discussion of science, technology, and equipment, be it military or civilian.

Benjamin Fox, a rough-around-the-edges grump, had a soft spot for Kai. Sam wondered at any history of romantic relationships there but thought perhaps not, as Fox continued to chase after Lev, the ship's second. His advances toward Sam did not go unnoticed either, although she mostly ignored them. She had learned her own lesson from years in UMF. Flings and missions didn't mix. After the stress and final adrenaline, however...there was therapy and release in that practice.

She spent most of the trip observing their antics and repartee, which was a great distraction. She fielded random questions left and right from Nas, who was eager to learn all about Ursus and the latest versions of holopads or weapons they employed—which, to his dismay, were mostly the same as Station.

Her brother joined the larger group occasionally and would retreat to his corner when the interactions became too much. Sam noted that he and Yuri would separate together, a budding friendship ever since they found out the second also had a proficiency for sign language. At first, she was annoyed that Scott would befriend the overly chipper marine, but pushed it aside, just happy that it could be leverage for her to convince him to stay in UMF later.

The trip had been smooth, except for some rough patches of turbulence over heavy waves as they passed the earth's equator. The team was lucky with the weather and the absence of heavy storms. Sometimes, Sam could glimpse thin slices of the coast and the barren land on the horizon through the ship's little windows. If she looked hard enough, she could see the skeletons of buildings far away that once made up cities. The colors of the peach sunset had glowed and painted the inside of the cabin some hours before, a magnificent reminder of the time change, much earlier than their bodies were used to. It was pitch black now. Though the ship was skimming parallel to the coastline, no lights or life were visible to the human eye.

A core group had mainly stayed inside the galley, entertaining themselves with conversation, a quick rest here and there, and now, card games. Scott sat on the same chaise lounge as before and engaged his commcuff, swiping through old notes and messages. Fox slept on a red couch nearby, legs up, a large forearm splayed over his eyes.

Around the table, Miriam, Sam, and Kai played a strategy game. There were three empty seats across from them, cards on the table in front of two. On the other side of the galley, Nas leaned against the wall. He ate the last of his stashed chocolate between cursory leg stretches.

A loud alert chimed across the ship.

All but Fox looked up as the intercom cracked to life. "Thirty minutes to dock," a voice stated over the ship's system. "Thirty minutes to dock."

With another chime, the message ended.

Scott gathered the small, cluttered items around his space

and walked over, pausing next to Sam. She continued to carefully study the table.

"Yeah," Sam said without looking up.

Her brother left the galley. Miriam and Kai returned to the game, although obviously intrigued by the siblings' style of communication.

Nas rejoined them and picked up his cards. He groaned and rubbed his forehead as he perused them—it was the same hand he had left before. Fox grunted loudly behind them, and Miriam glanced at him, then to the remaining face-down stack on the table.

"Ignore his grumpy ass. He's not good at cards, but he's especially not used to getting beat in darts." Miriam tilted her head at the opposite wall and board where Sam had previously outplayed the rest of them. "Oh, and deal Yuri out. He's probably not coming back."

Fox rolled over to his side and tried to shift into another comfortable position.

Sam smirked. *Sore loser*.

4

COEFFICIENTS

CAFFEINE WAS A WONDERFUL DRUG. But even that stimulant had its limitations. Sam was grateful as the boat neared the coast, and the prospect of another new location brought a second (or third, or fourth) wind. She knew the burst of excitement was a fleeting energy. A crash loomed beyond it.

Compared to Station City, Temunco Outpost's port was minuscule, with only two dock platforms facing the ocean. The outpost sat near a wide estuary where a river veined inland. Smaller waverunners meant for short expeditions lined a pier on the river-facing side of the port. The entire area dedicated to ship arrivals and departures could fit in a tight corner of Command's secured harbor.

Through the dim compound lighting, Sam could make out the figure of a four- or maybe five-story tower in the center of the compound. From the outlines of the large equipment along the side and a suspended red light blinking above, she knew it to be the communications building—the only link between UMF posts and the wider network. Surrounded by other modest structures, it was the tallest point of the outpost.

It was late in local time when the scout cruiser locked into one of the two platforms, the other landing dock already occupied by a larger and older ship, a layer of its armor visible underneath the chipped paint. Two dock workers, their faces unseen in the shadows cast by the suspended lights, waited for the Station ship to unfold its ramp.

At the entrance of the gangway, a capped figure in a neat officer's uniform watched, with hands clasped behind their back. They stood with their spine straight, shoulders pulled back. An air of authority churned about them.

Krill was the first to step out of the ship. As he walked down and off the platform, Sam and the others heaved their gear over their shoulders. The thick scent of saltwater and sulfur filled their noses as they stepped onto the metal ramp.

The officer approached them. "Vayen Krill?" he asked with a thick, regional accent, the double *L* in the first name becoming a *Y* in the cultural shift.

"Yes." Krill shifted his bag and offered his right hand.

The man clasped his upper forearm, their arms touching. Krill stiffened, but quickly adjusted and mirrored the greeting.

"And this is Echo." He gestured back to the others as they filed out of the ship.

The officer looked past the team as if he were expecting more to step out. He waited until the eight marines made their way in front of him.

There was a ruckus from somewhere within the compound, and Echo swiveled their heads to locate the sound. The officer remained undisturbed as overlapping shouts burst out and then died down.

The man shook his head and raised a hand. "Apologies."

He didn't elaborate.

"Welcome to Outpost Temunco. My name is Diego Cordeiro Sandoval. I am First Officer here. CO Otueome is sorry she could not meet you. She is currently engaged on a different matter but will catch you later for the brief. I know you are tired, but if possible, I would like to check you in with the TOC." He smiled grimly.

Krill surveyed the team around him. It was a long journey, but most of the marines were temporarily energized from the arrival.

He gave the officer a quick nod. "Sure, we can do that."

"Good. Please follow me."

First Officer Sandoval started into the quiet compound. Echo trailed after him, east toward the tower, the center of the base. A mismatched combination of white and yellow lights threw soft shadows across the buildings, accompanying the marines in. Sam thought she heard a light chorus of insects chirping near and far away, welcoming them to the south.

◯

Six Echo marines, including the two recon specialists, waited outside a windowless building. Their packs, equipment, and weapons were neatly scattered on the ground around them. Fox lay on the pavement, his light machine gun tucked into the nook of his arm like a resting pet. Nas and Kai, next to him, excitedly discussed the species of insects and animals prevalent in the south, things not found as much in the northern continent. As they delved into a discussion about environmental resilience, Sam turned away to yawn. Her brother reclined next to her against the wall.

YOU'RE MAKING FRIENDS. Scott smirked. He added, IT'S NICE TO SEE.

Sam snorted. THEY'RE GREEN, BUT THEY'RE NOT BAD SO FAR.

Were the Echo teammates "friends"? It had only been one

day, mostly stuck on a ship together. She didn't think she needed many friends. She always had her brother.

GETTING OUT OF URSUS IS GOOD FOR US.

She gazed up at the red light at the top of the tower. It was so high up there. She moved her hands and fingers without looking. AND GETTING OUT OF UMF IS GOOD FOR WHO?

She felt Scott's stare. She knew he was trying to read her face in the low-light. As she glanced back down, he bit his lip, caught himself, and pressed his mouth into a line instead.

Sam waved away a small bug as it buzzed near her. She wasn't trying to be passive-aggressive. It was a valid question.

SAM, Scott signed. He didn't finish.

A door squeaked open and harsh, white light spilled from the interior hallway. Yuri exited and held the door open for the team lead. A scrawny teenager dressed in a loose uniform followed. The kid fumbled for his garrison cap, unfolding it and placing it on his head as he crossed the threshold. His face was soft and unlined—very young. As the door shut, the group was thrown back into muted darkness, the only source of illumination coming from the yellow light above the building exterior.

Sam kicked off the wall and gathered closer to the others. The new face glanced around the group. Realizing he was the source of attention, he dipped his head and rubbed his arms uneasily.

"We'll have another brief here at zero eight thirty. Temunco will help monitor, let us know if anything changes." Krill turned to the kid, a stark change in physicality compared to the rest of the special operations team.

The lead grimaced. Sam realized he had already forgotten the marine's name.

The kid bowed nervously, then straightened. His dense

black-brown hair bobbed with the quick movement. "Junpei Matias Hikari-Rezin."

"Right." Krill clapped a hand on the kid's shoulder. "Er, Rez...Hikari here is from New Zapala and will join us on our trip. The CO said he's a pro at getting through the terrain. Thanks for waiting up for us."

Their Temunco guide pasted on a somber smile.

"They've set us up in temporary quarters just up the way. Let's get as much shuteye as possible. We start the trek to Matam tomorrow. Remember, zero eight thirty brief."

The kid lifted a hand close to his narrow jawline. "I can show you to the dorms," he said in a feathery voice.

Krill nodded at him.

Junpei Matias Hikari-Rezin waited patiently for the group to gather their things and, once ready, led them toward a row of long barracks further down the road. They passed a few parked rabbits on the side and a roving sentry who stared after the group.

Next to Sam, in the rear of the moving marines, Fox swung his assault pack to his other shoulder and leaned toward her. He threw his stubbled chin at their Temunco guide. "A little young, int' he? Think he's the same age as when you joined?"

Sam shrugged. She doubted it but didn't feel like saying anything in response. Hikari-Rezin's young age wasn't a surprise for her, but it was probably more startling to the Station marines. UMF's home base tended to recruit older because of the educational institutions and alternative opportunities in the city. Kai and Miriam were the only ones of Echo who had attended higher university, and Yuri, Nas, and Krill had all attended uni. Fox, like her brother, had dropped out before graduation. Sam was apprehensive when she had learned Echo's backgrounds and compared them to her own. She was the only one who hadn't sought education past standard school, and even then, she graduated two years early with UMF's pull and oversight. She was still relatively young, but with almost eleven official years in the military, she felt like every recruit did look younger.

Hikari-Rezin guided the team into one building and through a long corridor with stale air. He cut a glance at Nas, who tugged on door after door as they passed. *Nosy.*

Stopping just past a chipped metal door, Hikari-Rezin waited for the rest to catch up. He showed them the code for the small panel on the side console and pushed the door open by its handle. It was old technology. Sam realized the Temunco marine didn't even have a commcuff.

The living quarters inside had two rows of five cots, with a pillow and blanket folded at the foot of each bed. Two windows dotted the wall, and both were propped open, allowing the cooler night air to circulate within. The SOG team filed in and claimed their areas, dropping their gear as territorial dibs and markers.

Krill threw his items onto the first and second bed on the left. Nas and Kai stepped further into the room, taking the end beds in the same row. Scott moved to the opposite wall and sat on the cot in the corner across from Nas. Miriam paused in the middle of the room, considered for a moment, and set her pack on the one to the left of Scott's, leaving an empty cot in between.

Sam automatically took it, neighboring her brother. Her heart kicked at the thought of sleeping in such proximity to Miriam. She set her items down but didn't sit. Instead, she ignored her body's weariness and moved back to the door, hoping to explore until her sudden spike of nerves settled.

Second to last to enter the room, Fox passed by their young guide who waited outside in the hall. The Temunco marine bowed his head politely. "I am young, but I *am* a good marine."

Fox's eyes widened.

Sam slipped out of the room, hiding a laugh behind her hand.

○

Sam normally showered in the morning, but she made an exception then. It was late, and some of the others had already fallen asleep. Warm recycled water slid over her, washing away the soap, sweat, and oils of travel. The water temperature wasn't hot enough to steam, but it was enough to help clear her mind. Between the long journey, her morning interaction with her brother, and new teammates, she was drained from the emotional ups and downs.

She was grateful to have the whole dorm bathroom to herself, and Sam basked in the moment of privacy—she didn't expect to have much of that in this mission with Echo. The shared community facility at the end of the hall was meant for all the marines of this barracks, but at this hour, it was quiet. On her brief self-led tour, they seemed to be the only inhabitants, anyway.

The spigot above her stuttered, tutting impatiently. It signaled the coming end of her rationed cleansing. She sighed, but remained where she was until the water flow turned into a drip and then nothing. A shiver ran over her skin. The room itself wasn't cold, but now wet and without the lukewarm stream, she reached for the thin, raggedy towel and dried off.

Draping the towel around her shoulders, she stepped out of the booth. She couldn't wait to succumb to the crash her body desired. Her clothes were waiting where she last put them, on the long bench in front of the row of showers, and she pulled fresh undergarments on. She threw the wet towel onto the bench and reached for her T-shirt.

"Hey."

Sam startled and turned to the voice, gripping her shirt to her chest.

Miriam leaned against one of the end partitions, a gray towel thrown over a shoulder. She wore only her sports bra on her torso, her midsection bare. Sam swallowed and averted her eyes, focusing on Miriam's face instead. Worse. She tore her focus away to a stain on the wall behind Miriam, darting between that and those light-brown eyes. Sam felt naked, despite the layer of clothing she already wore.

The medic's mouth twitched upward, and her eyes blazed. She raised her hand. "Sorry. Didn't mean to scare you."

Sam weaved her arms as speedily as possible into her shirt's sleeves, suddenly conscious of her body. "You're maybe the quietest person I've ever met."

Miriam snorted. "Quietest? That's new. And coming from the *actual* quiet one…"

Sam pulled the shirt over her head. "You know what I meant."

"Sure. I'll make more noise next time."

Sam wanted to say more, but she didn't know what. Her headspace, cleared by the shower, had returned to mush. They had shared only a paltry amount of time alone, and she wanted to know more about the woman.

Miriam's gaze penetrated her, unmoving. Sam then realized that even if she asked Miriam something, it would probably turn back to her. She didn't want to be asked about herself. She wasn't sure if she had anything impressive enough to talk about. Sam didn't know why, but she desperately wanted Miriam to like her.

"Well, goodnight…Tanner," she said instead.

Another time then.

"Goodnight, Valkyrie."

Sam moved toward the exit.

No. Now. Something had been chewing on her mind since the trip, and she turned back to Miriam, who had already started kicking off her pants. Sam's cheeks warmed, and her eyes flicked back to the smudge on the wall.

"You mentioned before, back on the ship…you're not planning on staying with UMF." Sam stole a glance at the woman and immediately regretted it as warmth flooded her cheeks. Her attention locked on the wall stain. She tried to keep her voice even. "Why not?"

Miriam heedlessly pulled a leg free from the uniform and studied her. She thought for a moment, then spoke. "There's more to life than the marines, right? I'd like to travel, get out, explore if possible. Plus, my parents manage one of Station's medical centers. I guess there are expectations for me to help run it with them."

"So why the military? You didn't have to join with that kind of cred—" she stopped herself. *Idiot.* "Sorry."

The medic gracefully flicked her discarded clothing up with a foot, catching the garment and placing it on the bench. She stood there, confidently, in nothing but her black undergarments, deep in thought. Then, Miriam shook an open hand and shrugged. "I don't know, stage of rebellion? Postponing the suffering with my parents?" She chuckled. "I thought this would be a good challenge, I guess. Something different."

"Oh," Sam uttered softly.

"I don't hate it, you know. It's an interesting chapter of my life. I've met a lot of good people." She paused, considering. Miriam shrugged again. "How about you?"

"I just renewed, well, put my request in. It'll be my fourth contract—"

"Fourth!" Miriam exclaimed, her eyes wide. "How old are you?"

Sam didn't know how to respond to that. She wasn't sure if she liked that Miriam didn't know about her. She thought her reputation as the youngest SOG marine had reached Station. It did, at least to Krill and Fox.

"Twenty-three," Sam muttered. "You?"

Miriam's eyes glazed as she did the math in her head.

"I joined when I was twelve."

The other woman whistled. "Hell." And then, as an afterthought: "I'm twenty-eight. Shit, I should've figured you for a masochist."

Sam didn't feel like a masochist.

"I, I like UMF."

"Sure, you'd have to, I guess. But what are your plans after? Can't do it forever, right?" Light-brown eyes pierced her. "Who do you want to be?"

Miriam's questions continued to bounce in her head, edging out other thoughts as Sam retreated along the lonely corridor to the dorm room. She had fumbled out of answering that question and slipped away with another muttered goodnight. By the time she got to her bed, her mind was a blur. Insecurity blanketed her as she replayed snippets of their interaction over and over.

Why did she have to open her mouth? *Idiot.*

Who *did* Sam want to be? She was a marine. She never wanted anything more. Why did she have to be something else?

⏚

Despite the turmoil raging inside her head, Sam fell asleep almost immediately. Some hours of uninterrupted sleep later, she felt refreshed. It wasn't a lot, but it was enough.

She had woken up at the sound of Scott stirring six minutes before her alarm buzzed against her wrist. Half the team had already scattered off to shower and prepare for the day. She looked sideways to Miriam's bed, but it was empty, the sheets rumpled and thrown back. Sam felt a pull of disappointment, but also relief. The scene from last night replayed again in her mind, and she cringed.

Sam rubbed the sleep out of her eyes. Her spine popped satisfyingly in a deep stretch. She remembered where she was as she pulled on her boots and fixed her hair in a high bun. The excitement grew in her gut. This was another part of the world she had never explored, and although the brief back in Station had mentioned a tough journey ahead of them, she looked forward to it.

The chow hall was easy to find as Echo followed the flood of UMF personnel starting their day and the trickle filtering away, the night shift returning to their quarters to rest. Once inside the facility, it was noisy, filled with laughter and the scraping of metallic utensils against plates. Conversations carried on in a mix of accents and the local dialect. The demographics here were not as diverse as Station headquarters, and most of the population had similar tanned skin tones and dark hair.

The SOG marines sat at their own round table in the center of the busy room—too small to fit the group of eight, yet they squeezed together with borrowed chairs from other areas. Krill joined the group from the long food line and set his plate down, maneuvering into a seat next to Yuri and Miriam. Sam scooted her chair back in an attempt to make space for herself, a little more breathing room for her comfort.

Kai leaned in as best as she could. "Is it just me, or are they staring?"

Sam looked up from her half-finished plate and glanced around the room. The siblings had been on the receiving end of many stares in their lives, but this was intensified. The Temunco marines were either blatantly watching or unsuccessfully pretending they weren't. Echo wasn't exactly camouflaged into the scene either. The Station marines were still wearing their lighter uniforms, but color aside, their clothes looked sharper than the faded uniforms around them. The team and recon duo had pulled off all their black tabs and any SOG-identifiers on the ship, but they stood out. They *were* Special Operations Group. Plus, it must've been a comical image as they crammed shoulder-to-shoulder around the table.

"They're starin'," Fox grunted without looking up, his mouth still partially full of the porridge-like mush. He shoveled another spoonful into his face, to Kai's disgust. Fox rolled his eyes and stuck a pasty tongue out at her.

"We're in the country now. Of course they're confused by us city folk," Yuri added warmly.

Fox's eyes shifted to Sam and Scott. He spoke out of the side of his mouth, food still inside. "Maybe the *golden twins* should cover their heads."

Scott ignored the comment and stabbed at a biscuit-like shape on Sam's plate. Sam raised an eyebrow at Fox, then separately to her brother. *Really?*

Fox swallowed his food and winked back.

She batted away Scott's hand and returned to her plate. Her Echo teammate wasn't wrong though. Sam knew their blond hair was an unnecessary spotlight. She felt Scott's touch on her knee and brought her bouncing leg to a stop.

"I don't think they're used to seeing Station show up this far south," Yuri said. He took a small bite, chewed, and swallowed. "They seem to be pretty self-sufficient, probably try to keep things in-house."

"Apparently not sufficient enough to do these settlement ops on their own. Not that I'm complaining. I'm not complaining," Nas said.

Kai reached for her cup of filtered water. "Well, the food is good." She poked a lump on the plate in front of her. "Doesn't look the best, but it's better than that artificial chicken wrap they serve at the DFAC."

Fox gruffly responded, "Nothin' is better than chicken tender wrap Mondays." Small flecks of slurry flew out of his mouth as he talked.

Kai's lip curled and she covered her plate in defense. "Fox!" she admonished.

Sam stifled a laugh. She agreed with Kai, though. Whatever beige-white, starchy pulp the cooks served here was savory with hints of spice and seasoning. She couldn't place the slightly sweet aftertaste, but the meal was rich and delicious. With all things UMF, Sam was sure it was pumped full of lab-engineered nutrients and calories. It didn't matter; it was hot and better than the bars and ready meals in their packs. She missed Elly's coffee on board the scout cruiser. The bitter swill in the mess left much to be desired.

"Let me know if we need anything else for today. Don't forget. TOC brief in thirty," Krill told the group. It was a reminder to be done and ready outside in fifteen minutes, if not earlier.

⏀

The Tactical Operations Center was a dark space illuminated by multiple screens along each wall. First Officer Sandoval stood behind five watch officers and specialists who manned the terminals while the teenager from the previous night and two others stood stiffly near the back.

A dark-skinned woman with short dark hair strolled in; her officer's uniform was fitted and immaculately pressed. She took her place at the console in the center of the room. With a tug on her sleeves, she peered around the room and nodded at Echo.

"Good morning. I'm Amalia Otueome, Commanding Officer of Temunco." She had a Station accent—not from the region. "Is this everyone?"

"Yes, CO," her second-in-command stated.

Disappointment flashed across her stern face. "I ask for an entire company, and Command sends just one SOG unit. Typical." She raised one hand to the group and rubbed her neck harshly with the other. "No offense, not your fault." She turned to Sandoval. "Alright, take it away."

"Yes, CO." The officer blinked at one of the watch officers, who pushed herself away from her terminal and stood.

The watch officer looked down at her holopad and read out loud. "Regarding the incident from last night, MP is processing the marine now. All evidence and correspondence were gathered this morning and will be sent to the judges. For missions, as of zero seven this morning, Matam route is green, no reports. Palguin route holds at red, continued conflict consistent with previous reports." She looked up from the holopad, her morning report done.

"Thank you, Sofi," CO Otueome said.

The watch officer sat back down.

The Temunco CO scratched her head and addressed Echo. "Another fresh recruit with Charon propaganda trying to radicalize others. The goon ran when he was found out."

That explained the fracas the SOG marines had heard on arrival.

"We're already having trouble with numbers. Now add on finding potential marines with *clean* records… What a mess. Is Station having the same issues?" It was a rhetorical question as she didn't wait for a response. "Resources aside and Command only sending one unit…" She muttered something unintelligible. "Station's probably cracking down on the Charonites more so with that summit."

"Yes ma'am," Krill responded.

"But I digress. You're not here to help with our recruitment issues. I don't even know what can be done about it myself… Let's get back to it. Diego?"

Unfazed, the first officer stepped forward to the center console and tapped a button. A holomap appeared, stretching out in front of the room.

"As Sofi mentioned, the Matam route is green. Mal and Juancho are your prowler drivers." He wagged his finger at the two marines next to Hikari-Rezin. "It is one, two hours' ride through the mountains to the last drivable point. From there, it will be another hour or so by foot and cable lift. Jun will be your guide. Matam SecTeam cannot provide rabbits at this time, but the road shouldn't take long through farmlands to the west gate. And you are lucky. No rain. Yet."

"Thank you, we appreciate the support and the lift," Krill said.

"Call in when you are heading back, and we can send drivers to meet you. Do you know when you will return yet?"

"No, but we'll give a heads-up as soon as we know."

"We normally send our marines to Matam for rest and relaxation via the river, but we've been having more scuffles with Charonites and alterados along that route. I sent it up the chain to Command requesting support, but…here we are. It's not worth the headache going that way without reinforcements," CO Otueome added.

"Sorry, ma'am. I don't know much about that. Should *we* be concerned?" Krill asked.

Sam felt guilty that she had thought little about the mission after Krill's initial brief in Station, but now in the TOC, she grew uncertain. It was a large objective. Look into the issues in the settlement, monitor Children of Charon involvement, and keep them at bay, specifically anything that could endanger the upcoming summit with the Altered. The talks were in less than a week. If this was a concern, UMF should have sent units to the south much earlier to scope and control the situation.

"I've told Command." The Temunco leader's hands fluttered up. "Just know that the settlements and people around here tolerate us. And barely. They're certainly not fans of UMF operations in their little fiefdoms. Whatever Command has you doing here, getting each settlement's SecTeam support may be best. Or not. You do what you think is right." She eyed the team and their uniforms. "Either way, I recommend a change of clothes if you have any. Diego, have you gone over the comms with them?"

First Officer Sandoval nodded and steepled his hands underneath his round chin. His eyes flitted to Yuri. "Yes." He peered at the rest of the team. "But for the others, please remember that the terrain here differs from yours up north. Each prowler is outfitted with its own long-range repeater. You will need the portable for the extra boost when you go on your own. It is your direct line to us and Command. The settlements have their own versions, but as the CO mentioned, they are not fond of UMF. We do not have consistent communication with them, if any. However, we will send a message to Matam to give their SecTeam notice. They dislike surprises. I will also let our repair squad know you are heading out there. They left for Zapala some days ago to help fix their communication system. The lead, Ari, is very good. He and his guys can show you around. If they finish early, I will have them meet up with you in Matam."

Krill thanked the first officer and turned to his team. "Greg, you've got our repeater?"

"Yes. I'll stop by the tower and do some last calibrations, too," Yuri responded.

Krill looked back at the two officers. "We'll have Tan, our medic, stop by your clinic as well." To Miriam, he said, "See if there's anything else we need to bring. Just remember we won't have prowlers for the last portion."

The commanding officer rubbed her neck. "There's a clinic in Matam, but...it's the south."

Echo understood. Even if UMF had a good relationship with the southern settlements—which they didn't—the medical equipment wouldn't be as modern and updated. The difference with the north's technological capabilities was already evident in Temunco.

"So, thirteen hundred at the south garages?" Krill looked at the two drivers and Hikari-Rezin.

They nodded affirmatively.

"Good. Gives everyone time for lunch before. Eat up, get your energy."

CO Otueome gave a weak smile. "Let us know if we can help. And I apologize for the earlier lack of enthusiasm. It's been some time since I was last in the city, and it really *is* nice to see Station faces here, even if it's you SOG lot." She grinned wider now. "Our home is yours. Leave whatever you need to in the dorms. It's yours until you return; grab whatever gear you need as well. Diego can assist." She crossed her arms.

The brief was over.

5

EXPEDITION

"A FULL DAY, MAYBE!"

"What?" Yuri shouted over the wind and the engine's deep grumble.

Mal, their prowler driver, yelled again, "A day!"

Yuri's head bobbed in the passenger seat. "Crazy!"

Sam was grateful for the all-terrain vehicle and cable systems built long ago. If not, the trek by foot would have taken far too long. Mal had explained there were pedestrian-accessible shortcuts, but as Sam watched the topography change in their ascent, she questioned what southerners considered "accessible."

"If it rains...two days! More!" the driver hollered.

The prowler hit a bump, jostling five marines within its open cage.

"Glad it's not raining!" Miriam shouted from the middle row.

Sam was also grateful for the cloudless day. The harsh sun stood high in the sky, and the weathered route up and through the mountain had been relatively monotonous minus the occasional bump. The prowler's large, treaded tires bit easily into the gritty incline now, but Sam imagined rainfall would cause significant issues on the steep and winding path.

Sam stuck her hand out of the vehicle, pressing it into the current and letting the warm air dance between her fingers. Outside, the scenery had changed wonderfully. Although she was used to the northern woods, Sam and the others were in awe of the forest and its thick vegetation. The strange climate and a plantation effort by multiple generations before must have allowed this lush land to thrive. To the Station marines, this was something never experienced where they lived, only seen on the network and holopads.

Sam thumbed her rifle stock and rubbed a spot on her stiff pants leg. She preferred her worn-in UMF-issued clothing. They weren't too flattering, but she missed the large pockets. It was just more functional, more comfortable.

With the commanding officer's recommendation, the SOG marines and Hikari-Rezin had changed into civilian clothes. For Sam, this meant a simple T-shirt over tighter, less-pocketed pants. They had left a set of uniforms in the dorm, and their packs were roomier now. Nas, of course, filled his space with candy bars bought from the compound commissary. Echo looked less military but still just as much tactical mercenary. It was only slightly improved camouflage to blend in, but with the SecTeam and Children of Charon further south, it was better than the recognizable UMF clothing. Over their new, local look, they were kitted up in varying hybrid armor—a mix of low- and high-profile rigs. They kept their rifles slung in plain view.

As briefed, the drivers dropped them off at a flat section over two-thirds up a large mountain. A sad, lonely shack sat in a small roundabout. This was as far as any vehicle could go. Cliffs and steep mountains stretched beyond, and the paths forward were too small for even a smaller two-seat rabbit.

The team unloaded and adjusted their gear from the back of the prowlers, including the mobile long-range repeater inside a slim case attached to Yuri's pack. It was exactly 1500 hours on Sam's wristcuff display when the prowlers sped away, leaving behind a trail of dust.

Led by a baby-faced marine whose large pack, a multitude of additional supplies, and rifle accentuated his scrawny body, the SOG marines trekked forward. They were on their own in a new world of trees and towering natural structures in the distance. Sam took up the rear as they ventured further, where the wide path transitioned into a worn rocky trail.

"Junpei…er, Jun. When you go home, how long does it take you?" Kai said. Sam was impressed and realized that Kai had caught on to the South's preferred use of first names. Sam had noticed back in the TOC brief but couldn't quite shake the discomfort in immediate informality. She preferred Station's last name or Ursus's callsign customs.

Hikari—no, Junpei, raised his voice so he didn't have to turn around. "Maybe a few hours from NZ to MT and another few from MT to Temunco. With transportation. Without? Maybe a day. More. But everyone usually stops in MT."

"Hell. And that's in good conditions," Kai said.

"Yes, in good conditions," he repeated. Junpei jumped from rock to rock.

Sam carefully stepped into a small section of large boulders with a sudden awareness of her shorter breaths. The altitude was much higher here, with thousands of meters difference from their coastal living. She needed to acclimate. She wasn't sure how people made this trip normally. Did they have porters who carried packages between settlements? In the north, they had delivery services, an entire industry with dedicated personnel and rabbits to disperse trade and goods across settlements. But in the north, they at least had some kind of infrastructure and road system in place—something built on the previous generations' work. Here, she started to understand how the settlements and outposts were fairly independent, sustaining their own operations with necessary services. Movement was doable but limited in the Andean region.

"Do you see your family often?"

The teen pondered. "I joined yoomy—I mean, UMF, two years ago with my friends. This will be my first time back in a... long time." He paused, and in a softer voice, he said, "My sister sent a message a while ago. My mother's cough is getting worse, so this trip is..."

"Two birds, one stone," Fox grunted as he grabbed a tree trunk for support.

Junpei stopped and tilted his head. He didn't understand the saying and looked to Fox for an explanation. It *was* an older phrase that had stuck around, although there were little birds left, mostly just the memories of them in the digital archives.

Fox shrugged.

"That'll be nice to see your family," Kai said.

A row of slightly crooked teeth flashed. "Yes." Sam noted a shade of pink crawling up Junpei's neck before he spun away.

Unaware of the effect of her attention, Kai continued, "Do you know more about Temunco's...issues? What CO Otueome mentioned this morning?"

"Oh. You mean the recruits," Junpei started. He hooked his hands tensely underneath the straps of his large pack. "With the Charonite migration, it is getting harder for post."

"Migration. Because of Legion?"

The teenager shrugged, a casual attempt to hide the change in his posture. His voice lowered. "All the alterados."

Before anyone could ask what he meant, the forest opened into a clearing with calf-high grass. With no trees to block the view, the landscape was overwhelming with its mountain peaks, cliffs, ravines, and gullies below. Sam exhaled and marveled at the sheer size and untouched greenery around them.

Her attention shifted to a metal structure that stood out on a flat man-made slab on the edge of a steep decline. They had reached the first of two aerial lift systems on their route. It was a rudimentary design, but the most elementary things seemed to be timeless and best. A thick pillar served as one base, connected by thick steel track cables and a separate propulsion line to another mountainside roughly two kilometers away, and then another one further out. After activating her hololens, Sam could make out the last thick metal trunk, a gray thumb sticking out, mirrored across the way. A cable car was a speck on the other side.

Junpei skipped forward and opened a console box on the base station. He flipped a switch, and the cables creaked and whined in the track as they moved. The kid had done this several times before.

In the wait, Fox sat on a fallen tree trunk, set down his heavy weapon, and rolled his shoulders.

Sam leaned against a nearby boulder and watched the cable car slowly return. She had never taken an aerial tram, and though she understood the concept, Sam still had doubts. The cables were thick and sturdy, but the enormous distance and drop below seemed impossible. She picked up a small stone, running her finger over its jagged edges to placate her growing nerves.

"So, how old are you exactly?" Nas asked Junpei. He peeled open a candy bar. Kai shot her teammate a look, and he shrugged back. Nas wasn't diplomatic like her, nor was he trying to be.

Junpei's shoulders drooped, and Nas quickly splayed his hands at the visible change in demeanor.

Sam understood Junpei's reaction. She recalled the backhanded teasing and words passed in hushed tones about *her* age when she first joined. As she lazily threw the rock at a rotted trunk, she wondered if Junpei was often teased for how young he looked. The stone landed softly inside a small hole in the middle of the rotted stump.

"Sixteen…" Junpei responded, jutting his chin out. "But I know what I'm doing."

Sam's eyes quirked up. She would've guessed much younger. Or she just felt much older. Junpei must've been around fourteen years old when he enlisted. It was two years older than when she had enlisted herself, but still much younger than the other Station marines were used to.

Fox exhaled. "Fuck me."

"I'm not the youngest one at Temunco," Junpei added, his chest puffing.

"Who's the youngest? A damn baby?" Fox chucked a loose fist at the teen's shoulder. Junpei rocked back, unsure at first, but at the sight of Fox's grin, he let a smile slip.

"They do start them young outside of Station," Yuri said over his shoulder. He stood closer to the ledge, admiring the scenery below and beyond.

Sam felt Scott's gaze on her, and she faced him. He looked away. She wasn't the youngest anymore, not with Kai, Nas, and now Junpei around. She was one of the more experienced marines despite her age. Sam picked up another rock, letting it roll around in her palm.

Junpei shrugged. "I like it."

Fox muttered back, "Course you do." To Sam's recollection, Fox had joined UMF at a relatively young age, too.

"My mother said it'd be safer for me in Temunco. Less gangs. Less Legion," Junpei said. He spat to the side at the mention of the Altered military and security force.

Sam tossed the new rock at the dead tree. It landed again in the hole, a nice clack as it met the previous stone. When she looked up, Miriam and Fox were watching her. Fox nudged his boot at a pile of large rocks, a competitive glint in his light eyes.

Nas nodded and crossed his arms around his rifle, hugging it to his chest. "That's right. The Legion post to the south. Is it border fighting?"

"I think so. When they raid, the NZ gangs will mess with them too, now and then. Those are bad days, but...they do not last long. The fights."

A cable car sailed to them only thirty meters away now, a quiet whirr along the thick cables.

Fox gave in and picked up a rock, measuring it in his palm. Junpei and the others watched him. He looked at the tree stump and considered, but the thought petered out as a hushed screech signaled the impending arrival of their ride, and he chucked the stone to the side. He shot Sam a smirk as if acknowledging some unsaid challenge.

She ignored him.

The tram slowed to a smooth halt before the base station, and Sam moved toward it with the others, peering into one of its windows. It was a rounded capsule, spacious enough to comfortably fit twenty civilians. It would be plenty for the nine marines. The interior design was simple: some vertical bars for structural integrity and no benches. Standing room only. It was simply a container to move people and things from one point to another.

She looked around at the group and then at the vessel. Everyone and everything seemed too big, too heavy for this to possibly work. Sam was not the only one skeptical of the lift system.

As they stepped into the car, Krill spoke up. "This *will* hold us, right?"

Junpei laughed. "Should!"

It wasn't a comforting answer, but the cable system did its job. Despite Sam's clenched grip on one of the bars, the trip across the divide was smooth with minimal swaying. Junpei tried to assure the team that these systems were entirely safe, even in lousy weather. Fox had found that to be the opportune time to test the teenager's claim by trying to rock the cable car, pumping his legs up and down. This was immediately stopped by stern glares from the others, although his antics received a quickly stifled howl of laughter from Junpei.

A while later, the team stepped out onto a new mountain and traversed a small stretch to the other side of the range. Although Sam decided she was not a fan of being dangled in a metal box over a steep drop, she was grateful for the efficiency and alternative to long bouts of rocky inclines and declines. Whoever had engineered and installed these systems years before was a godsend.

So, when the team arrived at the next cable base station, they were shocked. Like the previous one, this system had its tower. *Unlike* the other, the car rested on the dirt platform, and its thick cables hung off the tracks over the lip of the mountain. The opposite post sat like a middle finger protruding from the mountainside only two kilometers away. Just beyond the stretch was their destination, or at least the outskirts of Matam.

"Well, shit," Fox grumbled. He and Junpei crept toward the edge to peer over.

Had the cable snapped after all this time? Was maintenance regularly done? What if the previous cable car had broken while suspended above the gap? How did one even build these things? How would they repair it? Sam stilled the onslaught of questions and paths her brain was sending her. The most prominent question was "how," but looking at the thick steel cables, the more important questions were "why" and "who."

"Could it have broken on its own?" Kai said.

"There's no way. See how thick these cables are?" Nas responded.

Kai narrowed her eyes. "I know, but I have to ask before we move on to what we're all thinking."

Scott signed to his sister, SOMEONE CUT THIS. DELIBERATE.

Sam nodded and scratched at the rough patch on her thumb. The first and obvious answer to "why" was to sever the route, the connection from Temunco to Matam. Echo had barely started their mission, and it was already evolving in front of them.

Miriam echoed Sam's thoughts out loud, "Did this just become an investigation op?"

Nas pumped a fist close to his chest, and he shared a look of glee with Kai.

Krill said nothing. His forehead furrowed. After a long moment, Echo's team lead turned to his second. "Get the long-range up. I'll message it into Command…and the outpost." Then, he turned to their young guide. "Hik…Jun, are there any other ways across?"

They hadn't even made it to Matam yet, and they already had something to investigate. But first, they needed to get out of the mountains.

As Yuri worked on setting up the case, Junpei fell into silence, his tongue darting out of his mouth. Sam imagined he was plotting maps and points in his head, calculating times and routes. The Temunco marine paced without a word between the different trailheads that branched away from the clearing.

Finally, he returned to the group. "There are other ways…

but this one…" He pointed at an overgrown, narrow path leading north toward a cluster of tall cliffs. "…will be the fastest. Another few hours, maybe less for you." He looked around at the special op marines. Sam eyed the other trails warily and looked down the south path, which led downhill to the river and winded away from their destination.

"And the others? How long would those take?"

Junpei raised six, then seven fingers, and shrugged. "Más o menos. I have never been through the others. There are supposed to be bridges, but it is close to the river. The river is not a good place right now."

Krill cursed under his breath and looked at the cuff on his wrist.

"We don't want to be out here when the sun goes down," Yuri reminded.

Sam nodded. Hiking in this landscape in the dark, with only their lights and visors to see would be deadly. The terrain was already difficult as it was.

The lead closed one eye and pinched his mouth. "Is it safe?"

Junpei's side-eye and shrug kicked up some doubt.

6

DEVIATION

"THIS IS A JOKE, RIGHT?"

Kai peered over the edge, her neck stretching as far as her body would allow, feet firmly on the path, one foot away from the cliff ledge. Strands of loose, dark hair whipped in a frenzy around her as a gust of air churned against them.

A ravine tumbled below. Thousands of meters plunging straight down. The ground at the bottom made Sam nauseous if she stared at it too long. The air, light of oxygen, meant dizziness and fog edged constantly at her mind.

She wiped a line of sweat with her shirt before the wind could take it. It had been an arduous hike to this point with rocky and ankle-twisting scrambles and treacherous drops. Their hands and knees were already scraped up from the sharp edges along the steep trail.

Junpei, on the other hand, didn't look a bit winded. He replied to Kai with a loud chirp. "It'll be okay. I've done this once before."

The others around him were still catching their breath, beads of sweat glistening on their foreheads. The altitude was a cruel stranger to them as well.

"For Temunco?" Yuri shouted incredulously, a crack from his usual chipper demeanor. This detour was not ideal.

Junpei shrugged and squeaked, "For fun."

Sam groaned. *Fantastic.* He had never done this with full gear and weapons.

"Fuckin' hell," Fox muttered as he shuffled closer to the edge.

Sam was inclined to agree. The hike up had been breathtaking—a show of how little they were compared to the natural behemoths around them—but it was also incredibly dangerous and difficult.

Now, the path in front taunted them—a narrow ledge etched into the face of a daunting cliff. To the left was a sheer wall of vertical rock that stretched up into the sky—at this close distance, she couldn't see where it ended—only a small lip hung over the footpath, not much cover for any rockslides from above. To the right of the path was a straight drop. At its widest, the ledge looked to be about half a meter wide. At its most narrow point, less than a third. The path looked like it had been worn down by the elements, not so much by foot traffic. Metal handholds were bolted to the wall in a scattered line at varying heights and distances. Across the cliff face, roughly ten meters away, Echo could see where the path opened and widened on the side of the mountain. Sam doubted many people took this route intentionally.

"Do we have rope?" Kai asked. Sam could see her already mentally constructing a safety line across.

Junpei was undisturbed. "It looks worse than it is," he promised. Then he swung his rifle behind him and nimbly darted forward to grab a handhold, positioning his feet on the path. "See. Not bad." He maneuvered forward with youth and the lack of fear that came with it.

At the midpoint, he looked back at Echo with a quizzical expression.

They stared back at him, unmoving.

"Come on."

Sam determined that Junpei, as shy and demure as he had initially come off, was very much in his element now. She hesitated, fished her gloves from her pack—glad she had brought the pair with a better grip—and waited for someone else to take the first step.

Anticipation was a bitch.

Nas watched her and nervously slipped on his own gloves.

Krill eyed the cliff. It was apparent the new leader was second guessing his decision, a nervousness that he brought eight others to their expedited death, well before they even started toward their objective. "Do we even *have* rope?"

They all knew they didn't, at least not enough for this feat. No one had been expecting this. Sam was both grateful to the individuals who had installed the cable lifts to bypass these nightmarish routes and simultaneously indignant at whoever had possibly cut the cable lines forcing them to take these paths.

In the pregnant silence, she could hear the others calculating in their minds how the crossing would work with their much larger bodies and heavier gear. Sam was doing the same thing. The longer alternative path sounded like a better option, even if it meant they'd be stuck in the dark at some point.

Junpei was almost to the other side when he leaned back, his arms fully extending like a casual canopy. He looked questionably at the group again and cocked his head to the right as if to say, *let's go*.

Anticipation was a dirty bitch.

Her brother was the first of the SOG marines to move. Scott

silently rearranged his rifle around his gear and took out the remaining slack in the strap. Sam held her breath as he squeezed her shoulder and eased to the front. She held back from grabbing him, from pulling him away from the danger.

She was equally in awe and terrified as she watched her brother grab the handholds and pull himself sideways onto the thin ledge of rock. He maneuvered much slower and more cautiously than Junpei, but he was moving.

Past Scott, Junpei reached the end and jumped off to the wider trail. He leaned outward to grin at the group from across the way. He was showing off, glad to have something over the SOG marines.

Sam felt a twang of jealousy, of his lack of fear in this situation. Humans and Altered, she could manage—they were mostly predictable. Nature was another thing. No matter how many man-made handholds were hammered into the cliff's surface, there was a lack of safety, of security in this beautiful, haunting place.

Scott's motions seemed to stir the group. It was one thing to watch the much smaller and youthful Junpei cross the path, and another to see an older and larger teammate perform the same action.

"Shit…" Fox mumbled against the wind. His mischievousness and boldness in the first cable car was gone. There was no metal cage around him to act as a buffer. He adjusted his equipment, balancing his heavy weapon across his chest, and awkwardly followed Scott, not to be shown up by anyone else. Fox was laser-focused on the placement of his feet as he shimmied forward.

Krill was next. He cinched his rifle strap taut against his chest and moved to the first handhold.

To Sam's relief, Scott reached the end of the path without incident. Leaning outward to see around Fox and the others, she watched Junpei grab her brother's pack in support, pulling him into the other landing.

Several seconds later, Fox also reached the end of the track, having found confidence as he moved along. He shuffled to a stop and looked back at the others. "Ain't too bad!" He shot a grin at Sam.

She narrowed her eyes. *Show-off.*

However, as Fox reached for the last handhold, his right foot slipped on a patch of loose rock. Pebbles scattered below him into the chasm and his eyes widened as he fell backward.

Sam felt a gasp escape her mouth. Her heart skipped in dreadful suspension, feebly watching from afar.

But Junpei's hand was on Fox's wrist, pulling the much larger man back before his heavy weight could bring him down. Scott grabbed a shoulder strap, adding more pull back into the cliff.

Fox gripped the handhold and stabilized himself. With a pale face, he murmured something Sam couldn't hear over the draft of air and hurried onto the landing to join her brother and Junpei.

"You okay?" Krill shouted.

Fox provided a weak thumbs-up. Even with the distance, Sam could see his elevated hand trembling. She felt the group exhale in relief with her.

Krill hesitantly continued his shuffle, and as he reached the middle of the path, Nas readied himself on the first rung and looked back at Kai expectantly.

She closed one eye in a grimace. "I just need a second." She took a couple of deep breaths and then nodded to herself in whatever internal affirmation and encouragement she found. She followed Nas onto the thin ledge.

Sam scratched at her thumb, but was unsatisfied with the motion, her gloves a layer between her skin and nail. Her hands grew clammy underneath the fabric, and she scanned the cliff face again. Her eyes dropped as she followed dirt disturbed by Kai's foot, trickling into the gaping abyss below. She set her jaw and glanced up, meeting her brother's eyes. His hands made small, but familiar motions. YOU'RE OKAY.

Not asking. Telling.

Her eye twitched, a small show of irritation that he had crossed first without her. But she nodded, inhaled deeply, and then slowly counted out her exhale.

I'm better than okay. And she was.

At her side, Yuri motioned his hand forward to Miriam. "Ladies first."

"You're so kind," she sneered, but positioned her hands and feet, and started the shuffle forward.

Sam followed Miriam after she had moved a few steps in. She didn't dare look over to track where Nas and Kai were, afraid that her attention would fall on the emptiness behind and below her. As she moved sideways, she was immediately glad about her judgment on the gloves. Though the handles fit well in her hand, the extra grip was another layer of confidence when she moved further from safety. She kept her eyes on Miriam, using the woman as a marker, stepping where she stepped, alternating from handhold to handhold.

Not even to the midpoint, Sam heard an ominous clattering above them, and her eyes looked up in dread. A shower of loose rocks accelerated toward them. Her stomach sank, and a clammy vise wrapped around her body as the noise thundered louder. Closer. Sam averted her gaze and strengthened her grip against the holds, pressing herself as close to the stone surface as possible.

Next to her, Miriam frantically hugged the wall, flattening herself as much as possible beneath the thin lip protruding above them. It would maybe provide some deflection and cover.

Sam watched the rocks hail past out of the corner of her eye; she felt some of the smaller ones bounce off her pack. She heard them hit the tough fabric of Miriam's next to her.

Sam wanted to close her eyes, wanted to wish herself out of this situation. She wanted to be on the other side, in Matam, back home, anywhere but there at that moment. She wanted to be somewhere she had control, and she wanted to violently harm whoever had messed with the cable lift system and pushed them into this detour. Her anger speared at Krill for his decision, at her brother for going without her, and then she was mad at herself for being weak. She adjusted her right grip as the brunt of the danger passed.

Sam's hearing adjusted, and she heard the others cry out. Had her teammates been shouting the entire time? Even if temporary, perhaps she had started to call them friends.

Right then, a large rock tumbled down, a stray from the pack. It caught Miriam's bag, knocking the woman off balance into the open air. Sam's heart dropped as she watched Miriam lose her grasp on the steel handhold and her right foot slip completely off the ridge.

Miriam fell.

And suddenly, every muscle, tendon, and ligament screamed. Every fiber tightened and strained to support the sudden and full weight of a marine and her gear from her right arm. Sam clenched her jaw so hard from the exertion and pain that she thought her teeth would shatter. With her left hand, she gripped one rung, trying to contort her wrist and forearm in a better brace. She held onto one of the medic's pack straps with her other hand. And at the end, Miriam dangled, locked in with her chest strap and buckles. Her legs hovered in the air. Sam could barely make out the trees in the forest below as they rushed up to flood her vision. Her mind careened, and she felt her breath catch as the edges of control disappeared. Her heart raced in her ears with its strong, muffled whump after whump.

Pain. So much pain. This wasn't sustainable. Sam's arm felt like a coil unraveling. It was excruciating, but what was her other option? Let go? She couldn't.

Miriam was looking down, paralyzed in her own trance of fear.

Sam needed to get her attention. "Tan…"

Her joints groaned as she tried to tighten and flex. Her shoulder threatened to pop, to dislocate. And her knees buckled as her legs tried to find a more advantageous position. What if she fell? How long would it take for her to hit the ground? Her arms trembled, her own limb threatening to betray her.

No.

She had control.

She wouldn't let go.

"Mir…" Sam tried again.

Miriam looked up, her eyes following their connection, grazing up Sam's wrist, her tattooed forearm, and then to her face.

Good, Sam had her attention.

Miriam was panting, breaths shallow, but as their eyes snapped together, Sam saw clarity return and the realization of where they were.

"Can you…reach…" Sam said. Her breath grew sharper, more laborious. Hot, flashing pain surged through her whole body now.

Miriam eyed the narrow ridge just above her head and the handhold another meter above it. She gulped and stretched out her other arm to grip the ridge. The motion pulled then alleviated some weight, and Sam groaned at the little relief.

She dug into her last reservoir of strength and lifted the

woman up. Another pop of warmth flooded her shoulder and down her arm. She ignored it and didn't let go of Miriam's pack until she was back in a stable position, both hands holding the bars.

Miriam pressed her forehead to the side of the cliff. A wave of stuttering hyperventilation came over her, her body shaking dangerously.

Sam panted, and her hand struggled to lift and grab her own rung. She forced a wrist around it to maintain her balance for now, and stabbing lightning shot through her shoulder as she moved. Sam fought to control her body as she felt the incoming adrenaline surge. It was good for one thing, though—masking the anguish that was her entire arm and shoulder.

"Are you hurt?" Sam gritted her teeth. Beads of sweat had formed on the crest of her forehead.

The others were calling to them, but she disregarded the noise.

The medic didn't respond.

"Miriam."

Miriam snapped out of her daze and looked up. Sam anchored her gaze and let herself fall into those light-brown eyes. She could feel Miriam's breath slow in their proximity. The panic dissipated from the medic's eyes, and her head bobbed gratefully as the muscle memory of SOG training returned.

"You're okay." Sam nodded. *You're better than okay. You're beautiful.* She swept away the abrupt thought. "We have to keep moving. Just a bit more." She tried to put a reassuring hand on Miriam's shoulder, winced at the motion, and readjusted herself. Sam looked past her, breaking their connection. Most of the team was there, watching her, beckoning encouragingly. Their mouths were open, but she couldn't make out their words.

Sam wanted off this death walkway, but she couldn't move, not with Miriam still frozen there. The other woman's hands were white-knuckled around the handholds, her bent arms tensed.

"Mir. It's okay. I'm here."

Miriam shuffled to the side, her feet finding security first, then planting. One foot after another. One more handhold after the other. Sam pushed through, focusing on one hand, one foot, one hand, one foot. She was so concentrated that she startled when the weight from her pack lightened.

Scott.

He clenched an exterior strap and helped pull her onto the wider platform, away from the edge. His eyes were distraught. She could see the white scar on his palm as his fingers reached to check her shoulder, her back, her arm.

She shook her head. *Don't touch it*. She inhaled a hiss with a clenched jaw to keep her teeth from chattering. Sam reached with her good hand back to find the cliff wall. Solid. *Safety*. She leaned into it, waiting to catch her breath and her composure.

With each controlled inhale and then exhale, she pulled and pieced herself back together while her brother hovered close by.

"Close, too close," Nas said.

"Everyone okay?" Yuri said as he jumped to the path, the last one to cross.

Krill's eyes flitted back and forth between Sam and Miriam, alarm and guilt dancing in his dark pupils. His gaze lingered at Sam's hold on her injured arm. It was her dominant arm, her gun hand.

No one answered.

The lead whipped around to their Temunco guide. "Are there more passes like that?"

Junpei gulped, but shook his head, his playfulness gone.

Relief swept the group. There was no going back now, anyway.

"Okay. Take a breather, but I want to put distance between us and here as soon as possible," Krill said. He gave Sam another look.

She nodded, then winced. Krill responded with a mouthed *thank you*, then stepped to where Miriam sat on the ground. Kai kneeled next to her and offered her water. Miriam's hands trembled as she received the container.

"You alright?" Yuri said as he carefully weaved back to the siblings.

Sam wove her left hand at him. She'd live. When Miriam had her breath back, the medic would help patch her up. Or at least enough to get to Matam to get better care. Sam needed that arm.

Past the others, Nas flexed his biceps at Fox and Junpei, and glanced back at her. His eyes widened apologetically when he saw her watching, but Sam shot him a soft smirk, and he returned to hushed gestures and chatter with the other two. Apparently, her reputation would live on.

"People do this for fun?" Kai shouted to Junpei.

The Andean native only shrugged.

7

WELCOME

AS THE MARINES descended the last mountain toward the settlement, the forest opened in various clearings of smaller, thin trees, sprouting out from charred and dead tree clusters. The group approached a fork in the path just beyond one of these graveyard nurseries. The left and north-facing route declined into one valley of farms, and the other led to a small, metal bridge across a gorge. Patches of green farmland quilted another valley beyond, and a wide river wound through it like a venomous snake, bordered by yellow plots of land. Matam sat in the distance, apart from the waterway. It was a dense spot of brown structures.

A family of four, dressed in faded neutral colors, crossed the bridge in a single line with several items on their backs. An older, bearded male, with an old revolver tucked into his belt, led three of what seemed to be his children, similar in their crooked noses and weak chins. The second in line was a stout, young man, a walking rectangle. Trailing behind was a skinny teenage boy younger than Junpei, and an even younger girl, perhaps eight or nine years old. They looked to be returning from a supply run from the nearby settlement. It was a strange scene, with packages extending five heads above every individual.

The marines stood to the side to let them by.

"Ho," the gray-haired father grunted at the group.

Junpei and Krill returned their greetings. The rest of the team observed with various nods and looks of polite acknowledgment.

The eldest son looked at the marines. His eyes narrowed as he passed Fox, who stood the tallest with his LMG slung over his shoulder.

Sam fought back a laugh. Male machismo. Brave, but stupid. Fox could break the young farmer's bones easily. She was confident she could, too, even with her shoulder braced and pain-blockers in her bloodstream. She could still feel where Miriam's hands and fingers had touched her.

The son's heavy cargo wobbled as he tried to maintain eye contact with Fox, and he raised one of his arms to steady his burden. As he lifted his limb, the folded tunic sleeve fell back and revealed a dark tattoo of a black lantern on his tricep. It was quite simple: two curvy lines made up the body of the hand lantern, with a top and wide base.

The second son gawked at the marines, his lower jaw slackening and showing a crooked row of bottom teeth. His head swiveled as he passed, staring at the strangers and their tactical gear.

Behind him, the girl was just as curious. She stopped in front of Sam and stared up at her, eyes like saucers. A smudge of dirt streaked her forehead.

Unlike her cool stares at the rest of the procession, Sam smiled warmly down at her. The girl's knotted fingers reached up for Sam's golden hair but fell short. Sam cautiously crouched to meet the child at her eye level, gently bracing her right arm to minimize movement to the thin medical bandage.

The girl pulled her hand back but remained. Her eyes shifted focus to the visor, hololens, and commcuff.

"Ven aca ahora!" the father snapped. His sharpness froze the girl, and she jerked back, running to catch up with her family. Her father smacked her across the back of her head with a free hand as she passed.

Sam's stomach twisted. A wave of emotion—anger?— rolled over her. She squeezed her right arm, her fingernails biting into the scar. She stared after the departing farmers and picked at the edges of that unidentifiable feeling, trying to unravel what it meant. But it was too murky, too far away.

A warm hand touched her left shoulder.

You okay?

She shook her head, shook the feeling away. "Yeah."

Scott's eyebrow raised.

Sam gave him a brittle smile and slowly signed back, I'm okay. She'd be better than okay when her shoulder was fully fixed.

She moved forward across the bridge after the others, and Scott followed at her side. At the end, Miriam had stopped to wait for them. Sam remembered the careful touches as the medic checked the length of her arm, the soft "thank you" in her ear when Miriam bandaged her shoulder. She thought of the warmth in those brown eyes as she stopped the pain with an injection. She saw it again now.

Scott tussled her hair, messing up her bun. She felt a tenderness in the motion, that closeness with her brother. The feeling, however, cut short and the invisible wall shuttered back in place as he left to catch up with Yuri, leaving Sam alone to walk with Miriam at the group's rear.

"You might've been her first blonde," Miriam said.

"Hm?"

"The little girl."

"Probably..." Sam replied. She reminded herself to purchase a hat or some kind of local headgear to hide her hair. It was too much of a beacon in the land of brunettes.

Her self-consciousness increased now, with the medic walking beside her. Unsure of what to say, Sam scanned the changing scenery of terraced farmland with their neat aisles of pods and irrigation lines.

"How's the arm? Let me see."

Sam obliged and angled her body to the medic. Miriam carefully patted a corner of a gel bandage down without breaking her stride.

"Whatever you gave me is working." The injury worried Sam, but she didn't want that concern to show.

"Good. I'll see if Matam has a MedJet. We'll fix you right up."

"Thank you."

"No," Miriam said softly, "thank *you*. I wouldn't be here if you hadn't..." Her eyes dropped to Sam's tattoo. "Thank you."

Sam watched those eyes, and then the light freckling in a small splash across the bridge of her nose. She wondered if Miriam felt the same electricity coursing through her body now.

"You saw the big kid's tattoo?" Fox's voice broke the spell.

Nas nodded vigorously, a frown contorting his brow. "Charon's mark."

Kai called out, "Jun, the Charonites. How large *is* the presence here?"

The teenager threw his voice over his shoulder. "Big."

"We *are* closer to the border," Nas added.

"And in the south," Miriam said.

"I heard that Charon himself grew up in one of the southern settlements. Before all the 'humans first and only' stick," Nas said.

Kai turned to him. "And who did you hear that from?"

Nas shrugged.

"I wouldn't be surprised," said Miriam. "His words are like wildfire in the outer settlements."

"Is his mantra really that terrible?" Fox said.

Kai's head whipped to him. "Humans first and only?" She emphasized each word separately.

"*We* are humans, Kai," Fox said.

"So you support kidnapping, torturing, raping, and executing innocent people?"

"Are alties actually innoce—" Nas cut off as Kai's intense glare stabbed at him. He flinched. "Add on how they treat sympathizers. COC doesn't care about collateral damage."

Fox raised his hands in defense. "I d'int say I agree with how they do it. They're nutters anyhow."

But he had already stoked a fire. Kai's face flushed, and her steps became heavier against the dirt road. "They're criminals. Terrorists. They're on the same level as wunbies. 'One blood, one promise' drivel."

Fox pumped his hands again. "Oy. I don't support the COCsuckers, Kai."

Kai sighed, her ire dissipating. "Why can't we just coexist?"

"Yoomy and COC? Or humans and alties?" Nas snorted. "Things are okay with the alties right now, I guess. But only because of Station. And maybe the current Sovereign."

Yuri, who like Krill, Sam, and Scott, had remained quiet but was following the conversation, called out now. "Nas, were you even alive during the last Sovereign's reign of terror?"

Nas mock laughed and stuck out his tongue. He wasn't immune to the age jokes from the team, even with Junpei there.

The team's second winked back.

"Well, we're doing better now, at least," Kai said. "We have the summit, so that's a big step. We have City Center in Station. If only we could get the south to play nice..." She perked up. "Jun, what are the settlements really like? Any equivalent of diplomatic centers or efforts here?"

Fox rolled his eyes. "If they did, we wouldn't be here, would we?"

Kai shot a look at him.

Junpei shrugged. "We have the governor and other leaders. But I do not think anything diplomatic like you say. My mother used to tell me and my sister stories about the old times, when it was more peaceful. She said the towns used to be run by old women. Elders or something... They were more diplomatic, I think."

"Matriarchs?" Kai asked.

"Yes. Those. She said they kept the peace a long time ago, but then the alterados came and...no sé. They're just stories now. I guess the people wanted more security. More power."

Yuri chimed in. "Sounds like they became scared. Fear does drive people..."

"And hate," Miriam said.

Kai shook her head. "So they turned to the Charonites?" She pondered for a second. "I guess you can't blame them. Legionnaires *are* pretty intimidating."

"Have you met one?" Nas said.

"No, have you?"

Nas shook his head. "I think I've only seen them from afar. That armor though...wish I could get a better look. I'd love to see a praetorian too..."

"I could take one on," Fox said. "Get rid of all that tech and armor? Yeah. I could take on a legionnaire. Think you could, too, kid." He patted Junpei on the back.

Sam didn't have to scoff. Kai, Nas, and Miriam did it for her.

Junpei looked at Fox, the others, and then back to the large marine. "I think I am good. The regular alterados are already…" He quieted.

"Nah, Legion ain't too bad. It's just their armor, but once you get through that, easy peasy," Fox grunted back, but with a softer smile reserved for the kid.

Sam raised an eyebrow. Fox was wildly understating, but Junpei's shoulders relaxed.

The path flattened out into a road barely wide enough for two rabbits side by side, or six of Echo shoulder to shoulder. Small fencing on each side of the lane separated the throughway from rows of vertical pods with fresh greens. Irrigation and fertilizing tubes ran between each pod, and micro-solar panels covered the tops of each rack. The north had similar structures, but Sam had never seen this many farms together in one place.

Loud voices and commotion turned her attention further down the road. Sam could make out a group of men smudged with dirt and dark stains huddled around something, struggling to drag it into the road from a perpendicular path. Beyond that, Sam could make out a bridge over what she assumed was the river.

"Hey, hey." One scrawny, especially dirty man with mangy hair nudged one of the others and nodded at the marines who had come to a stop meters away from them.

Fox quietly pulled Junpei, who had gone stiff, behind him.

Sam realized the large bag on the ground was, in fact, a person. It was a bloodied man with a swollen face, and scrapes and welts showing all over exposed skin where the clothes had rolled up or torn. A breeze lifted, and she could smell a metallic copper twang mixed with another foul scent. She wasn't sure if it came from the person on the ground or the hoard of men surrounding him.

A tension suspended in the air as the gang turned to face

Echo. Sam angled herself toward the right side of the road, almost standing in the ditch shoulder to watch everyone. She knew her brother had moved to the left, mirroring her.

There were six people. Sam monitored as two of the men furthest away moved their hands to their waistbands. She could spot dark shapes of ink on different parts of the individuals' skin. Children of Charon lamps.

She touched her right thumb to cool metal and slowly manipulated the safety off on her rifle, keeping the weapon in a casual position against her chest so as not to alarm or telegraph her intentions. She could hear a few soft clicks around her as the other marines had the same idea. They hadn't even reached the settlement walls and were already face-to-face with their target.

Krill held a hand out in a greeting and placating gesture, not touching the weapon still slung on his shoulder. He called out in a steady voice, "Good afternoon, gentlemen."

One of the gang members, a large birthmark stamped on the side of his bald head that looked like a single horn, dropped the leg he was holding and straightened up much taller and wider than Echo's team lead, almost the same height as Fox. He puffed his chest out and looked menacingly up and down at Krill and the heavily armed group behind him.

Sam fought the urge to roll her eyes. The bull had bravado.

A knotted, smaller hand curled around the man's forearm at his lamp tattoo. At the touch, Bull took a small step to the side, although his threatening glare settled on Fox. A spindly woman with a small, sharp nose, a shrewish face, and a short haircut that stood up at odd angles stepped forward. A long revolver hung loosely in a tattered holster on her skinny waist.

She addressed Krill in an equally shrewish voice steeped in the regional accent. "Good afternoon…"

Sam was confident Krill's greeting of "gentle" did not suit the group in front of them.

The woman flashed a cruel smile, and Sam saw red gums and yellowing teeth. Her eyes were dark black, but they blazed with something furious and crazy, asking to be challenged. Her skinny neck showed a red patch of irritated skin—scratch marks.

Sam quickly scanned the others, and she found more of those scrapes. Her lip curled. She recognized it. She had seen it many times before. This woman, this shrew, the leader of this band of misfit Charonites, was a stim junkie. Dilated eyes proved they were hopped up on it now. Sam raised her guard a tick higher. She disliked the Children of Charon, and she hated junkies. The combination…

Behind Shrew and her pet Bull, the person on the ground groaned and flopped over onto their back, the bloody and bruised head lolled to the left. Black and gray hair stuck out in tufts, matted with thick blood. He opened his eyes and looked at the marines.

A flash of blue, green, and brown.

Heterochromatic eyes.

Altered.

8

BULLIES

KAI GASPED THEN STEPPED FORWARD, but Krill put his hand behind his back, fingers splayed. *Hold.*

It was the right call. Sam could see four other figures further down, walking in their direction. They were coming from the bridge, another body dragged between them. Sam caught more movement in the corner of her eye, behind the marines. She turned her head only slightly as to not attract attention. Two young adults were trying to sneak up behind Echo.

It would be twelve against nine. With UMF's armor and high-caliber weapons, the marines had better odds, but it was too early for trouble. Matam was just beyond this group. Sam could make out the perimeter wall and the people that milled around.

She glanced at Scott over her shoulder, and they shared a look. She knew he had also detected the flanking individuals. They slowly angled their bodies to face outward. As per their usual routine built out of years working together, Sam knew if anything happened, she would handle the male on her left and Scott, the other.

"Can we help you?" Shrew asked.

"We're on our way to Matam," Krill said.

The Altered man in front of her groaned, and Sam stole a glance to the side and down. The man was bloody and raw, skin missing all over his body from the grit and ground.

Bull kicked him in the ribs, and the Altered grunted.

Kai inched forward again.

Shrew squinted and examined the marines. "Qué tenemos aquí…" The Charonite's voice became a nasal hiss. Her eyes raked over the others, Scott, then Sam. "You are not from Temunco. Too pretty for Temunco…" Eyes widened then narrowed again as another member whispered into her ear. "Que interesante. So why *are* Command marines out here, so far away from home?"

So much for blending in. Sam didn't have high expectations, but still.

"We don't want any trouble," Krill said.

"Nem nós," Shrew snorted.

The men behind her echoed in soft snickers.

"You still have not answered my question? Are all you grunts estúpido?"

The gang's laughter grew.

Sam's fingers rubbed against the stock of her rifle. She was a bit taken aback by the audacity and outright confidence of the gang. The Charonites here were different from what she and her brother were used to.

She checked on the two individuals who had wrapped around behind them. They had stopped approximately ten meters back from her and Scott, leaning against the fence. One, sinisterly handsome, picked at his fingernails.

"What did he do?" Krill motioned at the Altered man who was now watching Echo, slowly blinking those strange multicolored eyes. "What did *they* do?" he corrected as the four others stopped shortly behind the gang with their own package. The other body was smaller than the first Altered but just as bloody. A boy no older than Junpei.

Without the obvious difference in eye coloration, the two victims were indistinguishable from any other human. They bled and probably felt pain, like humans. They were not exempt from violence, like humans.

"Just digging out *ratas*. There is a constant infestation here. No help from you grunts." She spat on the Altered man with the last word.

Kai snarled under her breath, "Six to one. Terrorist filth."

Sam gripped her rifle. She was grateful Kai at least had the tact to whisper it. If the Charonites heard her…

"Whajya say?"

Sam's stomach sank.

One of the flanking men behind them loped onto the road, somehow much closer than she had last checked. A rusty pistol raised at Kai in an outstretched hand, a dirty finger twitching dangerously over the trigger. The Charonite junkie wore a disheveled shirt and ripped pants that hung off his bony skeleton. Thick, gnarled hair covered his head like a mop, and red marks gouged his neck.

Scott already had his weapon up and pointed at the man, the tip of its barrel only a couple of meters from its target. Sam mirrored her brother, holding her sights on the other male, who had hiked up his shirt to reveal the butt of a large sidearm in the waistline of his pants. He, unlike the other, continued to lean carelessly against the fence. One hand picked at its fingernails while the other pulled a long finger across his cheek and stared flatly at Sam. A pink tongue flickered out to wet his lips.

She could hear the gang, now behind her, pulling out their own weapons. She figured it was a mix of blades, clubs, and additional small firearms from their sounds. Someone thumped theirs against an open palm. Probably Bull. She recognized the sound of a few pistol hammers cocking. Sam's shoulder stretched and protested at her upraised position, but she ignored it.

The man holding his gun on Kai opened his mouth and flicked a tongue out between his surprisingly straight yet yellowing teeth. He took a step closer to Scott as if daring him to pull the trigger first.

Her brother didn't waver.

"Back up," Sam growled. It was easier to ignore the lumbering pain in her arm as her pulse quickened. She swung her barrel, adjusting slightly to aim at the man and then to the other who still lingered back. The man's eyes were black, his pupils oily and wide.

Junkie. Fucking junkie.

"Jus' wanted to hear what the little zorra said." His hand shook, and his lips twitched.

It was a standoff. The marines were better armed, but they were also nine to twelve, sandwiched in the middle. Sam knew she could easily take down her target, but it was still too high a risk. Echo wasn't in a good spot. Saving two Altered farmers wasn't their mission. The Children of Charon were, but not in this situation.

Shrew crowed, "We really going to do this?" She sounded entertained, almost excited.

The junkie crept forward again. Reckless.

"Back. The fuck. Up." Sam gritted out.

She heard Krill call out behind her. "How do you see this going? What, you shoot us, we shoot back?" He paused, but no one responded. "You shoot, and Command will only send more of us. You want that?"

It was a bluff. UMF Command was preoccupied with the

summit and its preparations. They had only sent eight SOG marines to deal with whatever clusterfuck was happening in the south. But the Charonites didn't need to know that.

With a quick flick of her eyes, Sam could see the entire team, except for Krill, had their weapons in a high-ready position, their weapon stocks drawn into their shoulders, barrels up.

"Maybe have your people stop pointing their weapons at mine," Krill encouraged.

As Shrew and the Charonites considered their situation, the junkies' teeth clicked against each other in the lull.

The afternoon sun blazed at Sam's skin, and a breeze tugged at her hair. A bead of sweat dropped in a line down the side of her face and her heart boomed in her chest steadily, a little elevated but still very much in control. Her breath was even.

This wasn't her first standoff. And it wouldn't be her last.

"Basta," the gang leader finally commanded.

As the other weapons lowered, Sam watched her team cautiously lower their own muzzles as well. She and Scott continued to hold theirs on the junkie in front of them, the initial and last remaining Charonite still with a raised gun.

"Flaco, déjalo."

The man gnashed his teeth, flashing both rows at Scott and then her like a mad animal. He punched his weapon out again, his grip so tight his hand shook, finger still dangerously on the trigger. Flaco then pulled the gun back and scratched his head with the slide. He spat a dark gob to the side and narrowed his eyes into thin slits.

Sam and Scott carefully brought their weapons to a low-ready position, muzzles at a downward angle, the rifle stocks still in the nooks of their shoulders.

The other male remained leaning in the same position against the fence. His dark eyes never left Sam during the ordeal, and she felt a crawling sensation over her skin now. It was unlike the strong repulsion she felt with Flaco. She felt violated in the way he fixated on her. *Creep.*

"Are we good?" the gang leader shrilled.

Sam heard someone—a marine—behind her inhale sharply then exhale. She heard Yuri say the team lead's name, hesitant and warning.

"What did they do?"

Flaco snarled but didn't raise his pistol. He was twitching, still amped-up.

"Is it your business?" Shrew said.

Krill gave no response.

Sam fought the urge to twist around and see what was happening.

A hoarse cackle whipped into her ears. "You have no authority over us."

UMF did. However, their authority did not seem to mean the same thing in certain regions, the south included. Sam knew arguing with this drugged-up Charonite gang wasn't worth it. It would fall on deaf ears. She knew the Echo lead knew it, too.

"Krill. They'll kill them," Kai murmured loudly.

Sam shot a glance over her shoulder.

"You an alt-lover, puta?" Flaco vehemently spat out.

The blood in Sam's veins iced at her mistake. As she turned her attention back to him, Flaco lunged forward and whipped up the pistol, pointing past Sam.

Sam lifted her carbine, neglecting the dull knives in her shoulder, but it was too late. Reaction against action was always too late. Motion blurred in Sam's peripheral vision, but her focus was on the man's finger on the thin metal trigger.

A deafening shot cracked out.

Ears ringing, Sam didn't dare turn back to see the killing blow.

She didn't have to.

There was none.

In hindsight, Sam didn't know if Flaco had meant to shoot, if it was the drugs and the lack of control, or if he had actually wanted to kill someone right then and there.

Instead, Scott stood above the junkie, who was now splayed out on the ground, pistol thrown to the side—a thin wisp of smoke drifting from its barrel. Her brother's rifle muzzle pressed into the Charonite's chest, pushing the fabric deeply into the man's sternum, outlining the bony ribs. Flaco's face distorted in confusion and pain, his breath knocked out from Scott's quick movement and resulting drop.

There was motion in the corner of Sam's eye. The second man, Creeper, had moved swiftly away from the fence and had closed in, only two meters from her.

Sam was ready this time. She raised her carbine and aimed at the man's torso, although it did little to deter his movement. He sidestepped to her left, maintaining a distance. His empty hands taunted her, but his weapon remained in his pants. She followed him with small pivoting steps, facing outward. She hissed air between clenched teeth. A warning. It didn't faze him as he continued side-stepping, still facing Sam, until he stopped on the group's right side. Sam angled herself to keep her weapon sights on the man but could now see the rest of the team and gang, her back to Scott. She didn't know what Creeper was doing but didn't trust him one bit.

Now with both groups in her sight, Sam saw the standoff had returned with a vengeance. And this time, every marine including Krill had their weapons up and trained on the Children of Charon group around them. Echo's team lead pointed his rifle right at the woman, whose own weapon remained in its holster.

Shrew groaned and shuttered her eyes. She mumbled something garbled, what seemed to be a stream of curses directed at Flaco. Then, she raised her hands in a conciliating gesture at Krill, unmoved by the gun in his hands. "Okay okay. That was our fault." She rubbed her hands along the back of her head, mussing her short hair. "Mira. You go on your way. We go on our way. Everyone happy. No one hurt. No one dead."

But Krill had enough. He growled, "Leave them."

The gang members behind Shrew snarled and pressed their variety of weapons forward. The marines didn't falter. Fox took a step forward. The brandished LMG looked light in his arms.

"And if we say no?"

"You lost that choice when your man tried to shoot one of mine."

Shrew tilted her head upward and sighed. "Fine."

Her group protested, whispering and shifting their surprised eyes back and forth between their leader and the marines. She rolled her head to the side as if she was bored, and then raised a limp hand to hush them. The gang dropped their weapons to their sides. It was a smart decision. The Charonites would live to hunt and torture Altered another day. Another day they'd avoid UMF's pending attention.

Echo cautiously lowered their weapons in response, although Sam held hers longer on Creeper before she relaxed. Her lip curled in disgust as his tongue flickered out and then pursed his lips at Sam. He rejoined his group and Sam took steps to the side to re-angle herself.

"Mute."

Scott looked up at Krill, his face devoid of any expression.

Then, he stepped three paces away from the man on the ground. His rifle relaxed and rested in one hand.

Flaco scurried up and glared sharply at Scott. He flitted around the cloud of marines, maintaining a safe distance, almost bumping into the other side's fence, and scrambled to join the rest of the gang.

Shrew jerked her head back to the settlement. "Just know, you are in our town, in Matam. We will be watching."

The threat was not subtle.

She turned her back on the marines and walked through her frozen crew. Sam heard her growl expletives at Flaco, as he scampered to follow her. Bull gave another hard, swift kick to the Altered's rib cage in passing. The rest of the Charonites retreated, although many of them didn't turn their backs on the marines until they were far enough apart, and even then, Sam watched them twist back with withering glares and obscene gestures.

As the gang shrunk with distance and disappeared past the gates of the settlement, the marines and the two Altered remained on the road. The first bloody figure on the ground stirred first. With a wary eye on the team and their weapons, he crawled painfully toward the other individual.

Kai stepped forward.

Sam moved to stop her. Her bleeding heart had already done enough. But Fox was there first, with an arm blocking the engineer. "Wait."

An injured Altered was still, after all, an Altered.

They watched, instead, as the man brushed his hands delicately over the other's still frame. The blood in their open wounds had already clotted and crusted. He cradled the head, matted in thick tufts, and ducked his head to touch their foreheads together.

Sam looked away briefly and swallowed. Her throat was dry.

Kai pushed past Fox's outstretched barrier and reached around her pack to grab a water pouch. She kneeled a few paces from the two Altered and offered the container.

Colorful eyes amidst broken red vessels looked up, and a raw, shaky hand took the gift. "Thank you." It was a raspy whisper that the marines would have missed if they were not all concentrated on the scene in front of them.

"Can we help you…back…" Kai asked.

Sam wasn't sure where *back* entailed. It was an offer Kai shouldn't have made, especially not to Altered strangers. The marines knew nothing about them except that Children of Charon had wanted to do extensive harm. Renewed caution and skepticism replaced Sam's initial sympathy.

"No." The Altered's voice was louder this time, with pained breaths between every other word. "Thank you… Just need…a moment…"

Sam wondered how many ribs had broken.

The man placed a hand tenderly on the other figure before attempting to sit upright. He slowly undid the top of the pouch and took a small sip, wincing at the motion. He then offered it to the younger male, gingerly cupping the back of his head with one hand.

In the middle of the group, Miriam swung her bag around to her front and retrieved a packet Sam recognized as general medical gel. Krill and Nas turned at the rustling noises and gave soft sounds of protest.

"Wait," Sam started, but Miriam had already approached the Altered. Sam tugged her rifle closer.

Kai looked up as Miriam passed her and kneeled closer to the injured figures, offering aid.

She was too close.

The Altered put up a weak hand, declining.

Yuri shifted his rifle to his side. "Where…"

The man looked warily at him.

"It's okay. We're not going to hurt you." Kai said.

The bloody man glanced around at the marines, finally settling on Kai. "Past the river." He pushed himself to a standing position, and Sam's fingers tightened around her rifle grip. Miriam took some steps back. Even injured, the Altered was daunting as he stood. It was his tri-color eyes and what they represented—a history of hostilities and strife.

The other individual on the ground moved and suddenly recoiled, his entire body jettisoning into a crouched position away from the marines. Blue, red, green, and brown flashed, the centerpiece of a scathing glare from a dirtied and torn face. Two large gashes split the second Altered's forehead and left cheek, from ear to nose. They were nasty cuts, and Sam could see the clotted blood and dirt in the ripped skin. Barely dried streaks formed a layer on all the exposed skin from the neck down into the tattered tunic. A rusty-brown color stained the fabric like an inconsistent dye. His intense eyes, one bloodshot with head trauma, turned to Sam. The hatred in his glare was heavy.

She felt the hair on the back of her neck rise.

She heard her callsign.

And then, her name.

She pulled her stare away from the Altered to the voice. Miriam was standing and had one hand raised to her. The medic softly pumped her hand down, and only then did Sam realize she had somehow raised her rifle, trained on the young Altered.

She lowered it and stepped back.

"Why did the Charonites—" Yuri started but cut off when the older Altered turned to him.

"My son and I...are just farmers... Our home is...past...the river—" the man said between breaths, gripping his ribs.

The son snapped his head up and hissed. "Don't tell them anything."

Kai motioned. "We're not with—"

The young Altered bared white teeth at her and scowled as he shakily stood up, his arm hanging at an odd angle. "Let's. Go," he growled to his father and limped backward to the perpendicular road. His eyes darted around to the Matam perimeter wall and back at the marines.

The father looked between his son and Echo. He gave them a curt nod and offered the water pouch back to Kai, who kindly declined.

The marines shifted to provide a safe berth between the Altered and themselves, and the two farmers walked slowly back down the road they were only recently dragged on. Colorful eyes watched the marines—one set a mix of gratefulness and curiosity, the other filled with something darker. Echo watched as they stumbled away.

When they were in the distance, Kai turned to Scott and said softly, "Thank you."

Krill also gave Scott an appreciative look similar to the one he had given Sam on the cliff passage. That was now twice the Ursus recon specialists had saved his teammates.

Their teammates.

Sam ignored the ache in her shoulder and swelled with pride. Her brother was too good to leave UMF—Echo saw it as well. She'd have no problem changing his mind before they were done with this mission.

As the marines resumed their stroll toward the settlement, Sam hoped they wouldn't run into any more trouble there, although she was doubtful. Their confrontation outside its gates teased at what lay ahead. It didn't matter, past or future—humans always found a way to violence.

PART 2
ACCELERATION

9

MATAM

"CAN you please point us in the right direction?"

The SecGuard looked in their twenties, large as could be—bigger than Fox. Their chest and shoulders were wide, barely restrained by a tight tan uniform threatening to burst at its seams. A large patch with an emblem of a shield and three crossed swords sat over the left breast pocket. They looked like a block of stone, their sleeves straining against muscles.

They glared at the nine marines standing in front of them, judging. Strangers. Foreigners. Military. Though no sounds came from their mouth or movement from their hands, the interaction was as accusatory and hostile as Echo's confrontation with the Charonites before.

The SecGuard's peers at the perimeter station did not seem to share as extreme of an attitude toward the arriving group, but Sam kept a cautious eye on them. She fought against the comfort of holding her rifle. It was probably better anyway. Her shoulder hadn't appreciated the sudden action before, and she braced it rigidly against her side now.

"Temunco messaged ahead. Can you tell us where your main office is?" Krill repeated with a smile that fell flat. He tried to remain calm and professional, but his patience was understandably wearing thin after their previous encounter.

The androgynous boulder stared at him for a beat. Then, they wrinkled their nose and sniffed. With a jerk of their head at their colleagues, the SecGuard turned and stalked into the settlement.

Krill looked after the moving wall and glanced back to his team. Sam watched the muscle above the lead's upper lip twitch and then relax as Krill followed. The marines tagged along behind.

Just inside the perimeter gate, a row of repair and maintenance shops welcomed the group. The narrow streets, barely wide enough with the encroaching stalls and kiosks, were layered with decades of grime and grease. Softer notes of soap and fabric replaced the smell of oil and metal as they passed into a crowded residential area. The rattle and noise changed as townsfolk scrubbed their dishes and washed clothes in small tubs on the narrow landing in front of apartment buildings made of old brick and concrete, patched up in layers over generations. Stares, more cautious than curious, followed the marines as they maneuvered through the small street in a single-file line behind their burly guide.

This town stretched horizontally instead of Station City's more vertical landscape. They had been walking for ages when Sam noticed a growing pattern of color in her periphery, flashes between each passing alley. Deep crimson red posters with dark ink plastered the walking seams between each housing block, barely visible from the main throughway. Even from the off-angle, Sam recognized the familiar lamp under a fresh sheen of glue.

Her jaw clenched.

Propaganda. They were deep in the territory of the Children of Charon.

She glanced at her brother behind her, and he nodded. He had seen the posters, too. He motioned discreetly, and she scanned the area, pretending to take in the sights and people. She caught a glimpse of two familiar faces slinking a distance behind them. Flaco. And Creeper. She monitored them until she lost their presence several blocks in. They wouldn't try anything here. Not with witnesses and the SecGuard so close by, right?

The market announced its presence two blocks before the group reached it. Fresh produce, spices, butchered meats, and then the savory smells of different street food. Sam's stomach grumbled. She couldn't remember how long it had been since she last ate—was it breakfast? Did she have lunch? The hunger only intensified after the arduous detour they had taken.

Plus, soreness was setting deep into her muscles and joints. Her shoulder ached again as the drug's effects wore off. It'd be time for another dose soon.

The traffic thickened as the road filled with stalls and booths showcasing leafy greens, powders in small translucent containers, and different cuts of meats and organs. The area was a clamor of business as vendors called out their wares and people bartered for goods. There were woks of all sizes, colorful tapestries, small animal hides, and jars with strange items floating in fluid. Children, who must've just left school, ran through the streets between the sea of legs, and Sam subtly pulled her rifle tighter to her body. The atmosphere distracted her from her usual dislike of crowds, and she stepped carefully behind Nas, who stuck his head into every alley and kiosk.

The noise, the odor, and the colors were overwhelming. Not unpleasant, but the new settlement enveloped Sam. It was unlike the northern towns—chaotic, but in a way where she felt like she had taken a step back in time, to how life might have been ages before the collapse. This market, Matam in general, was like someone had hit pause on time and preserved a lifestyle against all odds.

She would have missed the quick turn into a quieter and less occupied alley if not for her brother herding her by her good shoulder. As much as she wanted to experience more of the bedlam, she was glad for the relief. The group fell out of their single-file line and morphed back into an amoeba-like shape, the SecGuard a short distance in front.

As a native of the region, Junpei looked unimpressed, but he relished the team's expressions as they took everything in. His face lit up, and he threw up a finger at Fox. Before Fox could react, the teenager disappeared into a narrow, winding alley.

"Hey! Kid!" Fox yelped and halted abruptly in the middle of the alley, Kai and Nas just stopping before they collided with his pack.

Krill, Yuri, and Miriam turned at the interruption, but Junpei was already back with a giant grin. In his hands, he carried multiple skewers with hot, thin slices of greasy meat.

Junpei passed the sticks around to the others, and Fox and Nas ravenously bit into theirs, a line of juice slipping down their chins. At Boulder's stony glare, they continued moving forward. The group hushed as they chewed on their treats.

Sam delicately pulled a chunk off a stick and passed the rest to Scott. The meat was lean but tender, rich, and salty. It was a moment of ecstasy as she swallowed. She hadn't had real meat in years.

After a cursory wipe of his mouth with the back of his hand, Fox gripped both of Junpei's shoulders and heartily squeezed him. "Kid, we're keepin' you."

Junpei's grin grew as Nas clapped him on the back. He blushed as Kai reached over to ruffle his hair.

"What is this? It's delicious," Kai said.

Sam agreed silently as her stomach warmed. Real meat was

a delicacy, a rare treat. The south had life, trees, and actual animals that the north did not. Much of the destruction from previous generations had left the western coast of the southern continent relatively unscathed. Apparently, the governments here before weren't threatening enough in the past wars of the world. The north and Station's protein was mostly lab-engineered or plant based. It was a subtle contrast, especially after her years of routine diet, but tasting the real thing now made a world of difference.

The teenager smiled. "Cuy."

"Of course, the south has guinea pigs," Miriam said, delighted. She laughed after she swallowed another morsel.

Junpei looked pleased with himself. "My sister cooks it better. We'll have you over for dinner soon."

◯

The rest of the walk through the settlement passed faster, with Junpei happily picking up more street treats for the group. Their stomachs were full when the SecGuard led them into a semi-open space, similar to a square or town plaza. In this less-trafficked area, they stuck out more with their gear, despite their civilian clothes. Eyes followed the unit the entire way as they passed scattered vendors and SecGuards on their breaks.

Sam had purchased a light headscarf from a kiosk, and it now covered her head, her golden locks tucked safely underneath. Her scarf was solid black, unlike other locals' with multiple bright colors, but the fabric was airy and cool. Scott had picked up a simple gorra and thrown it over his short hair.

Boulder stopped at the door of SecHut, a brown, four-story building. It was the tallest structure in the entirety of Matam. Communication hardware stuck out from the top of the structure. This was where the settlement's main communications and central network system was. Other buildings around the city had been set up with repeaters, but this was it. It would also be one of the most armed spots of the settlement.

Their burly guide distrustfully glanced back to confirm if Echo was still behind them as they entered the main double doors into a lobby that had a stale metallic smell. SecHut was barren and quiet, except for the light tip-taps of a white-haired and spectacled man focused on his screen behind a rusting desk in the middle of the room.

Boulder ambled up to the counter and stood before the typing man, waiting. When the man did not look up, they kicked the desk soundly with their boot. The screen shuddered.

Only then did the receptionist look up and startle.

"Good afternoon," Krill said, stepping into view.

The man squeaked an unintelligible greeting back as he acknowledged the team lead. His gold-trimmed glasses almost slipped off his nose as he peeked up to see seven heavily armed individuals and a scrawny teenager wielding a rifle too large for his frame.

Boulder turned and faced Krill. They took a last scathing and sweeping look at the team and strode for the door. Junpei lurched to the side to avoid their path, and Sam turned to watch them leave. She caught the bottom of a dark lamp inked on their tricep, peeking out from underneath the taut sleeve.

"We're here to talk to your commander," Krill said. "We're from Station on important business."

Another soft squeak bubbled out of the man's mouth, but he leaned forward to press and hold a button on a keypad in front of him with one hand. With the other, he adjusted his glasses nervously, his eyes never leaving the marines. Sam wondered how often Temunco or UMF frequented the Matam SecHut. Rarely, based on the man's reaction.

Something whirred above them, and Sam fixed her eyes on a camera device in the room's corner. It swiveled down, its lens aimed at the group.

She then met Scott's gaze and subtly signed to him. THAT GUARD HAD A CHARON LAMP TATTOO.

He nodded. THIS WILL BE AN INTERESTING MISSION.

WILL? IT ALREADY IS.

Scott's lips pulled into a thin line. IT'S DEFINITELY DIFFERENT FROM HOME.

Home didn't have Children of Charon messing with Altered so close to a settlement. And she was pretty sure the north settlements' SecTeams didn't have Children of Charon amongst them. At least not yet.

HOW'S YOUR ARM?

She shrugged and touched her shoulder cautiously. She *was* worried about her dominant arm. It ached and was stiff now—her neck was also tense from bracing it in place. It was too early in the mission for an injury, and their encounter with the Charonites only forecasted more of its kind.

IT'LL BE FINE.

He gave her a dark look. Of course, he didn't believe her.

Sam dipped her head at the back of Miriam's head. SHE'LL FIX IT. IT'LL BE OKAY.

She turned away at the sound of heavy footsteps as they descended the stairs. A man with a large head and a wide midsection stopped short of the last step. He wore an ironed navy-colored jacket, but his tan pants and shirt underneath were wrinkled as if he had been sitting in them for a long time.

His arms opened to the group. "Station UMF! In my city. Or, what is it the young ones call it now? Yoom? Yoomf. Silly. Never mind." He wheezed and looked over the marines as if they were a new set of toys. "Please. Come up to my oficina! Come. Come!"

He gestured for them to follow and trod back up the stairs. Even at the ground level, still near the door, Sam could hear his harsh breaths at the top.

The marines exchanged uncertain and amused looks amongst themselves. This was a startling change from the hostile welcome they had received to this point.

Echo climbed two sets of stairs to the third floor and slowly and politely followed the short man down a wide hallway to a room at the end. In front of Sam, Nas twisted door handles as they passed. Halfway down the corridor, one of the handles squeaked loudly, and Krill glared back. Nas's head and ears sunk to his shoulders, and he stopped. Fox and Yuri shook their heads at him.

The corner office was quite large for a SecTeam official, but what space it potentially had was cluttered with lavish items on the floor, on end tables, and piles of dusty books. Two plump chairs occupied the space in front of the desk, along with a small area where Sam could've laid down comfortably.

The man diligently wobbled through the pillars of books and squeezed himself into a gaudy chair behind a desk. He waved one hand, beckoning, and with the other, he dabbed a cloth at his face.

Krill set his gear and rifle down outside of the office. He whispered to Yuri, and the second put down his items as well. The two shuffled into the room and sat in front of the desk. When they sunk into the chairs, both were noticeably lower to the ground than the commissioner across.

The rest of the team remained outside and settled where they were in the wide hallway. Sam had already slid her rifle off and was now cautiously extricating her right shoulder from her pack. A metal chair leaning against the far wall had her name on it, as long as the others didn't get to it first. She was ready to rest her body after the trek.

"Echo," she heard Krill call out.

Fox, already relieved of his own equipment—LMG and pack dumped haphazardly on the floor—popped into the office. When he turned back to the hall, his face pinched in concern and confusion. "He wants us all in there," he whispered loudly.

Kai mouthed *what* back at him, and her incredulous expression matched the others'.

Fox only shook his head and grimaced. He disappeared into the office.

Sam, rid of her heavy pack, moved for the door with Miriam and peered in. The space was far too small and only made smaller with its cheap show of opulence. Nine marines surely wouldn't fit.

Undeterred or ignorant of the fact, the commissioner waved emphatically at them. "Come. Come." His head dipped dramatically with each word.

Sam and Miriam hesitantly slid next to Fox and crammed themselves behind Krill's chair. As the others and Junpei joined in, their faces flickering with fear and uncertainty, they pressed and distorted closer together. Soft grunts and expletives murmured in the doughy tangle. A mix of sweat and street scents punctured Sam's nostrils as skin touched skin in violated personal space. She pressed awkwardly between Miriam and Fox and hugged her arm as close as she could, protecting it. If not for the pressure from both sides, she wouldn't have been upright or balanced. She strained to look to her side to see how her brother was faring, but it was a wasted effort.

She was deeply uncomfortable. This had to be a joke. Or a power play.

Satisfied, the commissioner clapped his hands once. His thick accent rolled over his shiny lips. "Diego messaged and said you were coming! It would have been nice if we had more notice, but UMF does what UMF wants, no?" The man chuckled to himself, though it caught, and he ended up coughing to the side. When the fit had passed, he adjusted his shirt collar that seemed too tight around his pale neck. "You are all very impressive. Big. Strong."

Sam didn't feel impressive, not in the compressed knots they were stuck in.

Yuri and Krill shifted uncomfortably in their chairs, attempting to subtly scoot closer to the desk for the others behind them.

Krill cleared his throat. "Yes, sir. Thank you. I am—"

"Ah, porra! I did not introduce myself." The man straightened in his chair, and Sam thought he intentionally puffed out his chest. "My name is Yosef Wilfredo Macias Laxa, head of the extraordinary Security Team of Matam!" He leaned forward. Sam could see the shine of wetness in his small, dark eyes. He added lightly, "And I am also running for governor soon. I have a good chance, they say." He leaned back in his chair and threw his arms to the space behind his desk. "Welcome to my city."

Someone's arm shifted, and it stuck in Sam's left rib cage. She couldn't tell if it was Fox or Miriam at this point. She didn't dare move her head.

"Thanks for having us. I'm Vallen Krill, the lead for Razor-Echo from Station. This is my second, Yuri Gregov. And my...team."

Commissioner Yosef scanned the group before him and tapped a finger to his bulbous nose. He didn't seem to notice or care how cramped the marines were. "Ah! And a Temunco marine, I assume?"

Sam felt the pressure against her body as someone, probably Junpei, tried to raise his hand in greeting. She was grateful when he gave up the motion. Cradling her arm, she was already being pushed inward at an angle facing Miriam.

Under the aroma of earth and sweat, she could still note the fading fragrance of cinnamon. She tried to shift back, extremely conscious of her forced proximity, but her body was pinned.

"We see many of you young Temuncans here. Hanging in *love alley* and the bars." The commissioner wiggled his fingers. "You be good now, ay? We do not need any more little bastards running around. Protection is key."

Before Junpei could protest, the man chortled to himself and wiped his eyes. "A magnificent team. Very strong. What does Station feed you?"

Sam shifted. *Please get us out of here, Krill.*

The lead stammered, "Er, thank you, sir. We are—"

"And what can I help you with? Why so far from Station?" the SecTeam commissioner interrupted again.

Krill cleared his throat. Sam could see the strain in his posture as he suppressed a growing irritation and frustration. "Command received a couple of reports in New Zapala and Matam—"

"From Matam?" the commissioner cut in. His round face squinched. "No...not from me or my team."

"—regarding COC and alty activity," Krill pushed through, his voice teetering dangerously into a monotone. "With the summit preparations in Station, we're here to help." He paused then quickly added, "Help *you* and your team secure the situation. You and your SecTeam are the experts here, absolutely."

Commissioner Yosef put his hand under his chin, and his eyes glazed over.

The Echo lead continued hesitantly, but in a light tone. "If you have any information on where the COC base of operations is, we'd appreciate it. We want to be prepared to address whatever issues..." None of Krill's words seemed to land. He waited to be talked over again, but for once there was nothing.

He moved along. "But we can discuss that more later. We plan to stay for a few nights to rest and get acquainted with your city. It shouldn't be too long. We'll head to New Zapala afterward."

Echo waited again for a response from the commissioner, but he was still. Sam wasn't sure if he had heard anything Krill said.

"If you could help direct us to nearby quar—"

"Who from Matam provided these reports?" The commissioner's voice had lost any of its previous warmth.

Krill's body went rigid. Sam could see his hand claw into his thigh.

"UMF should know SecTeam has the Charon situation well under control. We do not have any issues aside from the usual city squabbles. We surely did not ask for any assistance in this matter."

Yuri's head moved as if he were about to interject but stilled.

The commissioner continued, his tone brightening. "Although you are probably here because Zapala has been having a rough time with the Legion post set up nearby. Raids, so many raids. Their SecTeam is not as good at diplomacy and defense as we are. Ah, and Zapala cannot even maintain their own network. Did you know I tried to help that excuse of a colonel over there? Pah! He would not listen. He is just as incompetent as their current governor. If I were there, not that I would want to be, the alterados would run away! Did you know Diego had to send a unit to assist in their repairs? I gave his men safe passage."

He leaned back to catch his breath and steepled his hands, elbows on his chair's plush armrests. His stare turned cold, almost challenging to the marines squashed together opposite him.

"Me and my SecTeam are the *only* things keeping this city from chaos, you know…"

Someone stifled a cough, and the office fell quiet.

Yosef threw up his hands. "Stay a few nights if you need. You are welcome to use this SecHut while here. You will see we have everything under control. Let your Command know we are friends of UMF." He waved his fingers dismissively. "Check with Bogdan downstairs about temporary quarters; he will assign a sergeant to you while you are here."

"Sir, we don't need a—" Krill stopped himself. "Thank you, sir. We'll take our leave."

Both leaders were done with the other.

The marines mumbled their own acknowledgments as they untangled themselves and escaped from the office. Sam couldn't decide which was more suffocating: the cramped space or the man's ego. If it hadn't been made clear by the Charonites, it was now crystallized with SecTeam's unctuous welcome: Matam did not want them there.

10

LA POSADA

SAM DIDN'T KNOW who was more irritated: Krill or their mustached SecTeam babysitter. The two marched individually ahead of the group with distance between to blow off their own steam.

Sergeant Nicolau Baluyot's strides were long and heavy. He was unsubtle about his resentment, displeased about his assigned role as the marines' chaperone while they were in Matam. Echo had been audience to his loud protests to Bogdan, but the older receptionist indifferently waved him off. In the end, he had accepted what the SecTeam commissioner ordered, but he didn't have to like it. Nicolau had barely grunted at the marines before he marched ahead, guiding them to the small posada, the inn, that Bogdan had referred them to.

Aside from the tension, it was a lovely evening. Streaks of peach and strands of gold painted the sky between the cracks of the dense roofs and panels. As the town dimmed, lights turned on, casting soft yellow and orange glows in the narrow alleys.

It was almost enchanting, if not for Sam's uncanny feeling that they were being watched. She smoothed her headscarf and glanced back. A small man was hunched over, invested in a kiosk's wares. His spine protruded through the thin fabric of his shirt. He looked up to watch Fox and Kai, then across the street to another man whose eye peeked out over an old-generation tablet. He lowered the device, revealing the other, scarred-over eye. These stalkers were good, but Sam was better. She labeled them Spiny and Cyclops and kept an eye on them discreetly as they followed a good distance behind.

At the ragged door of an old, half-brick, half-stucco building, Nicolau pulled to the side, motioned, and said a curt goodnight over his shoulder. He mumbled something about meeting at SecHut the next morning, then promptly turned tail back in the direction they came, avoiding any further conversation with the group. Not that there had been much effort for interaction in the walk there.

As the team entered the structure, Sam noted their followers had hung back a block down. With the team's lodging known, they disappeared into the shadows. She'd have to keep an eye out for any signs of future trouble.

The inn itself was old but quaint. The smell of tobacco and dirt lingered in the small lobby, which was big enough for a counter, one armchair, and a thin, dusty floor lamp. A creaky staircase led up to the second floor, where Echo booked three cheap rooms near the end of the hall, away from any prying ears and general guest traffic. A community bathroom with three shower stalls was available at the far end, with a hovering hint of must and sweat in the air. Sam noted a small window where a decrepit and rusting ladder descended into a dimly lit back alley below. It wasn't much, but they had expected little to begin with. It had a contingency exit, and Sam could live with that.

The group split into three. Each living space contained two small, narrow beds and a foldable cot. Three marines per room. Yuri, Scott, and Nas took the first. Krill, Fox, and Junpei took the second one two doors down, and the women took the room directly across.

After they dropped off their gear and used the facilities, Echo and Junpei reconvened in their team lead's space. Nine people inside a room shared with the beds and minimal furniture still felt more spacious than Commissioner Yosef's office.

Fox sat on his bed furthest from the door, loosening his boots. Junpei perched cross-legged on his lower cot, close to the foot of Fox's bed. He blinked heavily to ward off fatigue.

Krill walked into the room, drying his wet hands on his pants, and closed the thin door behind him with a hooked leg. "Let's make this quick. Not sure I can deal with cramped spaces anymore after that...weird mess." He shuddered. "We'll convene at SecHut tomorrow morning. I have a feeling SecTeam isn't telling us...well, a lot, and we'll probably get the bare minimum if we ask around." Krill pinched the bridge of his nose. "This Sergeant Nicolau fellow doesn't seem to like us very much, but it'll be worth a try. We just need a better lead so we're not scattering out with nothing."

"And the cables?" Nas said.

"COC, cables, alties, why SecTeam is so up themselves, whatever. Command didn't exactly give us the most specific tasking. Not moaning, I just don't want to overlook anything," Krill replied. He glanced at Nas. "Everyone, just keep your eyes peeled and ears to the ground. Maybe a bit more subtle, though. Anyone who is willing to talk with, or at least tolerate us. Jun, you too—you know this place better than we do. I don't think I can handle another moment with that commissioner just yet, and if we can get a good source elsewhere, let's do it."

"We'll have to be careful. SecTeam isn't off our radar for... whatever Charonite activity we're looking into. There's too much influence here," Yuri said. He had probably seen the tattoo on Boulder as well.

"We can start from the farmlands and then work our way in. There might be some resistance if we start here." Krill looked around the crowded room. "We're all tired. Get settled. Go see the town if you feel like it but grab a buddy. I don't trust this place. Shower. Rest. You deserve it."

Sam hung back, waiting for the others to depart the room first. Goodnights were mumbled throughout the group as Nas and Kai filed out. Fox grabbed Junpei, and the two waltzed out, talking about the different food and shops that would still be open. It was still relatively early in the night, and venturing through the streets did sound interesting, but Sam was worn-out. The hotel bed was waiting.

Krill fell back onto his mattress and sighed loudly. He draped an arm heavily over his eyes and head. "Greg, let me know when you're ready. We need to send a report up."

"Give me ten," replied Yuri.

Miriam moved by, patting the lead's boot hanging out.

"Good job, bossman," she said tiredly, "good job."

Krill grunted, too exhausted to protest.

Outside the room, Scott touched his chin and motioned downward with his hand. GOODNIGHT. Sam returned the motion and mouthed a goodnight to Yuri and Miriam. Her brother hooked a left, and she had just put her hand on their room's doorknob when she heard her callsign.

She turned to Yuri's worried frown and saw that Scott had stopped in the corridor as well. "How's the shoulder?"

Concern and guilt flashed across Miriam's face.

"It'll heal." It wasn't a lie. Sam could already feel the gel working as elevated science sped up the process. The pain itself was manageable with the drugs Miriam injected. The medic was already monitoring it closely, and Sam was content with the extra attention.

"I'm heading out to find a clinic. But I don't know..." Miriam trailed off.

Sam understood. After seeing Temunco, she had expected the south to be a step backward in time, but not this much. This region seemed untouched and isolated still. The technologies they were privy to in the north now seemed like blessings they had taken for granted.

Whatever medication or gel bandages should do, Scott signed.

Yuri nodded. "Any medication or gel bandages, Tan," he repeated out loud. His eyes softened at Sam. "In the meantime, please rest."

She was planning on it.

⏀

After they had split up, Sam stood alone in the inn room. She was depleted but suddenly restless—a feeling aided by the lack of company, she had quickly gotten used to being around Echo. She liked them. A lot. Sam loved her team back in Ursus but found herself more comfortable with the Station SOG marines, like she fit in just a little better.

For the second time in a long while, she showered at night. The posada's shared bathroom tiles were molding and slimy, and she spent as little time as she could in the cold water, but she felt clean again.

She attempted to lie down but sleep evaded her, taunting from a near distance. The others had returned, and she now sat on the edge of the lumpy mattress, a fresh coat of gel bandages stiffening around her shoulder and another dose of drugs swirling through her veins. The throbbing ache dwindled.

She blinked heavily as she took in their lodging for the next however many nights. The women's windowless room was a mirror image of the other. The only illumination glowed from a tiny lamp beside the bed on the far side. Two beds and a cot. Kai had happily taken the cot, quoting how she was the most junior and youngest of the three. Sam didn't object, although it mattered little to her. She could've fallen asleep anywhere in practically any position, or at least she had thought she could.

Parallel to her bed, Miriam lay on her side facing Sam. She glanced up from her commcuff as Kai walked into the room, having changed into a fresh shirt and pants.

Kai stashed a small pouch into her bag and sat on her cot, combing her fingers through her dark hair. She had something on her mind. "I know there's a bigger COC presence here, but I didn't think it would be practically everyone and everywhere."

Sam nodded slowly. "The SecGuard…" she muttered.

"Those farmers, too," Miriam added, sitting up.

Kai made a face. "And that group. With the alties…"

A door slammed in the background, barely muffled by the thin inn wall.

"Do you think maybe those Charonites, that specific gang, is the reason we're out here in the first place? That they could actually mess things up for the summit?" Kai asked.

Miriam swept a stray hair out of her face. "That was only, what? A dozen people? From what we've seen so far, that seems like a fraction of what's actually happening here."

The Charon lamp tattoos. The posters. The settlement was a Children of Charon sanctuary.

"We're not in Station anymore," Miriam continued. "This *is* the south. It's almost lawless. I think this is as extremist as you can get. Charon represents strength and hope for these people."

"In a sick and twisted way," Kai sighed, falling back onto her cot. She kicked her legs up onto her pack leaning nearby.

Sam agreed. From her experience, people could only take so much before they grasped at any semblance of hope. Even if that hope made them lose touch with their own humanity.

Laughter drifted into the room from the hallway.

"It's not just the south."

Miriam and Kai turned to Sam.

She hadn't meant to say that out loud. Sam cleared her throat. "They're also gaining momentum in the settlements north of Ursus. Our leadership is quietly monitoring." She scratched at her thumb and looked down to see how raw her skin had gotten. "But the ones we ran into before are different from the Charonites in the north. They're more...intense. And they're using. That combination is trouble."

"Using?" Kai's voice cracked.

"Stims," Miriam answered.

Sam nodded. "We've seen a new strain popping up in the north, but I've never seen this many people on it. There are the usual signs—eye dilation, spastic movement...but look for the scratch marks. That's the new one. Supposedly makes the skin crawl."

Kai shuddered and scratched her arm absentmindedly. "I need to tell your brother 'thanks.' Again."

Good. Sam needed all the fodder she could to remind Scott of his skills and what he was doing for others. UMF needed him. She needed him.

Sam looked up and found Miriam staring at her. She swallowed.

"And the marines? Any issues like Temunco's recruitment, Charon radicalization?" Miriam asked.

Sam shook her head and willed herself not to break eye contact. "We've had too many ops against them. They're violent but amateur and unstructured. More like a nasty pest that won't go away. We're not worried about it." *Yet.* She looked down and fumbled with her fingers. She felt like she was speaking too much. "How about Station?"

"Command hasn't directly addressed it yet. I've seen one or two pop-ups of Charon graffiti in the city though. Nothing like here…but still." Miriam shrugged.

"My friend in District's SecTeam said it's the same for them," Kai said. She rubbed her eyes with her fists. "It's terrible. If this grows, it'll divide us, you know? We have to be a united front. Especially going into these talks with the Royals. It could be better. Everything could be better."

"I don't know if that's possible."

The two women looked at Miriam.

"There's too much history. Plus, with the current Royals, there's no common enemy for people to rally against. The north and south only came together because of the last Sovereign's hatred and violence against humans. Once the Court booted him out…well…" She rubbed her neck. "We're not good… we're not comfortable with peace."

Sam pinched and rubbed the space between her eyes as the room quieted. The settlement was falling asleep. A wave of lethargy passed over her, and she fought a yawn. Between Kai, the aspiring, hopeful diplomat, and Miriam, the realist, it was such a change from the usual marines Sam knew. Aside from her and Scott's team, most of the marines at Ursus didn't look outside of life and politics in the north, outside of their own settlements. Maybe she was guilty of that as well. It all seemed so mundane and trivial now. Sam inhaled deeply at her own realization and judgmental finger inward. *The irony.* Scott was right. Time away from Ursus, from the usual outpost folks, was good.

"Earlier today?" Kai's voice rang out. Her hands propped

behind her head while she stared up at the stained ceiling. "The Charonites and alties. I...I didn't think it was fair, you know? Why I..."

"No need to be sanctimonious," Miriam teased. Her tone softened. "Don't worry. You don't need to explain."

"No, I...it's important to me that you know I have your backs. When it comes down to it, yeah? I know I put us in a bad spot, a dangerous situation... It's not that I'm an *alty-lover* or anti-us, anti-human, I just..."

"You hate bullies," Sam affirmed. "It's okay. It worked out. We were going to stick out no matter what, anyway. Now we stick out *and* they know we don't mess around."

The others chuckled softly.

Sam yawned. She carefully lowered herself into the bed and heard the others nestle into their own. She stared up at the ceiling and the mottled texture splotched with stains that seemed to move as she fought against her drooping eyelids. This was that delirious stage as she evaded sleep, or maybe it was the other way around—sleep was avoiding her. Sam chuckled at a growing thought.

"What?" Miriam asked, amused.

Sam shook her head into the rough pillow. She fought against the words but felt especially comfortable with her company after an excruciatingly long day of shared weariness. Was it the pain medication? Her exhaustion? Both? It was a different intoxication.

Hell, she'd say it.

"Kai, you know what I first thought when I met you?"

"Oh?" Kai rolled up on one elbow to look at her.

"I...I thought you were some upper-class snoot who got into SOG with family connections. Just another stepping stone to whatever future you have in politics." Sam grinned at her, but her expression faltered as she immediately regretted it. Her impressions and judgment were best to stay inside her head, behind all the filters and introversion.

Miriam coughed, her eyes widening.

It was too late; it was already out there. Sam searched Kai's face frantically, hoping she had gauged their rapport correctly. It was too much. Why did she say anything at all?

Kai's face distorted, then slowly transfixed into a grin. Her almond eyes crinkled. "I mean…you're not wrong." She fell back onto her cot and laughed heartily.

"Shit, Valkyrie. Don't hold back." Miriam's echoing laughter was a sweet chorus to Sam's ears.

Kai's rolling fits subsided. "Hell, I'm glad we're finally cracking you open. You're a tough one. Maybe we'll get your brother talking next." She wiped a tear from her eye. "And what do you think about me now?"

"Shit, *I* want to know what you think about me," Miriam said.

Sam ignored Miriam and shook her head. "No, there's more to it…" She looked back at the ceiling stain. "I respect it. You're SOG, so you *had to* pass the usual physical and mental tests. And you're obviously smart. Probably much smarter than most UMF. There's just…there are other options to get into politics and diplomacy."

Kai pondered for a moment. "I guess the other methods seemed so dull in comparison. This is…real-time. I'm not reading it on the network days after. I feel like I'm doing something, even if it doesn't have a huge impact yet. Maybe it'll build into that down the road, you know?"

"Getting your boots dirty," Miriam said.

Sam touched her face. The engineer and future diplomat was the biggest bleeding heart she had met in her time at UMF. She wasn't just getting her boots dirty. She'd have blood on her hands one way or another. Kai's constant desire for peace and working in SOG didn't match. To her, SOG was the tip of humanity's spear. They were the necessary defense, the necessary violence, that *helped* pave a path for some politician or diplomat's peace treaty. Maybe *Sam* didn't understand politics. Or diplomacy.

She blurted out, "When you pull the trigger, will that eat away at you?"

"Does it eat away at you? Fox and Nas say you're Ursus's poster child. Hell, maybe even UMF's. One of the youngest marines to join. *The* youngest to join SOG," Kai responded.

"Well, no," Sam started, then paused. She hadn't expected the conversation to turn to her. She stared up, avoiding the eyes of whoever was watching her now. "I don't know, I don't think so. I've been doing this so long."

"Did you have a choice?" Kai whispered. Sympathy. Pity? Her question felt eerily similar to the one Miriam had asked in Temunco.

An insect chirped softly from within the wall.

The two were still waiting for her response, and Sam didn't know what to say. She joined the military because it was all she had. She joined because her brother did. She joined because she was good at it. *Did* she choose? If she thought past the surface, she wasn't sure if it was the truth. If she said it out loud, would it *be* the truth?

Miriam rescued her. "We choose what we do with what we have. And *I* choose to sleep now. As should we all. We've got long days ahead."

Kai chuckled, and Sam turned her head. She hoped the medic could read the gratitude in her eyes.

Miriam pulled the blanket out from under her. She smiled softly at Sam and turned back to turn off the lamp, leaving Sam to stare at her back in the darkness.

"Good night." Kai yawned loudly.

"Night," Miriam responded.

Sam mumbled her own goodnight as she still tried to process an answer to Kai's question. To Miriam's question. Did she choose UMF? Why did she join? Who did she want to be? What were her plans after? The words piled up and cluttered her mind—an overwhelming and claustrophobic cloud of unanswered questions.

Kai's voice broke her thoughts. "Are we really not going to talk about that ridiculously tiny office?"

11

TRACTION

IT WASN'T the ideal setup, but the second-floor conference room in the SecHut was a better place to organize their investigation than the small inn they stayed at. It had taken the morning for their arrangements as nervous Bogdan was little help, and Sergeant Nicolau had not shown. The room had been a mess, filled with boxes of evidence and other equipment that were promptly tossed into another empty room by reluctant SecGuards plucked away from their normal duties. Most guards had an attitude just short of hostility toward the UMF group, but they kept their distance.

Sam was not excited about the situation either, as she and the others held their own suspicions of the settlement's security enforcement organization. How were they going to monitor the Charonites if their hosts were also in bed with their subjects of interest? It felt like Charon lamps peeked out wherever they went.

When Echo settled into their temporary workspace, Krill went off to make a round of reluctant pleasantries with their host, and Miriam and Kai chased down a second cup of coffee in the surrounding area. Fox had already claimed one of the chairs, his boots planted on the tabletop, fingers laced behind his head, and was staring out the window.

"I'm the muscle and guns, kids. Point me'n the right direction, and we'll be done an' outta here," he grunted.

Nas swallowed the sweet bread he was chewing and laughed. "Notice he didn't say brains. Which is quite intuitive for the dumbest one here." His snicker cut off when the burly man shot him an icy stare.

Fox's chuckle started where Nas's stopped. "True. But I could crush all of you in a fight." Fox winked at Junpei, who just timidly smiled.

He didn't want to get involved. *Smart.*

"You sure about that?" Yuri took a seat, having finished setting up a mobile holoscreen console. He raised his eyebrows at the two siblings at the other side of the room.

Fox scoffed. "Together, maybe."

Scott signed to Yuri before he sat down next to him. DON'T BRING ME INTO THIS.

PRETTY SURE YOU COULD, Yuri grinned and motioned back.

HE WOULDN'T EVEN GET PAST MY SISTER.

Sam followed their silent gestures with amusement. It was still strange to see her brother so actively communicating in sign with someone other than her. It had only been a few days since they left their home outpost, and Scott, who was far more introverted than her, had already nestled into a friendship. He was more relaxed than usual.

Sam felt a twinge of doubt again. Did he already accept he was done after this mission? Would she be able to change his mind to stay? Was she doing the right thing? She pawed the thoughts away.

"Oy. It ain't fair with your secret language," Fox grunted.

"Not that secret. We just haven't learned it," Nas said quietly.

Fox glared at him.

Sam suppressed a snort. "They're saying you are, indeed, the superior fighter."

Fox raised an eyebrow at her, and his eyes glistened.

She rolled her eyes back at him, extricating herself from the pissing contest Fox was baiting them into. When she looked back at Yuri, his mouth was agape dramatically in exaggerated betrayal.

HE NEEDS TO HAVE SOMETHING, she signed to him with a shrug.

To her surprise, her brother and Yuri laughed, and she smiled. She tried to remember the last time Scott had been so at ease.

Fox narrowed his eyes at the three of them. "Damn right I'm superior," he finally said. He tightened a bicep, and Junpei laughed. Fox grinned wider.

Sam watched the two laugh, Junpei flexing his own muscles, dwarfed by Fox's giant arms. When she was little, Scott used to joke and play with her like that.

Yuri's eye twinkled, and he shrugged. He had caught her watching them. The second was damn intuitive. HE HAD A LITTLE BROTHER. MAYBE JUN REMINDS HIM OF HOME.

It made sense. The large marine was softer, a bit less crude, around the teenager.

After some time, Kai and Miriam rejoined the others. They were followed by Krill, who looked rejuvenated since the previous night, with their SecTeam babysitter in tow.

Sergeant Nicolau also seemed to be in a better mood. The deep scowl on his face had eased up into a permanent frown, and annoyance lingered at the edges of his face.

"Morning, Sergeant," Yuri said, leading a low chorus of

greetings to the uniformed man who posted himself just within the limits of his tolerance, to the right of the door.

The sergeant was in his thirties, but the mustache and wrinkled lines on his forehead from habitual furrowing made him look much older. His eyes were just as dark as his hair and mustache, which looked like he had barely combed them. His shoulders hunched as if a great weight had settled there. Nicolau held an old, scratched thermos like a weapon. Steam wisped up from the open container.

"Good morning." It was neither hostile nor amicable but indifferent. But at least he responded, unlike the block of muscle the previous day. As he raised a hand to take a sip under his mustache, Sam looked for Charon ink on any of his exposed skin. None that she could see, but at this point, she was just as wary of their chaperone as he was of them.

"So what's the plan, boss?" Yuri asked as Krill examined the mobile holoscreen.

The lead glanced at Nicolau. "With yesterday's encounter, I'm thinking we head out to the farms—"

The sergeant grunted.

Krill straightened. "Something you'd like to share?"

Sam held her breath.

"They won't be at the farms." Nicolau took another sip. He must've heard about Echo's encounter with the Charonites, or the commissioner had told him why UMF was in the area.

If it bothered Krill, he didn't show it. "That's okay. We'd like to talk to some people in the outskirts first. Get a better idea of the climate, the usual happenings." Krill tried his luck. "But if you know where we can find the Charon base of operations in Matam…? Your commander didn't seem to want to provide that information…"

The last sentence wasn't entirely true. The commissioner

had seemed more preoccupied that someone in Matam had reported to UMF without his knowledge.

"Which farms?" Nicolau didn't take the bait.

"We'll start with the closest ones and work our way out. Bogdan mentioned earlier that you could help us with some transportation. And then we'd like to head past the river and chat with some locals there." Sam knew he was referring to the Altered farmers they had encountered the previous day.

Nicolau's mouth twitched. "We do not go past the river, not with the…"

"No worries, that's what we're here for." Krill shrugged and held up his hands peacefully.

"And what exactly *are* you here for?"

Krill paused, guarded. Sam knew he was trying to determine what to divulge. They were in a tough spot. Command had given them a broad mission: monitor the Children of Charon and ensure they weren't up to anything that would endanger the summit. That was understated. The entire south seemed to be either COC or in cahoots with them, even their temporary SecTeam host. But how could they do this with only eight SOG marines—nine, with Junpei?

They needed help. They needed to start somewhere, and so far, all they had was the Charonite gang they ran into, their victim Altered farmers, and the cut cable wires from the trek over. They were leads, but frankly, it was still too large of a net to cast in their limited time. The summit was gearing up, and if Intel's suspicions were correct that COC would try something to derail the peace talks, Echo needed to disclose something to the sergeant. And then there was the question looming in front of them: Did they trust this Matam SecTeam sergeant?

"COC…Charonites. Are you tracking anything significant?"

Nicolau took a long sip from his thermos and scowled. "What do you mean?"

"Why has activity spiked here?"

"Be more specific." Nicolau blew air sharply out of his nose. "There has always been a large presence here. Charon... protects," he said lukewarmly.

Bullshit.

Sam wasn't the only one. Kai spoke up from the back. "UMF protects. SecTeam is supposed to protect. The Children of Charon are...criminals."

The sergeant scoffed. "UMF? Your Command is more concerned with their *peace* with the Royals. You northerners do not see what the alterados are doing. You are far away from what they consider *their* frontier. They encroach on our farms, they kill in the night, and take land away from us centimeter by centimeter." He paused and took a breath. Kai had touched a nerve. "When I was a child, the farmlands went lengths beyond the river. This was all ours," he said, calmer than before. "And what can SecTeam do? My job is to maintain order in the settlements. We have enough on our hands. Now we must protect from these bloodthirsty invaders?" Nicolau looked around the room. "Did your Command send you here to stop the south from defending themselves? And for what? For some peace documented on paper only to be ignored in reality?"

Kai squinted, and her arms crossed tightly against her chest.

"Do you support Charon?" Fox was blunt. Direct.

Krill turned to Fox, his eyes wide. Sam held her breath. They were toeing the line of antagonizing their chaperone. Echo needed the rapport with someone with authority or information, or at least the foothold to start somewhere.

Anger flashed over the sergeant's face, and his mustache bristled. "I do not."

Krill tried to reel the conversation back in. "I apologize for my—"

"I was born and raised in Matam. The Children were here

before UMF was. It may seem foreign to you northerners, but Charon is entrenched in this city, whether or not you believe in his teachings. I am *not* a Charonite nor do I support their methods, but you will get nowhere if you do not understand that they are now the only ones effectively standing between our enemies and our ways of life. *They* are part of the south. Your Temuncan marine is from the south, *he* can tell you that."

Sam and the others looked at Junpei.

Fox straightened but glared at Nicolau instead.

Junpei recoiled under the weight of attention and stammered, "I...I do not know all of this. My mother sent me... I-I have not been back in NZ since..."

Nicolau's face softened, guilt flashing quickly through his eyes. "Your family sent you to UMF, to Temunco to protect you."

A joint on a chair squeaked.

Krill raised his hands placatingly. "Sergeant...UMF, no—" He paused. "You're right. We don't understand this situation fully. But we're here now, and we're trying. We're the eyes on the ground, and we'll report what we see up. If the COC isn't the issue, Command must know. But if Station doesn't know, how can they change? We can't do this without help. Without you."

It was a plea and a good strategy. Especially now that the sergeant looked partially remorseful for dragging young Junpei into his rant.

"We'd like to start at the farms outside of Matam," Krill continued. "Just the farmers to start. But if you have a better recommendation, I'm all ears."

"How far?"

"Sorry?"

"The farmlands. How far out?"

"However much we can. Starting with the southeast ones.

But I want to get over the river sometime as well," Krill said warily.

"I cannot take you."

Sam tensed.

Before anyone in the room could protest, the sergeant raised a finger. "Yosef," he said the name with spite, "ordered me to stay with you. But he also does not want SecTeam outside of the walls anymore." Nicolau muttered something in the local language, then inhaled deeply. "I can have someone provide you with vehicles for the day *if* you can help look into something for me."

"What is it?"

"My case, well, my old case. I was taken off it to come…" He gestured at the group bitterly. "I have a feeling they are trying to bury it or punish me…" His face cracked into something jarring. A weak smirk. "No offense."

Krill snorted and waved a dismissive hand.

"A missing farmer. Her place is to the far east, but if you see or find something…if you can just be on the lookout."

"Alties?" Nas asked.

Charonites?

Nicolau shrugged. "Não sei. The violence has forced farmers away from the river, but they relocate. The neighbors have not seen the woman… She is some recluse far from the settlement, almost between here and Zapala, but Zapala SecTeam does not look into these things. They are too busy keeping the peace on the border. Plus, she is a daughter of Matam. This is a favor to an old friend. You probably will not go that far yet, but if she moved or you hear anything…"

Nicolau's demeanor shifted, lifted now with his own investment with the marines. He paused and tilted his ear to the door. Whatever he was listening for satisfied him, and he continued in a hushed voice. "The commissioner thinks it is a waste of time and resources. He is not fond of that...family. He thinks it is the daughter's fault for leaving the settlement and venturing so far off by herself. But who else will look for her? Is that not SecTeam's duty? My duty?"

Sam wasn't sure if he was looking for an answer from the group. Her jaw clenched. Impassioned speeches aside, Sam still didn't know what to make of their SecTeam chaperone. He seemed to genuinely care about the settlement, at least his missing farmer case, but what he said earlier had merit. The marines had to accept they didn't understand the full picture. They were foreigners trying to police something completely different from what they were familiar with. Maybe they didn't even have the picture correct at all.

⏀

The sergeant split away with Krill and Kai to call for vehicles and handle other logistical items. In the past minutes, Nicolau had thawed a bit, now with his own interest involved.

The rest of Echo retained their reactions and emotions as they hovered, waiting in the hall and conference room. With the summit looming, they had come to the south with a muddy idea and mission, only for it to be slightly clarified but simultaneously more complicated. The Charonites *were* an issue, but they weren't unwelcome in the south. Echo was still blind, but they were trying to see. That was a start, right?

"Yuri." Nas poked his head into the room where Echo's second, Fox, Scott, and Sam sat. "Come with me," he whispered. And then he was gone.

Yuri remained seated, his mouth turning down.

Nas reemerged in the doorway and stared incredulously at the group. "Guys. Over here," he said, hushed and urgent. He jerked his head to the corridor.

Sam and the others reluctantly followed the marine into the hall and around a corner, away from the stairs.

Fox grunted. "The fuck is this—"

Nas twisted and hushed him. He looked around to make sure they were still alone and opened a door.

Sam peeked in. Shelves lined the walls of the closet. The only light came through a narrow horizontal window high on the opposite wall, but it was enough to reveal the clutter within. Boxes, metal parts, and different items she didn't recognize stacked chaotically. It looked like a cleaning closet or something where random maintenance items were kept. She quickly glanced around, unsure of what was drawing Nas's attention. She pulled her head back and let Yuri by.

WHAT IS IT? her brother motioned.

Sam shrugged.

The second poked his head in and then turned to Nas. He must've had the same experience as her. Yuri lowered his voice. "What?"

Nas hissed through his teeth. "It's right there. Seriously?"

Yuri furrowed his thick brows. "Tell me what I'm supposed to be looking at."

Nas threw a hand toward a metal piece of equipment. "That's a shear."

Sam didn't work a lot with shears, but she figured she could recognize it if she saw it. The ones she had seen were always in the outpost maintenance shop but were quite large. She would've seen one if it had been in that small room. Sam peeked in again, along with Fox and Scott.

On second look, she still wasn't sure what Nas was talking about. The machine Nas wildly gestured at was slightly covered by a folded tarp and was shorter but wider than her carbine rifle. It almost resembled a pistol, but instead of a barrel, it widened out into two prong-like frames.

Nas looked at the surrounding faces and frowned. "Come on. Seriously? That's a plasma shear."

"Why the fuck are we lookin' at a plasma shear?" Fox grunted. "And why the fuck are ya even openin' random doors, ya snoop?"

Nas pumped his hand. "It's alty tech, you half wit."

Voices echoed from a connecting hall, and Yuri quickly pulled Nas away and closed the closet door. As the door shut with a soft click, Nicolau and another SecGuard turned the corner. The marines pretended as if they had just stopped mid-conversation in the hall. Yuri waved to the two, and the sergeant hesitantly returned it, his face twisting quizzically.

"I will meet you downstairs with keys," Nicolau called, then turned in the other direction.

The marines were alone again in the corridor.

Yuri pushed the group back toward the conference room, and once they were all inside, he closed the door gently behind him. He turned to Nas. "Alty tech?"

"Yes," Nas said excitedly. His face fell as he looked around at the others' unimpressed and confused faces. "Am I the only one that follows Intel's updates on alty tech and advancements?"

The marines murmured, and Scott shook his head. Sam usually skipped to the section on weapons and the latest reported Altered arsenal. Big Intel's product was hundreds of pages long with technical details that went over her head most of the time. She surely was not looking for any industrial equipment or, specifically, shears, in those lengthy records.

"Why are you even openin' doors in the first place?" Fox said.

Nas ignored him. "*That* can cut through metal. Easily through *cables*."

"But why does SecTeam have it?" Sam said out loud.

It was the question on everyone's minds, and they turned to Echo's second.

Yuri kneaded the skin around his temple. "I don't know. Let's tell Krill. We have to be delicate about this. We barely know what we're even dealing with here. I hate to say it, but…" He held an inhale and then sighed. "Command screwed us with incomplete information. Temunco is hours away, and we just don't have enough time or resources for this."

WE ACCUSE PEOPLE, AND WE'RE GONE. IF WE'RE GONE, NO ONE IS LOOKING INTO THIS.

Scott was right.

"I'll go find Krill." Yuri patted Nas's shoulder. "You did a good job."

Fox grunted. "Sure, but stay out of my shit."

The door opened, and the group quieted. Miriam strode in. Her eyes narrowed at the sudden change. "What'd I miss?"

12
———————

FARMLAND

KRILL SPLIT the group up to cover more ground. With Nas's discovery of the Altered shears (and Kai's subsequent check of the latest Intel report to confirm), the lead tasked his intel stand-in and engineer to help poke around the various SecTeam posts in town. Nicolau begrudgingly followed out of obligation—although they had yet to ask the sergeant about the tech in SecHut's closet to Nas's disappointment.

Yuri led the five others to the settlement's perimeter gate, retracing their steps from the previous day. Leaving the crowded streets behind, Sam felt it easier to breathe, taking in the open air as they drove down the dusty road into the farm enclaves in borrowed rabbits. Instead of taking the road to the bridge and river, they turned the other way.

At the first farm they came upon, Yuri, Junpei, and Miriam disembarked and approached the small house via a narrow, pebbled driveway. It was the only route to the residence otherwise ensconced in layers of vertical pods. Fox sat in the first rabbit, and Sam and Scott stayed behind in the second vehicle, angled where they could watch the road and down to the front door.

"We don't need you scaring anyone off yet," Yuri had said.

"Just a meatshield," Fox had grunted, but he hid a smile when Junpei stifled a giggle.

Scott now stared intently at the vertical pods, which contained sprouts of some kind. Another row had leafy greens, and another, long blades. He was uncharacteristically unfocused on surveillance.

"Hey."

He turned to Sam.

"You okay?"

Scott's eyes gleamed. He rested his rifle between his legs, its barrel leaning against the steering mechanism. With both hands, he started to excitedly sign. THEY HAVE...

Sam didn't recognize the last motion. She raised an eyebrow at him, and he fiddled with his commcuff. Hers pinged shortly after.

> S. RECKERT: Seedlings.

Her face scrunched in response.

BABY TREES.

"Those are baby trees?"

THEY'RE RE-PLANTING. Scott paused, his eyes alight. PERHAPS THE FOREST? THEY'RE ACTIVELY MAINTAINING LIFE HERE. NURTURING.

Sam knew little about replantation efforts, farming, or trees.

But Scott apparently did. He pointed eagerly at a row. AND HERBS.

She squinted to see the point of his attention. The little leaves looked like some plants in her brother's apartment.

Scott combed through his commcuff and shared picture after picture of different plants, herbs, and vegetables. Sam could barely read the labels over the pictures as he swiped through. Basil. Chard. Chives. But she could feel the smile grow on her face. She didn't recognize most of what he showed her—these were all foods she had never seen as individual pieces on her meal plates, but now, the variety of savory food in the south made more sense. She had never seen her brother so invigorated.

THE SOUTH IS BETTER AT FARMING. THE NORTH DOESN'T HAVE ENOUGH OF THIS LAND.

"What do you mean? We have plenty of land. Farms."

TOO MANY WARS. CONTAMINATION. IT'S IN THE SOIL. AROUND URSUS, IT'S BETTER, BUT IT STILL TAKES LONGER TO PROCESS.

She'd have to take his word for it. "I didn't know you were so into this stuff."

IT'S FASCINATING.

Sam took him in now as he continued to gaze at the vertical pods with a burgeoning grin. She thought she knew everything about him. She was learning she didn't.

She checked back on Miriam and the others. A farmer was talking to them through a sliver of the door. Junpei had taken point and his hands bounced in a pleading motion.

"Two more contracts, and you can get some land to do your own farming," Sam said.

Scott stilled next to her, and his face returned to a neutral expression. He didn't respond but wrung his hands instead, his thumb rubbing over the scar on his palm.

ϕ

The six marines had hit at least twenty farms on this side of the valley by the time the sun sat low on the horizon. Of those, only one or two had been cooperative. Even then, the information provided was irrelevant to the marines. And none knew or remotely cared about the farmer woman who had gone missing. The group found that the further they went from the settlement, the more the farmers became belligerent and closed off. Doors had been shut or slammed in their faces the moment the residents realized they were UMF. One had squeaked that he didn't want any trouble. "You marines have morals and rules. They don't." Talking to UMF meant drawing unwanted attention from the Charonites. Their "guardians." It had been a frustrating day of no answers.

For the siblings, after their terse conversation at the first stop, Scott hadn't motioned about farming and plants again. Sam hadn't pried further, and both returned to their normal dynamic after some time.

As they returned to the settlement, the marines took a left at the intersection and inched closer to the bridge and river. Everyone was on guard.

The rabbits motored past several plots of rundown vertical pods. Yellow wilted leaves spilled over the lip of individual containers, unscavenged. It was eerie after traversing kilometers of lush green rows of plants. There was no point stopping by the houses for these respective areas. The buildings were as deserted and broken down as the surrounding land, now mere ornaments in a diorama of abandonment. It stretched out, only cut off by the river in the distance.

No man's land.

"Yuri, do we go further?" Miriam said into the visor, her voice resounding over the putter of the vehicle's engine.

They rolled to a stop right before the stone and metal bridge. Dried leaves and dirt settled on top of it. It wasn't well-traveled. It was an invisible wall, a marker of territory.

Sam could make out a rundown structure two hundred meters down on their side of the water, close to the riverbank.

With her visor engaged, she could barely recognize the nose of a boat sticking out. Abandoned.

The sound of the river was soothing as its currents swept down its path, and for some seconds, Sam let her mind go with it. Relaxing, if not for the dead, ghost farms around them.

She remembered the Temunco brief. The river was dangerous.

"The alty farmers will be somewhere down this road, past the bridge," Yuri responded. "But it'll be dark soon."

Fox's voice jumped onto the channel. "We can handle it."

Sam was positive they could take on Altered farmers. But she also preferred being prepared.

"I don't want to get caught out there without a plan," Yuri said, echoing her thoughts. "Let's head back. I'll give the others a heads-up."

Fox's groan was audible over the engines and river.

◇

The Echo lead and second huddled closely around the long-range case in between the two beds in the inn room. Sam leaned against the wall on the other side, observing while the others conversed quietly. Krill straightened and silenced the group.

"Good evening, Vayen," a voice wavered loudly from the repeater.

Yuri adjusted the volume and looked up at Krill. He mouthed the first officer's name.

"Hi, Diego. The situation's as you mentioned. Worse actually," Krill said.

"Yes. Any updates on the cable system?" The technology isolated his voice, although Sam could picture him standing in the busy TOC back in Temunco. UMF felt like a world away.

Krill rubbed his eyes. "We've identified alty tech that could have been used to cut through the cables—"

"It definitely cut the cables," mumbled Nas from the back.

"But we're still trying to figure out who's responsible. Our contact doesn't know why it would be in SecTeam's possession, but he's looking into it."

Nas harrumphed. Whatever the three marines had worked on with Nicolau that day hadn't gone the way he wanted.

"Thank you. We have already held back some marines who want to go on leave. Have you heard from Ari or the others yet?"

Krill's face contorted.

Yuri mouthed, *Repair unit.*

The lead nodded. "No, sir."

After a moment, Diego responded. "Odd. We could not pick them up on communications. They should be on their way back from Zapala by now. I still cannot bring up the SecTeam there, but they are not known for their response. Regardless...you are closer than us. Can you try to reach out to Ari?"

Sam and Scott shared a look.

"We'll try a few hails and keep an eye out."

"Okay. Anything else?"

"Nothing more from what was last sent. We'll update when we can."

"Roger. Be safe."

Shortly after Krill responded, the little green light in the box's corner blinked off. He looked up to his team staring intently at him, skepticism on their faces. Was this another potential curve?

"Yeah, yeah. I'll let Nicolau know," Krill said.

⏚

Sam dug her fingers into the tight muscles at the base of her neck. She felt vulnerable without her rifle. She had left it back at the inn, locked up behind a flimsy door. She had only a thin sense of security as her sidearm pushed into her midsection underneath her shirt.

Lay low, Krill had instructed.

Her leg bounced as she watched the street. Sitting on a rickety bench, Sam felt eyes on her still. She thought she saw a familiar face in the crowd—Cyclops, maybe—but lost it on a second look. Sam tugged on her head covering, then checked her commcuff.

Her brother had ventured out of her sight into a vendor's stall full of seeds, and she fought the urge to go with him. Ever since Krill had called it a day, most of the marines had scattered into the settlement. She struggled against the need to keep track of them all, especially Scott.

Beyond a querulous customer at a neighboring food stall, five young children played with trash in the road on the market's periphery. No parents were in sight. One bigger kid wore a large tin over his head, like a bucket helmet. Someone had roughly cut slits for the little eyes to see out. They laughed and giggled as the helmed child chased them around, a flimsy sword made of scrap metal swinging up and down.

Sam had few memories of settlement life as she had grown up in a military outpost. She had been teased in her basic class for not understanding norms and general settlement culture, but even when she learned what they were teasing her about, she shrugged it off, not too concerned. While other children played with made-up armor and weapons, UMF exposed her to actual firearms. Taught her how to respect them, wield them. As she watched the children play, she wondered about their carefreeness. How could she feel about something she never knew or thought she needed?

"Valk."

That familiar voice pulled her back.

She looked away and back to the food stall she sat in front of. Miriam handed her a small plate with what looked like a couple of baked buns. Sam muttered her thanks and glanced back around, looking for her brother again.

It was strange watching him so at ease. She thought about how disengaged he had been out at those first farms and now in the market. Sam didn't recognize her brother. Was she losing him?

Miriam sat down next to her, positioned inward, facing the stall's table. Sam felt a warm touch on her knee and looked down.

Miriam's hand.

"He'll be fine," Miriam said. She slid a container of local beer to her and gestured for Sam to turn and face in. "I don't think Charonites are going to jump us tonight. Want to eat like a normal person?"

Sam peered at their surroundings one more time and sighed. She hesitantly rearranged herself to face the counter, her back to the street. If they *were* jumped, she'd make sure Miriam received an earful. She paused and shot one more glance over her shoulder.

"He can take care of himself."

"Hm."

"What's wrong?" Miriam asked.

Sam thought about the last time she had been physically separated from her brother. Back in Ursus, in the previous mission. She thought about telling Miriam of her worry of losing Scott, about him leaving, about her uncertainty. She wondered if Scott had already told Yuri. If Yuri had told Miriam...

No. If others knew, it'd be real. And she didn't want to

release that reality. Not yet. She still had time to figure something out.

"It's just..." Sam picked at the food in front of her. She felt the flood of thoughts come, and she quickly forced a dam up. After a moment, she finally said, "One of our last missions. Near Ursus. We were separated."

Miriam looked at her.

"We were chasing our subject and..." Sam had been so scared. He had chased their target and then she lost him in the chaos. She didn't know where her brother had gone. If he were dead or alive. "I don't know. It's okay."

She bit into one of the bread buns to gap her awkwardness and startled at the savory meat inside. She chewed and swallowed as Miriam continued to watch her, waiting for more. Sam shook her head and motioned with the food. "This is good." She had reservations about Matam but had to admit the south and its delicacies had soul and charm.

Yuri roared with laughter, and both women's attention turned further inside the stall, something jovial shared with the attractive shop owner at the counter. Sam couldn't help but smirk even though she didn't know what the conversation was about. The second seemed to get along with just about anyone.

"The locals are quite friendly once you get past their tough exteriors. They're wary of us but still quite hospitable." Miriam had caught on and indulged Sam's desire to change the subject.

Sam looked away and picked at the second bread. How did this woman read her so easily?

"Did someone forget to tell the sergeant? His hospitality could use some improvement." Sam twisted to search behind her. "Where is our babysitter, anyway?"

"I think he's dodging us as much as he can. Especially since the commissioner isn't watching... And with Krill back at the inn, I don't think the sergeant really cares."

"Krill's still sending reports?"

Miriam raised an eyebrow. "Maybe to a certain pilot. And Kai's consoling Nas. I guess some words were exchanged earlier with the SecGuard. Baby Echo's all riled up."

By the time Sam and Miriam finished their meal, Fox and Junpei joined them, their own street finds in hand.

"Hello, you two." The large marine winked at the medic.

"Fox." Miriam glared, then softened. "Hey, Jun. What do you have there?"

Junpei raised a skewer of charred, semi-translucent balls. "Jellyfish takoyaki! Want some?"

"Oy. Don't give Tan any," Fox teased. He turned to Sam. "I'm willin' to give you a couple of mine, though, Valk. If you consent."

Sam deadpanned and scoffed. "I'm good. Thanks."

"Fuck's sake," Miriam muttered and rolled her eyes. She leaned into Sam. "I'm going to get Yuri. That dolt is always making friends and his food is getting cold. You going to be okay with this heathen?"

Sam nodded, the last piece of bread in her mouth.

The medic placed a hand on Sam's left shoulder, leaning softly against her to extract herself from the table. Sam fought a blush at the contact and looked away before the others could see. When she composed herself, she watched Miriam swap positions with Yuri. A slender hand directed him to his plate of meat-filled bread, and he lumbered to the shop's entrance.

"Ho, Scott," Yuri said.

Sam didn't need to twist around to see her brother joining them. She recognized his footsteps.

"Want some?" The second offered one of his breads.

"I'll take it."

Yuri deftly pulled back, evading Fox's swiping hand.

"It's good. Have some," Sam said over her shoulder. She

craned her neck before her brother could answer to ask Miriam to order more. Sam still had room in her stomach, especially for these delicious treats.

A knot clenched in her belly as she watched Miriam lean across the tall surface to the shopkeeper. The woman behind the counter blushed and her fingers inched closer to Miriam's casually splayed arm. Sam felt a sharp knife plunge into her gut but couldn't tear her eyes away.

"Casanova!"

Miriam's head whipped to Fox.

He threw four fingers up. "Four more!" He looked at the others. "Anyone else? Jun? Valk?"

Sam swallowed and shook her head, the room in her stomach now gone.

Fox twisted his hand and lowered three digits so that only the middle finger was still erect. He grinned at Miriam. "That's it, thanks!"

Thin metal scraped against the pavement, and Sam returned her attention to the children playing in the street, glad for the distraction. Two older boys, still prepubescent, towered over one kid, who was now sprawled on the floor. The tin helmet lay strewn across the alley, closer to the shop where the marines sat.

Sam watched as one older boy took small, exaggerated steps in a clumsy pirouette. A Charon lamp was hand drawn in soot on his bare forearm. The boxish outlines were unmistakable and intentional. The smallest kid, perhaps six years old, scrambled for the tin helmet and swung it into the bully's legs. Sam saw a faint line begin to color and bleed. And then the group scattered, a chase deeper into Matam's market and alleys that Sam's eyes could not follow.

Was this a childhood she missed out on? There was

freedom to it, an air of unlimited imagination. But also cruelty and violence.

She felt a nudge in her side. Her brother's elbow. She hadn't noticed him sitting down where Miriam had previously sat. In the corner of her eye, she saw his inquisitive look.

"Nothing," she muttered. "Just kids being kids."

13

THE WILD SOUTH

WHATEVER QUALITY TIME KRILL, Kai, and Nas had spent with the sergeant seemed to have changed the team's rapport in a positive direction. The marine's morning check-in at SecHut was considerably less hostile. However, the same couldn't be said for Nas. His lips pressed into a thin line, his arms crossed across his chest, and his hands kneaded into his muscles with irritation. All aimed at the sergeant.

"Anything with the granjera?" Nicolau asked.

"The gran-what?" Krill said.

Junpei whispered in his ear.

"Oh. Your missing farmer? No. But we're planning on getting out again in the afternoon."

"Hm. Okay. I tried hailing Zapala's team." Sergeant Nicolau shook his head and petted his mustache down. "Even *if* their network is working, it is a fifty-fifty chance they answer. The last time I heard a transmission from them, it was like a child who did not know how to use it."

Krill rubbed his chin. "We'll give it a bit. See if the marines show up today."

"What about the cable system?" Nas scowled. The room turned to him—a decent morning on the verge of turning foul.

Sam still wasn't sure what exactly happened between Nas and the sergeant while she and the rest had been out of the settlement.

Before Krill could say anything, Nas cut him off. "What? I don't want to dance around it anymore. He's not telling us everything. In the land of outdated tech, why is SecTeam hiding alty shears?"

"Nas…" Krill growled. He pressed a clenched fist to his forehead.

Nicolau grew stiff. "You already accused me yesterday. Are you still accusing me now? I do not know what that is."

"I'm just saying you have alty tech sitting inside a closet and—"

"Nasiri." Krill's lip curled up. "Out. Now."

Nas stared defiantly for a split second, then stormed out of the room.

Yuri gestured subtly to Kai for her to follow him.

With the two marines gone, Nicolau raised an eyebrow at the lead.

"We are not accusing you, Sergeant," Krill said with a sigh. "But…"

"He said 'cable systems.' What did he mean?"

"I didn't tell you yesterday because—"

"I get it," Nicolau harrumphed. His lips pinched, and his mustache twitched. "What happened to the cables?"

After an explanation of what Echo had found on the trek from Temunco, the sergeant stared at the holoscreen console, then Krill. "Your man thinks that technology he found here…he thinks that is the tool responsible. And you think someone *here* sabotaged the cable system."

Yuri stepped in. "Yeah. He's fairly certain. He can get a little too passionate…" He winced. "But he knows his stuff."

"Did you tell anyone else here?" Nicolau asked. He pondered for a moment and answered his own question. "No… I guess not if you did not even trust me." He nodded slowly. "I…cannot be offended. Not with my colleagues. But I did ask around after our conversation yesterday. Apparently it was confiscated from the Children recently. The SecGuard who took it did not know what it is, either."

Krill's eyes flashed. "It's just another thing on top of a growing pile of things that don't add up…" he said. "About the Temunco unit—we tried hailing them, and we got nothing as well. But Jun says the route can be tricky if they don't have a ride. I'll give it another day before I get worried. And the comms… We'll check it out when we get to New Zapala."

"And when is that?"

"Trying to get rid of us?" Krill folded his arms, but his face cracked into a grin. "We're going to head out across the river later today. Sure you don't want to join?"

Nicolau stared back. "Funny. SecTeam going to meet with alterados? That is a death sentence now." He tilted his head to Echo's second. "You still have keys to the rabbits?"

Yuri nodded.

"Okay." The sergeant lowered his voice. "Do not tell anyone where you are going. There are eyes and ears everywhere in this place."

Sam's eyebrow raised.

"And the commissioner is already unhappy with you all… And me. But I can deal with him."

☥

Echo rolled in a three-rabbit motorcade past the abandoned farms up to the river bridge. A full squad of nine marines felt like overkill, but there was safety in numbers. They didn't know what to expect past the river, especially with the vague caution from Temunco's brief and Nicolau.

Just before they crossed, Krill hung out from the passenger side of the front rabbit and waved at the others behind. His voice came clear over their visors. "Heads on a swivel. Keep an eye out." With that, he leaned back into the vehicle, and they moved past the tangible territorial marker.

Sam activated her visor's hololens. The farms were a mirror image of where they had just come from. A strip of fields of broken vertical pods, tubing, and panels were still erected, yet to be picked up by the intentional scavenging human. Sam looked down and pulled back her rifle charging handle to ensure a round was in the chamber.

At the first fork in the road, the vehicles turned into the path branching further south. According to Kai (relayed by Junpei), the one to the east was an old route in the direction of New Zapala. The technological shift in the vertical pod structures and their panels was the first indicator they were headed in the right direction. The smell of ammonia and dirt grew stronger.

"See those capsules? That's tech we don't have yet," Nas said over the visor.

INJECTION POINTS AND FILTERS, Scott motioned from the passenger seat in front of her.

"I think they're filtration systems," Nas said simultaneously in her ear.

"Keep the channel clear." Yuri's voice was sharp over the ambient noise of the rabbit's wheels against the dirt. She glanced at him in the driver's seat. He flashed a grin and a wink at her, then said out loud to her and Scott, "Nerds."

The first farm they came upon was abandoned, although the stalk pods looked to still be active. They quickly moved along and came upon the open entrance of a small lane that led down into the rows of Altered farming tech. When they rolled to a stop on the side of the road, Sam could make out the roof of a flat structure at least a hundred meters down within the sea of green.

Krill popped out of the first vehicle, and over the visor, he directed the group. "Kai, Valk, Mute, and Nas, on me. Nas and Kai, drop your weapons. The rest, keep an eye out."

Once all had adjusted themselves, the five moved down the path with Krill in the lead and Sam and Scott at the rear. Sam glanced back at Miriam, Yuri, Fox, and Junpei who watched their surrounding angles. She lost sight of them as they turned with the path toward the structure.

"Let's look as unthreatening as possible, yeah?" Krill's voice came like a whisper in Sam's ear. She slung her rifle behind her and adjusted her chest plate. Scott did the same. They were the only two armed of the split group. Before they reached the building's small perimeter fence, she patted her pistol in her leg holster to ensure it was still where she left it. It was, as always.

The building was a dark shade of beige. Closer now and able to make out more details, Sam saw the house was constructed out of matte, metallic panels. Her hololens showed the invisible lines between poles uniformly placed to form a perimeter several meters away. The lines danced up and down as if they were electrified and alive.

Krill hesitated, having seen the lines through his own visor. But then he carefully stepped forward between a pair of the poles. He passed through the invisible barrier with no issue, patted himself, and then shrugged.

"Selective barrier? Alarm system? Or both?" Nas said quietly. "Interesting."

"Valk, Mute. Hold here," Krill said, after Nas and Kai followed him through.

The siblings stopped just outside the fence. Sam would rather be inside the barrier if something happened—she'd be able to protect her unarmed teammates better—but she obeyed the lead. Her mind whirled as she mapped out contingency plans.

Krill, Nas, and Kai walked a short distance to the front door, and Krill raised a fist to knock. Before his knuckles could contact, a voice rang out.

"What do you want?"

Echo had performed a quick hood brief before they departed Matam on this exact scenario. What would they say to the Altered farmers if they were there?

"We just want to ask some questions. We're UMF. Not looking for any trouble."

It was a safer route to go with their military identities. The Altered were probably already suspicious of the humans in the region. After all, it wasn't UMF beating and dragging the genetically engineered people away from their homes.

"Your friends back there don't look like it."

"It's for our safety, too. You know that."

Kai stepped forward. "We'll be out of your hair if you can chat with us for a few minutes. If it makes you feel more comfortable, we can talk this way. It's a bit difficult, but we can manage."

Always the peacekeeper.

The voice didn't respond. As the seconds passed, the five marines exchanged uncertain looks. But the door slid open, and the three inside the fence line took a step back, giving a wide berth to whatever was going to come out.

"I remember you."

Sam saw the heterochromatic eyes first—blue, green, and brown. And then a face followed by a lanky body. The bruises were yellowed, the scrapes and cuts already closed. It had only been two days since they last met the Charonite's Altered victim and he was only recognizable now by the fading marks. He stepped out, and the door closed behind him. It wasn't enough time for Sam to scan into the house. She inched closer to the poles, and her visor crackled with static. She stepped back again, and the static disappeared. A barrier to communications? She was glad the three others were within talking distance.

"If it's okay, we'd like to know what happened the other day," Kai said.

The farmer gave them a cold stare. "Your kind attacked us while we were minding our own business. They kidnapped us, and then you showed up. What else is there to know?"

"We aren't with the Charonites."

He stared at Kai, unreadable.

"Why did they attack?"

The Altered blinked.

"How long have you been here?" Nas asked.

Nothing.

"What brought you here? This is Matam's land. Human land."

That sparked something.

"Am I not human, too?" the Altered responded.

The marines said nothing.

"Am I not allowed to find and make a place for me and my own?"

Kai stammered, "But you *have* land. The, the Royal Sovereign—"

"What does the Sovereign know? What do the Royals

know? This land here is still fertile and uncharted. I am free from the Royals' reign here. I can make my own living, my own future."

There was no point in arguing that this land was "uncharted" to the Altered because it was, and continued to be, human territory.

Nas folded his arms. "These alt—these farms, do they require shears or cutters of some kind to build structures?"

The farmer looked at Nas. It had to have been an odd question to him. "For these kinds of structures and work, yes. How else would I do it? Mechanical saws?"

The Altered thought *humans* were primitive.

"Do *you* own a shear?" Nas asked.

The man's eyes narrowed. "Yes." He crossed his arms. "Do you want to see it?" If the Altered was curious about their specific questions, he didn't ask. It was perhaps a perk to Echo for being *inferior* as simple humans.

The Altered and the three marines walked around the building. Sam and Scott followed as best as they could at the fence's exterior.

A wide, roll-down door punctuated the middle of the wall. The farmer pounded his fist into a barely visible console, and the door rolled up, revealing a workshop roughly the size of their inn room. Two workbenches lined one wall, cabinets and shelves on the other, and a series of mounted equipment faced them. Parts from an enormous machine were laid out on the floor.

The Altered walked in, stepping around the pieces of equipment. He scratched his head after pacing around and muttered something indiscernible to himself. Then, louder for the others: "It's not here."

"Did you perhaps lend it to another alt—neighbor?" Krill offered.

The farmer glared at him. "No. Your kind's memory may be flawed, but mine is good." He opened one cabinet to peer inside. It was full of gardening tools from what Sam could see around his body. "We used it only a couple of weeks ago. The barn..." He trailed off, muttering to himself again.

Sam glanced at a partially erected structure in the distance. Its beams were a rough sketch of a wider building. It wasn't finished, but it looked like it had been recently worked on. She looked again into the open workshop. One workspace was neat and organized, and the other, next to it, was littered with wrappers and drawings. She noted a tarp draped over a wheeled chest underneath the messy bench. It looked like something the shear tech could fit in.

Nas saw it, too. He pointed. "And that?"

The man turned. "I assure you it's not in there."

"May we look inside?"

The farmer's lip twitched, but he held his tongue. "My son's. He's off gallivanting with his worthless friends now." He closed the cabinet door. "Will you leave if I show it to you?"

The Altered took the group's silence as an affirmative, pulled the box from beneath the desk, and shook away the tarp. He muttered to himself again and searched his son's station, lifting a tablet and swiping foil wrappers to the side. Eventually, he found what he was looking for in the form of a thin rectangle which he inserted into the side of the thick chest. It opened, and he scoffed as he looked down into it. He kicked it forward, letting it slide across the floor to the others.

There was no shear or any Altered tech inside, not from what Sam could see with her hololens.

"May I?" Krill said, squatting next to the container.

The farmer grunted.

Krill lifted a white garment out. A long-sleeved shirt.

Sam recognized the color of the Altered military.

"Your son is a legionnaire?" Krill asked.

The Altered snorted. "My son can't be a legionnaire even if he tried. Doesn't hit the requirements. We're the wrong make, bastard class and all. Maybe years ago, he could've tried for the army, but that's long gone. He's a dreamer, though."

"And the uniform?"

"Who knows? Off the black market or stolen by one of his friends, no doubt. It isn't even the proper uniform, just an undergarment. Where are the pants? The armor?" He scoffed.

Krill dropped the shirt back into the chest and closed the lid. He attempted to push it back as the Altered man had easily done, but he could only move it a meter.

This obviously amused the farmer, but he was wise enough not to comment.

Suddenly, the farmer perked up. He cocked his head to the side and shushed the marines. His eyes scanned behind Sam and Scott, and his nostrils flared. Sam realized he was trying to smell something, and she looked around at the rows of vertical pods. The Altered was picking up on something she could not. Her visor read normal, but she strained to listen for anything unusual. A gentle breeze rustled the plants and leaves hanging out of the individual pods.

Nothing.

The Altered's eyes darted back to the marines, and he said in a lower voice, bordering on a growl, "If you're satisfied, I'd like you to leave now." He pushed past them, and they staggered out of his way. He palmed the door shut and headed back inside the house without another word or farewell.

Krill, Nas, and Kai rejoined the siblings at the fence exterior with confusion on their faces. Sam narrowed her eyes as she continued to scan their surroundings, willing her hololens to find something. *Something* had spooked the Altered farmer. It was reasonable for them to be worried as well.

"Coming back to you, Greg," Krill said over the open team channel.

No response.

"Greg."

Again, nothing.

Krill's forehead furrowed. "Fox?"

The five marines exchanged glances and quickened their pace back for the rabbits, with Sam in the lead and Scott taking the rear. Sam wasn't sure what to expect. Why wasn't anyone responding? Her heart rate began to climb, and her body tensed. The safety on her rifle was already off.

Sam turned the corner first.

Into a colossal figure.

She pushed back and her muzzle rose into its chest.

"Fuckin' hell, Valky!"

Sam startled but a wave of relief flushed through her at the familiar voice and face. Her heart had only started pounding in her ears. She lowered the weapon quickly and shot a glare then an apologetic look at the man.

"Fox! Hell!" Kai exclaimed behind Sam, clutching her rig.

"What happened? Why weren't you guys responding?" Krill demanded. He peered around the marine to locate Miriam, Yuri, and Junpei still with the vehicles, watching them—their own relief replacing the anxiety on their faces.

"Why weren't *you* respondin'? We were callin'. I came to check on you," Fox said irately.

At that moment, a soft buzz and whoosh turned their attention back to the Altered's house. A semi-translucent barrier went up and over the building. And then it disappeared, invisible again.

Nas's eyes lit up and widened.

Fox grunted. "Fuckin' alty tech."

Sam breathed out in relief. At least there was a reasonable explanation for why they had temporarily lost communications.

"Anything suspicious out there?" Krill pressed as they walked to the rabbits and the others.

"Nah. Nothin' on this road for ages," Fox grumbled.

"Eyes on a swivel," the Echo lead said to the group.

"My eyes have been swivelin' this entire time, boss."

Yuri leaned out of one vehicle. "Any luck?"

"No," Krill answered with a sigh.

"Are we pushing on?"

"I don't know. Probably not. This is a dead end, too."

Although the marines were back together and they settled into the rabbits, Sam felt eyes on her again. She didn't know from where. She looked around at the rows of pods, but her scans were fuzzy and unclear now. Something to do with the activated barrier. The hairs on the back of her neck stood on end. Only a few hours of daylight remained. Whatever Krill decided, they didn't want to be on this side of the river come nightfall.

14

RESISTANCE

"I HAVE SOME NEW INFORMATION, but I do not think it will be good news."

Sam looked up as Sergeant Nicolau closed the door to the temporary team room, pulled a chair, and sat. Something was different. His shoulders sagged, and the lines on his face were deeper than before.

Krill sat across from him. "Tell us."

The sergeant spoke down at the table. "I asked around. There were a couple of bodies that turned up east of the city. Close to the river, outside the perimeter. They were taken to the mortuary, and I sent one of mine to stop the process until you can get there. But you will have to be quick. The people here are not...patient."

"Are they the marines?" Yuri asked.

"Não sei. They were...naked. And mutilated. No belongings found." Nicolau sighed. "You should go before they cremate. Matam burns bodies fast. Yosef does not like bad news to spread. The mortuary is paid..."

"Human?" Kai said.

"Yes."

"Where's the mortuary?" Krill questioned.

"Southeast." Nicolau held out an open hand to Yuri, motioning at his commcuff. "I can give you the location."

Yuri poked at the device and turned the display upward. Using one finger, Nicolau dragged the map until he found what he was looking for. "There."

Krill looked around the room. "Greg, Jun, Tan. Head over there and get whatever information you can. Jun, if they are… If you can identify them…"

Junpei pushed back from the table and bowed his head.

Fox abruptly stood up. "I'll go, too."

Krill didn't object, and the four promptly left the room.

Sam watched Miriam disappear into the hall. *Be safe*, she wanted to say, but they were gone.

The sergeant placed his hands on the surface, and he sighed again. "Tomorrow, I am reassigned to patrol. Sergeant Martín will be with you instead."

Krill gave the man a questioning look.

"Martín is one of Yosef's…and a friend of the Children."

"What happened? Why?"

"Someone found out about your excursion across the river." The sergeant sighed. "I did warn you."

Nas stood up. "To the alty farmer? It's part of our mission. Did *you* tell—"

Nicolau slammed a hand down. "I did no such thing." His sneer was convincing. "But someone knew. And it got to Yosef." His lip curled up.

Sam knew it. She knew they were being watched. They had been ever since they entered the settlement.

"It looks poorly on him, you see. Yosef fears the Children. He needs their numbers for political favor."

"But what does that have to do with us, Nic?" Krill asked.

"UMF talking to alterados? Under his watch? It does not look good."

"We need all the information we can get," Krill said. "From all sides. You know this."

The sergeant shook his head. "There is only one side in Matam." He snorted softly. "You are being leashed. Like me."

Krill lowered his voice. "Nic, what can we do?"

"I care about this city. It may not be as peaceful as it once was generations ago, before all the politics and the alterados, but it is our lives, our ways. The Children came, saying they were here to help. An enemy of our enemy is a friend, and they did help. Matam loves them for it. But the Children grow and grow, and I watch my friends, my colleagues, and family become something they are not. I do not recognize this place anymore."

"Where is the COC base of operations? Is it in Matam? New Zapala?" Krill pressed.

The sergeant shook his head. "No, not Zapala. Matam is the major city here. I do not know though. Maybe they are hidden—some old-town, secret passages. Only the older generations knew of it completely." Nicolau sniffed, his mustache raising with his lip. "And it is bases. It is not just one. There are many, supposedly. But find one of the Charon council, if you can. Tread lightly. Yosef is not happy, nor are the Children."

"Did Yosef—"

"The commissioner does not interfere with the Children."

Sam's jaw set.

"You came here to stop whatever they are planning. But they are too much, too many. The only way to rid the Children is to rid the alterados or find some kind of peace. But a true peace that extends to the south. Your Station summit is a dream, an unrealistic and distant hope. But if what you are doing here can make it more real... Do what you came here to do. Help."

Sam still wasn't sure what they were there to do. In that Station team room, their mission had been to journey to the southern settlements and figure out what the Children of Charon were planning—to prevent the derailment of the summit with the Altered government. It was overwhelming. They were here now, but the problem was too vast for one Station SOG unit, two temporarily assigned SOG recon scouts, and a young outpost guide to tackle. So far, they had run into sabotage and figured out the spike of Charon numbers and activity was due to Altered encroachment into their land. But the more the marines tried to investigate, the more the answers eluded them. It was an impossible task.

For the first time, Sam was angry at UMF Command and their ignorance. She understood Temunco's frustration; she felt Nicolau's irritation with his own system. She felt helpless.

$$\oplus$$

Back at the inn, Krill, Fox, and Junpei's place was now Echo's new team room following the loss of their SecTeam chaperone and the subsequent loss of any remaining trust in Matam's security component. SecTeam was not the marines' primary suspect, but they were still affiliated with the Charonites.

Unfortunately, their suspicion of the washed-up bodies was also confirmed. Junpei recognized them, despite the mutilation. Miriam had brought up their images on her commcuff holodisplay in the center of the room. On the pale bodies that were still intact, there were marked signs of blunt trauma, drag marks, and cuts despite the bloating. The other corpse was less of a body and more of a water-damaged torso and stumps where limbs had once been. Its only identifying indicator was a tattoo on the back shoulder: the Temunco version of the UMF shield sigil and outstretched wings. The skin was ripped, but the ink was still recognizable. The violence of the missing body pieces was grotesque.

"Hell," Kai whispered, her face turning pale.

Sam was no stranger to gore and gruesome scenes, but she was grateful when Yuri covered Miriam's commcuff, and the display blipped out.

"Where are their clothes? Their gear?" Nas asked and shook his head.

"We need to tell Temunco," the second said flatly.

"And Command," Miriam added. "We need support. An actual investigations unit. Better intel. Something."

The sound of a beep interrupted the growing murmur in the room. The marines stilled and turned to the case on Krill's bed. Yuri hurried over. His fingers danced over the long-range repeater.

"Krill. It's Station."

"Speak of the devil…" Fox grunted.

Krill's hand remained over his closed mouth, but his eyes darted to Yuri. Sam could see his jaw clench. He gave a curt nod and his second connected the call.

Yuri hovered over the case. "This is Razor-Echo."

"Yuri? Where's Krill?" A male voice rang out.

Sam was taken aback. This wasn't usual Command formality. The other Echo teammates were also momentarily confused but seemed to recognize the voice.

Krill stepped forward. "Jace? What's going on?"

Jace? Sam mouthed to Miriam.

The medic mouthed back, *Old teammate. Intel.*

"I was going to ask *you*. Why is COC attacking Legion?"

Echo's team lead shook his head and looked concerned at the repeater. "What are you talking about?"

A second of silence stretched, then the man's voice came back. "Command will send a formal report soon, but I wanted to reach out first. Station Center is panicking. Says the Royal emissaries received a distress call from their Legion post near you. COC attacking or something."

The marines looked around the room at each other.

Junpei sat up straight in his cot. He squeaked, his voice cracking, "Is NZ okay?"

The voice came back. "Is that a kid? Look, Krill. They've settled down now, but Station and Command are worried they've lost leverage for the summit. You need to get a move on. Take the COC out if you need to."

"Easier said than done…" Fox muttered.

"Jace, we've got other issues, too."

"We all do. Just giving y'all a heads-up. Gotta go. Stay safe."

And with that, the line disconnected, and the room was thrown into a long bout of silence. Sam had been wrapping her mind around the confirmation of dead Temunco marines, and now this?

"Krill," Yuri said, the first to break the pause.

The marines looked to their lead. He was frozen.

A chorus of voices erupted in the void.

"The fuck was that?" Fox said.

Miriam crossed her arms and then uncrossed them. "We need backup. A settlement full of Charonites? Dead marines? Sabotage? And now this?"

"We don't need backup."

"Are *you* trained in proper investigations, Fox?"

"There ain't time for a proper investigation."

Kai joined in. "We have to consider that the Charonites will move on us like they did the other marines."

"We don't know if it was the COC," Nas said.

"Krill," Yuri said again.

"You just heard Jace say the Charonites attacked Legion! You saw how they brutalized those alty farmers. They wanted to kill us too. They've maimed innocents just because they thought they were alty-lovers."

"We don't know anything yet," Nas urged.

Sam shared a look with her brother as the pandemonium grew. The siblings, Krill, and Junpei were the only ones quiet. The team lead's eyes were unfocused, staring into a middle distance. They needed one voice. Authority. They needed something that made sense.

Krill's lips moved, but with the wave of other voices, it was drowned out. He spoke louder. "We're going to talk to them."

The room quieted.

"We have to talk to them," he repeated.

"Command?" Miriam asked.

"The Children."

A violent murmur rippled around the crew.

"We're dancing around." Krill raised his voice, and the whispers came to a halt. "We just need to face it and talk to them. Directly."

"How?" Nas said.

"They already know what we're doing and where we are. Let's call them out. Hope for the best."

Yuri balked. "Hope for the best?"

"What, say their name thirteen times, and they'll pop up? I don't think it works like that," Miriam said.

The team lead turned sharply, and Sam flinched at the sudden attention. Krill's eyes glimmered. "How many are following us?"

"Following us?" Kai repeated.

"One when we first arrived. Another in the market," Fox said.

Yuri waved, and they quieted.

Sam swallowed. With all the attention on her, her confidence wavered. "Today or overall?"

The other marines murmured again.

Overall, then. Flaco and Creeper were a pair, and Spiny and Cyclops were another. Sam said four at the same time her brother raised his fingers, matching her answer.

Eyes widened around the room. Sam was surprised but not shocked. The Charonite surveillance team, since their first encounter outside of Matam, was decent. They had some kind of training. Plus, the marines were preoccupied with their own matters.

"Think you can grab one?"

"Krill…" Yuri didn't think it was a good idea.

Sam didn't either. There was a high chance that blatantly antagonizing the COC would result badly for the crew. But there was also a chance it'd do what their lead wanted. And if what Echo's old teammate in Intel said over the call was true, they had little time to salvage whatever leverage they could for Station's summit.

Sam glanced at her brother.

He nodded. It was doable.

"Yes," Sam said.

Yuri waved his hands. "Whoa, I know we're grasping for anything right about now, but that's a shit plan, boss."

"Do you have something better?" Krill said flatly.

Nas jumped in. "We can move on to New Zapala. See what we get there and come back."

"The Temunco marines *were* in NZ," Junpei offered shyly.

"No. And you heard Nic. If it's COC, the directions are coming from here, from Matam. Something is going on. I, we, just can't piece it together yet. We have to go directly to the source. I have a feeling." Krill put a hand on Junpei's shoulder.

"You can head to New Zapala if you'd like. You've done a lot for us here already. I don't want to keep you."

Junpei thought for a moment, then shook his head. "I want to help."

Sam understood his response. He was part of the team. The mission, camaraderie, and acceptance were addicting.

Fox clapped his back.

Junpei blushed.

"We'll head to New Zapala soon," Krill promised. He glanced at Sam and gestured a chin at her shoulder. "How's it feeling?"

"I'm good," Sam replied quickly. It was mostly true. She had fully committed to the gel bandage and medication routine in the last few days, and only a dull ache remained in her arm. If anything, adrenaline would help. As long as she didn't run full speed into a wall, she'd be fine.

Yuri still wasn't fully convinced. "It's your call, boss."

"Let's just get this done," the lead said.

After the growing mess of unanswered questions, Sam was just glad for a decision. She hoped it was the right one.

15
___

MOMENTUM

SERGEANT MARTÍN WAS a thin wire of a man. He stood outside the inn like an animal waiting for its prey. His conversation was not unpleasant, and his manners were courtly, but Echo heeded their previous chaperone's cautions. This man was one of Commissioner Yosef's, and Yosef was in the pocket of the very people they were after.

Through strategic, split movements, Junpei's clever distractions in conversation, and using Matam's own confusing network of alleys and narrow streets, Echo had succeeded in losing their SecTeam warden. The Station marines met discreetly in the shadows of an alley in the settlement's northeast sector, behind a butcher's shop that smelled of copper and rot.

"Martín?" Krill said quietly, his voice sharp through the visor.

"Gone. Should've learned how to stalk like our Charon tails," Fox said.

"Mute. Valk?" the lead whispered.

Sam keyed her visor. She leaned against a knee wall before a busy tailor's shop and adjusted her head covering. "Two marks. One on the other side of you. Your six o'clock."

Spiny squatted on the streetside between a kiosk and a large bin, watching the alley in which Echo huddled. She glanced diagonally across the street at her brother, who kept his hooded head down. His arms folded across his chest, and a finger subtly pointed to another figure further down the road. Cyclops.

"Another one two blocks down."

"Okay. Kai, Jun, get back to the inn and stay there. I'll leave this channel open. Hail Temunco if things go south," Krill commanded.

Kai wouldn't be happy about that, but Sam agreed. Other than keeping the Temunco marine safe, the engineer's presence could have adverse effects on their plan. Kai had been too emotional in their first COC encounter. They couldn't risk another verbal mistake, or worse, have the Charonites use her bleeding heart against them.

A minute later, Sam watched the young marines scamper out the alley and back toward the inn. Spiny and Cyclops perked up as they decided whether the two were worthy targets to follow. They didn't take the bait.

Sam pushed down the growing anticipation in her gut and almost reached for a rifle that wasn't there. She resisted the urge to pat her sidearm concealed in an appendix holster, tight to her core, just underneath her low-profile armor. She picked at her thumb instead.

"Valk?" Krill checked.

Spiny and Cyclops were still there, waiting.

"Situation remains."

"Okay." A pause. And then, "Let's go."

Krill and Fox emerged first from the narrow corridor and turned east for Sam and Scott. About seven seconds later, Yuri,

Miriam, and Nas took to the west. Spiny waited for Krill and Fox to pass before he slowly stood up and sauntered carefully after the two. As he passed, Sam dipped her head. He didn't notice her or Scott, intent on following the Echo lead. Cyclops took after Yuri and the others, and the siblings moved stealthily after him. Spiny was smaller, but Cyclops had a better weakness to take advantage of.

By the time Yuri, Miriam, and Nas maneuvered into another quiet, empty alley, Sam and Scott had incapacitated and gagged the Charonite tracker. They left him in the darkness of the settlement's labyrinth with the three SOG marines and moved to another position where Krill and Fox were circling back to bring Spiny into his own trap.

It was quick.

The two Charonites glared from their bound, sitting positions. Sam watched Fox, slightly concerned he'd break Krill's command not to harm the scouts. UMF didn't need any additional ire and antagonization from their already brazen attempt to make contact.

Yuri handed one of the two small hand radios they had retrieved from a thorough search of their two detainees to the team lead.

Krill crouched down in front of Spiny and Cyclops, who glared up at the surrounding marines. "Where is your base?"

Fox pulled the gag down from Cyclops' mouth. It hung stiffly around his chin as he stretched his mouth and licked his lips. His brown eye stared defiantly at the lead.

"We won't hurt you. We just want to talk with your leader…or council."

A scowl was his only response.

"Let me work 'im," Fox grunted.

Sam saw a flicker of fear as Cyclops eyed the large marine.

Krill shook his head. He turned to the other bound captive,

who returned it with a stare that could beckon death itself. The scouts weren't going to talk.

Fox rearranged the gag back over Cyclops' mouth.

Krill sighed and raised the small communication unit close to his mouth.

He hesitated. And then, "This is the UMF lead."

⏀

The plan worked.

But as they walked, surrounded by a pack of Charonites, they could only wonder if it was still a good plan. Every individual around them bore the lamp tattoo on some exposed or partially exposed skin. Sam saw the bulges of concealed weapons underneath their clothing, and the scent of raw tobacco lingered in the air around them. The SOG marines were stripped of their weapons and tech and were walking into the unknown. Willingly.

Even without her sidearm, Sam took some solace in her close combat skills, but she knew hand-to-hand would always be the loser in a gunfight. Her brother hadn't bothered with the elective training back in Ursus, showing no interest after checking the box for it in initial and annual refresher trainings. She hoped the three other SOG marines were not rusty. They'd need everything in their arsenal if the situation devolved.

Sam's brain was working furiously, trying to remember each turn they took, but after the twentieth deviation, she was certain their escorts were intentionally bringing them on a circuitous route. Sam didn't recognize any of the streets and cursed their lack of time for area familiarization. In their short time, Echo hadn't ventured too far into the north sector, where Children of Charon propaganda and painted signs were ubiquitous, plastered on every imaginable surface.

She and the others were surprised when they arrived in front of a decrepit building, which looked more like a large shed connected to a series of appliance repair shops. One Charonite loosened a large chain around the door.

Krill turned back to the team; his face etched with an expression that said he hoped he hadn't killed them all by bringing them down this path.

It was too late now.

They entered the shed in a single-file line and walked down a cement staircase where the middle of the steps dipped, worn down by the many years and people who had passed through. Cool air and a musty smell of stone and stale water enveloped the group as they ventured further.

At the bottom, the stairs opened into a network of tunnels lined with large pipes that Sam figured could only contain the settlement's waste and sewage. The walls had decades, if not more, of stains and looked wet to the touch. The corridors curved away, and their ends could not be seen from the group's position.

Sam recalled Sergeant Nicolau's mention of secret passages —they were in one now. Matam extended underground, and the Children of Charon were the underbelly's patrons. She wondered if the townspeople knew of the elaborate system beneath their homes. UMF sure didn't.

Add that to the list of things UMF doesn't know, Sam thought.

The marines were led into a small tunnel with only dim lanterns threaded few and far between. Unease grew in Sam's gut. Though none of their hands were tied, she resisted the muscle memory of activating her visor hololens—which wasn't there.

Naked. She was too vulnerable.

The procession came to a stop in front of a barren door. A Charonite shouldered his way past the line of marines, and the two individuals in the front moved aside. The Charonite rapped his knuckles lightly against the metal.

A muffled response came back.

The door opened, and Echo followed the man in. Sam squinted into the bright lights, and she waited for her vision to adjust. The room opened in front of them, a lengthy bunker-like space with a low ceiling. A large table with a motley of old chairs sat twenty paces into the room. Three individuals stood on the far side in soft shadows, engaging in a hushed conversation. With the marines' arrival, one of the people, still unrecognizable, walked out a side door without even a glance toward the incoming group, clutching a tablet to their chest. The smaller of the two remaining figures straightened and rested a hand on their side holster.

The taller of the two walked past the table. Sam examined his slim features as he approached. The man had one hand in his pants pocket, and the other held a lit cigarette, a line of smoke dancing from its glowing tip. He looked refined, in a clean linen shirt with its sleeves neatly folded to his elbows and plain dark pants. Deep lines were etched into his face, but his eyes were bright and deceivingly charming. Sam couldn't figure out his age, but his wavy, gray hair said he was older. He was also surprisingly barefoot.

The man waved two fingers in the air, and the Charonite escorts scattered back the way they came. The five marines were left alone with the man and the other woman, who remained on the other side.

"UMF plays a risky game." His voice pitched forward and resonated.

Sam narrowed her eyes. His accent was of the north. Closer to Station.

The man took a long draught from the cigarette and exhaled, filling the space with a thin, cloying smoke.

"We're not here to play any games," Krill assured him.

The man leaned against the table's edge. "Oh? Perhaps the pawn…" He scrutinized each marine with a piercing gaze. Sam felt her skin give way under her scratching nail as his bright eyes wandered over Scott, then Sam. "No…you're SOG. You're not a pawn, no, maybe UMF's knight. Yes…perhaps you knights don't recognize the board you've been set upon."

Sam was never interested in the old chess game, but she knew enough that it was a snub, although said without any condescension.

After a pause, Krill lifted his chin. "Perhaps. And you? Are you the king? The queen?"

The man laughed, adding more lines to his face. "No. I am just another pawn." He chuckled more. "So you seek Charon's council… You'll be dismayed when I say we're not much of a council, not in the traditional sense at least. You'll only be getting me. The others will think I'm a fool to entertain you, Mr. Krill."

Sam gave credit to the team lead. If he was surprised the man knew his name, he made no show of it. Krill was also far more patient with playing the Charonite's game. If it were up to her, she would've demanded answers—possibly throttled him for them.

"I want to know the truth."

"Whose truth?" the man asked, his tone light. He dropped the cigarette and crushed it under the ball of his foot, then stuck his other hand into his pocket.

Krill's jaw set.

A water drop blipped somewhere within the room.

"You're an intelligent man. You have an intelligent team. In your time here, have you not seen the truth for yourself?"

"I see brutality and cruelty."

"Ah." The man sighed. "You've seen Chibuzo's work. She

runs her…crew more aggressively. But all within reason, of course. She and hers don't like you very much, by the way." He chuckled.

Sam knocked herself on the head internally. The two duos following them, Flaco/Creeper and Spiny/Cyclops, were from different Charonite groups. It was so obvious now.

"You all wear the same mark. I see no difference."

"True. A downside of our structure, of course. What one hand does, the other may not know of…or like. But we are all guided by a collective purpose."

He paused. "Station is concerned Charon threatens their peace with the Altered." It was not a question.

"Yes."

"Good."

Krill's forehead furrowed.

"What does that peace mean for Station? Trade? Technology? What does it matter when we continue to lose our land? Our freedoms? The Altered are wiping us out, and Station is blind to it. They move with force against us and our neighbors. Are we not entitled to push back?"

Sam shifted from one leg to the other. They weren't here to discuss the reasonability of COC mantra.

The man pulled his hands out of his pockets and crossed his arms. "Station doesn't know. They underestimate the south. They fear what they cannot control. Your Station government is too concerned with peace with the Altered in the short-term. They would give all of humanity up in the long run." He pushed away from the table to stand upright. "Do you see it now? The Altered are dividing us. They are making it easier for them to conquer. You should be with us, fighting them, not trying to make peace."

The marines were silent.

"But you are all but pieces on the board, set on the spaces that you are limited to. Go forth and transform, my friends."

"And violence is the way?"

"You see the humor in that statement, no? Does UMF seek violence?" He waited for a response but received none. "Do *you* seek violence?"

Krill's chin lifted. "No. I don't want violence, but I am prepared for it," he said. "Enough of the games. Legion. Why did the Children attack them? And our Temunco brethren. Why did you kill them?"

His eyes waved slowly over Krill, his face without emotion. "Are those accusations?"

"They're questions. The Royals say their Legion post was attacked. Our marines were found dead and mutilated. And we've seen firsthand the cut cables between Temunco and Matam. Severing access is one thing. Provoking the Altered and killing ours is another."

The man fell quiet, his dark brows furrowing and his eyes following Krill's face as if trying to decipher some coded message there.

The seconds passed and Sam stole glances at the others. She was growing nervous at the silence and how still the room had gotten.

When he finally spoke, the man's voice was low, almost a whisper. "That wasn't us."

"SecTeam said they confiscated alty tech from you—the same alty tech that cut those cables."

The man's face remained stony. "I don't know about this. We fight against the Altered. Sometimes our people nick shiny things—we don't always have the brightest...minds. They wouldn't dare, anyway. And Legion, your fellow marines... It wasn't us," he said. He touched a hand to his chin and his eyes darkened in thought again.

Oddly, Sam believed the man. Despite his refined wordiness, he was a Charonite to his core, but he didn't hold himself like the others, the ones she spent so many missions chasing down and capturing. There was no false bravado. No, this man was certain and convicted, and underneath it all, profoundly tired.

"What one hand does..."

The man gave a thin smile at his own words used against him. "Mr. Krill, we may not like each other, UMF and Charon... but we *are* on the same side."

"And what side is that?" Krill asked.

"Humanity, of course."

16

MOTION

"I DON'T BELIEVE HIM."

Sam adjusted her commcuff on her wrist. The Charonites had returned their devices and weapons after depositing the marines in an unfamiliar area after another circuitous route. She checked her location service—they had ended up somewhere in the east of the settlement, far from where they had originally started. Although she didn't recognize their surroundings, Sam felt better back out in the dense settlement's open air, a place she had only days before thought was claustrophobic.

"About the marines. And the cable. I still don't know why anyone'd try to attack a Legion post, though. That's plain dumb," Fox said.

Sam believed the well-spoken Charonite, but she didn't say anything. The five marines had gone deep into their opponent's bowels and returned having made little progress. Sam secretly hoped they'd move on to the next settlement, but she wasn't in charge. A nervous sensation creeped into her skin with the nameless man's words. She wanted distance, needed something fresh.

Whose truth?

Sam removed her sidearm magazine from its catch. *Thieving bastards.* She stared at the one bullet, then checked her other magazines. Three total bullets. She swiftly consolidated the rounds in one magazine and slid it back into her weapon. The pistol was limited in potential, but it still meant security.

A look at her brother and the other three confirmed they had all been victims of ammunition theft. At least her devices were still working—of course, they'd have to run diagnostics back at the inn.

Fuckers.

Sam snorted softly at her brother. She would've used a harsher insult.

"Greg," Krill said once he fixed his visor into position.

Yuri's voice cracked in her ear. "Glad you're alive. Had us worried for a bit there."

Sam checked her commcuff. They had been gone for almost two hours.

Krill checked his as well. "We're...somewhere in the east quadrant. Coming back now."

"Tracking."

Then, Nas's voice came on. "Pick up some food on the way back, yeah?"

Scott smirked and Miriam chuckled.

The weaving streets were similar to the areas Echo had become familiar with, with painted Charon lamps to remind them of whose town they were in. Conversations died as the marines neared and then returned in murmurs after they passed. A shiver crawled up her spine, and Sam adjusted her headscarf as they passed a couple of SecGuards, who glanced at the five and whispered.

As they turned into another alley, all the hair on her neck

had risen. There were no townsfolk. Even the street's clatter had faded.

At the front of the group, Fox's stride slowed. His left hand inched for his sidearm, his right behind his back, signaling to the group. *Caution.*

Caution.

Sam placed a hand on her pistol and wished it were her carbine. This wasn't an ideal situation. The buildings were too tight around them, and the path narrow. The marines had taken this route to connect to another major throughway, but a figure with a familiar birthmark stepped out at the end of the small street, blocking their way forward.

Bull.

Sam's eyes shifted around. There were only two entrances to smaller alleys, one on each side—Sam wasn't sure where they led. They could turn back now. But from the way Scott shifted behind her, she knew they had also been blocked from behind.

An ambush.

Sam heard a rapid fire of clicks over her visor. It was a signal to the others for help, but she didn't know how useful it'd be. The five of them were still some distance from the inn and the rest of their team.

"You in our territory now, cabrones."

Sam remembered the voice.

The gangly man emerged from the right alley onto the side of the road. He leaned against the wall, scratching his neck.

Flaco.

"Where is the other puta, the alt-lover?" he said.

Sam counted at least a dozen Charonites as they moved out of the corners to surround the marines. All were armed with various weapons—bladed, blunt, projectile.

Shrew—Chibuzo—joined her gang in the front. They were

back for revenge after their first humiliation, their first encounter.

Miriam inhaled sharply. "The rifle."

Sam found what the medic was looking at. A man next to Chibuzo hugged a recognizable weapon to his chest. It was a UMF-issue. She could barely make out the small etched letters, the same ones that the human military loved to put on everything.

Chibuzo's crew killed the marines.

She was wrong. The nameless Charonite man lied. He had set them up.

No. That was an issue for later.

She slowly pulled her head covering down and stuffed it into a pocket. Blending in was a lost cause. She'd need her full peripherals. Nothing to block her vision.

As the Charonites settled in around them, Sam *really* missed her rifle. She pondered whether she and the others should act first. Action was always quicker than reaction. She quickly calculated where every Charonite was and how many she and her brother could take down. There were at least seven in front, closer to Fox, Krill, and Miriam. At least five combined behind her and Scott. Sam steeled herself, her muscles tensing, ready to spring.

"We don't want any trouble," Krill said in an even voice, but his hand betrayed his words as they gripped the handle of his pistol.

"I think they want trouble," Miriam muttered in front of Sam. The medic had already drawn her sidearm but held it to her side.

"What'd you talk about with them ratas?" Chibuzo called out.

Sam's suspicions were confirmed. They had been followed across the river.

"Just trying to figure out what's going on." Krill stalled. "We're moving on tomorrow. You won't have to worry about us anymore."

"Gon' let them keep doing what they're doing?" the Charonite woman drawled.

"Jefa, they stallin'," whined one acolyte.

"Yo sé," she snapped back.

A deafening crack exploded in Sam's ears. She didn't know who shot first, but suddenly Krill's arm was raised, pistol in hand.

Fox lunged to the side, grabbing and launching a Charonite at the man with the rifle. He was their biggest threat.

The sharp staccato of bullets lanced at every hard surface of their small arena, ringing in Sam's eardrums. Her sidearm was out, and she was moving. She jabbed a sharp elbow into a jaw. One trigger pull at close range. One down. A swift heel into the center mass of another. A warmth blossomed on her side. She staggered, compensating for the momentary loss of balance. Second bullet. She didn't know if it hit its mark.

Sam was suddenly in someone's grip, her arms pinned. The world went sideways, and her right shoulder crunched something awful as it met a concrete curb. White-hot pain shot through her body.

Sam struggled her gun hand away and pressed the pistol into flesh. A shot, and the embrace slackened. She broke free and pulled the trigger again.

Nothing.

Fuck.

A rough hand tightened around her wrist, and Sam was pulled back toward her assailant. She grabbed the pistol with her other hand and hammered it into his face, bone crunching underneath metal. Fingers loosed and flailed to protect its owner. She kicked away. She had to get back up. The ground meant death.

Sam scrambled back and rose to her feet. It was bedlam around her. A scrawny woman clung high to Fox's back, her arms wrapped around his neck as he wrestled with Bull, the rifle in between them. A couple of writhing bodies littered the ground. Krill and Miriam had somehow moved away, almost into the other alleyway, and were fending off their own pack together.

Sam reeled around to find Scott, who had already put one Charonite into the ground and was in a dance with two others, one wielding a club and the other, a machete. Sam flung her pistol at the one closest to her, Machete.

Her shoulder screamed at the jerking motion.

Fuck. That wasn't good.

Machete's head snapped to the side with a sick thud, and the siblings launched forward. Sam swept Machete's legs and followed with a fist as he fell. His skull cracked against the ground. She pressed on, not giving the Charonite time to recover.

The small victory was short-lived as she was suddenly lifted off her feet by what felt like a block of stone. Her world slowed as she moved sideways in an awkward position. Time returned to normal as a pile of trash broke her fall. At least it wasn't the hard pavement.

She tried to rise and almost panicked. Her vision was gone.

No. It was just dark. Somehow, she was in one of the alleys.

As she willed her eyes to adjust, she was crushed back. Kicked. Sam braced her arms in front of her face. Kicked again as she tried to touch her device, activate her visor. She saw stars as she took a blow to the side of her head and was on the ground again.

Hello, ground. Hello, death.

Sam curled her arms around her head, bracing against the blows. And then, the flurry of hits stopped. She tried to find her breath, tried to get back up. She was kicked over again, trash scattering in different directions.

"Hola, chica," a hoarse, abused voice sang out.

Sam peeked up.

Two Charonites.

Fuck.

Noise from the main fight seemed far away. She was by herself, no rifle, no pistol. Only herself. One against two.

Fuck.

"Let her get up. It will be more fun." His voice was a hovering blade.

Sam narrowed her eyes at the speaker.

His tongue flicked out.

Creeper.

She picked herself up. Her shoulder was raging, her head throbbing, and the rest of her body crying out in a hundred different ways. She willed the pain out of her mind. She could do this. She was the Valkyrie.

"You're very far from home, bonita," the first Charonite said, taking a small step forward. He held a knife in front of him, and it winked wickedly as it trembled in his hand. Knife was thin and tall, taller than Sam.

Creeper hovered behind at an angle, his pistol shaking slightly in his grip. Both of their eyes glimmered from two meters away. Both junkies on stims.

Sam clenched her jaw and lifted her chin.

Fucking Charonite junkies. *Dumb* junky scum. They had made a mistake. By taunting and playing with her, they were giving her time. She was okay with that. Her mind raced as she weighed her options. Creeper's gun was an issue, but Knife and his blade were closer. Deadlier.

"You were right. She's feisty," Knife said. He flexed his trapezius muscles, an attempt to make himself bigger, more impressive.

An unexpected wave of humor moved through Sam, and she suppressed the urge to laugh.

Not well enough.

Knife's face contorted. "What's so funny, marine?" He flung the last word like an insult. Emboldened, angered, he took another step forward.

Creeper snickered, raising his pistol-wielding hand to his head to scratch it.

Knife twisted his head back at his comrade with a glare.

Now.

Sam lunged forward, deftly folding her fingers around Knife's wrist, twisting, and punching an open palm into his bony knuckles. The blade fell from his grip and into her own. She sliced it forward and felt it tear into Knife's, now Knifeless's, chest. She kicked out into a kneecap, feeling it dislodge.

He crumpled with a howl.

A sharp crack, and something whistled by her ear. She dropped herself with Knifeless's off-balance body, using him as a shield, as more shots lashed out. The ground ripped apart around her, and she keeled to the side to fling the knife at the gunman.

Creeper recoiled; his hands flew to protect his head. The blade slashed across his forearm, and the gun clattered to the ground.

That wasn't Sam's plan, but she'd take it. Luck was on her side.

Sam burst past Knifeless's writhing body, but Creeper's attention, briefly distracted, returned. He weaved to the side, striking her as she stumbled past. His dexterity was surprising.

Sam wheeled around, their positions now changed. She was close to the alley's entrance, her back to the main fight.

Creeper cocked his head and raised his bleeding forearm to his face, dark eyes never leaving Sam. He licked the wound; the blood smeared around his mouth. A predator. Wounded, but wild and still hunting.

Sam's foot touched something heavy and solid, and it clacked in the motion. She glanced down at the pistol.

A mistake.

In an instant, she was back on the ground, a rush of air leaving her diaphragm as the firearm spun away. Sam hadn't caught her breath before she was met with a flurry of strikes against her head. Her torso. Her head. The hands were everywhere. She managed to grab one wrist and then wrestled with the other.

The Charonite hovered over her, his eyes black and oily. It was a dangerous position. A dangerous individual. Sam tried bucking her hips to offset his balance, but he read her motions and rode it out, pulling one hand free of her right grip. He slammed his palm downward, and she jerked her head to the side. She felt the loud smack, the vibration from the force on the ground next to her. His hand came down again in a wide haymaker, and her right arm bladed up to block. It partially worked, taking the brunt of the impact and dampening the blow to the side of her head. However, the pain that rippled through her limb overrode the lightened strike to her temple, and a groan escaped her mouth as her shoulder gave. Sam didn't have time to process the injury as she felt intense pressure to her right ribcage, and a fresh pain bloomed out.

She needed to stop the barrage or get on top. Or both. Her stamina was waning. She braced for a second strike. It didn't come. She bucked up again and her assailant's weight moved over her head. Success. Sam had a small window. She shot her arm out, ignoring the searing pain, and folded Creeper's arm at the elbow, bringing his face closer to hers. His breath was hot on her. She braced her forearm across his chest with the momentum and shifted her hips to flip over. She had him now, she'd have the upper hand in the turn.

Before she could complete the motion, the weight on her was gone. Creeper was gone. Only air now.

Sam's heart thumped in her ears. On her side, she watched her brother stab a knife over and over into the figure below him, the man who had just seconds before been on top of her. Creeper's mouth suspended in a small *o* as the blade plunged in and out of his neck and torso.

A single shot rang out in the main street behind them.

Scott's bloody hand wavered above the knife grip, left protruding from the body.

Sam eased herself up, avoiding weight on her right arm. She peered around her brother at the body. The Charonite's face had lost its charm in death, contorted and eyes open, gone to the world as crimson slipped silently and stained the ground.

"That's enough," a feminine voice bellowed.

Sam looked to her side.

The nameless man's marshal from their underground meeting raised her revolver in the air, a wisp of smoke escaping its short barrel. The nameless man stepped into the street and over a whimpering Charonite. His dark eyes took in everything.

To her other side, Sam was surprised but grateful to see Yuri, Nas, and Kai with their rifles raised. Their eyes were wide, and their heavy breathing and unbloodied clothes indicated their recent arrival.

With a click of the marshal's tongue, the Charonites that were still alive and mobile slowly picked themselves up. Chibuzo stood hunched next to the marshal, her own face and arm bleeding. The gang members retrieved their unconscious, injured, and dead brethren, including the one underneath Scott, and scuttled away, lowering their eyes as they passed by the man, his marshal, and their gang leader. Like children who had been caught red-handed.

Relief hit Sam as she found the other marines, bloodied but alive, scattered among the exodus of Charonites. Miriam had a gash and a growing welt above her brow, but she stood next to Fox, defiant.

The gray-haired Charonite looked around until he located Krill, a trail of blood painted a third of the marine's face. The man's words came slow and lingered in the air. "Stay the night —another day. But I recommend you and your team move on to your next assignment."

Krill spit to the side and glared at the man, then Chibuzo. "She—the rifle—"

The nameless man turned to his peer.

Chibuzo rubbed her neck, refusing to look anyone in the eye. "Found it near the river. Finders' keepers."

Someone scoffed.

"Leave," the man said, and the Charonite scampered away, after the rest of her broken crew. He gazed back up at Echo. After a moment, he spoke carefully. "There is nothing else here for you. I cannot guarantee your safety."

Safety. Sam wanted to laugh and scream at the man, but she was too frazzled—her body shook as the adrenaline crashed like a wave. What could this man guarantee? He tried to guarantee a victory, stealing most of their ammunition and then notifying the other Charonites, Chibuzo's gang. Why hadn't they stolen all of their rounds? What kind of crazed, sadistic people were they dealing with? Their loss, either way. They had attacked them almost three to one—some on stims and still lost.

"Yoomy will—" Nas started but was cut off by the man's impassive look.

Fox scowled, and Krill stared back stoically, his eye twitching.

Echo had been ambushed. Echo had been attacked without any provocation. Sam knew the team lead was fighting back a myriad of reactions, for she was also biting her own tongue, holding in her spewing anger as it bubbled now that the immediate danger had gone. In the end, Krill's jaw clenched, and he dipped his head once in a shallow nod.

The marshal tutted her tongue twice more, and the gray-haired man and the other Charonites left. Only when they had all disappeared, did the marine reinforcements lower their weapons.

The street in front and behind them slowly returned to its normal bustle, although time seemed stuck in their narrow, blood-stained alley. They had escaped an ambush with their lives intact, but it still felt like defeat.

Krill kicked a metallic can into the wall, startling the band of marines. They watched their leader as he paced to the street and back. He raised his head, a deep scowl across his bloody face, "I..." he started. His hand clenched. "Get back to the inn." He turned his back and stormed away.

"Krill—" Yuri reached out.

The lead spun around. His face was a mix of rage and guilt. "I...I just need... I'll be back." And that was that.

Echo looked on as Krill left.

"Kai."

The engineer nodded at Yuri and jogged after the lead.

Sam and Nas moved to help Scott up, but Sam was closer.

She offered her left hand to him. "Thanks, but I had that."

Her brother looked down to the ground at the patch of blood beneath him, his fingers unfurling and shaking over his thighs. Sam knew it was the adrenaline rush coursing through his body and limbs, just like hers. He ignored her and got up on his own.

"Mute," Nas said. "Glad you're on our side. You're a fucking killer." He cocked an eyebrow and clapped Sam on her back. His face distorted apologetically as she grimaced at the wave of pain that coursed through her limb.

After it passed, Sam brushed dirt off her pants and shirt with her good arm and braced the other carefully against her body. Nas got it. Echo saw it, too. They understood. Her brother was too good, too skilled not to renew his contract.

She motioned carefully with her fingers. SEE? UMF NEEDS YOU. YOU CAN'T LEAVE ME.

Sam ambled over to her pistol, still on the ground where it lay. From a cursory glance over its surface, it was fine. She'd do a meticulous clean when they got back to the inn.

Nas grunted behind her, and she turned in time to see her teammate regain his footing. She caught her brother's back before he disappeared around the corner into the main street.

"What's his problem? It was a compliment," Nas muttered.

Sam stared after Scott. That was odd. She began to follow him, but Yuri held a hand out to her.

His brow furrowed. "It's okay. I'll go." He jutted his chin to her braced arm. "Get to the clinic with Tan and Fox. Get yourselves looked at. Nas, go with them." He glanced at the others, nodded, and backed out of the alley in the direction her brother had taken.

With the four of them left in the alley, Nas threw up his hands. "Should we really be splitting up like this right now? That doesn't seem safe!"

Sam looked away from where Scott and Yuri had last been and peered down at the puddle of blood on the ground. She didn't think the Charonites would mess with them again anytime soon.

◯

The small medical center, once open and amicable to Miriam, had been cold and avoidant of the bloodied marines. Only until Fox made a loud and not-so-veiled threat did the staff finally provide a private room and basic supplies. Another menacing intonation conveniently resulted in an older generation MedJet, which helped speed up their recovery process. They had been lucky. Between the three who had been in the ambush, there was only: a hole in Fox's shoulder, a shallow stab wound on his thigh, a gash on Miriam's face, a broken finger, a bullet graze and cracked rib on Sam's side, and the torn fibers in her right limb. Sam's shoulder would need more time to fully recover, but the pain had subsided with two rounds in the MedJet, Miriam's pills, and medicated bandages. Sam could move and raise it without grimacing. It was doable.

It was dark by the time Sam and Miriam returned to the inn. The Matam clinic had taken much longer than expected, and the others had gone to find food with Junpei. Safety in numbers.

As the two women walked down the hall to their room, Sam only thought about the shower she desperately needed, and the sleep she'd embrace, no matter the lumpy mattress. She was still worried about her brother—he had acted so unlike himself—but she found momentary relief in affirming messages from Yuri. He was with Scott, and they were back at the inn. All was well.

Two doors away from their room and pending rest, Sam heard a voice, muffled but recognizable. She froze in surprise, and Miriam crashed into her, bracing herself against Sam's left arm and right hip. Sam would have blushed at the accidental proximity, if not for her shock.

"—can't do this anymore."

Her brother's familiar rasp.

Miriam opened her mouth, but quieted when Sam held up a hand. Her mind, frozen before, was now racing. Scott was in his room. And talking? With whom? Yuri? Why was he talking? She leaned carefully into the door, straining to hear through the thin material. It might have been a second; it felt like an hour. Sam knew it was rude to eavesdrop, but she was bewildered. Scott hadn't spoken the entire time they'd been with Echo. Or had he, and Sam was too distracted to notice? Had she imagined his voice? Him talking?

Miriam noiselessly moved to the other side of the door and leaned in, her curiosity piqued by Sam's behavior.

"And does ... know?"

Yuri *was* in there. His voice was low, and she had barely caught those words, but his tone was sympathetic.

Sam's brows compressed together, lines forming in between. She knew Yuri could understand sign. What was happening inside? What couldn't she see?

"No. I...I don't know."

It was definitely her brother's low, scratchy voice. Something that she had gotten used to only hearing in close moments. And even then, his verbosity was rare. Her head tilted again. What was going on? Why was he suddenly so close, so talkative to Yuri? Not her?

Her brother continued. "I haven't told her."

Her? Sam? She knew he wanted to leave UMF. She had been trying to change his mind—perhaps more passive-aggressively than she wanted—but until now, she was pretty confident she was getting to him. What else was he holding back?

"I...can't tell her."

Sam felt a warm touch on her left shoulder and turned. Miriam's lips were slightly parted ready to say, or mouth something. Those light-brown eyes had filled with doubt and concern, and they cautioned Sam, mirroring what she already knew. Sibling, best friend, or not, they were violating a private moment.

Sam disregarded it, too invested, too curious, and turned her attention back to the thin door and the hushed words beyond it. Just a bit more and then she'd leave, she told herself.

But there was nothing. Just another insect chirping in some wall in the inn.

Maybe the conversation had ended. Or maybe they had moved back to their silent array of words within the motions of their hands.

Sam had only begun to pull away when she froze again.

"She thinks our father was…killed by…by…"

Sam tensed. *Thinks?*

"I killed him."

17

FRAGMENTATION

A BUZZ FILLED Sam's ears. She took a step away from the door, her head reeling. *Scott killed her father? That wasn't true. It couldn't be true.*

Her right elbow bumped loudly into the wall, but she didn't notice. Didn't care that the motion stung her shoulder. She glanced at Miriam.

The medic's eyes were wide. Concerned. Searching.

Miriam reached out for her, but Sam twisted away and briskly backpedaled to the stairs. She needed air. The walls of peeling paint felt like they were moving in, crushing, constricting her. She saw her name on Miriam's lips, but she turned her back, turned away.

She had to leave. Get away from that room, that hall, that inn. Her legs were heavy and slow, like she was caught in a dream, one she couldn't escape from. But she kept moving, one foot after the other.

Scott killed her father? Their father?

Her head was still spinning when she left the settlement through its main gate. She didn't remember how she got there. The entire way had been a blur.

She stood outside in the open, no dense buildings around her, no panels to block the cloudy night air and sky. She felt the humidity on her skin, forecasting a coming rain, nearly oblivious to the stares from straggling passersby. Her headscarf had fallen away and hung around her neck, her light blonde hair free and unkempt. The glow from a nearby lamp bounced off Sam's face as she stared into the dark farmland beyond.

In her storm of thoughts and questions, she found a slight comfort in glints of green in the distance. Fireflies. She would've loved to see them closer, to chase them and hold them in her hand. It was a life that didn't exist for her, a childhood experience that she never had in the north.

And then Sam wasn't there. She was back in Ursus, in the settlement nearby. Memories swept up around her, within her, rushing back to stab and haunt her like a shattered mirror. Fragmented shards cut into her mind as they came hurtling back.

Her brother killed their father.

No. Her father was killed by addicts. Junkies. That's what Scott said. That's what he had told her all those years. She hated junkies. She hated them so much.

Scott made her an orphan. He made them both orphans.

No. He saved her.

There was a sharp sensation in her forearm, and she clutched it, her fingers digging into that fleshy scar line. She remembered the pungent scent of alcohol, the smell on his breath.

Her father didn't want her.

She remembered a warm home stained and littered with pill casings. Pipes. She remembered a plate of cookies. A mattress on the ground.

Scott lied to her. Scott didn't want her.

Stray pebbles bit through fabric into her knees, her shins. Sam grabbed her head.

That wasn't true.

Scott wanted to leave UMF.

No.

He wanted to leave her.

No, no, no. That wasn't true.

Her father was killed by junkies.

No. Scott lied to her.

Her father was an addict. A junkie.

Whose truth?

A moan.

A wail.

And then a broken whimper.

Whose truth?

⌽

It was late when she returned. Sam didn't know exactly what time it was. She had disabled the wrist device after what felt like the hundredth buzz announcing message after message from who knew whom.

When she pushed into the room, no one was there. Kai's cot was gone, her things still on the floor where it once was. *Good.* Sam didn't think she could bear to talk, or explain, when she couldn't even process her own state of mind.

She found herself on the edge of her bed and let her body take over. Her boots came off and she changed her outfit, folding the soiled clothes neatly and to the side. Order. She needed order. She reached for a rifle that wasn't there—someone had moved it, perhaps Miriam?—then to the sidearm still in her holster. She held the sturdy weapon in front of her.

As much as she wanted to dismantle and clean it right then and there, she put it away.

Sam sat there alone in the room, suddenly without anything else but an emptiness. Her only company was the settlement's ambient noises far in the background. She didn't know what to do with her hands, so she pressed them firmly underneath her thighs, locking them in place. She stared into a small stain on the side of Miriam's mattress.

Numb. She was numb.

Sam didn't hear the door open and close. She barely felt the dip of the bed keel to her left, although her body automatically balanced and compensated to the right.

Go away. Leave me alone.

She heard her name in the distance.

Please go away.

Her name, again.

Scott gave her that name: Sam. Short for nothing. Sammy when he was feeling particular.

She felt something warm on her thigh, and she blinked, looking down at a hand. Slender. Sam blinked again and stilled, suddenly aware that she was rocking.

"Hey, it's okay."

Sam wasn't okay. Far from it.

She looked back at the small stain and let out a shaky breath. "He was an addict." Her own voice was alien to her ears.

She was five again.

Sam inhaled through her nose, biting her bottom lip, and huffed out a breath. "Scott... He told me..." She didn't know how to finish. She pulled her hands out from under her thighs and held them out in front of her. Shaking. Sam's eyes glazed, trying to focus on the scar on her forearm. She'd had it for as long as she remembered.

Passing memories flashed again, and she slipped under the surface. She was fracturing, falling apart again. Her chest tightened and she couldn't breathe. The walls were closing in. The stain taunting and suffocating her. She squeezed her arm, fingers closing over the pale scar. The memories pierced her one at a time, slow, spaced out.

She couldn't reach the cupboard in the kitchen. A cup, a vase, a can? Something knocked over. It startled her, scared her.

The smell of alcohol was suddenly there. All around her. Her father.

That scared her more.

Go away.

A blow to the head, and then a sharp pain in her arm.

Fracturing.

She wanted to cry, but her brother had taught her not to. Never make noise. Stay out of his sight. Sixteen-year-old Scott had said he'd be back. He wouldn't be long. She flinched—he'd be angry she left the room. He had told her not to.

Even now, Sam felt the pressure grow behind her eyes and her nose, but no tears came.

Who was she? Who did she want to be?

Don't cry. Stay out of sight.

Who did she want to be? Had she ever had a choice?

Don't make a sound. Stay out of sight.

Hey.

"Hey."

That voice. It pulled at her.

Sam turned her face away.

"It's okay."

There was an engulfing warmth around her.

Her voice and words tethered her, even though they were lies. They held her insides, her outsides, everything together as Sam threatened to fall apart again, and again.

"You're okay. I'm here."

Sam felt fingers through her hair. She felt lighter with each stroke.

Each stroke closer to nothing.

Each stroke dulled the stabbing pain in her chest.

Each stroke pulled her back.

She leaned into the faintest scent of cinnamon. Sam curled into it, into her embrace, her warmth. When she thought about her, everything else fell away. She wanted everything else to fall away.

18

ACCESS DENIED

A DOOR SLAMMED SOMEWHERE down the hall, outside the room.

Sam stirred and moved to rub the sleep out of her eyes, but her arm was met with light resistance, and then a resulting stiff ache. Panic, as quick as it came, subsided as she saw an arm draped over hers. As she followed the limb to the woman behind her, her panic bubbled again, softer this time.

Miriam.

Sam slid away from the bed, carefully maneuvering herself from under a protective arm. She stared at the medic. Why was she in her bed? Sam looked at the bloody clothes folded to the side, patted her own body and garments, and then looked over again at Miriam, who was also still clothed. Sam must have fallen asleep, and Miriam had dozed off right next to her in exhaustion after...

Reminders of the night crashed into her head.

Her father.

Junkie.

Her brother.

No. Stop. No more. She lifted a hand to her head to block the thoughts, but winced at the sharp, unpleasant sensation that came with the movement. She raised her left hand instead.

Her hair was greasy underneath her fingertips. Dirty. She felt dirty. A mild embarrassment crept into her mind that Miriam had fallen asleep next to Sam, with her…like that. The trip to the room and the showers last night had been interrupted by Scott's overheard confession.

Sleep had helped temper the hurt and onslaught of memories, and she wasn't ready to face it just yet. She needed a shower. A shower would help. And then a good, long clean of her rifle.

With a plan—or at least a semblance of one—in place, Sam grabbed her things from her pack, careful not to make any noise. She resisted the urge to touch the slumbering woman's face as she slipped out of the room.

$\oplus$

The team met later than usual, a recovery from the events of the day before. Sam had kept to the side, her gaze down, not wanting to look anyone in the eye—look her brother, specifically, in the eye. Even after a shower, she wasn't ready for that yet.

Scott, for the most part, obliged and gave her the space she needed, lingering around the edge of wherever she occupied.

As the nine marines walked to SecHut in a loose cloud, Sam tried very hard to think about the coffee and the last piece of bread in her hands, glad the pain medication had kicked in. She still had a lasting recovery-throb in her shoulder, a sign of the Matam MedJet's antiquity, but it was a thought in the background.

Even the normally bubbly Yuri was quiet. Sam was aware of Miriam's subtle glances between her and the second in the back, who was already concerned, watching Scott. The others, although oblivious to what happened the night before, respected the shift, their own conversations slow moving.

If Sam kept her mind on her brew, its artificial milk swirling like the thoughts she pressed away, she didn't have to think about the memories or the guilt clawing its way in. The morning and shower had helped her distance and realize the craziness of it all. Her brother lied to her, but her father had also tried to kill her. Scott had saved her, right? Did that negate everything else? A lifetime of a big lie. Or was it protection? Did Scott hate her? Did he hate that he had to kill his own father for her?

Something clawed within her chest, but it drew away when she felt a hand on her bicep. Miriam. Sam opened her mouth to speak, found nothing she wanted to say, and closed it again. Instead, she gave Miriam a soft look, hoping the thanks within was obvious enough. Miriam's hand dropped and Sam immediately missed its touch and comfort. The warm ghost of a handprint faded.

Sam forgot why they were going to SecHut. The previous day's recommendation—or threat—to move on to the next settlement returned to her but nothing much beyond that. She continued step after step, foot after another, and only noticed the first, sporadic drops of rain as they kissed her face.

Clouds hung dark and heavy in the plaza—precipitation on its way. Outside of the building's main entrance, the marines were met by the scowling faces of Sergeant Martín and a band of uniformed SecGuards. Sam could feel herself and the others tense at their receiving line. Her mind cleared and sharpened as she braced for another bout of hostility—grateful for it, like a swift dose of cold water to wake her hazy mind.

"Everyone's a lump of sunshine today," Fox said.

Krill shot a glare, then turned to the SecTeam sergeant. He

said in forced politeness, "Good morning, Martín. What's the meaning of this?"

The sergeant stared flatly back. "Commissioner thinks it's best if you move on."

Krill's shoulders tensed; his jaw clamped down. A vein presented itself on his temple.

"This about your buddies yesterday?" Fox grumbled.

Sergeant Martín disregarded him.

"Twelve, maybe thirteen armed COCsuckers to five unarmed marines was a fair fight. What are y'all thinkin'?"

Yuri and Miriam looked to their team lead, but Krill made no motion or sign to stop Fox. This was a bridge, a relationship being burned before their eyes, if not already incinerated. UMF wouldn't be happy.

Fuck that. Sam hadn't fully realized it until that moment, but she was angry with UMF, too. Command had sent them into a field chock full of landmines without good intel or a map of any sort.

Emboldened by Krill's silence, Fox stepped forward and made a show of counting each SecGuard. "Fifteen," he said, then counted Echo. He planted himself in front of Junpei, a subtle move to block him from any resulting trouble. "Versus nine. Not too fair, is it?" He smirked impishly. "For you…"

Sam slipped a hand over her pistol. Round two. She welcomed a fight. Even if it meant the entire settlement's security force. It was a good distraction. Violence would be her salvation.

But not at that moment.

Heavy boots slammed against the pavement toward the marines and SecGuards. Nicolau, panting and breathless, stopped just short of the large gathering. His eyes widened at the spectacle before him, bouncing back and forth between the two sides, a trigger pull away from combusting.

"Qué carajo..." he said between shallow exhales.

Martín's scowl deepened. "What do you want, *Sergeant?*"

Nicolau ignored the emphasis on his rank. "Why is no one answering their radios?" he demanded. "East gate!"

The other sergeant's eyes narrowed.

"East gate!" Nicolau repeated. "People are coming in! Too many. We are trying to hold them for now. Why is no one answering?" He stared at his colleagues.

"Alterados?" one SecGuard finally shouted out.

"No! People. Zapalans!" Nicolau said.

Sam looked around. Confusion filled both marine and SecTeam faces.

Krill moved forward and grabbed Nicolau's shoulder. "Show us."

$$\oplus$$

The roar of multitudes drowned everything out, including Sam's thoughts and emotions, as the marines approached Matam's east perimeter. A SecTeam unit dressed haphazardly in riot gear, holding clear shields and more equipment, ran past the group. One gate door was closed, and the other wide open —pushed back by the edges of the pulsing mob. The only retaining line was two compacted rows of SecGuards, linked by their arms, holding the mass back.

"Nic! What is this?" Krill shouted over the raging noise.

"Não sei! But they're all from Zapala," Nicolau responded.

"Why aren't you letting them in?"

"Are you loco? There are too many of them. We need order!"

"Is there another way out? We need to figure out what's going on!"

Nicolau didn't seem to hear Krill as he pulled a stray

SecGuard and shouted something to him, drowned out by the clangor. The sergeant then worked his way closer to the gate.

"Sergeant!"

Echo lost him in the chaos.

Sam looked around. They needed a higher vantage point. Her brother already had the same idea and was scanning the row of buildings behind them. They could break into one and get on the roof. Maybe they could get a better view to understand what was happening. Her eyes connected with Scott's, and for a second, the hurt, pain, and guilt came hurtling back. And then it was gone. They needed to talk but now wasn't the time.

Before Sam could suggest a new position, the sergeant burst out from the crowd, dragging a petite, frazzled woman behind him. She bore layers of garments around her shoulders and a large bag across her back.

"Follow me," the sergeant yelled as he moved past them, away from the clamor. The woman stumbled behind him, eyes wide at the marines.

The group followed the two southerners and found refuge from the chaos in a nearby empty restaurant with an unlocked door. The din of the crowd was far from obscured, but here they could talk without stressing their vocal cords. The woman collapsed into a thin chair and tried to find her breath.

"Nic?" Krill said.

The sergeant ignored the lead and lowered himself in front of the woman, meeting her at eye-level. Miriam hastily grabbed a water packet from her pouch and offered it. The woman ripped the top open and tipped it back, taking in the crowd around her as she drank.

"She's from NZ," Junpei squeaked, pointing at her colorful garments.

"It's okay," Nicolau said. "What happened? Why are you here?"

The young woman wiped her mouth with the back of her arm and hiccuped. "Zapala," she started nervously. "Legionnaires."

"A raid?" Junpei said, pushing his way forward.

"Retaliation for the previous attack?" Nas asked in a low voice.

The woman shook her head and shrugged.

"But how many people are outside those gates? Would Legion attack a human settlement just because COC provoked them? The summit..." Kai mumbled, trying to make sense of it.

"Forget the summit. The hell is goin' on here?" Fox said.

Nicolau touched the woman's hand gently. "What happened?"

She hiccuped again. "No sé. Too many. My husband, he told me to leave with the others."

"Where is your husband now?"

"Gavin stayed. To protect our shop."

Nicolau patted her hand and stood, taking a few steps back to engage his small handheld radio. "Cristina. Beck. Check in."

Static hissed in response.

"Sergeant," Yuri said, "do you have any contact with Zapala's SecTeam?"

Nicolau shook his head. "No. I do not know. Their communications have not been working for some time."

Sam remembered the images of the mutilated Temunco marines.

"Is there any way we can contact them?" Echo's second pressed.

Nicolau strode to the door and tapped the radio to his mustache. "Try the long-range again. There could be a mensajero close enough with a device...but..." He shook his head and looked over his shoulder. "I have to get back." He turned to the Zapalan woman. "You can stay here for now. I will come back, okay?" And then he was gone.

Krill pointed at his second. "Greg—"

Yuri already knew his instructions. He tapped Kai and backpedaled to the door. "Already on it, boss. Kai, let's go."

The chances were extremely slim that a runner from New Zapala was close enough for the long-range to connect with, but Echo had to try something.

As Sam watched their departure, she found herself speaking out loud. "We need eyes on."

Junpei nodded. His cheek crimped with concern.

"Tan, pull up a map," Krill instructed.

Miriam poked at her commcuff and her holodisplay projected outward. The team gathered around, their backs to the Zapalan woman, whose hiccups continued.

"Jun, where's the New Zapala SecHut?"

The teenager pointed at an area just south of the settlement's center. "Here."

"Okay. And the Legion garrison is here." Krill indicated a spot several kilometers southeast of the town's perimeter and neighboring river.

"Yes. But they've never raided past this point," he said, voice wavering. Junpei drew a finger back to the settlement's edge. His hand trembled.

"Kid." Fox's voice was soft. Kind.

The young marine glanced away from the team, a shine in the corner of his eyes.

Fox continued. "Hey, where's your place?"

Junpei swiped his palms across his eyes and looked back, raising a finger at a cluster of dense contour lines in the north of the settlement. Fox and Miriam breathed in relief. It was a respectable distance away from the Legion post.

"Okay. They're far from the alties, yeah?" Fox put a comforting hand on the teenager's shoulder. He turned to Krill, and his voice turned harder. "Valk's right. We need to go. Now."

Krill stared at the holomap, then around at the six other marines. "We don't know what the situation is over there."

"Recon. We'll jus' do recon. We don't all have to go." Fox looked to Sam and Scott. "We've got two of the best right here. Let's do our job, Krill."

Krill rubbed the back of his head.

"I'll go," Nas volunteered.

"Me too," Junpei blurted. But then he said it again, more confident. "I'm going."

"No," Krill said. "Both of you. It'll be better if you stay. Some of us should stay. Help keep order and figure out whatever else we can. We can't go into this blind. We can't…I can't have another incident like yesterday. Give us your address, and we'll help find your family, okay?"

"The kid knows the place better. It'd just take us longer and you know it. I'll watch him," Fox rebutted.

Krill closed his eyes tightly, then sighed. "Shit." He bit the inside of his cheek. "Fine. But this is only recon, okay? *Only recon.* Any sign of trouble, you get out, get back here, and we'll figure it out together."

Krill keyed his visor. "Greg. Send updates to Command about Zapala. Temunco, too." He looked back up at Fox, then to Sam and Scott. "Are you good? Shoulder? Your arm?" He looked at their bandages.

Sam touched her shoulder. She'd be fine. The MedJet and medication were a godsend. Plus, she couldn't sit this one out —this was her and Scott's line of work and they were two of the strongest, if not the most experienced. She ignored Scott's stare and nodded to Krill.

Fox nodded as well.

"Okay—" Krill started.

"Wait."

Sam turned to Miriam.

The medic returned a look of concern and glanced at Scott.

Sam tried to plead with her eyes. Physically, Sam would be fine—not one hundred percent, but she was functional and recovering well with advanced medical science. She watched Miriam with the others, hoping she wouldn't betray her. Sam needed this. She needed the mission.

"If they're going, I'm going," Miriam finally said. "MED."

"Okay. That settles it, then. Fox, Jun, Valk, Mute, and Tan." Before Nas could interject, Krill said, "I need you here, okay?"

Nas tried to suppress a pout.

"Get your gear and the case from Greg when he's done. We'll work with Nicolau on using the long-range at SecHut somehow…"

Sam folded her arms and scratched at her thumb from within the nook of her limbs. She could hear the soft pattering of drops on roof panels and the pavement outside as a light shower began. After all the hostilities and unanswered questions in Matam, they were finally going to New Zapala.

19

COMBUSTION

THEY MADE GOOD TIME, considering their options. Thanks to Nicolau, they had managed to borrow two SecTeam rabbits and two guards to drive to the border settlement. The trip normally took less than two hours, but with the midday downpour, detours from broken bridges, and the congestion of New Zapalans on the road, a few hours had already passed. Fox and Sam had agreed it was safer to disembark a few kilometers away from the southernmost human settlement. Their drivers were content to stay with the vehicles at the pass, shielded from the rain and away from whatever was happening. The flux of refugees boded nothing good.

This meant one more uphill climb between them and Junpei's hometown. Sam was grateful the incline was more moderate in comparison to the terrain between Temunco and Matam. At least it was a worn path. With the weather, it would probably take them another hour.

Sam and the others were drenched despite their water-resistant cloaks and hoods. If she wasn't soaked from the heavy drops above, she was saturated from the mud below. She gazed ahead, using Miriam's back as an anchor. The medic walked side by side with Fox, and both were at least twenty paces behind Junpei, who briskly led the way. The teenager's dark hood turned each way, searching each passing refugee for a familiar face. He was on a mission, and Sam understood the feeling.

Solemn stares from passing townsfolk followed them. Echo's armor, rigs, and daypacks were hidden underneath their cloaks, but their rifle barrels peeked out with each step up. Sam pulled her hood further down and kept moving forward, intentionally keeping distance between herself and her brother, who held back at their rear. He had tried to talk before, in the rabbit, but she snapped at him. She wasn't ready to talk.

What did she have to say? *I'm sorry you got stuck with me?*

She wasn't good enough for him.

I'm sorry you had to choose between your father and me.

Was she worth it? Would he have had a better life?

The mission.

Focus on the mission.

Her mission was to free her brother. Scott wasn't trying to leave UMF. He was trying to leave her.

No. That wasn't true. What was true? Why did she snap at him? They just needed to talk this out.

No. She couldn't handle the reality. Not yet.

Focus on the mission.

Sam was mad at herself for the maelstrom in her head. There were too many emotions. Too much conflict. One thought immediately countered the other. She didn't trust herself with anyone right now, especially not him, so she trudged forward, ever aware of the growing distance between the two of them.

Perhaps that was worse. Being aware.

Her thoughts were interrupted near the top of the incline as Junpei straightened, then shot forward to a group in long, dark coats, carrying multiple bags and belongings. Sam mimicked the others and jogged forward to catch up with the teenager.

They found Junpei in the embrace of an older woman, her head covered by a large-brimmed hat. Drops of rain sloped from its sides like a beaded curtain. She looked up at the group in surprise, her face wrinkling.

Junpei pulled himself away, his hood falling back from his head. "This is Tía Clau," he told the four marines. "Our neighbor down the road." He turned back to the woman and her family, who nervously stood around, glancing behind them. "Why are you here?" Junpei said. He had been so excited to finally see a familiar face that he must have almost forgotten the situation.

"Legion raided the south," the woman shakily responded. "Up to the mercado. We had to get out…"

Miriam bowed courteously. "Where are the legionnaires now?"

"The mercado…our shop…they burned it. It's not safe." The old woman's eyes glazed.

"Tía." Junpei held her hand. "Mi familia. Where are they?"

"They said the Legions would go back. They always go back. I told them it wasn't safe…"

"Tía," Junpei pressed.

She didn't respond, lost in her own world. Sam couldn't fault her. They had just left everything behind.

Fox shifted, visibly uncomfortable as he made the connection. "They stayed," he muttered. "We need to go now." He walked forward, but when Junpei didn't join him, he turned around. "Come on, kid."

Junpei tapped the old woman's hand to his forehead and whispered some parting words to the family with a quick bow; his drenched hair whipped a small arc of droplets. Then he hurried after Fox with the others.

As they reached the top of the ridge, Sam glanced behind her. The old woman stood in the same place, watching the marines. Her own family had started trickling in the opposite direction with all their items in tow. The woman's hand reached out.

Not that way. It wasn't safe.

⊕

The settlement of New Zapala was on fire. Sam saw the thick plume of smoke as the marines curved around the bend. It was an ominous hand of gray connecting into the dark clouds above, no wind to blow its tendrils away and resistant to the ongoing downpour. As they moved down and forward, they could see streams of people trickling away from the settlement in different directions, but most coming their way for Matam and the other small towns.

Sam thought she could make out the sound of sirens, although they were too sporadic and eerie. Screams, she realized. They were screams. And gunfire. Explosions. How did a Charonite attack on an Altered Legion post turn into the burning of an entire settlement?

She didn't have time to think further. Junpei took off running toward the town. His pack bounced on his back as he gained speed on the downhill slope; his hip straps untethered and flapped behind him.

"Kid, no!" Fox bellowed, sprinting down the path.

Sam cursed and gave chase, her own rifle shifting at her side.

Fox was surprisingly agile, but he was no match for the native teenager who had run these routes, these slopes, his entire life.

She heard Miriam shout after them, her own boots

slamming into the slick ground.

As the terrain evened out, Fox came to a halt. Between heavy pants, he hoarsely called out again. But Junpei was too far ahead, already disappearing into the heavy curtain of smoke, New Zapala's looming gate and the town's incline beyond it.

Sam caught up to Fox, out of breath. She and the large marine shared a look. The man's eyes were wide, and Sam saw fear in them.

Scott and Miriam joined them, steps and seconds behind.

Fox breathed out, "I have to go after him."

"You don't know what's in there," Miriam said.

Sam inhaled. The bitter essence of smoke filled her nostrils. She took charge, didn't let herself consider any other options—not when she needed her head clear. "Scott, Mir, stay here. Watch our six. We'll get him, we'll be back," she uttered. Sam caught her brother's surprised eyes and then looked away before he could protest.

She dropped her daypack on the ground in front of him, turned on her heel, and ran forward. As she patted at her chest rig to ensure her armor and magazines were tucked away, she felt a slight tug in her chest. Sam ignored it and heard Fox behind her, sprinting with her into the unknown before Scott or Miriam could stop them.

Only recon. Krill's instructions and words dissolved behind her, left with her brother and the medic. The recon mission had turned into a search and rescue.

She and Fox charged past the gate and into the smoke, their legs straining as they fought against the sloped streets. It was disorienting. Even with her visor's hololens engaged, her sight was severely limited. Her eyes, her nose, and her throat burned, and she fought against the tears as she held her sleeve against her face. Every now and then, Sam would encounter a pocket of air where she could make out buildings. Screaming and gunfire erupted sporadically. Close. Far. She couldn't tell anymore.

Ash and rain fell from the skies in big clumps that gathered in every nook of the settlement. She could feel it disperse in contact with her exposed skin. She coughed as tears streamed down her cheeks.

Fox took point, and she followed as close as she could. North. Junpei's home was north. Dense topographic lines meant they had to go higher. Sam chased after her teammate, or who she believed was her teammate, as he ran forward, shouting for Junpei, choking as well. It was difficult to see, hard to make out details until the shapes lurched into view. She stumbled over and through cadavers of furniture that littered the streets.

Then panic set in.

She lost Fox.

She was alone. Alone in this burning hell.

She left Scott.

She left Miriam.

No. She was protecting them.

Sam hacked against the soot lining her throat. Her foot caught as she staggered forward. Somehow, she had found herself in a level area where the smoke stayed along the periphery. She was relieved with the brief respite as she blinked the tears out of her eyes and her vision adjusted.

Ahead, she saw Fox's colossal frame in an embrace with another. Junpei? No, too large, too broad for the teenager. The person was even larger than Fox.

Fuck.

Some meters in front of her, an axe lay on the wet, cobbled ground. Fox's LMG splayed on the other side, its stock underneath a burned panel. The tangled pair turned, and Sam saw the armor: white with smudges from the ash and flame. A legionnaire. The blade between the two gleamed as Fox struggled to keep the pointed tip away from his neck.

Sam's eyes widened. She swung her rifle up at the Altered soldier.

There was no clear shot. The legionnaire was fully suited, from helmet to greaves. The ricochet of her bullets would hit Fox, or she'd hit him first. She looked for an angle, for some break in the white armor.

"Valk! Shoot!" Fox hollered, and shifted his weight as far back as he could. He pushed the knife away in a burst of strength, opening as much space between him and the legionnaire.

Sam fired precisely at the side and back joints of the Altered's armor, hoping the force and angle would be enough. Her shots deflected off the matte plates, but it distracted the assailant.

Fox notched a foot against its inner hip and kicked. The blade cut forward just under his collarbone in the motion but flitted away as he careened backward. Fox cried out, but with the separation, Sam emptied the rest of her magazine into the legionnaire, hoping the armor would break.

It didn't.

Fox scrambled for the closest weapon in her barrage and Sam's rifle locked. She transitioned smoothly to her sidearm, but Fox was already pushing off the ground, lifting the axe by its handle, then swinging it back down with all his weight.

The legionnaire saw the movement a split second too late and raised a hand to block the weapon. The sharp blade swept cleanly through the gauntlet and severed fingers before lodging into the side of the Altered's helmet.

Fox stumbled back toward Sam, where she shoved her pistol into his welcoming hands and reloaded her rifle, her heart rushing. The adrenaline was already causing a loss of fine mobility in her fingers, but her muscles paid no mind, remembering their consistent, almost obsessive training.

Sam had only seen legionnaires from afar. Their uniformity was intimidating, even to seasoned UMF marines. She had never fought one or needed to. Legionnaires did the Royals' bidding. They were the Altered's military elite, UMF and SOG's counterparts. They had never been in open conflict, not since before Sam was born.

The legionnaire reached up with its opposite arm, grabbed the handle close to the axe head, and ripped it up and out of its helmet. A line of blood leaked along the white surface. Fox had struck it, but the helmet had taken most of the cleaving blow. The Altered lowered the weapon to its side.

"What…the fuck," Fox gasped under his breath.

Sam's heart thundered in her chest. What was this monster? The combination of the armor, the soldier's size, and this gruesome act was too much. Junkie Charonites, Apostate bomb makers she could take. This was different. This was a new horror.

The legionnaire faced Sam and Fox; its point of focus was obvious but obscured by the dark visor. It took its helmet off, and the indent caught on something flesh or bone, but the soldier tore the helm away, a strip of skin ripping vertically up its cheek. The Altered winced, its only show of pain—something that felt wildly under exaggerated for that type of wound.

"What the fuck," Sam echoed. She already missed their fights with Charonites.

Unmasked and bare, the legionnaire looked at them curiously. One eye was blue; the other, a shade of green. It blinked, and a third translucent eyelid shuttered from the side.

Its ear was decimated, the lower section hanging from the side of its head. The cut extended into its cheek, and Sam could see the white of the bone underneath. It sent shivers down her spine. Crimson blood dripped like a sheet down its jaw and to its neck, where a freshly scabbed mark blazed against its skin: a triangle with a circle around its top point.

Sam tensed and felt Fox box up next to her. She kept her rifle trained on the behemoth in front of them, Fox mirroring her with the pistol. The legionnaire's head was unguarded now. The Altered soldier took a step forward, and she squeezed the trigger. Center mass of its human-looking face.

Sam felt the weapon recoil into her shoulder. She expected the Altered to drop, but it didn't. She had missed. How? She was confident in her aim.

There was no time to dwell on it. Sam and Fox let loose and fired a steady stream of bullets. In a lightning movement, the legionnaire raised its axe to block the barrage from its face; the rounds ricocheted off its blade and armor.

Within seconds, both marines had run out of ammunition. Sam scrambled for another magazine out of her kit, but her fingers couldn't quite catch the edges. The Altered soldier lowered the axe and stepped forward, one foot after another. The panic choked up her throat. There was no time to reload. She braced herself as the armored behemoth came closer.

She wasn't ready to die.

Or was she?

An uncanny calm washed over her. Better her than Scott. He could live his life how he wanted now. Without her as a burden. A debt paid, right?

A shadow blurred and streaked in the corner of her eye, disrupting her halcyon moment. It leaped and latched itself high onto the legionnaire's torso, wrapping one arm around the side of its neck and attempting to pin down one limb with its legs.

Junpei.

Jun.

Briefly startled by the sudden weight, the brute froze. It was less than a second, but in that time, Jun raised his free hand and slammed a dagger down at the legionnaire's already torn ear. The Altered pulled away quickly, and the blade buried deep into the back of its neck instead. A hiss of an exhale escaped its lips. Jun's weapon hadn't met its mark, but it was still a damaging blow.

So why wasn't the legionnaire down?

Sam clamped her lips together, a bout of giggles threatening to bubble out at the strange sight in front of her. The unkillable demon, a teenage boy latched to its body, her shattered illusion of calm, her adrenaline…everything was mixing in a wildly inappropriate response. She tried to regulate her breath. Sweat accumulated on her skin, a mix of the heat, the effort, and the fear.

The legionnaire ripped Jun off its body and threw him forward, the blade still stuck high between its shoulder blades, just at the lip where the armor ended and its white undershirt peeked out.

"Kid!" Fox shouted.

Jun picked himself up before the others, covered in soot and smudges. His face was full of rage, chest heaving, the corners of his mouth twisted down. Streaks of tears created two lanes in the layers of soot on his face.

Sam knew it then. She could see it in those haunted eyes. His mother whose cough had gotten worse, his sister who could cook a good cuy dish. His family was dead.

She thought of her family. Her *only* family.

Scott.

She still had so much to say to him. Things he needed to tell her. It was all so silly. It was all so clear.

They had to get out, but the legionnaire was too strong, too fast. Sam willed her feet to move, still delayed from her own realizations and renewed will to live. Someone else's grief had become her catalyst. *Move, dammit*. They had to move.

Her voice, hoarse with smoke, was alien to her as it thundered out: "RUN."

They sprinted back into the smoke. Sam was in front, then Jun and Fox. Her hololens helped cut through the terrain, but only barely, and the downward slope aided in their escape. She chanced a glance behind her shoulder. Fox was on her tail, close, his visor gone in the scuffle and his eyes narrowed, trying to shield from the smoke, rain, and ash. Behind him, she saw a patch of white in the gray. It was following them but at its own leisure, as if the legionnaire knew it would catch up to them no matter what.

They raced at the edge of their stamina. Fox slipped and stumbled over rubble but regained his footing. They tore past burning buildings, past alleys, and through the smoke. Sam ran, praying they were going in the right direction, putting all her trust in Jun who had somehow passed her and taken the lead.

Finally, a patch of cloudy sky peeked in front of them. They were at the settlement's edge where the smoke was dissipating. They were almost out. She could make out a head, then two in the medium distance.

Miriam. Scott.

She had so much to say to him.

The air shifted. Something slammed into Fox behind her. It knocked him past her, forward and down, and her pistol flew out of the marine's grip. Sam raised her rifle as the behemoth straightened up over her dazed teammate—the same legionnaire, its own blood coating the back of its white armor. Jun's dagger was gone.

The Altered soldier held its axe on Fox, the blade pressing

firmly into his back armor plate. It was curious, examining Fox, then Jun, then Sam. It even seemed confused as its third eyelid flitted away, and it looked over Sam's raised carbine and her gear. Its two differently colored eyes swallowed her whole.

Sam pulled the trigger, the barrel of her gun leveled at its face. Its reflexes were uncannily fast, but she doubted it could dodge a 1,200 meters per second bullet at that close of a distance.

The click was deafening.

She could see herself, tiny in those eyes. In the rush, she hadn't reloaded. She fumbled for a fresh magazine in her rig as the axe lifted. Indifferent. A killing blow.

She had failed. Fox was going to die. They were going to die.

Sam heard the sharp crack and hiss.

The back of the legionnaire's head opened, and liquid splattered on her face. The Altered staggered backward, then fell, like a giant tree toppling. Its blue and green eyes stared up into the gray hand of smoke above the settlement, a precise hole just above the brow. Apparently, no amount of genetic engineering could prevent death by gunshot to the brain.

"Get over here." Miriam's voice came over her visor. "Now."

Sam broke her stare away from the legionnaire, oddly beautiful in its stillness, the white and crimson a morbid work of art.

Unaware of Miriam's command—without a visor, Fox had already pulled himself to his feet, cupping the side of Jun's shoulder with a softness she had never attributed to the man. Fox pulled Jun in a close embrace.

"We have to go," Sam said. They weren't safe yet, still on the border of the burning town. She glanced back into the smoke and reloaded her rifle with a new heavy magazine. There could be more.

Jun pulled away from Fox and wiped his eyes with a wet forearm. It only added more streaks to his face.

"Sam," Miriam urged.

"Come on," Sam said to the two in front of her, and they reluctantly trudged back to Scott and Miriam, the ridge, and the path to Matam. Any urgency in Fox and Jun was left in the smoke and embers.

Twenty meters from the perimeter with Fox and Jun well in front of her, a chill ran up Sam's spine, and she looked back. She startled, seeing the slivers of white first. As the smoke wafted up and around, it slowly revealed another legionnaire, watching their departure, standing just beyond its dead peer. This soldier looked much smaller and only partially armored with a chest piece and gauntlets. It remained within the smoke, making no move to leave its post. Sam felt its eyes bore into her, a green glint like distant fireflies, as the smoke curtained shadows around it.

With her hololens, she could make out its translucent eyelids, engaged and shielding its eyes from the smoke. Underneath the third eyelid's matte sheen, its pupils were pools of black. There was a familiar pattern on its neck, like the dead legionnaire, paler than the surrounding skin. Fear drenched her like a wet blanket, and she picked up her pace, steadying herself for another sprint. The Altered wore no helmet. She hoped Scott had his reticle and sights trained on it just in case.

But the chase never came. It stayed there, a terrifying statue swaddled in wisps of gray. By the time she, Fox, and Jun reunited with Scott and Miriam, it was gone, folded back into the smoke.

New Zapala was lost.

20

REVELATIONS

BACK IN MATAM, the five marines dragged themselves through the inn's entrance. It had been a grim and quiet journey back. The rain had let up, and the sky opened, reflecting its gray-blues and the last of the sun before it dipped past the surrounding mountains. Its beauty was a slap to the face in their defeat.

Scott stopped at the door to his room, the first one in the hall that now stretched too long. He squeezed Sam's arm as she paused beside him. He had been angry with her outside of the burning settlement, but over the commute back, something had extinguished, though they still hadn't spoken.

That touch in the hall was a promise. It hinted at peace. She held her hand over his. An apology. A goodnight. His eyes were soft, and then he disappeared inside.

Krill was waiting for them outside his open room. He stepped aside, and Jun pushed past him without a word—the journey back had dried his tears. He was now a husk, tired of the day and world. Fox slunk into the room after him, not only his weapon and visor lost in New Zapala, but something more. Sam could hear the bed frames squeak as Jun and Fox settled.

The Echo lead looked into the room and back to the two women. He closed the door softly, remaining in the hallway.

Sam glanced down at the ground, wondering if she should say something, but she was at a loss for words, for any more thoughts. She took the steps toward the women's room by herself instead, but she couldn't bring herself to open the door. Sam was covered in a dried layer of grime and soot, a reminder of the settlement they lost. The people they couldn't save.

Her hand fell off the cool doorknob, and she headed to the bathroom at the end of the hall. She needed to wash this away.

Failure.

☿

Sam dreamed of smoke, and a dancing Charon lamp. The gray-haired nameless man laughed then became her father. Fire licked out and drowned in a deluge of rain. A plate of cookies broke, pieced itself together, then broke again. The brightness of white blinded her. The scar, the branded scab, and the triangle with a circle. Her own circle inked on her forearm grew around her scar. A knife impaled her, over and over. She tried to shield herself from the attacker above her.

Her brother.

She woke with a start, sitting up, and her eyes darting around. Her body relaxed as she remembered where she was. Miriam and Kai's beds were empty—Kai's sheets neatly folded, and Miriam's cluttered and wrinkled.

Shit. Sam looked at her commcuff. She had overslept, too exhausted from the previous days' exertion. From the look of it, the team had let her sleep in. Sam dropped back into the bed, her sheets damp with sweat, and crushed her eyes closed.

She saw the scantily armored legionnaire, its eyes a void that she kept plummeting into. Somehow it was more sinister than the much larger one that had pursued them. Its intimidation was not in its armor, but its intense vigil. Everything else Echo had dealt with, the Children of Charon, the cut cable, the summit, the farmers... It all felt so trivial now.

Legionnaires had raided, invaded, and destroyed a settlement. Killed thousands of humans and left many more without a home. The gravity of it all sunk in, and she shook her head, her eyes still closed. What was happening? She was just a marine, a recon spotter. What had Command sent them into?

Routine. She needed her routine.

As she dressed and donned her equipment, checked her rifle, her magazines, she felt her mind steady. She patted her holster, but it was empty. *Right*. It had been lost in New Zapala. She pushed away the feeling of unbalance, like she was not whole. She wondered if she had ever been whole.

When she was ready and exited the room, she could hear muffled voices down the hall—not from Krill, Fox, and Jun's room across the way—it came from Scott's room. She moved to the door and stilled.

I killed him.

She took a deep breath and rapped her knuckles gently on the door, and the voices quieted. Someone called out her callsign, and Sam walked in. Seated on the beds in a broken circle, seven SOG marines turned to her. All, but Jun.

Sam muttered a good morning and sat beside her brother, pushing aside his long rifle. His bed was a mess.

Krill continued their conversation. "We relayed the message to Command about New Zapala last night. And the legionnaires. They said they'd contact the Royal Emissaries in Station. We should have a response soon." He motioned at the case on the floor between them. "The summit—"

"Did the Royals condone this?" Kai said. "What is going—"

"I don't know." Krill sighed. "I'm just as confused as you are. COC attacks Legion and then Legion destroys an entire settlement in retaliation? I don't know what's going on."

Miriam shook her head. "This is an act of war."

"I know, but Command—"

"I still don't understand why the legionnaires did this. The Royals…" Kai said.

Nas murmured, "They're oppressors. They oppress."

"But why now?"

Sam looked around at the others. Yuri and Scott were quiet, but she was more surprised with Fox, who remained motionless. He looked angry, exhausted, and concerned.

"Did Command… Did we miss something?" Sam found herself saying. There was no way the summit would continue. They had come out here to monitor the Children of Charon. They hadn't expected Altered soldiers to attack an entire settlement.

The room stilled as the burden of guilt grew. Had they missed a clue? Had they been distracted by the Charonites and mundane, human squabbles? Something that they could have identified and been prepared for? Perhaps even stopped whatever chain of events? Sam thought about the cable lift, the Charonites' hostility, the Altered farmers, and the Temunco marines. She felt they were somehow connected but couldn't see how. It was a tickle, like a sneeze before it could manifest. The feeling that they were too close to it.

Whose truth?

The green light on the case lit up.

Yuri moved to it. "Station," he confirmed and looked up at the team lead.

Sam felt a hand on her knee. It was Scott. Her leg was shaking again but stopped with his contact.

Krill swallowed, then nodded.

Yuri engaged the long-range, and a voice came over its speakers. "Echo, Echo. This is Station."

"Station, this is Echo lead. Send it."

"More evidence requested."

Miriam mouthed a silent question laced with expletives.

Krill was confused as well. "Say again?"

"More evidence requested." The voice shifted, kinder and breaking the usual tone of formal communication. "We need more proof it was Legion. Royals deny involvement and any attack or Legion raids. They're accusing us of provocation and false accusations. Center refuses to endanger the ongoing summit. Command needs more evidence to confirm or escalate. Sending more via network." The voice shifted back to its cooler tone. "Send confirmation."

Echo shook their heads, incredulous. It was a betrayal from their own.

"Echo. Send confirmation."

Krill's brow furrowed. "Confirmed."

The green light blinked off.

There was a lull as the marines digested the information, and then the room exploded into murmurs. Krill ignored them as he watched his commcuff, waiting for the report.

Fox's voice was at the forefront. "What do they mean 'deny involvement'? We saw it with our own eyes! An entire settlement did!"

"They're taking the word of the alties over us? We're SOG! Yoomy doesn't believe us? What more evidence do they need?" Nas ranted.

Kai muttered, "Not Yoomy...Center..."

Fox's voice rose. "Do they think NZ did that to themselves?"

Words wound down as Echo realized they had an additional guest. They had been too distracted to notice his arrival. They looked at Jun now, his face still smudged from the day before. The skin around his eyes was swollen, the redness from the smoke replaced by a pink of grief. He sniffled. How much had he heard?

"What's next?" Jun whispered.

Fox stood and moved toward him, but Jun waved him away. Fox slunk back, slightly dejected, still worried.

"Is this another reign of terror?" Jun said louder.

No one answered.

Was it? History had seen this before. The previous Royal Sovereign had openly attacked settlements. But it couldn't be. The Royals had replaced her after the humans fought back. It was a bad time for both sides, but the humans, with their backs to a wall, were resourceful and came back viciously. Another reign of terror was too big, too heavy to comprehend.

"Are all alterados...alties like that?" Jun uttered.

No. The Altered and Apostates Sam had dealt with before were nowhere as terrifying as that behemoth. Everything felt unknown and uncertain then.

"No, that was a legionnaire," Fox said.

Sam thought about the Altered soldier's white armor. It was a legionnaire. But something in Jun's question made her doubt for a second. She remembered the second Altered's size and hollow eyes. The scabbed mark. The scar.

"Maybe. I don't know what that was."

The group turned to Sam, heads tilted.

"That was a legionnaire," Fox said again slowly.

The scar, the brand. She'd seen it before.

"Scott. In Ursus...our last mission, do you remember?"

Scott grimaced and nodded. Of course, he'd remember it. It happened less than a month ago, the last mission before they were sent to Station. Their Ursus team had been following a suspected bomb-making scheme, and Sam and Scott had chased a young Altered down, an apprentice to their tracked target. She had lost her brother in the pursuit, but then found the apprentice again, cornered her...

The girl.

"Yeah. Do you still have those pictures...before she..."

Before she blew herself up in that alley. In front of her.

Scott pulled up his commcuff terminal, and expanded the display so it reflected outward. His fingers whirled in a frenzy as he brought up an archive of folders. And then a surveillance picture they had taken of the girl walking out of a discreet shop. Her brother looked up, a confused and pained look on his face.

"Any more?"

He swiped through image after image until—

"Wait. Stop."

It was there, peeking out from underneath her shirt collar, but it was there. The white scar. The brand. The triangle with a circle around one point.

"Valk?" Krill asked.

"The mark," she whispered.

The others leaned in around the holodisplay.

"Wunbies?" Nas blurted out.

Krill turned to Sam. "What do wunbies...Apostates have to do with New Zapala? The legionnaire?"

Sam glanced at Fox and Jun, but they stared back at her like the others, perplexed. Had she been the only one to see it? She needed the others' assurance, but they gave none. They hadn't seen it in the panic of everything.

"Legionnaires," Sam said. "There were two."

Fox's brown eyes scrutinized her as if she had gone mad.

"Behind us, in the smoke...after..." Had she imagined it in her shock? No. She knew what she saw.

I saw it, too. But it just stood there.

Reassured, she squeezed her brother's hand. "Right. But you were too far to see." She looked around the room. "They both had that mark, that...brand."

"So the legionnaires are wunbies now? Terrorists?" Kai said slowly.

The marines' eyes darted around. Those implications were heavy.

Jun mumbled something, but his words were lost in the growing murmurs.

"Command?" Yuri asked.

Krill shook his head. "You heard them. We need more evidence."

"Let's say Valk is right." The second locked eyes with Sam. "How is that not more evidence?"

Sam shook her head along with Krill. It wasn't enough. If Fox and Jun hadn't seen it either, it was just one marine's word. Sam, the Valkyrie, had a solid reputation, but it wasn't enough to go to the Royals and provoke more problems, endangering their already shaky talks. She kicked herself for not taking a picture, even knowing that she wouldn't have been able to in their rush to get away. Hindsight was easy.

Krill echoed her thought out loud. "It's not enough."

"So...what? We have to go back and grab one?" Fox's hands knotted together. "Fuck me. That thing was..."

It was too strong.

"What does this mean?" Jun said sharply, a slight tremor at the end.

No one answered. No one wanted to be the one to put that thought into words.

"Are they coming here?"

21

SHIFT

SAM KICKED a pebble across the square outside of SecHut. Scott and Miriam watched it as it skipped along the uneven pavement. Nas and Kai had wandered off after a vigorous, hushed conversation, and Fox had stayed back at the inn with Jun. The SOG marines had expected to be turned away again at the Matam SecTeam building, but there was no resistance. The area was almost devoid of SecGuards, most of them too busy with the New Zapalan refugees. No one paid much mind to the marines and their rifles. Sam wasn't going anywhere in the south without her carbine. No more ambushes and no more getting caught in less advantaged positions.

"Your team told you that wunbies and legionnaires attacked Zapala." Commissioner Yosef's shrill voice pierced the early afternoon air through the open window above them. A vendor looked up from across the square, startled.

A muffled voice came back, which Sam could only imagine was their Echo lead.

"And you believe them?" the commissioner's voice cried.

Another incoherent voice.

"It is just another raid. Sergeant, do *not* dare interrupt me.

No. You are not from here. You do not know. This is legionnaires being legionnaires. Alterados being alterados."

Sam could picture the commissioner's cheeks inflating and turning a bright shade of red. Pointed fingers. Krill's irritation and attempt at self-control.

Now, she heard the sergeant's voice rising. "Sir, our people have seen scouts—"

The commissioner sputtered. "So let them come. They have and will always try to provoke us. You come from Station, which sits high and pretty and safe. You do not see what we see. You do not live what we live! We are stronger than you think! Get out of Matam. You do not belong here!"

A door from inside the building slammed, and the three marines waited with suspended breath. Moments later, the front door swung open, and a flustered Krill marched past them, his face a pink shade and mouth turned downward. Nicolau and Yuri followed but joined the three others.

"He won't evacuate," Yuri said. His cheek pulled back in a grimace.

Nicolau pulled his pipe out of his pocket and dangled it between his lips.

"Shocking. I'm surprised you even got a meeting with him," Miriam said.

Krill paced back to them. "He's an idiot," he seethed, before parading away, trying to dispel his anger. He strode back again. "Nic, who else will listen? COC?"

With a pinch of tobacco and a quick flick of his lighter, the sergeant sucked hard on the tube. He blew out a lungful of smoke. "They already know."

"The Charonites are going to fight," Miriam said.

The sergeant nodded. "I heard some have already gone to Zapala."

"They're dead," Sam said, remembering the armored legionnaire. "They're going to die."

Smoke puffed out of Nicolau's cheeks. "What about UMF?"

Krill shook his head. "Station wants Command to provide actual evidence of the wunbies and Legion working together. Apparently our word isn't enough. They're more concerned about the summit and offending the Royals. Temunco might be able to send reinforcements, but it leaves the outpost…scarce."

"It does not matter now. How much time do you think we have?" the sergeant asked.

Yuri glanced around the group. "We all still agree that Matam is next?"

Sam, Scott, and Miriam nodded their heads. There was no reason to believe otherwise. Not with Nicolau's account of white uniforms in the distance.

"We have to get these people out of here," Krill said. "Nic, do you think you can change any minds?"

"Maybe. Não sei. Some are already skittish."

Krill looked around. "Where's Nas and Kai? We can search for the tunnels, try to find…"

"I don't think that's a good idea, boss."

"We need to move people out of here. *Some* kind of exit strategy, Greg."

How were they supposed to defend an entire settlement that didn't want help? Defend them from Altered soldiers whose armor, speed, and strength even two SOG marines could not take down without help? Did they even have time?

Boots pounded on pavement and echoed off the surrounding buildings as Nas burst forward. He stopped and panted out, "Kai…"

Sam's grip around her rifle tightened. She combed the square and street behind him for their other teammate. What had happened now?

"Is she okay?" Krill said tensely.

Nas shook his head and waved his hand. "She's fine. We…"

"Catch your breath," Miriam said.

The marine attempted to inhale and then slowly exhale. "Kai and I…we might have something…the missing farmer."

As Nicolau stepped closer to Nas, Krill's shoulders sagged.

Sam's hand unclenched as well. Why did this matter now?

Krill sighed. "We don't have time for—"

"We do," Nas affirmed, his chin set and brown eyes gaping at them. "We do." His hands set on his hips, his torso leaning forward as he willed his body and breathing to normalize to pass along the message. "Remember Jun mentioned old matriarchs a while ago…what if they're still around? What if COC isn't the only player outside of the government here? They'd have to have intel, yeah? An information highway might still exist."

Krill's face scrunched in confusion. "What does this have to do—"

Nicolau's face set. "The matriarch is just a story. A myth."

"But it must originate from somewhere. Doesn't matter. We're grasping for anything, right? Kai and I—"

"Where is Kai?"

"What does this have to do with the missing farmer?" the sergeant said simultaneously.

Nas stared at them. "We went looking and asking around… and there was a mention of the woman. That Legion took her, but she's been found. She's here. Now. In Matam."

"How…" Nicolau muttered. His pipe dangled between his lips.

Krill's mind was working. "They're sure it was legionnaires?"

Nas shrugged.

"It could be something…" Yuri said hesitantly.

Command wanted evidence.

"Okay. Greg, go with Nas and Kai—"

"I would like to join," Nicolau interrupted.

But Nas held up a hand. "Can't. Only women."

"What?" Krill and the sergeant said at the same time.

"That's what they said. I don't know, but Kai is with the contact right now. We have to hurry." He peeked back toward where he had come.

"Okay…" Krill dragged the word sideways and gestured at Sam and Miriam. "Go. Get me something I can work with." He turned to the others. "We need to figure out how to get these people out of here."

"Yeah, boss." Miriam said as the two followed Nas, who had already broken out in a jog back for the dense streets. They left the others to address the looming threat of Legion.

Sam cast a long look at her brother behind her. He returned it with a small flick and outward motion of his fists.

Be safe.

◊

"How are you doing?" Miriam whispered, close enough to Sam for her to hear.

"Today? Or overall?" Sam chuckled. She sidestepped a slow-walking townsperson and kept an eye on Kai who followed closely behind the older Matam woman. She made a note of the latest series of alleys and turns they made.

"Today. Overall. Both."

"Things are great," Sam replied. "This is going great."

The medic shot her a look.

What was she supposed to say? She was trained for the worst-case scenarios. She was conditioned for the stress and pressures. Sam had been ambushed, attacked, chased, and all of that she had no issue with, but when she learned her brother had been hiding a truth, had been holding his guilt to himself, to what, protect her? She had broken. She had cracked. And the only thing holding it together was the mission and being useful. Sam dreaded talking to her brother. She kept putting it off, glad that the external factors were assisting her.

"Sam…"

She wanted to thank Miriam, tell her how much she appreciated her company, her presence. But as she opened her mouth, Sam almost ran into Kai.

In front, the Matam woman had abruptly stopped at what seemed to be a back entrance to a two-story stucco and brick building. She gestured at the door, looked around the alley, and hastened away without a word.

"Hey, wait!" Kai yelped.

Sam and Miriam glanced at the structure and back at each other. Sam moved to take point, but Kai shook her head. She unshouldered her rifle, keeping the weapon at her side in one hand, and cautiously pulled open the door. It was lit inside, a glow of lanterns reflecting into a small room, a foyer of sorts, windowless. Kai moved in, and the two others joined her.

The door shut soundlessly behind them and the three stopped short of a dull but strikingly curtained doorway. Incense filled their noses, strong but pleasant, and soft noises came from behind the curtains.

Sam activated her visor and pulled her carbine into her body. Kai glanced back, and Sam nodded. The engineer pushed past the curtains into a dimly lit room, the others close behind.

Kai made a soft sound of surprise. They weren't sure what they had expected—their guards raised because of the previous incidents. Her eyes would've needed to adjust, but the visor did it for her instantly.

The room was filled with at least twenty individuals—all

women—of different ages, dressed in beautiful colors and garments. They sat on faded cushions on the ground, tables in between them with foods that smelled heavenly. Was this the matriarchy or some remnant of the old order that the others had spoken about?

Heads turned to the marines, and both groups inspected each other. Sam's eyes narrowed as she caught one of the younger women standing at the side of the room sliding a hand behind her back.

Miriam stepped forward with her hands raised. "We mean no harm."

The seated women looked on, unmoved.

"We're UMF Special—"

"I know who you are." The voice came from an elderly woman seated at the head of one of the larger tables. Her shoulders hunched over with the weight of age and experience; she had an air of quiet authority. Her wrinkled hands delicately wiped against a piece of cloth. "Why are you here?"

Sam wasn't sure if the matriarch was asking why they were there in the room or there in Matam, in the south. It was pointed, but it was still the least hostile greeting they had in their time in the settlement.

Kai cleared her throat. "We were told a farmer was taken by...Legion, and they've been found. We'd like to talk with them." She looked at the elder for any reaction. "I believe they may have seen something related to what happened in New Zapala."

"It's important. Please, Matam is in danger," Miriam stressed.

The matriarch studied them with weathered, piercing eyes. Those knowing eyes betrayed her stooped posture. This woman was powerful.

She tilted her head, barely, to the side and said something

under her breath to a teenage girl seated close to her. The girl nodded, stood, and hurried out of the large room.

"Guess it wasn't just stories…" Kai whispered.

After a moment where no one spoke, the girl returned, holding the hand of an even younger girl who looked three or four in age. Her light-brown braid whipped as she quickly hid behind the other's legs, seeing the armed strangers. She peeked out and her eyes glinted, reflecting a soft green in the dim lighting.

Miriam gasped.

Sam held her breath as their mission and objective was momentarily forgotten. Her fingers closed around her rifle instinctually.

An Altered child.

The youngest one she had seen was the Apostate girl who had blown herself up, but she was about the same age as Jun. Older than Sam when she had started her first contract with UMF.

The woman at the side pulled a long, wicked knife from the back of her waistband and stepped forward to the marines.

"Ma'! Put it away," the Matriarch barked.

Sam's attention was diverted. She quickly moved her hand away from her carbine, putting her hands up, palms out in front of her instead.

The other woman lowered the knife but edged closer, vigilant.

"She's Altered," Sam stated, dipping her head at the child.

"Pacha is both." The little girl ran to the old woman, who pulled her gently into her lap with leathered hands.

Kai spoke. "Half-Altered?"

Next to her, Miriam whispered, "Half-human."

Sam blinked, then blinked again as she tried to make sense

of this. She had never seen or heard of a half-Altered, half-human before. A hybrid of two warring sides.

"Is she...? How...?" Kai said. She shook her head. "Why are you showing us this?"

"You are here to support peace, are you not?"

"Well, yes. The summit...between Station and Arshangol, the Royals..."

"And when that peace occurs, how does it sustain?"

Kai glanced at Sam and Miriam, then back to the matriarch. "Well, I guess...through regulations and oversight..."

"What about the people who disagree?"

The corner of Sam's mouth quirked. What was the point of all of this?

Kai pondered but continued to entertain the conversation. "There will always be people who don't like how things happen or why. For something like peace to actually hold...the people must believe in it. Or trust the future's potential..."

The old woman nodded once. "The south used to be more tranquil. There were some Altered here then, too. But no violence, not like the kind today. But pride...does not matter which side...it is a downfall. Sometimes we want the same thing. To just live our lives together. To share."

"Is that what happened with..." Miriam turned her chin to the girl in the old woman's lap.

"My granddaughter and her partner moved from this settlement, away from the hatred, to live a better life." She tucked a lock of hair behind the girl's ear and furrowed her thin brows. "She messaged me, my granddaughter. And then I didn't hear from her again. A friend of a friend was informed... But who can we trust now? When ego has corrupted so much already?"

She stroked the child's smooth cheek. "The women, they went to their home. My Amana and her partner were gone, but we found Pacha, did we not? My little waaj was hiding. Where her mothers told her to."

Thoughts spun through Sam's mind as links connected. Sergeant Nicolau's missing farmer was not just a farmer. An entire family. Human and Altered together?

"You said there was a message?" Miriam asked.

"Yes…"

"What happened to them?" Kai said.

The matriarch's eyes, soft and kind to her great-granddaughter, turned dark and cold. "Amana's partner said Promised followed them."

Miriam whispered, "Promised?"

"Apostates. Wunbies," Sam replied in a hushed voice, and clenched her jaw. Her mind reeled as it tried to understand what the matriarch was saying—she was still trying to process the half-human, half-Altered child.

"Imposters in Legion uniforms. And then I heard nothing more."

Kai gasped softly. "I'm so sorry…"

But Sam was focused on her words. "Imposters," she repeated under her breath.

"In Legion clothing…" Miriam echoed. She looked at the other two marines, eyes wide. "We need to bring this to Krill. Now."

They had something.

"The girl goes nowhere." The long, wicked knife winked at the marines, and tension filled the room as the misunderstanding dispersed.

Miriam raised her hands defensively. "No. No. We're not taking her away from you. We wouldn't…" She peered again at the little girl who stared curiously back, then to the old woman. "Do you still have that message your granddaughter sent? Please, we don't have much time."

The matriarch nodded once at the same teenager, and she disappeared back around the corner.

Sam stared at the little girl and the green glow of her eyes. They were getting what they needed. Evidence. But they had also been shown something else... Sam shook her head. UMF and humans—perhaps even the Altered—weren't ready for that kind of intimate peace. Why did these women trust them with this?

The young girl returned into the room, walked to Miriam, and held out an old communication device. Miriam smiled gratefully and took it. She linked it to her commcuff; Sam recognized the transfer process screen in the corner of her eye. On the other side of her vision, she watched as Kai took steps closer to the seated women, toward the little girl.

The door in the foyer slammed. The curtains behind them whipped out, and Miriam jumped to the side. A panicked and panting woman lurched into the room.

"Todo bien?" the knife-wielding woman asked.

The new arrival's eyes searched the room and settled on the old woman. "Avo! Matam is under attack!"

A collective breath was held in the room, then a klaxon sounded off in the distance. An alarm.

The women stirred and scrambled.

A knot grew in Sam's gut. They were too late.

The matriarch hissed loudly, and the room quieted. "Tranquila. Keep order. Get your familias underground. Go."

Sam, Miriam, and Kai moved to the side to allow many to rush out, while others assisted the more elderly women. The matriarch slowly stood up, leaning against the table for support, the little girl gripping onto her.

Kai turned to the other two. "We have to help them out of here."

"No," Sam said. "They can take care of themselves." And

she believed it. The matriarch and the den of women was its own sign of resiliency through the generations.

Miriam's nod was another affirmation.

Sam steeled herself, her thoughts already moving forward. If the legionnaires—no, the Apostates—were already in Matam, they'd come from the east, from New Zapala and their garrison. Their Echo teammates would move to the west perimeter.

"Sam," Miriam called over the room's chaos. Her hand cupped over her ear and visor, then talked into it. "We're still here. We're on our way.

"Let's go then," Kai said.

The three women ran out. They had the evidence they needed, and that UMF wanted, in hand. But what use was evidence when the enemy was already at their doorstep?

22

AGGRESSION

THE SETTLEMENT'S alarm wailed louder as the three marines neared the main thoroughfare, following the mass of people as it routed like creeks to a river. Sam hoped it was the right path, flowing outward toward the perimeter, for the sake of the townsfolk. The three weaved in and out of what felt like the crush of the entire Matam population. Sam wedged herself into the side of a food stall to avoid getting swept up, elbows and weapon held tight to her body to avoid the still-hot grill just on the inside.

"Which way?" Miriam shouted behind her. The medic had hooked herself just inside a neighboring shop.

Sam wasn't sure. She didn't recognize any buildings, stalls, or physical markers. Everything was transformed in the chaos.

Next to her, Kai checked her cuff, braced against her belly, while also trying to stay as flush to the stall as people shoved by. "I think we go right!" she yelled to Sam and then louder to Miriam. "Right!" She pointed a stiff, open hand at her chest.

An explosion, then another, boomed in the distance. Screams echoed in response. A new panic surged through the street.

Suddenly, Kai wasn't next to Sam, pulled into the stampede. Sam shouted after her, a hand too late, grabbing at the air where the engineer once was. Sam craned her neck to locate Kai but was forced to press back to avoid a new surge. She could feel the grill's heat through her shirt and kit.

Kai's head popped in and out of view as they tried to maintain eyesight of each other. Sam called out again, but she could barely make out her own voice over the roar of havoc.

"West gate." Kai's breathy voice came over the visor. "Don't worry. I'll see you guys there."

Two clicks in response.

Miriam.

Sam turned back to where she had last seen the medic.

WHACK. Her head snapped to the side, and her vision flooded with white spots. When her eyes adjusted, slightly blurred from the impact, Sam was falling into the crowd. Then, she was harshly pulled back, and firm hands stabilized her.

"Sam!"

She shook her head to clear the daze. It throbbed, and she touched her left temple. It was wet.

Miriam cupped her hands around Sam's face and tilted so she could see the impacted area. "Are you okay?"

Sam looked into the medic's eyes and then to her lips. She swallowed and refocused on the situation around them, pressing herself further out of the mob's reach. "I'm okay," Sam finally said. This was a dangerous place to be. They had little control.

"We need to get the case!"

The warm hands left her face, and Sam missed their comfort, almost leaning into where they had just been. Miriam shouted something else, but Sam couldn't hear, as another explosion and then gunfire ripped out.

Miriam tried again. "Krill and the others—"

Sam shook her head and then winced at the movement. "They're west!"

"Sam! The long-range!"

Sam squeezed her eyes shut, her head throbbing. *Well, shit.* She hoped that the others had notified Command about the attack, but if there was a chance they didn't, they had to retrieve the case or use the repeater at SecHut. It was their lifeline. And with the group moving to the gate, Sam and Miriam were probably the closest to both.

Sam keyed her visor to the open team channel. "Yuri."

"Valk! Where are you guys?"

"Do you have the long-range?"

"What?"

"The case!"

Fox's voice came faintly through in the background of Yuri's open transmission. Sam could hear scrapes and rambles of conversation for what felt like an eternity, but no response from Echo's second.

"Yuri?"

His voice came back quieter. "No. It's still in the room."

"Shit," Sam muttered and shared a glance with the medic. She keyed her visor. "Okay. Mir and I are heading there now."

"Wha- wait. No. It's too clo—"

"We'll be back in a bit," Sam interrupted. "Kai is heading to you."

"Val—"

She had already tuned him out. Sam had a new focus, a new task ahead. She nodded at Miriam, and together, they pushed against the flow of people until they ducked into a less-trafficked alley. The two moved toward staggered gunfire and explosions. Sam imagined SecTeam and the Children of Charon were fighting back. It was admirable, but she had a sinking feeling that it was useless.

The lights in the street outside the inn had been toppled, and many of the standing or strung-up lamps were snuffed out. The only light came from within the posada window, still on, a soft yellow.

Sam stepped cautiously out of the shadows, her carbine sweeping as she scanned around. Miriam stayed close behind her, rifle in hand as they dashed toward the building and let themselves in. The lobby was empty, and the building was quiet, like the rest of the area.

"I'll go." Miriam whispered, already moving up the stairs.

Sam reached around the counter to find the switch and doused the lights. She moved to a position near the inside of the closed door and window. The thin walls were poor cover, but she still felt safer behind something. Anything.

Gunshots cracked a few streets over. Closer. Sam wasn't sure if gunfire meant SecTeam, Charonites, or Altered. The legionnaire—the Apostate—in New Zapala, had opted for an axe. Did they even need projectile weapons with their armor?

Sam remembered the belt of disc grenades from Station and keyed her visor. "Mir."

Two clicks.

"Grab my belt, too."

Two clicks.

Some minutes later, Miriam reappeared at the top of the staircase, her full pack strapped behind her. Yuri's long-range case was attached to its side and Sam's pack and belt hung off her shoulders.

Sam adjusted her gear and rotated back into her position, Miriam to her side. They could go out the inn's fire exit from the second floor, but there had been no motion outside the way they came.

Sam cracked open the door. Her visor confirmed no movement outside. She nodded, then felt a quick squeeze on her shoulder. Time to get back to the others. Sam snuck out the door and quickly moved into darker shadows. She realized it would be pointless if they encountered Altered, but she didn't want to get shot by overzealous, amped-up Charonites or SecGuards. Plus, it was a habit. Stay out of sight.

The two made it without incident to the end of the street, back to the market. They only had to follow this route, which would spit them into the main artery straight to the west perimeter, the way they had gotten there on their first day in Matam.

She checked her left, then the area in front of her. Sam peered around the corner to her right, their destination. She could feel Miriam behind her and discovered a mix of comfort and fear. She wanted to protect her. Needed to.

Sam looked again to her left, and her body stiffened. Something had changed. Her rifle barrel crept up. There was no movement, but she willed her visor to scan and identify something, anything she could address. She and Miriam were in a dangerous place, hugging the right side of the street, completely visible to whoever, whatever, was down to the left.

Two reflective glows blinked owlishly at her, curiosity behind those orbs.

And malice.

Sam breathed out a curse.

Another pair of green glinted in the distance, much further behind the first.

Altered.

They knew they were there.

Before Sam could wonder how long they had been watching, she shot a burst of fire down the alley, pulling the weapon into her right shoulder to stabilize it as her left arm shot out, grabbed Miriam, and pulled her to the other side of the road. It was the opposite direction they needed to go, but right now, they needed to *not die*.

The quiet darkness shattered in blaring flares as bullets spit against the corner, hissed, and cracked against stucco and brick. When the barrage stopped, Sam chanced a peek around the corner, sending another concentrated burst down the street. She ducked back, quickly reloading as a hail of fire came back.

They needed to get out onto the main road. There were too many dead ends in the market, in the smaller streets. Sam patted the belt she had thrown around her neck and grabbed two discs from their loops. A glance down showed they were set on five-second timers. Five seconds was too long against Altered. Five seconds was also too short for humans.

The gunfire stopped. Sam wondered if that meant the Altered were moving closer.

"I'll cover."

Miriam nodded. "Okay."

She pulsed her closed hand around the two discs in a silent countdown. Sam squeezed the devices, leaned, and threw them around the corner.

Five.

Miriam peeled past her into the alley, sprinting her way diagonally across the aisle, rifle braced against her body and shooting down at the green eyes.

Four.

It was a distraction.

Three.

Sam popped her rifle around the corner and held down the trigger.

Two.

Miriam ran for the other alley further down. She had to get to the corner fast.

One.

The discs created concentrated explosions, and Sam knew it was a fifty-fifty chance whether or not they'd incapacitate the Altered. If it didn't, she hoped it was a good deterrent to keep them from advancing. The main thing was that Miriam was safely across.

Sam peered around the corner and didn't see or hear any movement down the alley. No green, no gunfire.

Okay. Her turn.

Sam grabbed another two discs from the belt and held them in the palm of her left hand, pressed against the barrel of her carbine. Her eyes locked with Miriam's as she took a deep breath.

Go.

She pushed herself off the wall and propelled herself forward into the open street, keeping Miriam's firing lane clear. She raised her rifle across her body as she shot a short stream of bullets at nothing in particular. Sam hoped the dynamic movement was enough to throw any lurking Altered off.

Bracing the rifle against her shoulder, cementing it with a firm grip, she dropped her hand away from its supporting position and squeezed the discs as she cocked the forearm back to launch them away.

Bright metal sailed out of the darkness and toward her. The blade flitted past her neck and grazed the surface of her skin. She stumbled, and a disc scuttled down the dark path. The other one rattled a meter away from her, its momentum lost.

Her eyes widened.

Fuck.

Major fuck.

She scrambled and catapulted her body behind the nearest kiosk. She was too close.

As the grenades exploded, Sam pulled her body as tight to her as she could, trying to fit it behind the little cover she had found. A sharp tug and searing pressure in her left calf was drowned out by the surrounding rattle.

Her eardrums buzzed as her hearing came back, her heavy breathing amplified in her head. Sam remained curled into herself and waited for more noise or gunfire, but there was none.

Miriam peeked around the corner, her rifle trained downrange. "Are you hurt?"

Sam patted her arms, her chest rig, and her abdomen. She was okay there. Just some scrapes from the leap to cover along the exterior of her arms. She continued her self-check and moved her hands down her legs. Agony fired from her left calf, and she grimaced. The fabric was already drenched with blood.

"Sam?"

"Leg," she hissed. Sam cursed herself. *Idiot.*

"I don't see anything. Can you get to me?"

Sam pulled herself into a modified crouch, careful to stay within the cover of the small space. She shifted onto her right leg to keep weight off her left. Even with the smallest movement, another scorching jolt shot through her limb.

"Yeah." Sam peered around the kiosk's frayed edge. She also saw no movement. "Are they gone?"

Miriam didn't respond, but Sam at least knew they weren't shooting anymore. No more ammunition? Were they injured? Dead? No green eyes watched from the shadows from what she could see.

"I've got you. Move."

Sam did her best to dash the distance to Miriam's corner. She was slow and overly exposed, but there was no further action or attack. Sam limped past the medic, her weapon aimed in the other direction, watching for any activity toward their destination. She was injured, but she still had a job to do.

Miriam peeled away from the corner and moved to support Sam on her right. They couldn't stay there. They had to make it back to the rest of their team. Together, they moved forward.

23

FAREWELL

THE WEST GATE was a bluster of exodus and activity. A SecTeam unit propped themselves against makeshift cover facing into the settlement, a reminder to everyone of where the threat was coming from. The stream of people stretched into the farmlands toward smaller settlements, or elsewhere. Many carried whatever they could grab in their hasty evacuation. The news of Zapala's fate had already spread like wildfire.

Worry drained from Scott's face as he and Yuri strode to meet Sam and Miriam. Sam's leg throbbed with each step. She was glad to have finally gotten to their destination and be able to rest, even if it was brief. The two women were the only ones with their packs; Sam offered Fox the belt of grenades from around her neck. She painfully shifted to her brother as Miriam slid her shoulder out from under. She tried to tell Scott she was fine. It hurt, and she hadn't seen the full damage yet, but it wasn't the worst injury she'd had. She was positive it would hold with whatever Miriam had in her medical arsenal.

"You two had us worried," Yuri said.

Miriam nodded. "We're okay." She unlatched the long-range case from her pack and extended it. "Here."

Yuri took it, but his face fell as he checked and opened the case. The equipment inside was damaged, almost unrecognizable.

"No…" Miriam breathed.

Echo's second examined the repeater's exterior. Two holes were punched through the metal. It was just scrap now. There was no need to zero it, wipe it of its encryptions, but Yuri didn't seem to care. He passed the case to Kai. Something else concerned him. He looked over at Miriam, hands out attempting to pat her down. Sam realized that the case, where it was positioned, had stopped bullets meant for her. Miriam didn't notice the contact and concern, her gaze still on their destroyed lifeline.

"Are you hurt?" Yuri asked. "Tan."

Miriam mindlessly patted her torso, sides, and then around her thighs. She was fine.

"Temunco," Krill huffed as he took the case from Kai's hands and tossed it to the side. "We need to go now."

Fox waved at the settlement. "What? No. We can't just leave them like this."

Sam looked back. There were sounds of fighting in the distance. Even though Matam hadn't been kind to the marines, there was still something unpleasant about leaving them to their own devices, their own futile defenses against a more capable enemy.

It was another New Zapala.

She thought about the individuals they had either killed or incapacitated when the Children of Charon were their main concern. It seemed like an easier time, although it hadn't felt like it then. She'd rather deal with the monsters she knew than the Altered demons coming after them now. SecTeam, Charonites, or both were still fighting. That was a good sign. Maybe Matam had a chance.

"Command needs to know," came the lead's flat response.

"SecTeam. Their repeater."

"We don't know if SecHut's system is working. We don't know if SecHut is even there anymore. I don't like it either, Fox, but we're going. Now."

The large marine balked and pumped an arm at the settlement, his mouth unable to formulate coherent words.

"Krill. People are dying," Kai murmured. "We can help."

Nas added to the overlap of voices. "We can't go back through those cliffs. That'll take us hours. It's a death sentence."

"Stop," Krill demanded. "If we don't warn Command, *more* people will die. Matam can do what they can to hold them off."

"They have more resources than New Zapala…" Yuri added with an apologetic look at Jun.

Miriam gently put a hand on Fox's arm. "UMF needs to know about the wunbies."

"We are going. *Now*." The team lead dared anyone to challenge him.

"How?" Nas shouted.

"The river," Sam said, remembering what she had seen on their first trip to the farmlands. It felt like a lifetime ago.

The others turned to her.

"There might be a boat. Near the bridge."

"Temunco said the riv—" Kai started.

"It'd be the fastest way back. Are you sure about the boat?"

Yuri answered before she could nod to the lead—although she wasn't as confident the boat was functional. "I think we saw it, too. The other day."

"Okay. Done. Greg, Nas, and Kai, take point and check it out first. We'll make sure it's watertight. If it isn't…we'll figure it out. Mute, Fox, take up the rear." Krill returned Fox's glare.

"You don't have to like it, but we *are* leaving." He made each word clear and brutal.

The lead looked at Sam's leg, then to Miriam. "Can you fix it?"

Miriam cursed, nodded, and shot an apology at Sam as if she felt guilty for not addressing it earlier.

Krill's jaw set, and without another word, he moved for the gate and the SecGuards there. Yuri, Nas, and Kai set off, headed for the intersection and the river, and Miriam dropped her pack to the ground to rummage through it.

Sam guided herself to a toppled chair in the dirt, an ornate piece of furniture that had been left behind. Scott picked it up and she sat in its rigid, polished wood, so homeless and alien outside of its element.

As Miriam cut away her pants and bandaged what she could, Sam squinted into the night's darkness. She could barely make out the mountain ridges with the little moonlight peeking out through the low, heavy clouds. Behind her, Fox and Jun stared back into Matam, a settlement fighting for its life.

◐

The rain had picked up again and pattered in a steady downpour against rotted wood and metal paneling. It was barely the definition of a roof, as water leaked through gaps and soaked the ground around the rusted boat. Its hull was surprisingly intact, and Kai and Nas were confident it could perform one last transportation job back to the UMF outpost. The others eyed the vessel but didn't challenge them on it.

The downpour and distance away from the settlement stifled any sounds of battle. At first, there were two or three refugees as they sought out a path along the river, but no one had passed since then. No one wanted to willingly cross the bridge into Altered territory.

The marines huddled together in split groups: Yuri and Nas in a corner already asleep, Sam, Scott, Miriam, in another, and Fox, Jun, and Kai half underneath the boat's bow and another patch of metal paneling. It was a decently sized boathouse, but significantly smaller with Echo avoiding the puddles and deluge. The dry spaces were just enough to sit comfortably next to each other.

"Here. Hold this for me." Miriam handed a lightstick to Scott. She rummaged through her pack and pulled out a red kit.

Scott moved the light over Sam's outstretched leg.

"Can you turn to the side?"

Sam obeyed and angled her body so that her calf was accessible to the medic. The hasty bandage had already bled through.

Miriam jutted out her lower jaw, concentrating. She carefully peeled back the layer and then prodded the area. "You are one tough cookie."

Sam grimaced. "It's the meds you gave me." She sucked in air between gritted teeth as the medic poked the wound with an extraction tool.

"Sure. The meds that probably wore off a while ago." Without looking up, Miriam motioned her head at the kit. "Right pocket. Blue jabber."

Scott transferred the lightstick into his other hand and pulled Miriam's pack close.

Miriam cleaned the affected area with a spray. "Okay. Jabber, thigh. Right there, yeah."

Her brother pressed the pen into her leg, needle piercing through the material of her pants. She felt the sharp prick, and within seconds, relief flooded Sam's veins. Her head sagged back, and a soft exhale escaped her lips. It was a calming warmth, and she fell into its embrace.

"Right. This may hurt," Miriam said. She didn't wait for a response, digging her tool into Sam's leg and working it around.

The succor was instantly gone as her body tensed with the distress, despite the cocktail of drugs. And then the pain left, replaced by a receding throb.

Miriam pulled away and showed Sam a piece of shrapnel, a metal fragment. She put the tool and the piece aside, grabbed a capsule from the kit, and rubbed its gel into the wound. Sam could feel the pressure as it sealed around her skin. Miriam sprayed the area again and then applied a fresh dressing.

"Done. That should be a bit more permanent than before."

Sam half grimaced, half smiled at her. "Thank you." She resettled into a more comfortable position, careful of her leg.

Miriam nodded and returned a weak smile.

"Where did Krill go?" Sam said. She didn't want the woman to leave just yet.

Miriam turned to look over her shoulder, still in a crouch. Krill wasn't in the shelter with the others. "Don't know, but not far."

"Is he going to be okay?"

Krill hadn't been happy to stop. He had only made the decision when Jun confirmed that navigating the river at night with a barely functioning boat was suicide. It helped that Sam had still been limping, although she thought she kept herself together pretty well. The team was drained and disheartened. They would have pushed through if the lead had told them to—they all understood the gravity of the situation—but they were glad for the rest. Jun was still grieving, although he hid his tears well.

Miriam sighed and didn't answer. Instead, she met Sam's

gaze. Sam didn't want the connection to end, but her brother cleared his throat, and the woman turned away to gather her kit.

Scott offered the lightstick back to her.

"Hold on to it," she said. Miriam shared a look with her brother and nodded.

Before Sam could ask, Miriam stood, her knees cracking. Sam winced with her. This mission had not been friendly to their bodies.

"Anything you two need?"

Sam shook her head.

"Okay." Miriam glanced again at Scott, then to Sam. "I'm going to check on the others. Get some rest." She gave the siblings another thin smile, then moved closer to the boat, shielding her head from the rain with the kit.

Sam stared after her before she felt a soft nudge in her ribs.

You like her.

She rolled her eyes and scoffed.

You do. I know you.

Scott smothered the lightstick in his grip, but the little glow showed his lined face. His amused expression softened, and his mouth twisted to the side as Sam turned her gaze to him. This was the first time they had been alone together in days, and the realization settled over both of them. There was so much to be said. To be fixed.

Sam started. "What was that with—"

"I'm sorry." He said it softly. Only for her to hear.

She stiffened.

"I..." He turned the light down and set it aside. His fingers went up to the light chain around his neck, and then back down into his lap. He wrung his hands. Are you still angry at me?

Her chest constricted.

You are. Scott bit his lip. I should have told you.

Sam turned as best as she could and looked at her brother straight on. She put both hands over his and whispered, "I'm not angry. I'm…" She didn't know what she was. "Why didn't you?"

Scott looked away, his mouth twitching. He gently removed her hands from his and threw a finger into his chest, paused, then rapped the knuckle against his sternum in a soft procession as he tried to find his words. He finally signed, You were just a kid.

Sam had skipped a normal childhood for all she knew. Straight into the mouth and hands of UMF. She wasn't a kid now. She hadn't been one in a long time.

24

THE BROTHER

SCOTT RECKERT HAD TURNED sixteen three days prior. He was going on a date with Jessica, the girl from the water filtration farm, who had finally broken up with the douchebag down the street. This was how he wanted to spend his break from university—he had finished his exams and had a short break before classes started again. It was one night when he didn't have to drag his kid half-sister along. One night to be a normal sixteen-year-old.

He left water and a plate of cookies on the crate beside his thin mattress. A black padded mat lay to the side of his bed, covered in mismatched blankets. The old lady down the street had thrown out a perfectly usable bed mat, and he had grabbed it before anyone else knew it was there. He was glad for it—his little sister was growing, and he wanted her to sleep in her own bed.

Scott patted her head and put his university tablet in her small hands. She eagerly grasped it, already opening a window to watch her programs. He put a splayed hand over the display to get her attention and told the five-year-old to stay put and stay quiet. She needed to stay quiet. He'd only be a couple of hours. A little over if he was lucky.

She nodded and didn't even look up as he closed the bedroom door.

Scott's hand hovered as he briefly considered locking it, but decided not to. He didn't want to deal with another pee accident when he returned.

He carefully walked past an open door, clothes and trash littered within the bedroom, and then past the kitchen to the entrance of the small flat. Their father was passed out on the table, his head smashed into the crook of one arm, the other hung over the surface with the usual drink in his clutch. Empty pill containers surrounded him. Scott made sure he was out for the night. Poked his back and called his name. His father was unconscious, but Scott didn't want to push his luck.

As he left the flat, he silently willed another reminder to his sister—don't make any noise. He'd be back soon. It was two hours. Two hours where he could pretend he hadn't become a de facto parent five years ago. It was only two hours.

And it was a good—no, fantastic—date. At the end of the night, he walked back to his flat, all teeth, beaming. Jessica had let him kiss her goodnight, and she had smelled like the good soap from the central bazaar, not the market down the street. He was proud of himself. She was three years older, already out of university, and a catch. They were going on a second date next week. He was floating, on top of the world.

And then he pushed the thin, metal door of his home. It was a steep drop from his emotional high as he saw the dark stain of blood on the dusty small rug his mother had bought when he was seven. The thick red color seeped through and spilled onto the exposed cracked concrete floor.

He stepped around it, speechless and confused.

And then he saw her around the corner.

His little sister was a limp doll, eyes shut, flat on the ground. Blood seeped from a big gash in her right arm. He tried to scramble forward, but he couldn't move. At first, he thought his body betrayed him, but then he felt his father's rough grip on his arm, holding him back.

The drunk slurred on about the damn child and good riddance. Scott tried to shake his father off, but the man was stronger. His father babbled on, apologizing to his dead wife, Scott's dead mother, don't worry, he was making everything right.

Scott watched his half-sister bleed, his little Sammy, whom he had raised for five years. She wasn't responsive to his cries, his sobbing of her name.

His father jerked him back.

And something ripped in him.

Scott turned, throwing his whole body behind a fist into a bony face. A face that had once been kinder, much softer. A face that wrinkled into a wide smile when a young Scott had told him he wanted to be just like him. A face that had creased and never returned to what it was when his wife became ill. A face of a man who had gotten another woman pregnant in an act of desperation and release. A face that turned to anything that would make him forget the look on his dying wife's face when she knew. A face that saw the new blonde addition to the family as a dud, a reminder of his guilt.

Scott struck his father with a hardened fist, a fist full of rage at the loss of a mother and a loving home. A fist of the sharp decline of respect for a once-great father. A fist of lost adolescence and forced adulthood. A final fist of all the bottled frustrations, neglect, and rage.

Tears pooled in his eyes; he didn't see the return blow coming.

Scott fell back against the counter, stunned. Dazed.

He couldn't even register it before he felt the vise grip around his neck, thumbs into his larynx, his back flattened against the unwashed dishes on the dirty counter. Tighter and tighter. The pain was suffocating. His breath was stuck in his body.

Dark spots first appeared at the edges of his vision, then began to grow inward, taking over. He was dying. He failed his sister, and he was failing himself.

He didn't remember grabbing the broken shard. He didn't remember striking it repeatedly into his father's neck. He only remembered the crushing pain of air and breathing. He remembered the spots clearing up in his vision and his own blood whooshing in his ears with each beat of his heart. It was all he could hear.

Each inhale felt like glass in his throat.

Air.

He needed air.

He headed for the door. Air was outside.

And then he remembered his sister. She was a pale doll in a sea of red. So serene.

Maybe it was for the best.

He could live his life the way he never could. The way he had thought he could those years before. Finish university. Work at the filtration plant. Marry Jessica. Build his own hobby farm full of greens, of life. A whole life, unburdened by others, awaited just within reach.

Without Sam.

It was a brief hesitation.

But it was a hesitation.

He couldn't do it.

He scooped her up in his arms. She was so light. So limp.

He ran out of the flat, not caring about the door he left open, the empty home he left behind. He ran as hard as he could, trying to shout for help, but his own voice betrayed him.

He needed to save her.

He had left her.

This was his fault.

Why did he hesitate?

This was his fault.

$$\oplus$$

It should have been a lot to process. But it wasn't.

Sam sat in silence as her brother signed and whispered.

His truth, in a mixture of motions and words, glued together the fragments of her fractured memory. This time, they didn't cut her like before.

"It was my fault."

Scott's hands stilled on his thighs, and he curled his shoulders forward, watching the rain drip down like long needles.

Sam rubbed the scar along her forearm, tracing it back and forth. "It's not your fault," she whispered back.

He didn't leave her.

She remembered something else. "And leaving UMF…"

Scott bit his lip.

"The kid. From the last mission." Their target, the Altered girl who had blown herself up.

He nodded.

"You did catch her…" Sam had been confused when she found the target by herself. "And you…let her go?"

Scott looked down at the ground and nodded again. "I couldn't…couldn't do it."

It didn't matter, anyway. The Apostate girl had died in that dead-end alley.

Sam saw it all clearly. Her brother, whom she had seen kill so many from a physical and emotional distance, hated himself. An image she had her entire life shattered, and she sucked in a deep breath. Even if Scott had chosen UMF in the beginning, at the age of sixteen—sister in tow—something happened along the way, and he didn't want to be responsible for death anymore. Every time she renewed a contract, he did, too. He killed to save her and continued to kill to protect her.

The guilt began to eat away at her like acid.

"I didn't know, Scott. I'm sorry." She repeated it with her hands. I'M SORRY.

She was. And though there was an unbearable anguish for her brother and her own guilt with her previous actions, something in her chest lightened. Sam had so much love for him, even more now. She had spent much of this—Scott's—last mission avoiding him, annoyed with him, and she sought to remedy that. No matter the Apostates, Charonites, the terrain, the south, or the road ahead, they'd be okay.

And that's all that mattered.

PART 3

FORCE

25

CONDUIT

THE MARINES GOT UP WELL before the sun to maneuver the boat into the thrashing river—its level high from the overnight deluge. Even Nas had held his breath when the mechanical lift lowered the vessel just off the bank, water already lapping against the rusted hull.

In the faint light of the blue hour, Sam could better assess the vessel's weather-worn features and makeup. The railings had been torn off and its side walls provided little cover, but the bones and main muscles were still there. A ridge created a bench that curved around the entire inside lip—a simple transport. Its control panel sat in the vessel's center, a box with switches and dials. It wasn't ideal, but if Kai and Nas could work their magic, it'd be significantly faster than the hike through the mountains. The memory of the cliff wall was so minute compared to the atrocities they had left behind, but Sam still shuddered at the thought.

In the distance, above the land of crop pods, she could make out the soft glow of a smoldering settlement, smoke dwindling and barely visible. The marines hadn't heard explosions or gunfire in the last hour. They were unsure of what it meant, although Sam had a strong feeling. Her expectations were low.

There was not much to pack with what little they had, and the team waited impatiently as Kai did a systems check, Nas to the side overseeing. Kai touched several levers on the panel, the tip of her pink tongue sticking out of the corner of her mouth. Something rumbled in distress. She flicked a few more switches and the engine sputtered, then fell into a solid thrum.

"Should be good," she shouted out. "Just need to disengage the lift." She pointed a multi-tool at the rusted arm still attached to the boat.

As Fox and Jun moved to work it, a rustle came from the row of abandoned pods behind them. Sam lifted her rifle alongside the others. They were nine strong, and all but Fox and Jun had their main weapons, but Sam wasn't sure if it was enough. She could put weight on her leg, but it still felt stiff. Another round of gel and drugs were working overtime.

Two battered individuals emerged: one injured man and a woman supporting him. The two startled, shocked to see the marines and the array of weaponry pointed at them. The woman cursed, but the injured man said something under his breath and calmed his companion down. He raised an arm weakly in greeting, high enough the marines could see the large, dark stain on the fabric over his ribs.

It was also enough to see the ink on his arm.

The man grimaced. "Ho."

Sam stared back. Politeness and courtesy had been shot to hell with Charonites.

The man dropped his arm and winced. He looked past the group at the boat and then to the others, ignoring the weapons still raised. "Can you fit us?" His words did not match the regional accent. The Charonites had come this far to join a fight they thought was worthy, and now, after all this, they ended up here, injured, and looking for the same thing—escape.

Tough luck. Sam bit back a scathing response and scanned their surroundings again. There could be more. She didn't trust the acolytes one bit. Sam glanced at Krill to see what he had to say, but the lead said nothing, his lip curling—probably irritated at the delay.

"Matam?" Fox asked.

The woman's eyes lowered, and she sniffed.

"You armed?" Kai said, her weapon trained on the two.

Sam's head whipped to her teammate. Kai wasn't considering their request, was she?

The Charonite man coughed. "Katrena. Give them your gun."

The woman started to protest but gave in with a sigh. She shifted him to a better support position and reached behind her back.

Sam tightened her grip around her rifle.

The woman pulled a revolver around, then hesitantly swiveled it forward, holding it loosely by the handle. "It only has a few bullets left. Take it. We won't be any trouble. Promise."

Fox darted forward, took the weapon, and stretched it back to Jun, who checked and pocketed it.

"Krill?" Kai said. When he didn't answer, she eyed Yuri.

"Kai..." Sam started. Were they really going to let these Charonites accompany them? She turned to Krill, Miriam, then Fox. The three had fought for their lives at the ambush as well. Were they already looking the other way?

"The boat has space," said Fox.

Something had changed in him in New Zapala. In Matam.

"We're going to Temunco," Yuri said, his own rifle lowering slightly.

The injured man coughed wetly and nodded.

Sam recalled Temunco's brief about the river—the conflict stretched along the water path and its nearby towns. Caches of Charonites. Their two guests would probably ask to be dropped off but were smart not to request it now, knowing they held no leverage.

Krill turned away. "Your decision, Greg. As long as we're on that boat in five, I don't care."

Sam looked at her brother for a sanity check. *This was crazy, right?*

But Scott's eyes softened, and she knew she had become the minority voice. With a sigh, Sam lowered her weapon and moved forward to check their two Charonite parasites for anything they could use against them. The marines would at least be smart about the whole thing.

⏀

The river ride, though rocky, was relatively quiet. Sam could make out pockets of thriving forests in the background as they moved closer to steeper terrain. The sun's warmth peeked out and the further the group traveled, the more the tension and anxiety released. The first town they passed had been still—it was early morning, after all. The two Charonites looked over at the few buildings but did not ask to be let off. Sam wasn't sure how the boat would've gotten across the water anyway, the river in this part was wide, and even if they could, they would've faced Krill's impatience to get back to Temunco.

Although Kai and Nas had brought the ship to life, the steering was minimal. The middle of the river provided a strong, unyielding current, and they succumbed to the whims of nature and its own channel. If they could get back to the outpost or within range of its comm tower, it wouldn't matter.

Jun assured them they were making good time back to his only home left, UMF and the outpost.

The boat's hull creaked and groaned. In deeper whitewater, the bow made disconcerting cracks, but it held up well for a once-abandoned craft now holding eleven people. Yuri and Kai weren't convinced as they gripped the sides, willing their bodies to remain glued to the bench against the choppy motions.

Across the way, Miriam opened her pack and threw small nutrition bars at Sam and Scott. She offered one to Fox, who waved it away, and then to the others. Sitting near the bow, Jun snatched one out of the air and considered the thin package with aversion.

Fox yanked the bar out of his hand and opened its wrapper. "Just eat it." He shoved it back into Jun's hands with a smirk.

The teenager took a wary bite, but in that moment, the vessel dipped, and the food missed its target, smashing into the space between his lip and nose instead. Fox howled with laughter. It was such a welcome sound. After New Zapala, both their demeanors had dimmed.

Jun frowned at Fox, crumbs and smudges pasted on his skin, but his expression slowly cracked. He wiped his face with the back of his hand. A hint of a smile was there.

Fox amicably swiped at the teenager's face. "Missed a spot. Several." He then leaned in for an exaggerated closer look. "What is this?" Fox teased, motioning at Jun's upper lip. Straggles of facial hair grew out in random patches of individual strands. Fox fell into a fit, which made Jun smile widely—the first since New Zapala.

The two broke into laughter.

"You tryin' to grow it out or somethin'," Fox said, gasping for air.

"Just like you," Jun replied.

Sam peeled back her nutrition bar. Although Echo carried bad news and the two Charonites had joined them, the day was off to a better start. Despite everything, she was hopeful, invigorated by her own talk with Scott. She bit into the bar as the river water sprayed up and misted over her. It tasted like clay with a hint of artificial strawberry. The water added a brackish seasoning. She already missed the fresh and savory food from the Matam market. She wondered if it was still standing.

As the cachinnation died down, Jun took another careful bite and slowly chewed.

Fox's brows furrowed. The moment had passed and gone.

Miriam tossed Fox a little pail from the corner of the vessel. He braced himself over the gunwale and scooped up water, lugging the container back into the safety of the boat. Miriam then broke open a package of small tablets and threw a handful into the full container. "Give it thirty seconds," she instructed.

When it was done, they passed it around. Kai took her turn and offered the pail to the two Charonites in the rear. The female muttered an incomprehensible thanks and helped herself and her companion to the cleaned water.

As the river widened and the current calmed, the group came across a second sign of civilization to their left: a small town with farmland along the banks and beyond. On the other side, another town lay quiet, with more modern structures and technologies. Sam could see marks of defense weaponry on both sides and was glad it *was* still early in the morning. She eyed a bolted station where a hooked, malignant harpoon loomed. But the boat and its occupants passed along without incident.

This was the divide. This was where conflict occurred. Humans on one side and Altered on the other. The idea of peace after the Charonites, New Zapala, the Temunco marines, the Altered farmer, the legionnaires, and Apostates seemed impossible.

Sometimes we want the same thing. To just live our lives together. To share. Sam thought about the half-human, half-Altered little girl. It *was* impossible, right?

When the boat passed more towns, the two Charonites did not speak up, and Sam pondered. These were little towns, much smaller than Matam or New Zapala, but large enough to have some Charon presence, especially with the proximity to Altered on the other side. But the two only huddled together without a word. The wounded male had significantly paled, and though Miriam had tried to help him earlier, they had waved her away.

"Jun, how much longer?" Krill called out.

"Not much. See the bridges ahead! After those." the Temunco marine replied, his energy rejuvenating.

Sam looked up and could make out the first bridge's platforms in the distance. It was missing its midsection, and Sam bemusedly wondered if it still constituted the label "bridge" if it was missing its defining component. It was coming up fast as the current picked up. A second bridge was further out, the mirror image of the first. Both looked like they'd been destroyed within the past year, another sign of the conflict in the south.

Jun stood and leaned into the front of the boat, bracing himself against the drift. "Do you smell that? The ocean!" He turned back to the others, his face split by a toothy smile.

Sam inhaled as a cool mist assaulted her face. It was true. There was salt in the air, a briny hint to the water. They were close to their destination. She exhaled and thumped her brother's knee.

Sam didn't hear the whistle or see the motion on the nearby bank until too late. It happened so fast.

The spear protruded so vulgarly from the teenager's side, his mouth still caught mid-smile, corners only starting to turn.

And then he was over the edge.

Under the current.

Someone wailed his name.

A hand above the dark water.

And then gone.

Sam recognized the white of the legionnaire uniform as they passed the first broken bridge. An Altered stood on the right platform watching them. Sam followed the bank further down the river and saw two more figures there. Both held something long in their hands, propped over their shoulders.

Harpoons.

"Right side! Contact!" Sam shouted. She let out a barrage of gunfire at the figures. Scott was at her side, shooting as well.

"Nas! Left! Go left!" Krill yelled.

The vessel careened sharply, struggling against the river current.

Another spear sailed between Sam and Scott, and lodged into the bench behind them, next to Kai. The siblings dropped to the floor, bracing against the boat's violent bobbing as the water crushed against the sides. They grabbed what they could to keep from sliding and hitting their teammates.

Sam willed the boat to move, to go faster. To get them out of there. She felt the fear regurgitate in her throat as she looked around. The others had taken refuge on the cramped floor around her. Nas was crouched behind the control panel, steering the boat as best as he could.

"Fox! Get down!" someone hissed.

Benjamin Fox sat unmoving at the bow, still in his seat. Unable to look away from the spot where Jun had been standing just seconds before.

Sam peeked over the boat's lip. They would come near the

harpoon-bearing figures in the next moments. The boat was moving away from the other bank, but too slowly. The currents were bringing them forward faster than the boat could propel itself sideways.

A curdling scream served as a siren.

The first harpoon hit its mark, tearing through the thin hull, skin, muscle, and bone. Its barbed tip stuck out centimeters from the Charonite woman's chest, just inside of her left shoulder. It missed the heart, just barely, but that was a lung gone. As Sam made sense of the image, the harpoon point pulled back into her body with a fleshy squelch. The scream stopped, replaced by a gruesome moan, as the woman fell into the shock before death.

The Altered were trying to reel the boat in.

"Nas!" Sam cried out, but it was for naught. She didn't know what else he could do.

Scott stirred to her side, and Sam realized he was getting up. She rushed to grab his arm, his shirt, but he darted away, his hands moving, his rifle up.

His weapon fired.

One Altered had just cocked a shoulder back, a harpoon in his grasp, and barely recoiled as a hole appeared in his torso. A small burst of color began to stain his white shirt.

Sam breathed. That one wasn't wearing armor. It was a critical shot.

But nothing changed.

Scott froze for a half second, confused.

By the time he aimed again, another harpoon sailed toward them. Her brother dodged, and the spear lodged itself into the interior wall of the other side, its line behind already tightening.

Now twice hooked, the stern began to keel perpendicular to the river. The waves crashed against the boat, and its inhabitants flew backward as the boat rocked dangerously.

Yuri leaped forward with his knife and sawed at the corded rope of the second spear. "Cut it!" he shouted.

Sam scrambled to her feet, pressing her thigh into the bench to stabilize herself as best as possible. They didn't have much time—they were either going to capsize or swing to the other bank, a place they really didn't want to be. She swung her rifle behind her and staggered over Miriam and Nas. She grabbed Nas's knife from its sheath on his body and pulled herself to the stern where the man was wailing. The woman's body was still, the harpoon's tip out of sight but pinning her in place despite the boat's violent movements.

She heard suppressing fire behind her.

Sam tried to get a better sight of the connecting rope, the other end of the harpoon somewhere in the water as it dipped from its pull. Waves parted, and she saw it, then lost it. The cord was too far out to cut with a knife.

The boat lurched, and the other rope whipped past her.

One down.

Sam braced herself, her thigh pressing into the bench beside the dead woman.

Think. What could she do?

She secured the knife in her chest rig and swung her carbine back around. Prayed and took a deep breath in. Sam exhaled as slowly as she could.

And took the shot.

At first, she thought she had missed. But suddenly, she flew backward as the boat rocked, free of its last tether.

The momentum and release drove the vessel forward, facing the other bank. Moments later, the boat rammed into the ground, and bodies and rifles slammed into each other as the bow shoveled itself upward.

Land. The boat rested on its belly in the mud.

They were across. Away from the Altered. Sam pulled herself from the tangle of gear and limbs, groaning.

"Get up! Move!" Krill's voice pierced the air.

Someone gripped her arm, trying to lift her. Nas.

She searched for her brother and pulled him to his feet. They both looked to the boat where two bodies remained, and then across the river, tracking their assailants.

When Sam confirmed the rest of the team had disembarked, she hurdled over the boat's side, quickly followed by Scott. Her boots stuck in the mud, and she fought to maintain her balance. She willed her legs to power through, trudging in the sludge until her soles touched on packed ground.

Sam glanced back.

A figure had made it to the split bridge. Two—no, three—others trailed at various distances behind. They were uncannily fast. Too fast, even for Altered. She was momentarily glad for the destroyed bridges—their attackers' way was blocked. She wondered if Altered could swim against the river's raging currents and felt a slight relief when the first individual remained at the edge of the other side's platform.

But her face fell in horror when the figure backed up. It vanished beyond her view away from the jagged platform edge.

No. It was more than a fifteen-meter gap. *There was no way.*

Sam clutched her rifle and turned, picking up her pace, and shouting for her teammates to go, to run faster. She had no time to watch the attempt. She hoped their Altered attackers wouldn't make it, but part of her knew they would.

26

THE CHASE

SAM RAN THROUGH THE FOREST, and her boots kicked off clods of mud in arcs behind her. As her legs met an incline, she slowed. Her muscles screamed agony, and her lungs tightened and constricted. Each thud of her feet echoed, falling out of sync with the louder thud of her heart. The group of SOG marines had slowed to an aggressive march led by Nas and Kai, losing momentum in the climb.

"How," Krill panted over the visor, "many?"

Sam stole a glimpse behind, past Fox who had slowed considerably, looking for the movement she knew was there. Four, she had seen four on the other side of the river. Now, she only saw trees and the broken brush trail left by Echo.

"Four," she gasped. Her throat was dry.

Scott turned, his eyes darting around while his shoulders heaved and sweat beaded his face. He raised a hand to his chest, palm angled at her. FIVE. His pinky and thumb touched, the middle three fingers upright. SIX.

Fuck.

He pointed the same hand and fingers at his chest

diagonally. Not behind them, not from the river. There were two more coming from a different direction.

"Six," Sam corrected out loud. "Two more. Four o'clock."

"How…much further?" Krill asked on the open channel.

"Thirty?" Yuri responded. "This ridge…and then…around."

Double fuck.

She could hear others echo their own curses in between breaths. Echo was reaching the end of their stamina, powering through on sheer will alone.

Sam looked up. She couldn't see the top of the ridge. The marines had the advantage of higher ground, but they were on a slope steep with slides and gullies. This was a terrible place of defense, even if they weren't tired and had proper levels of firepower and ammunition.

"Legion?" Miriam said, her voice sharp in Sam's ear.

Legionnaires. Apostates. Did it matter anymore?

Sam realized the medic might have meant to ask if they were armored like the one in New Zapala. She remembered the hole in the Altered's chest. "Some armor. Not all." She winced as her foot slipped. "Scouts?"

It was eight marines to six Altered, possibly legionnaires, who were chasing them down for some reason. Sam wondered if they had been following them this entire time. It didn't matter. They were spent. *She* was exhausted. Her injuries limited her. They didn't have enough ammunition. She hadn't seen the white legionnaire armor in the quick action, but she had seen how the one had been unaffected by a bullet to the chest.

They were royally fucked.

"I need another mag," Nas said over comms.

Miriam reached around her pack and threw two magazines to him. Nas stashed one in his rig and tactically reloaded the other. Sam checked her own ammunition. The cartridge was light—maybe four or five remaining rounds. She replaced it with the last full one from her kit.

A branch snapped behind them and Sam looked back. Something flickered out of the corner of her eye. Then another. She searched for a body, a face, something, but every time she tried to follow one shadow, it darted and weaved between the trees, and then another blurred by. They were getting close.

"Rocks. There."

Sam turned back around and saw the larger boulders Krill pointed at, a scramble thirty meters up and further to the right. It was dangerous, but it provided better cover than their current location. With the enticement of better defenses, the marines increased their pace up the slope.

Something whooshed and cut through the air to Sam's right. A small sickle planted firmly into the tree trunk in front of her. She burst into a sprint, her pain ignored and replaced by another wave of adrenaline. Why did these Apostate-legionnaires prefer bladed weapons? It was strange where the mind went in the worst situations.

"Run!" Sam hollered for the second, or third time in as many days.

Echo clamored up the incline. They moved as fast as they could while trying to use the trees around them as cover.

Another swish as metal sailed and sunk itself into the back of Nas's thigh. He stumbled. Scott rushed forward to drag him up. Kai and Krill reached the start of the rock scramble, Miriam and Yuri close behind. Fox turned, someone else's rifle in hand, and shot a stream of fire behind them.

Sam dashed behind the closest tree and did the same, trying to anticipate where one of the chasers was headed. They needed to provide suppressing fire, distract whomever from Scott and injured Nas. Sam kept her brother and teammate in her periphery, monitoring their progress toward the others.

She could make out their pursuers now. One was tall, partially armored with a white chest piece, but gaunt, its face ghoul-like, whereas the others—she only counted two—were smaller, and their white uniforms were sullied. One had a dark kit over his torso—something familiar. And yet, something was different with these Altered as their faces flashed in and out of view, their eyes almost too dark.

Demons.

Sam tried to track them. Shoot them.

Fear rose from her gut to her chest. She had never seen Altered move this fast before. The ones she encountered in Ursus were quick, but not this quick. They were taking the incline in dashes and jumps, impervious to the strain and effort it deserved. She heard her and Fox's names as the others beckoned them back to the group. But their attackers were closer.

One of the smaller—but still taller than her—Altered leaped at Sam, black hair swirling around its head like a dark halo, a large machete-like weapon in its hands. She pushed away from the tree and fired at the incoming attack.

Priority by proximity.

It paid no mind to her bullets and bounded up, slicing the blade down. Sam fell back and rolled with the slope. The weapon missed her, and she flattened herself out on her back, gripping the earth, grabbing a nearby tree root to steady her sliding body. She recognized the deep sounds of Scott's rifle rounds and watched the side of the Altered's body open.

The other partially armored Altered bolted forward and bore up to the rest of Echo in the patch of boulders.

Sam's attacker stood up.

Impossible.

A gaping wound in its ribcage poured blood down its leg.

Sam lifted her weapon and squeezed. One bullet cracked

away and pierced the Altered's chest with a meaty thud. Its body took the impact with little movement, and it kept stalking forward as if nothing had happened.

Sam had run out of ammo.

She threw her rifle to the side and reached for her pistol.

Her hand came up empty. Muscle memory betrayed her; the pistol had been lost in New Zapala.

The Altered drove the machete down in a barbaric chop. There was no technique, but who needed technique when critical wounds had no effect? Sam rolled, her rifle guard stabbing into her side. The attacker kept after her, bringing the blade down, then down again, although its speed was decreasing. Sam only narrowly missed the last strike, the edge cleaving through the cloth on her shoulder. It stuck in a tree root, and she kicked hard at her assailant's forearm, then at the weapon. It tumbled away, rolling further down the slope.

The Altered growled and raised its hands, about to grab at her, when a hole blew through its midsection. Liquid showered her. The Altered's face contorted, and it lowered its hands, its attention diverted. And then her attacker was gone and driving into Fox. Sam scrambled up, wiping blood out of her eyes.

The Altered and Fox wrestled with each other and crashed into another tree. It gripped the large marine's throat in one hand; Sam slid down the slope toward them. She slammed the butt of her rifle over and over into the Altered's arm, and felt the bone break. With one limb rendered useless, the Altered broke away, shoving Fox with the other arm and kicking Sam a meter back down the mountain face.

It picked up its machete and swung at Fox, its other arm whipping inefficiently around. Fox used his rifle as a barrier and parried some blows. Not all. Blood sprayed as the machete sliced the surface of his chest rig and his arms.

Sam grabbed the magazine she had replaced from her kit

earlier. There was chaos ahead of them in the rock scramble. She reloaded, her eyes never leaving her target. Sam tried her best to draw in a breath. She willed her heart to slow, whatever fine motor skills were left concentrated on her right index finger. She needed slow and steady.

Slow.

And steady.

Sam willed her body to be still for one second, warding off the shakes. Above her, Fox blocked another strike, but the motion stunned him and threw him to the ground.

She squeezed the trigger as the Altered pulled the machete back. Not at its chest. She had seen what little those body shots did.

She cursed as its shoulder took the hit, blocking its head. Sam watched the splatters of blood as her few bullets met flesh. Muscles burst as fire-hot metal tore through the sinews of the shoulder. She prayed that they had gone through and hit the skull, the brain.

But the Altered roared.

Failure.

It turned. Its weight slammed into her, pinning her rifle and hands underneath it. Sam struggled to maintain upright, the warmth of the Altered's body and blood already soaking through her clothes. She wriggled an arm free to guard herself as blood sloppily rained down. The Altered slammed its forehead into hers. White light sprouted in her vision. Her knees buckled.

Suddenly, the Altered was gone, and she fell forward at the loss of a counterweight. The ground blurred. When she looked up, the world spun. Fox had somehow ripped their attacker away. As she fought for her vision to normalize, she felt a grip on her elbow, pulling her.

She spun and looked up to see Fox. Sweat and blood

streaked across his face, his eyes staring past her. *If Fox was there, who had helped her? Scott?*

Sam turned in panic, staggering to her feet.

It wasn't her brother.

Or one of her teammates.

An athletic figure in a dirty white sleeveless top and equally smudged pants stood with their back to Sam and Scott. Short dark hair fluttered freely.

Temunco sent reinforcements?

The wounded Altered lunged forward. Sam wanted to yell out, but her throat was too dry. Their rescuer didn't stand a chance.

It happened so fast that she couldn't comprehend it.

The Altered scout flew into the air and came to a sickening crash in front of the two marines. Bones crunched.

Fox dove for the machete, turned and smashed it into its skull with a sickening thud. He was taking no chances and left the blade embedded in the Altered's face.

Sam looked down at the body, with its neck at an odd angle showcasing a pale triangle and circle brand. But her attention caught at the familiar crest of UMF pinned on its stained and tattered shirt like a trophy on display. The Temunco marines…

Sam shook her head and turned to the newcomer. She now faced them, fresh blood—not hers—smeared across her body and light clothes. The fabric's color and sheen were familiar. She overshadowed them now, higher on the slope, but Sam figured she was about the same height as Fox, though much leaner. Sam swallowed, her mouth dry, when her eyes met the other's.

One dark-green eye contrasted sharply against the other, a bright blue, almost gray, in the light.

Altered.

Legionnaire.

The woman turned to the others as their scuffle came to an end. Another muscular woman stood surrounded by the marines within the boulders and rocks, a familiar scythe in her hand. Her hair was dark and cut shorter than the first, a few centimeters from her scalp. She stood over the partially white-armored Altered scout. His throat was slit open, head dangling almost ninety degrees back.

Sam searched for her brother and found him, a gash across his cheek, but standing. Relief flooded her, and she counted the other marines. All six were dispersed across the spectrum of bloodied and broken, but they were alive. Sam saw Scott turn, looking, and his panicked face relaxed when he found her.

The air was quiet but for heavy breathing and sounds of the forest. Something rustled below them, and all eyes turned to a spot down the mountainside. A figure with wet hair and wet clothes stared up at them, face in shock and panic. Angry, but healing scars marked his cheek.

The Altered farmer's son.

Sam glanced back and counted the bodies, finding the other scout—kitted in what was probably a murdered Temuncan's UMF-issued armor—draped on the rocks that she hadn't seen before. Three. The Altered farmer's son was the fourth scout they had seen on the riverbank. He must have missed the jump over the broken bridge.

Before Sam could say anything, the farmer's son broke into a sprint back down the slope. And then he was gone.

Sam heard dirt shift behind her, and she startled as the woman who had saved them closed in.

No, she was bearing in on the boy. The farmer's son. The Apostate scout.

The other Altered woman made a sharp noise, and the legionnaire woman stopped abruptly, next to Sam. Her shoulders pulled back, and her chin jutted forward.

Sam looked down and noticed two fingers missing from the woman's left hand, fresh scarring over its stumps at the first knuckles. Sam carefully stepped to the side, trying to maintain distance. She was uncomfortably close to an Altered death machine who had somehow tossed another almost-immortal monster in the air like a rag doll.

"We will not hurt you," the Altered woman near the others said. She held the scythe out to Yuri, who stared at it uncertainly. "We are not with them."

The one near Sam spat on the scout's body.

"You're legionnaires," Sam said under her breath. She edged closer to Fox, pulling her rifle in front of her. It was a useless motion—she had spent her rounds and the weapon now only served as a comfort.

Both Altered women turned to Sam and examined her.

"We are Legion, yes." The one with shorter hair seemed to be the senior of the two.

"Why are you helping us?"

The senior turned her head to Miriam. "We are the only survivors of our post."

"Survivors?" Krill stammered.

"We were betrayed." Her lip curled up in disgust. "Apostates planted seeds. We didn't know until it was too late. They radicalized some, ambushed and executed everyone else. Our colleagues. Our friends..." The senior motioned to the other next to Sam and Fox. "Varya and I are the only ones left from our post. We escaped."

The legionnaire named Varya growled.

Echo knew about the Apostates in Legion—thanks to the matriarch and her granddaughter's last message—but this new fact sent Sam's head reeling. Apostates weren't organized. They worked alone. Maybe a small operation at best. But taking over an entire Legion garrison? This was too much to process.

"How did the wun—Apostates do this?" Sam said.

Both heterochromatic pairs of eyes seared into her again, and Sam swore she saw a flash of anger in Varya's eyes.

"We don't know," the Senior said, after a moment. "We need to contact our authorities. We couldn't…" She trailed off. She pointed at the body next to her. "We were following this one."

"Our komanda," Varya whispered.

The senior looked around at the marines then and said with a hint of surprise, "You handled yourselves well. I am impressed." She nudged the body in front of her with a foot. "These have ripped through every serf along the way, but not you. They were tracking you…" She scanned their rifles, their rigs, and gear. Her eyes narrowed as if she only realized that these humans were different. Not from the region. "Who are you?"

Echo looked at their team lead.

"Are there more coming?" Krill asked instead.

"Most probably. These are scouts."

Krill's face contorted. They needed to get to Temunco and warn Command. These two legionnaires were non-threatening at the moment, but…everything in this mission had gone sideways before. What was the next step?

"We are not Apostates. You are not our enemy…"

Sam waited for the "now" or the "yet" to finish the sentence. It never came. She touched the scratched surface of her rifle, aware of Varya's eyes on her.

"We are not yours, yes?" the senior asked.

Krill paused.

What other choice did they have? These legionnaires had saved them, but even their genetically engineered bodies were a threat. They'd have to take a chance. At least there were no brands on their necks.

"Not enemies, yes…" Krill hesitated, but then he stepped forward and extended his good hand. "I'm sorry…about your post. I'm Vallen Krill and this is Echo. We're with UMF."

The senior looked curiously at the team lead's hand. She hovered her palm across from his, mirroring it but not taking or shaking it. "I am Hadeon." She lowered her hand, and Krill awkwardly dropped his. "Your authorities. Are they sending reinforcements?"

Krill shook his head. "We haven't been able to get in contact…"

"We need to warn ours as well."

"The outpost," Nas said, still on the ground.

Krill shot a look at him.

"Then we should not delay any longer," Hadeon stated and stepped back.

Sam could see the looks of concern ripple around the marines. No one moved. These were two legionnaires. Altered. The other side. They couldn't just waltz back to Temunco. They were also sans Jun. Young Jun. Sam felt her heart drop. They hadn't been able to grieve for him. There had been no time.

Hadeon's brow raised, and she tilted her head.

Kai kicked a rock. "Temunco may be a little trigger-happy if we show up with…"

"New friends," Yuri finished. "I can try to comm ahead with the visor once we get closer. We might have a signal then." He muttered something about the topography.

"Let's get moving then. We're wasting time," Krill said.

Echo picked themselves up as the legionnaires watched from the side. With a large welt on her cheek, Miriam rushed around, pressing what medical aid she could into her teammates' hands. She tried to focus on Krill, whose arm dangled oddly, but he waved her away. With a wary eye on the legionnaires, Krill pushed up and forward.

"I have a question," Nas said. He winced, sandwiched between Yuri and Scott, as his leg dragged across the ground.

They were nearing the top, closer to the ridge. Beyond it, the downhill slope and a stretch of land were the only obstacles between them and the outpost.

"Just ask it," the second responded, shifting Nas to a better position on his shoulder.

"These alties..." Nas shot a look at their two recent additions. "Wunbies. Is it just me, or are they extremely difficult to put down?"

Kai turned around, walking backward. "We shot those things at least a dozen times."

Sam nodded behind them. She remembered vividly every critical shot, on the river and just before.

"It's the new synthetic." The senior, Hadeon, continued forward, her voice projecting out.

"New synthetic?" Miriam asked. "They're on stims?"

"If stims make one faster, stronger, then yes."

"Shit...and there's how many more of these guys?"

Nas's question stirred up other disturbing thoughts. How many had the Apostates needed to take over a Legion post? New Zapala? Matam? How many were behind them, possibly on the way?

The question seemed to stump Hadeon. After a moment, she responded, "We don't know. A lot. We barely made it away." Her voice was laced with frustration, the last bit in a lower murmur.

"Why didn't *you* take the synthetic?" Nas asked.

A low growl ripped from Varya's throat, and Nas glanced at the other legionnaire.

"Too damaging. Addictive," Hadeon said. "It isn't worth it."

"Dangerous." Varya spat to the side, glowering.

Sam could see their reactions only made Nas want to ask

more questions. She shot her teammate a look. *Don't test the lethally trained Altered soldiers.*

But Hadeon turned and saw expectant stares. "Aside from the unknown number of side effects, long-term effects...the synthetic seems to block and change the part of the brain that processes pain."

That was why the Apostates didn't go down.

"So they *were* dying but didn't know it?" Kai said slowly.

Those had been critical shots. The Apostates would have just kept fighting until they couldn't.

"Or they knew and still kept going," Miriam added.

As Varya said. *Dangerous*. For user and whichever victims. And right now, they were the victims.

Something else gnawed at Sam. "You said before they were tracking us," she asked. "Why?"

The two Altered looked at each other, and Hadeon dipped her head. "I believe their interest increased when you showed up on the border."

"Border?"

"New Zapala," Fox murmured, his eyes hollow.

Jun. The figure in the smoke. The weight of everything dropped on Sam. Had Echo triggered something?

"Did...did we do this?" Kai said in a low tone.

Sam cut in. "No. That last scout. It was the Altered farmer's son. From the first day."

Echo's morale had been on a downward slope for some time. They didn't need it to dive any further. Two settlements lost, and now Jun. Maybe the marines did expedite the Apostate attack and accidentally set something sinister in motion, but they couldn't dwell on it. Not right now.

"You let him go," Nas said.

"If he's on the synthetic, he is faster. And we..." Hadeon

glanced at Varya, then sternly at Nas. "We're the last of our garrison. We are not separating. Not again."

"But he'll get the rest of them."

"Yes."

The senior said nothing further.

Echo fell silent, digesting the information—what it meant and what it would mean.

They reached the ridge and paused—Temunco and the ocean were in the distance. Commcuffs slowly vibrated and pinged as connections to the network restored. They were back, barely within range of the outpost's tall communication tower.

"Call it in. We'll be there soon," Krill instructed Yuri. He glanced to the side. "With friendlies."

Miriam looked over the two Altereds' attire. The blood wasn't an issue—they were all covered in fresh stains and blemishes. The legionnaire white however… "Any chance you two have a change of clothes?"

27

FORTIFICATION

THE OUTPOST WALL was a welcome sight.

As they neared, it towered over them, almost eight meters high, fortified by a durable alloy resistant to most human weapons. The perimeter was also equipped with security features along critical areas, although most of them were hidden away. A turret emerged above the main gate as the group approached.

"Hold there," an unseen speaker boomed with the crackle of static.

From experience, Sam knew at least two marine sentries were in a guard station to the left of the gate, although there were no windows to identify it from the outside. They were being watched from a hidden surveillance system.

Krill stepped forward. "We're Echo from Station SOG. We hailed ahead. We need to get to the TOC and your CO *now*."

A long pause followed, and Sam felt the unseen cameras sweep over them. Her fingernail bit into her thumb. The marines had intentionally sandwiched the two Altered women in the middle, but their height remained a disadvantage. Sam stole a glance at them and winced. Hadeon and Varya were defiantly staring at what Sam figured was the main camera above the gate. She didn't have time to think about how they knew.

Another turret popped out above the wall and pointed menacingly at the group.

Sam heard someone behind her inhale and take a small step back. Echo hadn't come all this way to get decimated by their own.

The legionnaires maintained their confident stances.

Krill's shoulders sagged, but with a deep inhale, he stepped forward and raised his hands high. "Sentry. Stand down. They're with us. Check with your TOC."

The turret remained like a watchful snake about to strike. Sam was no stranger to weapons pointed at her, but there was something about facing down a two-meter-long turret, knowing a belt fed large caliber rounds into it. At this range, they'd be red mist. She hoped the sentry, probably junior and Jun's age, had their finger well clear of the trigger controls.

With a hiss, the turret returned to its perch within the wall, its panel sealing back over. The gate opened, and a familiar face was there.

First Officer Diego looked like he had just run to the gate and arrived a second before. His eyes widened at the legionnaires, who stared back at him. "H-hello." Diego turned to Krill, still glancing at the Altered. "We've got Command on the line. They're waiting for you."

Sam's body relaxed slightly as they filtered into the safety of the outpost, its familiar gray buildings and bustle of activity. The gate closed with a clang behind them. She could finally breathe, even if it was only for a second.

Krill nodded and turned to his team. "Greg, with me. You two as well." He gestured at Hadeon and Varya, who returned it with an acknowledging head dip. "Everyone else, get to the clinic if you need it. Then stock up and top off. Get whatever you need to help fortify this place. I don't know how long we have, but the wunbies are probably coming."

Diego cast a nervous look at the Altered again. "I'll let MED and the armory know you're en route," he said, and his fingers flew across his commcuff.

Miriam touched Krill's shoulder. "Stop by after. You need to get that fixed." She looked at his arm, still cradled against his torso. She stared at Yuri for accountability and the second nodded. Sam had no doubt he could physically drag the lead to the clinic if Krill refused.

"Get food, water, rest, if you can," Yuri replied to the team.

The five of them broke away and hurried toward the communication tower. With their lead and second gone, the remaining marines had a moment of stillness. Technically, Fox would have been the next in command, but he stood, hollow as before.

Miriam took charge. "Nas, with me."

Scott shifted the injured marine over to the medic, who braced herself with the new weight. She looked over the others. They were all scraped up in different ways but standing on their own. "Fox?" she said, eyeing the hasty bandages she had forced on his arms.

"I'm fine," he grunted and began walking in the other direction. "Armory."

Miriam turned to Sam.

Sam waved her off. "I'm okay. Thanks." She was beaten up and sore as hell, but she had nothing life-threatening. It could wait.

◐

When Yuri found them at the small armory, the other SOG marines had restocked their weapons and ammunition stores. Sam pulled a loaned pistol, an older generation, out of her holster. She seated it in and out again before she was satisfied. Her rifle lay out in front of her, its own lasered UMF label scratched to hell and waiting for its cleaning and maintenance.

WHAT'S THE NEWS? Scott signed to the second as he approached the vault door.

Yuri shook his head and cleared his throat. "How's Nas?"

Miriam looked up from the workbench. Rounds were scattered out in front of her. "Hey. It's a bit worse than I thought. He's in the MedJet now. Hoping the doc here can fix it. If not, he'll need more work back home."

Kai rubbed her forehead with the back of her hand. The medic had shared the news when she joined them a bit earlier, but the second time hearing Nas's update made the younger woman nervous again.

NEWS? Scott signed.

Yuri sighed. "They're sending support units down here."

"And?" Sam said apprehensively.

"Command wants us back at Station."

Fox's head lifted sharply from his focus on a large machine gun.

Kai let out an exasperated gasp.

Yuri continued before anyone could cut in. "I don't know. Maybe they want to get us in front of a committee? A transport is already on its way."

"That's ridiculous," Miriam retorted. She set her magazine mid-refill on the center countertop. "Come on. You know that's ridiculous."

"Krill isn't happy about it, either, but it's what Command wants."

"Fuck Command," Kai said. In the week with the woman, Sam had never heard her swear.

An empty ammunition box clattered across the room, a small dent in the wall where it had been thrown. Fox stood with his back to the others, his shoulders moving up and down with each flustered breath, face flushed.

Kai's voice raised. "I'm sorry, but after all this? Does Command not understand what's going on? We're already here. Support units will take what, another day to arrive?"

"We can't leave them," Fox muttered, almost a whine.

"I know," Yuri responded. He sighed. "I'm just the messenger."

"Has Krill responded?" Kai said.

Fox's anger seethed out. "Krill's a UMF boy. We're going home." He kicked the bench and sat down, head in his hands, tufts of his brown hair sticking out between his terse knuckles.

Yuri glared at him, but his gaze softened. None of Echo had broached the subject of Jun's sudden death. "Our lead hasn't responded yet. He wants us to meet back at the dorms in an hour. He's at the clinic now." Yuri looked at Miriam. "I'll tell him to check in on Nas."

Miriam's gaze stayed on Fox, but she acknowledged the second with a soft "okay."

"Okay." Yuri pulled his rifle around and set it on the table.

The armory was quiet.

Quiet enough to hear Fox's choked voice. "What the fuck are we even doin' here?"

Miriam cautiously sat down beside him.

Fox glanced up, his eyes sunken, bags under his eyes. His nostrils flared with a lash of anger, his brows twitched, and the corner of his mouth tremored. Then it was gone. It took an extra second for his eyes to focus on the medic, but Sam knew. She could see how deep the damage was.

⌽

"I wanted to talk with you guys first."

Krill looked tired. His arm was covered in a thin, rigid covering from MED's quick-repair system, and the shadows and lines on his face had multiplied and deepened. He sat on the dorm bed now, vigorously rubbing the stubble on his chin with his good hand. Nas was the only one missing, still at the clinic.

Fox, who had been prepared for a fight—verbally and physically—deflated. Sam was a bit puzzled, along with the others. She had also expected they would reluctantly follow UMF orders and ship back out to Station.

"I...I think we should stay and help." Krill started, his gaze dropping to the floor. His shoulders hunched slightly, and Sam thought she saw his bottom lip quiver for a split second. "I haven't made the best choices this mission, and this... It's not just my decision to make." He raised his gaze to his team, colleagues, and friends around him.

No one spoke at first. Sam realized that despite the surprise, she herself didn't consider this conversation insubordination, disobedience, or even disloyalty. In their time in the south, she had seen firsthand the misalignment of expectations and perspectives. Staying to help Temunco and the south was the right thing to do. They had already failed New Zapala and Matam, even if it hadn't been their responsibility or mission to start. Sam knew some of her teammates' stances would echo her own.

"I'm stayin'. No matter what. They can court martial me if I live, I don't care," Fox said, his arms holding themselves across his chest.

"Me, too." Kai raised a hand. "Nas would—"

"I checked with Nas. He agrees. Not how he said it, but... yeah." Krill rubbed his head and smiled sheepishly.

Miriam nodded.

And Yuri crossed his arms. "Okay. Let's do it."

All eyes shifted to Sam, who was paralyzed with the attention. She wanted to stay. Of course she did. But then, what about her brother? Scott would stay if she did. This was his last mission. He had a future beyond UMF, the marines, and fighting. All of it. He was so close to freedom, to a life spent creating and nurturing. Those demons, those stimmed up Apostates, would be death and destruction.

Sam turned to her brother at her side.

His hand was raised confidently, and he watched her with his kind, soft blue-gray eyes.

She puffed air out of her nose. "Yeah. I'm in."

In the windowless TOC, Echo mixed with a crowd of Temunco senior crew and leadership. Hadeon stood with Krill near the center console, and the senior legionnaire towered over him and everyone else. The Temunco marines gave her a wide berth.

They did the same for Varya, who stayed with Sam and Scott at the side of the room. Sam was glad for the extra space, away from the main congregation. She noted that many in the room glared between the two Altered women. One marine nearby muttered something under his breath. Sam couldn't catch all of it over the TOC's growing murmur, but it was a jab.

Varya, with her heightened hearing, must have understood it, but she gave no reaction. Sam was certain the legionnaires, who had been placed in the same empty barracks as Echo, had heard the team's earlier conversation from the next room over.

Although the Altered soldiers still made her uncomfortable,

they shared an enemy now. Sam felt sympathy for the two—she couldn't imagine what she would do if her brother, her team, Echo, or her home outpost, had been betrayed and executed in front of her. The legionnaires had been cut off from their own and were rightfully angry.

The ocean of chatter died as CO Otueome strode into the dark room, and marines parted for her. She stopped at the console and acknowledged Krill and Hadeon with a head quirk before turning to the TOC. "Most everyone here has already been briefed on the basics. We know what we're all here for. Let's get to it," she said. "Diego."

The first officer cleared his throat. "We've confirmed scouts along the southeast ridges."

Whispers rippled out but immediately silenced at a stern look from the Temunco CO. Echo were already expecting the Apostates to move fast and convene on the UMF compound. They had seen it in Matam. But the outpost marines had been doubtful, certain the Apostates would back off knowing that they had failed to stop the SOG team from arriving in Temunco with their message. Why would the Apostates attack now when UMF, Station City, and the Royals had been alerted? Sam understood their doubt. There was no strategic sense in attacking a fully aware and armed UMF outpost, but she kept her reservations to herself. Most of Echo's encounters in the south had perplexed her.

Diego directed his next question to Hadeon. "Do we know when or where?"

One TOC watch officer projected an overlay of the outpost onto the holoscreen. It radiated a blue-green tint on the faces near it.

"This is the most desirable place to control," Hadeon's voice boomed. Her finger pointed at the coastline and docks. "And this will be their goal." She stabbed at the command tower in the middle. "As for when, I don't know. But if it were me, my unit…" Her nostrils flared. "I'd attack in the darkest of night." She looked around the room, a faint glow of green in her eyes.

The Temunco marines collectively shifted.

A unit leader coughed. "I can set up my unit and bastions here and here." He pointed to the exterior north and south perimeter walls closer to the docks.

Krill shook his head. "You don't want any assets outside the walls." He looked up around the turning expressions. "Trust me. You don't want anyone outside." He held out his injured arm as much as he could. "They'll overrun it before you can blink. We need to use these walls to our advantage."

Krill looked at the CO, an unsaid request to take charge. She nodded. "If we focus on those areas, we're splitting resources. And that's on top of the already spread-out forces at the main gate and perimeter." He rubbed his chin. "They'll want to cut off our escape at the docks and take out our comms, right? So…what if we let them in?"

The TOC broke out in protests and waving gestures—it was an absurd suggestion.

A whistle screeched. Diego pulled his fingers out of his mouth. "Let him finish."

"We can't cover that much ground. And I'm telling you now, you don't want to get caught fighting separately. Not with these alties. We let them in, but we control where. Create a gauntlet. Bleed them out as much as possible. Route them where we want, on our terms."

So far, every fight they had on this mission had not been on the SOG marines' terms. An ambush and surprise every time.

"If they don't?" another unit leader called out.

"We can put some reserve units further back. And…" Krill looked around the room. "Kai?"

The engineer raised her hand, and all eyes turned to her.

"Get me all the mines, explosives, and materials you can. We'll make it difficult, buy time if needed."

"I'll send our sappers to you," Diego said.

Kai nodded.

"I'll go with her," Nas said, limping forward. His thigh was wrapped in a similar cast mold to Krill's. Kai shook her head and whispered something to him, but he pulled away.

"I will join as well."

Sam startled at Varya's voice next to her.

Krill acknowledged them, then turned back to the holoscreen. "I recommend we let them in through the main gate. It's got the most countermeasures right now. We'll try to mow them down before they even get close."

"Do we have an idea of how many?" CO Otueome asked.

The attention turned to Hadeon, and the legionnaire shook her head. "Our post was overrun with seventy, eighty Apostates. Maybe more."

The room murmured. How big had the Legion garrison been?

Her brow furrowed. "But some of us...turned. It'll be more." She fixed a steely gaze at the holoscreen.

Sam's jaw clenched, and her fingernail worked into her thumb. That meant up to a hundred Apostates, including trained and armored legionnaires who had radicalized. The attacks on the human settlements may have whittled the Altered down, and another variable was whether the Altered had chosen to hold the towns or if they were sending a full force to Temunco. It was unnerving not knowing how many they would be up against.

"They'll bring firebombs. That's what I would do."

"How do wunbies have firebombs?" Diego asked, bewildered.

A muscle twitched in Hadeon's neck. "They executed my

unit and many others. We did not give our post or arsenal to them freely." She glared around the room. "Be glad they don't have vehicles, armor, and more weapons. You can thank *our* fallen comrades for that."

A quiet filled the TOC.

"So maybe seventy? Less? We can handle that number," the same unit lead from before blurted out.

Hadeon focused on him, and he stepped back, bumping into the next marine.

Krill sighed and shook his head. "They're using some...kind of stim."

Sam recalled the oily blacks of the Apostates' eyes, their impossibly quick movements and strength even as holes appeared in their bodies. A shiver ran through her.

"The eight of us could barely handle three scouts without Hadeon and Varya's help." Krill looked around. "And that was in broad daylight. If they attack at night, they can see almost perfectly. We can't."

Sam felt Temuncan eyes turn and scan Echo. The SOG marines had since cleaned up, but their scrapes and injuries were prevalent. It put things in perspective.

"How many do you have here?" Krill asked the first officer.

"Combat-ready? A bit over two hundred."

Krill pressed his palm into the console surface. "Okay. This is doable. Command is sending reinforcements, but that's a day away. They'll probably hit us tonight. They wiped out New Zapala and attacked Matam and they're riding high right now. Arrogant. Greedy. But we have an advantage. We have these walls, and we have a shit ton of weapons. And most of all, we know they're coming."

Something in Sam's chest swelled—admiration? Motivation?

"We can push MED here." Diego pointed at a building

closer to the docks, further away from the expected conflict areas. "We may have some skiffs lying around, and we can move those to the main gate to funnel the assault."

Some leads whispered, but the mood of the room had changed. They had a plan, and with that was hope.

"Valk?"

Sam looked up at Krill, who watched her and Scott expectantly. She cleared her throat. "Mute and I will set up at the comms tower." It was the tallest building in the compound. She had identified it the first time they arrived in Temunco, and it was still the obvious choice. "We'll have clean angles to support."

"Which means they'll see you as well," Krill said.

Sam felt Miriam's eyes bore into her.

THERE WERE BARRICADES AT THE DOCKS, Scott signed to her side.

Sam nodded. "The dock barricades. Can we…"

"We'll move them for you." Diego gestured to a watch officer, who tapped away on their tablet. "We'll give you a unit as well. For security."

Krill pointed at the map again, at the main gate. "Greg, Tan, Fox, and I will support here. With your crew."

"I, as well," Hadeon said.

The TOC stirred, eager to get their defenses and fortifications underway. CO Otueome, sensing the energy, raised her voice. "It'll be dark soon. Distribute all the night-vision we have. Be safe and do what you must." Her eyes pierced the room.

"Ready the outpost."

28

FIGHTING DEMONS

GLINTS of muted green blinked like fireflies hovering in place.

A finger twitched, itching for motion.

A warm breeze swirled into the meadow, but the tall grass blades moved unnaturally against it. Two silhouetted bodies straightened and interrupted the grassland surface. They each lifted a cylinder onto their shoulders and tucked their temples into protruding viewfinders. Fingers moved for the triggers underneath.

A bullet sliced through the first figure's head.

The weapon fell with the crumpled body.

Another projectile pinged off the other's firebomb launcher, but it was too late. A brightness streaked out of the cylinder in a silent arc toward the outpost.

At the top of the UMF communications building, nestled between the roof's lip and the metal tower above, Sam watched from her prone position with Scott and a Temunco marksman. Her brother racked another bullet into his long rifle, his eye never leaving its position behind the scope. She followed his sightline to another Altered who had jumped forward to pick up the first launcher. The individual reappeared out of the grass with the tube on its shoulder. Scott let out a slow breath and began to squeeze the trigger.

At the same time, the first, still-airborne missile broke apart at the height of its curve and small bombs scattered down, pelting napalm against the perimeter wall. Sam could feel the crushing boom in her bones.

She watched as her brother's round missed its mark by centimeters and ripped off an ear instead. Sam glanced away as Temunco ground forces rushed to douse the fires that had made their way over the wall.

When she looked back up, Sam's stomach clenched as the Apostates charged forward out of the meadow grass with animalistic howls. The mass of shadows split in the middle and each side turned in opposite streams away from the main gate just like Hadeon had predicted.

Manned and unmanned turrets sliced down, focusing on the outer lanes attempting to herd the horde in. A second and third firebomb launched and broke apart over the main gate. Screams erupted as marines found themselves amid combustive incendiaries, their positions compromised. One unmanned turret exploded, and the other continued firing as flames licked up around it—until it didn't.

The main gate cracked open, and the attacking wave noticed, moving to the opportunity dangled in front of them. Some Altered continued branching out and around the walls, but the rest were culled and reemerged into one body. Whatever remaining turrets rained down sheets of blinding gunfire on the Altered as they stormed forward.

A series of firebombs brought down a turret, then another. The attacking mass shed bodies behind it, but not enough.

"Kai, Nas, you've got maybe six or seven coming to you. Five on the north side," Sam sent over comms.

"We're ready," Nas replied.

"Target the launchers." Yuri's voice came over the visor, calm, but Sam recognized the undercurrent of fear.

The same order must have been passed on the ground as Sam saw marines frantically waving. She could barely make out the concentrated shouts before another buzz of turrets and explosions drowned them out. The last manned turret swept to one of the launcher carriers and hailed fire, shredding the owner into pieces.

A bright, blazing globe detonated, and napalm consumed the horde around it. Those who were not immediately incinerated continued barreling forward like fireballs in the night.

The turret blew apart as a concentrated missile found its target.

"Someone take that launcher down!" blared a voice over the Temunco marksman's radio.

With no remaining defense mechanisms on the perimeter, it was up to the sharpshooters. The firebombs were not only a threat to the compound—it was also a matter of time before the Apostates were within range of the comm tower. The two barricades only served as hasty cover from small arms fire.

The radio crackled. "They're inside. They're inside!"

"Scott," Sam intoned.

The last launcher carrier was gaining ground.

Her brother's rifle sounded.

She watched through her scope as the bullet just missed the launcher itself, severing several of the operator's fingers. The Altered fumbled the tube but quickly recovered. Glowing eyes glared straight at them, and it lifted the launcher, now smeared with a dark stain.

Her chest constricted. "Scott."

Her brother was still. And then the long rifle released a loud crack.

Sam didn't need to follow with her scope. An orange flame flared its wings and engulfed the space, spreading bright light out and around. As it dimmed, she returned to her own steady, aimed shots as the Altered flooded the main gate. The outpost had at least cut down the attacking numbers by half, wounded many, and hopefully limited the Apostates' fight inside the walls.

Sam shifted her elbow backward, bringing the rifle to a better position against the roof's edge. Her shoulder and cheek dampened the heavy weapon's recoil, and she watched through the magnified scope and her hololens to confirm her shots. An Apostate who had jumped over the labyrinth of obstacles flinched and then barreled forward.

Damn these drugged-up demons.

Scott's rifle fire continued beside her.

It was mayhem.

"Valk," Yuri called out. Sam heard rallying cries over his open mic. "Some broke away. Two, maybe three. They're coming to you."

"Tracking," she replied. Sam reloaded the long rifle and pushed herself back, away from the ledge. Still prone, she gathered a box of ammunition, opened it, and pushed it within arm's reach of her brother. She keyed her visor—it would get through the deafening booms. "Scott. More ammo next to you."

He tapped the tip of his boot onto the roof twice. He shot again. He was in his zone.

Sam reached out to touch his leg but hovered just above. It would feel too much like a goodbye—and this wasn't a farewell. She was getting him home. This was his last mission. This was his last fight. Her fingers lightly rested on the fabric over his calf. His body muffled the energy of another shot as her ears rang with the same blast.

"I'll be back," she said. She couldn't tell if he heard her, but she scooted backward to the open hatch behind them. Her foot found the opening, and then the first ladder rung. Sam pushed herself backward into the hole. As she lowered herself, her brother's rasp filled her visor.

"Sammy."

She paused, one hand gripping the hold above her head.

"Be safe. Shout if you need."

She nodded, then realized he couldn't see her motion. She keyed her visor twice and descended the ladder.

○

Sam stood in the shadows next to the narrow staircase, her back to the cool wall. The glow of lights and explosions outside illuminated the outlines of the interior furniture through the windows. The Altered could see in the dark, but she hoped that the flashlights at the end of the marines' rifles would disorient their vision. Even for a millisecond. They needed whatever leverage they could get.

Two Temunco marines stood to her side, their night-vision gear on. She couldn't remember their names and could barely make out their faces, hooded by the devices, but they were both tight with anxiety. The other five from Diego's assigned security unit were on the ground floor, the first line of defense for whatever was coming.

Sam hoped Yuri was right. If there were more than three drugged-up Apostates, they were shit out of luck. She had meant to meet the others on the first floor, but she had made it to the third by the first barrage of automatic fire. Sam had made a quick decision and hit the lights before rushing back up to the top level to douse the illumination there as well. She hoped they were in a better position from their higher post.

Sam peeked around the corner and down the stairs, her hololens scanning. The stairwell was the only way up. She and these two marines were the last line of defense between Apostates and the communications equipment, and most importantly, her brother.

Yelps came from below, and then another series of rifle bursts. Furniture creaked and clashed with the sounds of struggle.

The noise stopped abruptly, and the lights went off on the first floor. The only illumination came from the second level and the fight outside.

"—north sector. I need help. Get me support!" Panic crackled over one of the marines' radios—Cody? Was that his name? Cody. Didn't matter. Sam shot him a look, but the stream was already silenced with a click.

A trickle of dread went down her spine. She motioned to the two marines, and they shifted, pulling their weapons deeper into their shoulders. The marine at the end was trembling so much she could see his barrel shaking. Sam couldn't deal with that right now. She had nothing comforting to say, regardless. She refocused on her own breath and tried to find her Zen before the inevitable course of adrenaline.

The lights on the second level flitted off, and now the building was devoid of its white luminescence. Sam's hololens constantly mapped and outlined the marines and shapes around her. Her ears bristled, her hearing at full power.

Movement. Below them. She couldn't tell how many. Hoped it was only two. Prayed for one. Hell, they were quiet.

Metal groaned from the bottom of the stairwell. It was that lower step Sam had noted when she first surveyed the building —the plating was a bit off-kilter. Fuck. They were quiet *and* quick.

Sam stepped out and swung past the open stairwell,

releasing a stream of bullets. Cody popped around the cover and did the same. Their rounds flowered in blooms of light from their barrels, flashing the blackness like an unsteady strobe. In the flickers, she made out bared, white teeth, thrashing and tangling of limbs, a hurricane of gasps, growls, yelps, flesh being pierced and ripped open.

Click.

The harsh sound was deafening over the noise. Multiple rounds were gone in what felt like a few seconds and somehow also an hour.

Sam transitioned to her pistol, guiding her carbine with her other hand to the side, and held her secondary weapon down into the stairwell. She couldn't sense any movement but noted the dark splatters on the wall that hadn't been there before.

Cody pulled back into cover, his magazine spent. Sam heard him fumble for a new cartridge and forget to release the empty one. His adrenaline was spiking. She knew his hands had already started to lose their dexterity, but he finally slammed the fresh ammunition into place and palmed the bolt forward. The barrel of his weapon lifted unsteadily into the darkness again.

With the marine's weapon back up, Sam glanced over—both Cody and his teammate were nearly hyperventilating—and swiveled back into her own cover to reload her carbine.

Before she peeked back out, she checked herself. She had an elevated heart rate; her hands and arms were tense. Sam took a deep breath, exhaled, and then took a second. Her nostrils and mouth filled with the sting of lead in that small, enclosed space. She prayed it was done, then shifted her rifle back out.

Glowing eyes leaped out of the dark.

Cody let out a spray of bullets, but in his panic, the rifle shot upward in a succession of recoil.

Before Sam could squeeze her own trigger, she was shoved

back into the wall, and the large silhouette was on top of the marine, pinning him down.

His teammate stepped back from the wall and raised his weapon at the Altered.

Sam shouted at him, but it was too late.

The marine screamed, or he opened his mouth to—Sam didn't know, she couldn't hear anything over the stream of bullets shooting into the Altered's battle-worn chest plate, the bullets ricocheting everywhere, but mostly into the marine below. Bullets came uncomfortably close to Sam's foot, and she pulled in, trying to make herself as small as possible, hoping she didn't die after all this time because of a frightened marine who had forgotten the cardinal rules[1].

The Altered roared at the marine and charged into him, slamming him to the ground, his weapon bouncing away into the darkness.

Sam swung her rifle around and tried to get a good shot. She didn't have one. She pulled herself up to her knees and swore, trying to get the Altered's attention. Her hand searched the floor, and her fingers curled around metal. It was Cody's water container. Sam slung it at their assailant, and it bounced off its head.

The Altered whipped around at her and snarled. He charged Sam, and they both smashed through drywall into another room. Sam shifted her rifle on its sling to block her attacker's barrage of haymakers. One swing caught her in the visor, and her hololens deactivated. Her disrupted balance was made worse by the loss of her holo-assisted vision. The only lighting in the room was now the faint glow of orange from the outpost fire through the large window.

The Altered ripped Sam's rifle away and tossed it to the side, throwing her onto a conference table in the process.

The other marine shot again at the Altered. It turned,

charged, and body-slammed him into the floor. Sam, still dazed, didn't see it, but she heard the sickly sound of the marine's body hitting the ground.

Sam pulled her pistol from her holster and attempted to shoot at the exposed joints of armor—midsection and neck. She didn't know how many times they had already shot the damn thing. She tried aiming for its head, but it moved too fast.

Before she knew it, the Altered crossed the room and swiped away her pistol. It grabbed her by her throat and crushed her against the wall.

The pressure was excruciating. The edges of her vision blurred and darkened.

She heard her brother call for her over the visor. It was so distant.

Sam grasped at the Altered's hands, trying to find its thumbs to break the hold. When she couldn't, she dropped her right arm to her knife on her rig, unsheathed it, and desperately stabbed several times at the Altered's side and stomach.

Nothing.

She stabbed up and underneath its armor. She was on her last breath, and with a final upward thrust, she plunged her hand and blade well into her attacker's chest cavity and under the ribs.

The Altered crumpled to the ground, bringing her with it. Its dead grip was still tight around her neck, but now Sam could gasp and pull away.

She coughed and heaved, but she was alive.

"Sam!" Her brother's voice rang in her ear.

Sam keyed her visor and tried to speak but found she couldn't. It hurt too much. She struggled to catch her breath and then keyed it again. "Yeah." It came out in a dry croak. She fought to find an even breath and added, "Stay." He was of better use to the outpost up top, at a distance.

She pushed the Altered away and grabbed her pistol from the ground. Sam checked it with shaky fingers; there were still rounds in the magazine. She re-holstered the sidearm and crawled on her hands and knees to the other marine. She would've stood up, but she had no confidence that she wouldn't faint. A copper tang sat on her tongue.

The marine groaned weakly as he came to. "Is it dead?"

"I think so." Sam could barely recognize her own voice. It came out raspy and broken like glass.

"Are there more?"

She didn't answer. She didn't *know* the answer.

Sam patted the marine's chest and pulled herself up against the table. Her head throbbed and spun, and she gripped the edge as she felt pressure flow over her body. The floor swayed beneath her feet, but she staved it off and stabilized herself. This wasn't the time to pass out. Sam couldn't afford it. She waited a few seconds for her blood to recirculate.

"Stay here," she told the marine.

He remained on the floor and groaned.

Sam tapped her visor, but the hololens didn't engage. *Shit*. At least the comms still worked. She stepped through the hole in the wall and stopped at the body at the top of the staircase.

The marine was dead.

She apologized under her breath as she took his night-vision goggles and placed it over her head and eyes, then picked up his rifle and stepped over the body. She still had to clear the building down.

The NVG illuminated a pool of blood around two dead Altered tangled together. Half of one's head was blown away, and the other had holes through its cheekbone and above its brow.

They had been lucky.

Sam stepped carefully around the knot of death and gore and looked around the floor. There was no movement, just the tense stillness and the battle sounds outside the tower. She moved to the second floor, doing the same until she reached the bottom. The area was a mess. Marines lay dead and mutilated, scattered all over the room.

Something moved outside the open front door. Sam raised her rifle. She was in the middle of the room with no cover.

A figure drenched in a dark substance stepped into the doorway and night-eyes glared at her. It seemed to be missing one hand, but a short blade was poised in the other.

She cursed under her breath and shot a stream of concentrated fire at the individual as it charged. Sam watched the bullets tear through its chest, neck, and shoulders to no avail, and quickly moved the rifle to block the incoming slashes.

The Altered was too fast, and she was already spent from the previous fight. The blade cut into her kit and then into her shoulder, and she cried out and twisted out of the way. Sam alternated to her pistol and shot from her hip. One bullet hit her assailant's hand, and the blade dropped.

The Altered slammed into her, and the NVG and rifle clattered away. Spots clouded her vision, and it took much longer to adjust to the sudden change. Not a good sign.

She found herself on the ground, the Altered scrambling for her, its blood dripping and spraying. Sam shielded her head. She was too tired from the previous fight. Too tired from the entire week. This was a losing fight. It'd kill her before it bled out. She kicked out, trying to make space, but it was useless. She moved her hand to grab one of its arms as it came down, but it was too strong. Her shoulder gave, and she cried out.

Sam was going to die.

CRACK.

Her assailant's body loosened against hers; the assault stopped.

She heard another meaty crack and peeked up. A dark shadow above her slammed the butt of a rifle into the Altered's temple again.

It screeched and pushed into the figure and away from Sam, a flurry of limbs against her savior. Breathing hard, Sam attempted to get up, but the stabbing pain and weight on her arm kept her down.

She watched as her rescuer gruesomely smashed their rifle once more into the Altered's face. While it was momentarily dazed, a deft blade sheathed into an eye socket.

Something touched her and Sam whipped around.

Reflective eyes met her.

Sam tore away violently, scurrying across the floor, preparing for another fight.

She heard her callsign from behind but ignored it.

It came again, louder. "Valk."

There was a cautious touch on her back, and she whirled to the side to keep the two newcomers in her line of sight.

"Hey. Whoa. It's me. It's Kai and Varya."

Sam breathlessly looked between them. In the dim light, she could make out Kai's form, her hands raised, and the tall, short-haired legionnaire.

Relief.

Sam let herself sit on the ground, then carefully lowered onto her back. The coolness of the hard floor seeped through her shirt and into her skin, almost soothing, despite the destruction and death around her.

She ignored the vibration of her commcuff on her wrist. A notification. Or a message. She didn't care.

Kai rushed to her side. "You're safe. It's over. We got most of them, the rest left. They're running. We did it, Valk. It's over."

Sam struggled to make sense of the words as she stared at the dancing shadows on the ceiling. Her chest rose and fell as she tried to regain her composure. Her neck and her chest felt like they had caved in. She tried to lick her chapped lips, but her tongue and mouth were just as dry.

She heard noise from above, and the others glanced up. Sam raised her hand to Kai and Varya, the motion turning on her cuff's display.

Footsteps came down the stairs with a beam of light leading the way. Scott. Behind him, the other marksman supported the concussed marine she had left upstairs.

The light washed over her and she squinted into it. She tried to sit up and stifled a groan as her beaten body protested. The floor felt better, so she laid back down. She raised her wrist again over her face and stared at the display.

UMF CONTRACT RENEWAL APPROVED

Sam stared at it for a moment.

And then she laughed. The motions hurt her throat and body, but she couldn't stop. She choked and then continued in a delirious snicker.

"Did we win?" the injured marine groaned.

No one responded.

---

1. Cardinal Rules of Firearm Safety—See Glossary

29

AFTERMATH

A LONE CLOUD hovered in the sky as if it had been painted there. Just underneath it, three UMF ship carriers interrupted the horizon. Sam could make out the individual blocky letters on the sides of their hulls from Temunco's dock. Tender boats dotted the water with their white tails in the swell, shuttling marines toward the outpost.

Sam winced as pressure tightened around her shoulder.

"Sorry, just one more adjustment," Miriam said as she fixed the bandage. "Sure you don't want another sit in the MedJet?"

Sam shook her head. "Others need it more." Her voice splintered in her throat, and she winced again. "I'll do it back in Station," she said.

Sam was ready to leave the south, but she was also anxious about returning home. Home was bittersweet. Home meant her brother was done with UMF, and he'd start a life beyond the military, something she was starting to wonder about for herself.

"Stubborn," Miriam grumbled, but there was a glimmer in her eyes. "But I guess you've done pretty decent, considering you've had a bum arm most of the mission. You could probably take on more Charonites with one arm tied up in a sling. Might be fairer for them in the future."

Sam scoffed, but accepted the compliment.

"I still don't get it. That attack was foolish." Nas's voice drifted in the salty air.

Sam and Miriam turned to their teammates walking down the platform. She noted that Nas's limp had grown considerably, his injured leg dragging behind with each step.

Fox followed at some distance, his head bowed.

"It's done. We won," Kai said.

"Yeah, but why did wunbies take out a Legion garrison, and then attack two settlements *and* an outpost in less than a week? They had to know that was a bad idea..." Nas came to a stop next to Miriam and chucked a chin upward at her and Sam.

Miriam glanced down at his bandaged leg. "Hadeon said they weren't expecting us in New Zapala. The wunbies panicked."

"Right. And Matam, Temunco suffered for it."

Heavy boots dragged against the platform and the four marines dropped into silence as Fox passed them. He didn't look up.

Once Fox disappeared into the ship, Kai hit Nas's shoulder. "But we destroyed most of the wunbies. Yoomy's going to help rebuild and recover what they can. Plus, the Sovereign and Royals know what's happening now. Hadeon said that Arshangol and other Legions are launching an offensive to weed them out. The wunbies are done."

Nas sighed and shifted his weight. "I guess. Just feels like we're still on the losing end."

Miriam looked at his leg again. Before she could say anything, Nas cut her off. "Tan, I said I'm fine. I already did a round in MED. I just want to go home." He turned and moved to the ramp. "Thank you, though," he softly added over his shoulder as Kai caught up with him.

Miriam's mouth twisted, and she caught Sam's glance. "You're both stubborn," she muttered.

Of course they were. They were SOG marines.

Sam looked back at the Temunco compound. The fires had been put out earlier, but the smell of smoke lingered. The outpost had taken some damage, but it was nothing that couldn't be fixed with time and UMF's core company of engineers. She thought about the rows of covered bodies they had lined up, more humans adding to the total death count of the Apostates' attacks in the south. What lives had those marines wanted outside of UMF?

The thought passed as her brother and Yuri walked toward them, both signing lackadaisically. Scott brightened as he saw Sam. He broke away while Yuri remained to wait for Krill, Hadeon, Varya, and Diego behind them.

Scott tapped a finger to his temple at Miriam, and she returned the greeting with a smile and nod. He then nudged Sam playfully on her bad shoulder.

She grimaced, more out of anticipation of the pain than the pain itself. Nursing her arm, Sam kicked at him; her brother dodged easily out of the way, continuing for the ship.

"You're the worst," she called hoarsely after him.

He turned around without breaking his stride. AND YOU STILL LOVE ME.

Sam laughed. The movement hurt her throat and body, but it was bearable.

The group of marines and legionnaires made their way closer, acknowledging Sam and Miriam as they paused nearby. The two women watched as the group said their last goodbyes.

"Our capital will do what they can. The Court sends their condolences," Hadeon said loudly.

Sam raised an eyebrow at Miriam. She had never heard of any Altered Royals sympathizing publicly with humans.

First Officer Diego waved a hand. "We do appreciate your help in the...attack. Both of you have safe quarters here if you need more rest."

Sam's brow notched higher. She had definitely never heard of UMF sheltering Altered. The outpost marines, especially the incoming reinforcements, were already uneasy with the legionnaires' presence. Sam knew they were all witnessing a pioneering moment. Many marines, humans in general, would have a difficult time combining generations-old mindsets with the new idea of Altered allies.

Hadeon looked surprised with the Temunco officer's offer as well. "Thank you, but we have more work to do. Our sister post is perhaps a three-day journey from here and we should be on our way."

Yuri snorted. "An unlikely alliance. Who needs the summit when we have Apostates to bring us together?"

Krill shot a look at his second.

Diego shifted uncomfortably.

But Hadeon smiled. "Safe travels to you and your team, Vallen Krill."

The Echo lead grinned back. "And you and Varya as well." Krill held out his hand, and Hadeon mirrored him, palms facing centimeters apart. Krill chuckled.

While the rest shared their farewells and parting words, Miriam touched Sam's arm and gestured to the ship.

Sam shook her head and whispered, "I'll be there in a bit." She wanted to feel the warm sun on her skin and face before she was locked into a metal vessel for the next hours.

Miriam nodded and left her on the platform.

Sam took a deep breath and inhaled. The damp ocean scent

mixed with hints of charcoal and ash. She felt someone's presence next to her.

"I hope we meet again."

Sam blinked and turned.

Varya stared out at the ocean, arms crossed casually across her chest.

"Fighting on the same side though, right?" Sam rasped.

Varya looked down and smirked, then extended an arm out, bent at the elbow, and hand raised—as if she wanted to arm wrestle in the air. Sam mirrored her, gingerly grasping the other's hand, careful of her own recovering shoulder.

In that simple motion, Sam knew that something had changed, had shifted in the world of humans and Altered. It was the start of something big, something better. A surprisingly optimistic thought.

30

STATION

SAM ROLLED over on the stiff mattress and opened her eyes. She forgot where she was as plain gray walls stared back at her and a covered lump stirred on another bed. For a second, Sam was back in Matam, in the inn, gazing at Miriam's back, but the thin blanket pulled away, and a head of blonde hair peeked out. Her brother turned, and one eye groggily opened at her. Scott sighed, then burrowed further into the pillow.

Echo had arrived back in Station late at night. The siblings had split off to spend the night in UMF's temporary housing. Sleep came quickly. The return trip had been quiet, but far from restful—serving as a period of reflection as each SOG marine finally had time to grasp everything that had happened: the Apostates, the Charonites, the human-Altered child, the attacks, Jun… The mission was neither a success nor a complete failure, and Echo was left ambivalent.

For Sam, she felt selfishly less conflicted. She examined her brother's face and was oddly content. Even though Scott would be out of the military, she experienced the small, thrilling sparks of another point in their relationship, and the opportunities they would have.

Her stomach grumbled. Sam checked her commcuff. It was closer to midday. In sleeping in, they had missed breakfast. Sam pulled up the message that Echo had received on arrival again. The mission debrief would be in the early afternoon, in a few hours.

She pulled herself to the edge of the bed. Her stiff shoulder complained with the motion, and she wondered if she had enough time to get to the main clinic before—Station's updated technology would fix her injury significantly better than Temunco's. Sam lazily drew a finger along the tattoo and scar as she considered whether to go. Better not. She didn't know how long MED would take, and she wasn't looking forward to sitting absolutely still in yet another round of the MedJet.

She listed what she could accomplish before the brief: shower, clean her rifle, organize her gear, perhaps another trip to the armory to replace lost items, lunch at the DFAC (she already missed the southern cuisine), and then off to the brief. Sam looked around the small dorm room and remembered their weapons and kits had been left in the team room. *Fine.* A bit more rest, shower, armory, lunch, and then off to the brief.

Sam held back a laugh.

There was finally some semblance of control back in her life after more than a week of chaos and uncertainty. She looked at Scott's resting face, already back asleep and lightly snoring. They would finally have some time to explore Station City after the brief—Miriam and Yuri had even offered to be their guides. Sam smiled. It was going to be a good—no, a great day.

◊

"Well, that's done and over." Nas heaved his armor and kit into his locker with a clang.

Echo had just returned from the debrief and was now

organizing and stashing away their gear, which had been discarded earlier in a heap. Sam and her brother sat to the side as they packed away their belongings.

Kai nudged her kit. "Wonder if we'll catch a glimpse of some of the Royals and emissaries before they leave the city."

"I think I'm good. I've had my fill of alties," Nas replied.

"It's just too bad, all of this, the summit being postponed…" Kai trailed off.

Miriam looked up as she hung her armor and kit. "Aside from all the…everything, Yuri's right, the wunbies were probably more effective than the summit. Look at us, we worked with a couple legionnaires *and* the Royals aren't trying to kill us."

"I guess," Kai said. "It's one good thing that came out of all this." She peered around the others at Sam. "I'm sorry you can't stay longer. I think it's pretty awful that Ursus is pulling you back so soon. We all need a break after that mission." Kai glanced over at Fox's equipment piled in front of his locker.

Sam picked at her finger. Command was sending her back to Ursus that night. She was already lined up for another priority mission. As always, good workers were only rewarded with… more work.

So much for her rest stop in Station City with Scott. And Miriam. She tried to hide her disappointment, but it was a flimsy attempt—her change in demeanor had already been registered by the entire team. At least Station was Scott's to explore for a couple more days—she'd ask him to bring back some treats for her.

Her brother nudged her now, watching her anxious scratching, and gave her a raised eyebrow.

Sam responded with a thin smile that didn't seem to convince him. JUST BUMMED ABOUT MISSING THE CITY, she signed.

AND A CERTAIN SOMEONE? he motioned back.

Sam glanced to see if Yuri, the only Echo teammate who could understand, had caught their silent communication. The second was preoccupied with untangling his own gear. Sam leaned back into the wall and threw a fist into her brother's shoulder, pushing him away.

He grinned. WE'LL COME BACK ANOTHER TIME, I PROMISE.

Sam tilted her head and narrowed her eyes at Scott.

He smirked.

Sam's eyes widened, searching her brother's face. He was going to give up his leave and rest days to return with her? She wove her hands and fingers to protest, but Scott put a large hand over hers, shaking his head. His decision had been made. Sam wanted to hug *and* hit him at the same time, but she did neither as she startled at a locker slamming shut.

"Duncan's in thirty!" Nas swung around and immediately winced at the movement. Like Sam, he had not gone to MED to follow up on his own leg injury. Stubborn, as Miriam said.

"Thirty?" Kai said. "I need a long, hot shower." Her nose wrinkled in Nas's direction. "*You* need a shower."

"What have you guys been doing this entire time?" Miriam jeered.

"I needed my food. And sleep," Nas added, scrunching one eye. "But with the golden twins heading out so soon, *we* are going to drink. We deserve it."

"We'll be there," Yuri said over his shoulder. "Someone message Krill and Fox?"

"Fox might already be at Duncan's," Nas replied.

Sam eyed the messy mound of armor and LMG accessories. Fox had kept to himself since they left the south and separated from the group after the brief without a word. Sam looked up and caught Miriam's eyes, who had also been staring at their teammate's items. Those light-brown eyes were filled with worry, then softened.

Sam held onto the connection as long as possible, giving the other medic a small smile. It felt like months had passed since the Ursus recon specialists had first entered this team room, since they had met Echo. A week of sweat, blood, and tears had transformed so much. Miriam was the first to break the connection as Kai approached the siblings.

The engineer placed her hands on Sam and Scott's shoulders. "Valk, Mute, you two better be there. Farewell and all."

Scott leaned his head down as if to speak, although Sam knew he probably wouldn't.

Kai tutted and held up a hand. "No no no. You have time for a couple of rounds. It's needed."

Sam's brows pinched together, and she started to object. She wasn't so sure about a social effort either. It was one thing to be with the team itself, but this "Duncan's" sounded like a bar, and that meant people. She wasn't ready for more people just yet.

"Two rounds, Valk," Kai emphasized, reading her hesitation. She held up her fingers. "Just two." She wagged her hand and grinned.

"Fine. Okay," Sam resigned. The woman wouldn't have taken a "no" anyway.

Nas slammed another locker shut and threw his hands up. Joining Kai, Sam, and Scott, he casually draped an arm over the engineer's shoulder and wiggled his eyebrows.

Kai laughed.

The weight of their mission had lifted, if only temporarily, with the promise of a few hours of festivities. A different future awaited, despite the grief of Jun and the loss of so many lives and so much land. But that was for another time. The next hours were for revelry and libations to celebrate their return home.

The two young marines left the room together, already giddy with anticipation.

"Shower, please!" Miriam called after them before the door slid shut. She turned to Scott and outstretched her hand. "See you soon. Mute…"

Scott stood up and gave her a hug, which surprised both her and Sam, but Miriam quickly relaxed into his arms.

"Be safe. See you around," she said. She looked at Sam. "You're coming, right?"

Sam nodded.

Yuri pounded Scott on the back, and the two friends pulled each other into a rough embrace.

DRINKS ON ME, Yuri signed, as they separated.

Scott snorted in response.

The second shrugged and clicked his tongue. "Hey, I tried." He thumped her brother on the chest and winked at Sam. "Don't be a stranger. I'll be checking in. Both of you."

The siblings shared a smirk and watched as their last Echo teammates exited.

As the door closed again, the room fell quiet. Sam returned to a cursory clean of her rifle. Rituals. As much as she felt different and lighter, she still liked her rituals. She rubbed the pad of her finger down her weapon across the scratches and scars from the mission's scuffles. They were cosmetic, and she could get it fixed when she returned to the outpost, but she decided to leave the marks—they told a story, gave her carbine more character.

To her side, Scott grabbed his bags, including his long rifle in its new case. He paused and watched her manipulate her weapon.

Sam sighed, shaking her head. She knew her brother; she

knew what he was going to say. "You know Kai and Nas will give me shit," she said. Her brother's eyebrow raised, and Sam sighed again. "I'll cover. Like I always do," she told him.

Scott responded with a muted scoff and smirk, and then a grateful nod. He walked out without a glance back.

"Twenty hundred! At the docks!" Sam called out after him.

Her brother waved a hand over his head before the door slid shut.

"Just the worst," Sam mumbled to herself.

$$\oplus$$

The neon light blasted "BAR" in fat, bright, bubbly letters. Sam stood in front of the rusted door; her nervousness was a distraction from her body's soreness after the mission's gauntlet of abuse. She smoothed her uniform pants over her thighs and hesitantly rested a hand on the cool metal panel. She could feel the vibrations of a muffled, punching bass line, and she heard shouting and laughter come through the cracks of the door. It was relatively early, the sun still in the sky, but there was already a crowd at the compound pub.

Sam pulled the bottom of her plain, black T-shirt out of her pants and then thought about re-tucking it again. The casual manner was alien, almost wrong, but she forced her hands away.

With a deep breath, she opened the door and walked in.

Sam was assaulted by the clash and wail of music but was pleasantly surprised that the bar was not as packed as she had imagined outside. To her relief, she could comfortably maneuver around the other off-duty patrons. Her boots crunched on the layer of littered crumbs on the grimy floor. She didn't need to search long for her teammates, as Yuri, Nas, and Kai waved their arms from the end of the bar. The drink in

Nas's hand spilled as he moved, and the marine was oblivious to the alcoholic shower he was giving himself.

Sam was fifteen minutes late. Echo had already started without her.

"The Valkyrie is here!" Nas shouted. He gripped Sam as she neared. "What's your poison?"

Sam chuckled. "How much have you already had?"

The young SOG marine winked and sloshed his beverage back into his throat. "Not enough! You need a drink," he said after.

Sam didn't feel like imbibing. She'd be nursing a headache on the long trip back. "Maybe a pop?" she said, leaning forward.

"What!"

Kai and Yuri cackled as Nas recoiled with exaggerated offense. He shook his head and pivoted to the bartender behind the counter. "A blender bender for Valkyrie!" he thundered, pointing his finger at Sam. He paused with the same digit now upright in the air, and then raised another. "Make that two!"

"Three!" Kai yelled above the thrum of the room.

Sam didn't know what a "blender bender" was, but she was confident the drink would have an absurdly high percentage of alcohol. It sounded like a giant, incoming headache. Sam waved her hand, cutting the air in front of her throat, but was ignored.

Nas hollered over her head, "Yuri? One for you?"

"I'm good! Still got this one!" the second responded exuberantly.

"No, Nas," Sam said. "I have to go soon. Maybe just a beer, then?"

It was Kai's turn to leer at her. "Even more reason to go hard!" she said.

Sam inhaled and let out a deep breath, steeling herself.

"Fine. Fine." She'd have to raid the ship's medical room or cabinet later.

Nas threw his hand up in celebration; Sam dodged a trail of alcohol as it flicked out of his cup. Yuri winked at her, and she chuckled again. Conceding to Kai and Nas's pressure was a defeat she wasn't too sore about. Sam settled into a stool next to the second and craned her neck to look around the bar.

"Where are the others?" she asked, as the bartender slid three metal containers to the group. Sam lifted one cup to her face, and her nose wrinkled. The smell of alcohol was overpowering. She took a small sip, and it burned every tissue in her throat. Her eyes watered as she swallowed. That was a *lot* of alcohol.

Kai motioned toward the corner of the room. "Fox went to the back. Bathroom, maybe," she said, then stretched her neck the other way and subsequently rolled her eyes. "Tan is schmoozing over there."

Sam followed Kai's hand and recognized the brown braid. Miriam leaned against a high-top table and was in deep conversation with another woman—attractive, with dark, heavy eyelashes. Something Miriam said made the other woman fold forward in laughter. Sam's stomach wrenched as a hand caressed Miriam's arm.

She tore her eyes away and found Yuri watching her. Sam's cheeks flushed. She took another swig from her cup, almost choking on the liquid again.

"Hello, hello." Fox's gravelly voice announced his arrival before the heavy fragrance of liquor hit Sam's nose. Fox stumbled into the counter, grabbed Kai's waiting drink, and took a lengthy gulp.

As his head lolled back, Sam reached out to stabilize him. Once he settled into a sturdier position, she stole another glance back at Miriam and the other woman.

"Where's Mute," Kai said—more a statement than a question.

Sam reluctantly turned back and shrugged. "You know him. He's not one for these things."

"Yeah...but we wanted to celebrate his last mission," Kai pouted.

Sam returned a reassuring smile. "Scott's never been great with goodbyes...or large crowds." She paused. The same was true for herself, but here she was, at Duncan's. "I think it was a good...well, not exactly how anyone wanted it to go, but it was a good, last mission for him."

And us.

She was going to miss Echo. The SOG team had grown so much on her. On top of it, they were now bonded through shared trauma and violence.

Kai frowned but nodded. "I'll send him a lengthy message. Berate him a little," she added.

Fox roused and grunted. "I see Tan's moved on, right back to it." He ogled the woman opposite Miriam and shoved a hand into the community snack bowl on the counter. "Surprised? Or mayb'not." He swung his eyes to the group and then back to the attractive woman. "She'd look better on me."

Disgust flashed across Kai's face and then again as Fox's hand dipped back into the bowl. Her lip curled. "Ew. Did you even wash your hands?"

The large marine shrugged and stumbled back.

Kai retched theatrically, and Sam chuckled, grateful for the distraction. She took another small sip, holding her eyes on the brim of her drink. She didn't want to watch the medic flirt anymore. That third sip of her beverage was no better than the first or second. She set the cup down, hoping that the physical separation meant that she wouldn't drink out of a need to fill time and space.

"Well, Casanova graces us with her presence," Fox muttered loudly.

Even if the music had stopped and the bar had quieted, Sam was certain she still wouldn't have heard Miriam walk up. The medic stood next to them now and mock bowed to the group. She punched Fox in the arm, and the large marine staggered back.

His face contorted into a look of snide pain. "So strong."

Miriam arched an eyebrow, raised a middle finger to his face, and grinned. "Fuck you, too."

Fox's eyes crossed to focus on her finger and then uncrossed. "Fuck. You." He laughed—almost genuinely. And then, a dark shadow—guilt, anger?—flared across his profile and his face fell. He turned to the counter and slumped against it.

The others quieted, their demeanor changing along with their grieving teammate.

Sam looked back at Yuri and signed, SHOULD WE TAKE HIM HOME?

They watched as Fox tipped the rest of the drink back into his throat.

WE'LL TAKE CARE OF HIM. DON'T WORRY, Yuri motioned.

Sam wasn't convinced. She moved her fingers.

"Whoa now." Fox whipped around, a smile plastered back on his face. "None o' this." The large marine's overly warm hands covered both Yuri's and Sam's.

Sam put her other hand over his, holding it there for a few seconds before she let go. She *was* worried for him, her teammate, her…friend.

Fox didn't seem to notice the extended contact—he was suddenly fixated on something across the bar and muttered incoherently about the music. He stumbled past the group.

"I can go watch over him," Kai said.

Nas shook his head. "Let him be for a bit. He's not leaving here anytime soon." He lifted his own cup. "And neither are we. Right now, we're all fucked up, and we're getting wasted. We deserve it." He knocked his alcohol back.

Miriam took Fox's place against the counter and settled in. Her thigh brushed against Sam's knee as she peered into Sam's abandoned drink. She picked up the cup and took a sip. The alcohol didn't seem to bother the medic. Miriam made an approving face and downed the rest in one impressive gulp.

Sam's eyes widened.

Miriam returned the look, her eyes alight with something Sam couldn't exactly place.

Before they could say anything, Nas rolled an open hand forward and feigned a poor, foreign accent. "So the mademoiselle didn't fall for your tricks?"

Miriam glared at Nas, then beamed. "What tricks?" She leaned forward. "You're just jealous." She pulled back, brushing Sam's shoulder in the movement. "Plus, we have the one and only Valkyrie for a little while longer before she leaves us." She gave Sam a wink.

Sam scoffed and shook her head, but a warmth grew in her stomach, either from the alcohol or the medic's direct attention.

She startled when Nas pounded his hand into the counter.

"Another round!"

⏀

Sam cleaned her hands in the ultraviolet station and stared at her reflection in the mirror. The bathroom was empty, and she was glad for the brief haven from the crowded bar. She brushed back a string of stubborn hair, trying to flatten it against the side of her head.

She inhaled and held it, hoping to release the small knot in her chest. After missions, Sam was always impatient to return home, to the outpost, but she felt an ache now. This mission had been tough, physically, mentally, and emotionally. Echo wasn't temporary anymore, and now she didn't want to leave. Sam exhaled slowly. She didn't want to go through another round of goodbyes.

The door opened and the music and background clamor filtered in, disturbing her quiet space. It was time to go. Scott was probably at the DFAC getting in a last Station meal before their long trip back. Sam would meet up with him at the dorm before they made their way to the military's secured docks.

A few strides out of the lavatory, she bumped into someone else. She hadn't heard them in the hall and mumbled an apology. A pleasant touch of cinnamon lifted in her nose as she looked up into a familiar face.

It was Miriam.

Sam realized she had automatically thrust out her hands to stabilize herself and the other woman. She released them now, her arms dropping awkwardly to her sides. She was too close and gingerly stepped around the medic.

"Hey," Sam said.

"Hey back." Miriam smirked. "Was I too quiet again?"

"Yeah." Sam's heart pounded.

"Sorry. I'll start whistling or something. Having a good time?"

Sam scoffed and tipped her head to the side. "Not as much as Nas and Kai."

Miriam laughed.

Sam loved that sound.

"They're all definitely letting loose. More than usual. It's been…"

"It's been tough. But we got through it." Sam nodded as she tried to ignore her heartbeat whooshing in her ears.

The medic looked at her for a moment. "You're leaving?"

Sam suppressed her surprise. How did Miriam always seem to know things? She shrugged. "It's getting close, and I still have a few things to pack. Maybe get some chow at the DFAC…" Sam paused. "Krill's going to meet us at the docks. I think I'm going to slip out." Sam closed her mouth firmly. She was talking too much.

"And you weren't going to say bye? To me?"

Sam tensed. "I—no, I—" she blubbered before she saw Miriam's growing grin. Sam relaxed a little, but her heart continued to race, and the knot tightened in her chest. "I…I already said a round of goodbyes. I don't think I can do any more."

Miriam scrutinized Sam with her kind brown eyes. "Yeah. Might be for the best."

They fell into silence again as the bass and beat in the main room slowed.

Miriam broke the spell first. "I expect updates, messages. Seriously, stay in contact. You—"

Sam closed the distance and kissed Miriam, pulling her core into the warmth of the other woman.

Their lips separated briefly as Miriam pulled back. Her eyes were wide and searched for a moment. Sam felt a flicker of uncertainty, but then it was gone as Miriam eagerly pushed forward and returned with a deeper kiss.

Sam melted into it.

31

THE MEDIC

INITIALLY, Miriam had a different idea of who their visiting teammates would be. Fox had mentioned "golden twins" and she understood the blonde reference, but the Ursus recon duo hadn't been twins at all. The siblings shared their hair color and some facial likeness, but that was pretty much it. The woman was pretty, slightly plain in the face, but very well-built. Miriam had worked with less.

"Tan."

She froze mid-step then pivoted back to her friend and peer. "Yes, boss?"

Krill stabbed a finger in the air. "Stop calling me that."

Miriam grinned and shrugged. "Mr. Bigshot got promoted."

"Don't…don't be a prick."

She shot a toothy smile at the Echo lead. Krill had deserved the contract, of course. But it wouldn't stop her or Yuri from teasing him. She shoved her hands into her pockets, innocent-like. "You know we keep you grounded. Can't let that head get too big."

He started to say something but caught himself. Krill sighed in resignation instead. "She's not another conquest. Can you *please* keep your pants on until we're done?"

Miriam jerked back. "I have no idea what you're talking about."

"I'm serious, Tan. I know you. Don't."

"You're not giving Fox the talk?"

He chuffed.

Miriam stared rebelliously at Krill. He didn't normally care about her social activities, but she knew this mission meant a lot to him—it was his first big assignment from Command since he started the new lead contract. She threw up her hands in defeat. Despite her love for a good challenge and the prospect of a fun romp, Miriam could be professional and hold off for one mission.

"Aye aye, bossman." *She leaned forward, saluted, then slipped out of the team room before Krill could throw anything at her.*

⏚

Brrt. Brrt.

Miriam Tanner stirred as a discarded commcuff trilled against the apartment floor. She turned over and ignored the juddering sound. Warm, naked skin skimmed against hers and she reached out to caress the smooth arm draped over her bare midsection.

Sam. The kiss.

Miriam smiled into her pillow and drifted back into sleep.

⏚

To her knowledge, the siblings still hadn't talked since she and Sam had overheard Scott and Yuri's conversation after the Charonite ambush. Miriam shielded her eyes from the rain and glanced back at the two: Sam trailed twenty paces behind, and her brother was further, taking up the rear. She thought about falling back, but hesitated. She had never seen someone compartmentalize so well. Sam looked fine now, but Miriam had been there in her breakdown.

"You haven't made a move yet," Fox said.

Miriam ignored him.

"Blondie. The Valkyrie."

She knew who he was talking about.

"She's nice on the eyes an' all, damn skilled, but a bit flat on personality, yeah?"

"That's harsh," Miriam grumbled.

"Oh, come on. I know you agree with me. You're just bein' nice 'n all cause you're tryin' to wiggle your way in. The Valkyrie only knows how to be a marine."

*"*You *only know how to be a marine."*

Fox laughed. "Exactly. So I know what I'm sayin'."

Miriam felt a pang of pity for the Ursus poster child. The Valkyrie. Sam.

Her teammate leaned in, unsatisfied with her lack of response. "Come on, you hit on everythin' with tits... And yeah, I am jealous. Because for some reason, they're always willin' to follow you back into the bedroom."

"I do not hit on everything with...tits." Her jaw set.

Fox laughed heartily. He was the only one who found it funny. "Are you fuckin' with me? Miss Womanizer isn't into the hot, badass blonde?"

Miriam picked up her pace. Maybe she could outwalk him.

"I'm just sayin'," he said as he matched her stride. "I'd try, but she's not into me."

Of course Sam wasn't. Fox was too rough around the edges. Or was she into that? Miriam's throat briefly constricted, but when she swallowed, the tightness was gone.

"She's not into anyone else for that matter. If anyone's actually lookin', it's obvious."

Miriam wasn't stupid. She was aware of Sam's attention and reactions—normally the time to pounce if it were anyone else—but Miriam had already backed off on her initial flirtations. Something about Sam made Miriam want to know her better, even protect her (if only emotionally) and maintain their friendship. Miriam didn't want to mess it up.

"She's a teammate, Fox," Miriam warned.

"Has that stopped you before?"

No, it hadn't. Miriam couldn't remember their names, but a slew of blurry faces, old peers, and colleagues sorted through her mind.

"Plus, she's only visitin'," Fox added. "Temporary teammate."

She glared at him.

"Oh, come off it. Are you hearin' yourself? Is this not the perfect scenario for you?"

Fox wasn't wrong. Normally, it would have been ideal. The likelihood of Sam returning to Station, to Echo specifically, was slim. But Sam wasn't just a conquest. Miriam didn't want to disappoint her; she had seen the look on the faces of her previous companions, and it was easy for her to brush those off. She didn't know if she could do the same with Sam.

"She's a friend," Miriam said.

Fox flashed another smug grin. "Is she just?"

"Yes. She's a friend," Miriam said again. "Can't say the same about you though."

"No no." Fox took a couple long steps to look her fully in the face. He squinted and paused, and Miriam passed him. He caught back up to her. "Shitfuck, Tan. You…like her."

Miriam rolled her eyes, pinched her mouth, and looked past him.

Fox chuckled as he drew closer. "Fine, I'll leave it." He lengthened his stride to catch up to Jun. A few meters ahead, he swiveled around. "Jus' think it's a waste, you know. She's fit."

If he had been closer, Miriam would've punched him.

⏚

Brrt. Brrt. Brrt.

Miriam groaned. The consequences of alcohol were now

hammering against her skull with each new vibration. She peeked an eye open, attempting to retain her sleepiness. The clock across the room flared with large, red numbers. It was too early. She had only fallen asleep a few hours prior.

Brrt. Brrt.

A small light blinked for attention from the ground below. Who was blowing up her notifications?

She shifted and searched for the cuff with one hand, hoping that if she kept her eyes closed, she could return to her slumber. Her fingers finally touched the cool, metal band. Holding the cuff close to her face, she squinted at its display.

A notification was pinned in all capital letters at the top of the screen. Her eyes shot open. Miriam read it again.

ALL STATIONS—URSUS UNDER ATTACK

The message had come in almost ten minutes ago. She ripped the blanket back, and the cool air in her apartment prickled her naked body. She ignored the curvy figure lying next to hers. What was her name again? The woman from the bar. She couldn't remember her face.

Miriam sprung out of the bed, setting the cuff on the stand. It continued to vibrate as notifications poured in. She ran to her closet.

The other figure mumbled and shifted, woken up by the sudden movement in the room. Miriam flicked on the main lights and rushed into the small kitchen to find her boots. In the periphery of her vision, she saw the woman in the bed slowly sit up, rubbing her eyes.

"What's going on? What time is it?" she said.

Miriam ignored her and shoved a foot into one boot. She rushed around the room, trying to figure out where she had tossed the other shoe. The commcuff continued to buzz. She needed to get to the team room.

She spied the familiar sole sticking out from under the bed and sprawled for it. Miriam pulled the remaining boot over her foot, grabbed her cuff, and sprinted out of the apartment into the warm, dusk air. The faint colors of the blue hour raked into the room before the door closed.

◯

Sam kissed her.

She hadn't expected it, and Miriam pulled back in surprise. When she did, the distance was unbearable. She closed the space again, her lips and tongue touching Sam's, dancing, meeting again and again. The dingy back corridor of Duncan's fell away, and time and space around her stood still.

Miriam touched Sam's face. Her jawline. Her neck. Everything was so soft, so warm. So…real and right.

Right? What was she doing?

She pulled away again, but hovered close enough. Sam softly exhaled, recuperating. The woman's breath was sweet, with alcohol at the tip of it. Her warm breath tickled Miriam's lips. Was Sam drunk?

Was she drunk?

Her voice was low and quiet as she stammered, "Sam… We… I can't."

Sam took another breath, deeper this time, and pulled away. Miriam held back from drawing the other woman to her—that space was too far, too distant. Sam sighed, and a thin smile pulled at one side of her mouth.

Miriam was suddenly aware of her hands still in the air, where Sam had once been, and she brought them back to herself.

"It's okay," Sam whispered.

Miriam's mind scrambled. The walls felt like they were expanding, and she had nothing to fill the space. She wanted to say something, but no words formed. She cleared her throat and tried again. "You're my friend. I'm sorry—"

Sam raised a hand with a wince. Miriam glanced at the dark ink on her forearm and the pale scar through it, the same arm that had saved her in the first days of the mission.

"Mir. It's okay. I'm sorry, I..." Sam paused, and her jaw clenched as she rubbed the back of her arm. "I have to get going." She motioned to an exit door Miriam hadn't noticed before. "I'll see you when I see you?"

The words hung in the air.

Isn't this what Miriam wanted? To be friends? She didn't want to mess anything up, right? What did she want?

But she *was* messing this up. "Yeah." And then she said it again more confidently. Miriam desperately searched for something else to say, but nothing came.

Sam took a few steps backward to the door. She paused just shy of the exit and angled slightly away, biting her bottom lip. Those blue eyes pierced into Miriam again, and she couldn't look away.

"Make sure Fox is okay?" Sam said as she palmed the door open.

Miriam nodded.

"Okay. Be safe. It was...really great to, uh, get to know you."

Miriam wanted to stop her, to say something and redo the dumb situation they were now in. Instead, she chuckled, and replied, "Yeah. You as well."

Sam flitted through the doorway and was gone.

Miriam's face fell as the door slid shut.

What just happened?

She clenched her hands, stretched out her fingers, then clenched them into fists again. Wordless emotions swirled in her mind, brewing and never forming into coherent letters and lines. She stood for a while staring at the door, blinking. Then she ran a hand over her hair.

"Shit."

32

PRIVATE MESSAGE
[TANNER TO RYAN]

M. TANNER: Are you guys okay?

Message undeliverable

M. TANNER: Sam, ping me when you can.

Message undeliverable

33

LESION

WHEN ECHO ARRIVED at the northernmost outpost with Station's supporting units, the last fire was still raging. They had gotten a full view of the destruction in the silky morning light as their airship circled and landed in a field some distance to the east. Ursus's airfield had been pocked with craters, rippled pavement where bombs had impacted.

Engineers, communication specialists, and other marines and medical teams flitted about the field in a hastily set-up camp. Boxes, equipment, and supplies were unloaded and loaded into shuttles and rabbits, whatever had space, as they hurried to the outpost's aid. The radiant sun and cooler temperature contrasted against the charred and crushed buildings in front of them.

Razor teams, Echo and Foxtrot, were the only SOG units amongst the other reinforcement platoons sent out—Miriam said a quick thanks to their former Intel teammate who had plenty of connections in Command. UMF had been concerned about sending too many troops away from the city with the still unknown reasons behind the surprise attack on Ursus.

Command was also limited, with several resources already tasked to Temunco and the south.

Echo now huddled in a small circle away from the large ships, closer to the tents and tarps that LOGS had hastily set up at the end of the vast field. The SOG marines were fully armored and kitted, and their stupor from their drunk shenanigans the night before had been turbulently ejected.

As Krill and Yuri talked about their search-and-rescue objectives, Miriam half listened and checked her commcuff again. Her messages to Sam remained undelivered, including her last text sent hours ago before they left Station. Yuri had relayed to the group that the attack had taken out the outpost's communication towers and other important network equipment.

She tapped in another line and sent it.

> M. TANNER: We're here in Ursus.

She stared at the message, waiting for the network response. The communications teams had set up makeshift equipment, and the long-range repeaters on the airships were helping boost the signal. She secured some stray hair behind her ear as a departing ship gusted air at them.

> **Message delivered**

Miriam's breath hitched as she watched the previous messages' status change to delivered one after the other. She waited, hope increasing.

But still no response.

Miriam pushed the wave of thoughts out of her head. There could be a myriad of reasons why Sam and Scott weren't responding: the attack happened too early in the morning, they might have left their commcuffs in their rooms on the way to the safe havens, or they were too busy with other efforts. Or maybe their cuffs had broken in the attack. There were a lot of explanations.

She stepped away from the group as Krill reviewed the logistics and outpost map. Miriam ignored Yuri's questioning eyebrow and keyed her visor on a direct line.

"Sam," she whispered. "Sam, come in."

Miriam waited, willing a response.

She tried again.

Nothing.

"Tan!" Yuri waved to her.

Echo was ready to move.

◯

Miriam had never been to Ursus, but the outposts and Station generally followed the same structure and layout. Even if she had known where she was walking, she wasn't certain she would recognize it. She couldn't tell where the roads and flattened buildings were indistinguishable from each other. Firebombs hadn't hit this outpost, like the wunbies' attack in Temunco. Something much larger, more sinister had impacted nearby and turned its surroundings into an apocalyptic horror. The burns and charred lashes seared across fallen walls, beams, and structures.

Miriam wandered away from Yuri and Nas and took in the severity of damage. Echo had separated into two to check this quadrant, what used to be on-compound housing, but within the first hour, she knew this place was too quiet, still smoldering with death. Whoever was still alive had already moved to safe havens while casualties moved to triage tents.

She stepped around a pile of burned debris and felt a fleshy squish under her foot. Dread rushed through her body. Miriam didn't want to look down knowing what was underneath, but she finally did. A scorched section of unrecognizable human remains had flattened underneath her boot. She pulled her foot away.

Sorry. She sent a prayer for whomever it had been.

Miriam Tanner was a combat medic and had worked on some terrible injuries and scenes in Station and its nearby towns, but this felt different. Since her training days, she had created a game in her mind, a coping mechanism perhaps to desensitize or separate herself. Treating someone and saving lives was a race against time. And she was fast. And effective.

But here, she was far too late. The race clock had long expired. She could smell death, and only death in this place.

She looked around again, and her attention caught on a pile of scattered debris. A patch of skin peeked out from under a large metal pane the size of a cot, and her breath fluttered.

She was wrong.

Oh hell, she was wrong.

Someone was underneath.

An urgency filled her, desperate for relief, and she pulled scrap away. Once cleared, she lifted the side of the panel.

The world froze at that moment.

Yuri called out for her in the near distance, but all the blood in her head had rushed away, dampening her hearing. Her heart had plunged into her gut.

"Tan!" he called out again.

Miriam blinked and turned slowly in her best friend's direction some ways off, a block, a kilometer away, she didn't know.

"Hey! We found one!" Yuri waved his arms at her, but she had trouble focusing on his moving limbs.

Miriam gave one last, long look and carefully set the metal sheet back down. She stepped away, stumbling over loose rubble.

"Coming," she whispered.

And she left.

She was a SOG combat medic, and she was needed. The game, the race against time was on with whomever Yuri and Nas had found.

But underneath that pane, Miriam had already lost.

If she had known herself a little better, she would have admitted she lost a part of her the second she set eyes on that bloodied body part.

An arm, alone, detached from its person.

Miriam knew it well. She had only spent the last week looking at it.

The circle and the scar.

ACKNOWLEDGMENTS

First and foremost, this book would never have happened without my lifeline and partner, Claudia. Thank you for your patience and tolerating my irritable change and transition back from Iraq. Even though I don't believe any of your compliments on this book (you're inherently biased and a *non-fiction* reader), your unending support is everything. Buckle up, I've still got at least two more books to painfully finish before I'm moving on from this "hobby." I love you.

To my dear friend, Katie P. for encouraging me throughout this process and continuing our silly high school banter. Thanks for beta reading, fielding all my random spurts of texts and memes throughout this process, and not unfriending me every time I voice my doubt. I will always value your feedback and opinion, but I'm not writing a spicy scene. Stop it.

To my gaming friend, Robin G., who I finally met IRL after some years (and in Paris of all places), for recommending me the web series that was my cringe catalyst. You are still the only person to have read my first and only screenplay draft, and let's keep it that way. Thanks for beta reading as well. Start writing your damn novel!

To my editors, Lauren H. and Paige L., for helping make this book digestible and easier on everyone's eyes. They say write the story you want to read, but after reading this 2,379 times, I'm blind to my mistakes (and just tired of it). This whole thing is a first for me and your professionalism and feedback was monumental.

To my other beta readers: Gavin E., Rob M., and Tessy D. for your amazing feedback to this new writer. As someone who doesn't know how to take compliments, I truly appreciate your critiques and constructive guidance.

To my friends and proofreaders: Jessica L., Samantha O., Brett B., and Chris G., for your eagle eyes. I'm sure there will always be typos and mistakes, but because of you, it's much less.

To my designer, Jason A. for your talent and expertise, especially taking this amateur graphic designer's concept and creating the final, amazing cover.

To my audiobook narrator, Savannah G. for your patience and wonderful performance. You elevated the characters and stories, and helped scratch an itch on my compromise from screenplay to novel.

To Cody S., who continues to not only be my sounding board, but also my work BFF and accountability partner. Your belief in me is crazy.

To Tom C., Carrie Z., Amy T., Amanda B., Sofi B., Juancho C., Mallory S., Dan E., Liv L., and all my in-laws, friends and trauma-bound colleagues who have checked in and provided encouragement along the way. How have I deserved this kind of love?

To my immediate family, who although not always verbally affirming (thanks, Asian culture), *do* support my constantly-changing interests even if they make fun of me or don't know what I'm actually doing. Your direct and indirect pressure for me to be excellent and never settle for less, has both shaped who I am and traumatized me. It's okay, we still love each other, and I turned out okay. Better than okay. If you're going to read any of this, just stick to the Acknowledgments and Glossary. I don't think I can handle the embarrassment.

To my former therapist, who got me to realize that this

fixation isn't healthy, because I don't know how to properly chill and enjoy "hobbies" as actual hobbies. It was what I needed to accept for my own mental wellness and see this as a "project," not a hobby.

To my former supervisor who contributed to this perfect storm, I guess a thank you is also at hand. If not for your micromanagement, condescension, and ability to plummet an entire office's morale, I wouldn't have lost all motivation in my day job. You broke me down in that assignment and all that productivity had to go somewhere (I threw it into this).

And to you, who gave this book and new author a chance.

Thank you.

Thank you.

Thank you.

OF ABRASION
SNEAK PEEK

The story continues in Book 2 of the Altered Earth series.

Miriam hadn't shared what she found in the early hours of their search-and-rescue effort. Even now, as she stood outside a hasty triage station where some of her teammates had just dropped off another Ursus colleague, Miriam couldn't find her voice. She couldn't bear the idea of saying it out loud to Kai, to Fox, or anyone. She was holding on to a fraying thread of hope that the tattooed and scarred flesh she had seen was only a dream. A figment of her imagination. It wasn't real. Not yet. So she held her discovery in, and it sat like a clump of lead in her throat.

"Guys!"

Miriam's eyes slowly focused and latched on to her teammate as he waved his hands, jogging toward her and the two others.

As Nas grew closer, his mouth turned downward in a frown. "Look," he panted as he thrust out his left wrist. His commcuff display was illuminated, showing a network feed.

Kai shook her head and deftly swiped two fingers across the

cuff, throwing the visual out onto a holodisplay. The four SOG marines watched as a white-haired man gestured his hands, his mouth moving.

Fox stepped forward to complete the huddle around Nas's wrist and holo. "What is this? Turn it up," he growled.

Miriam could smell the alcohol on his breath and skin. They had all been at Duncan's back in Station just the previous night. The night before all this happened. The night where she had been kissed and kissed back... Hurt spiked into her chest, and her breath caught at the remembrance of regret. If she hadn't pushed Sam away, would Sam have stayed in Station with her?

Nas's fingers fumbled with his device, and the man's voice grew clear. "Today, we say no more..."

Miriam blinked and shook her thoughts away. What she had seen wasn't real. It could've been someone else.

"No more to the falsifiers sitting on that hill, in that palace...'"

It *had* to be someone else. Miriam focused on the feed.

"No more to the unjust, criminal tyrants. No more to the oppressors. We shall restore our freedom, our rights to this world that we—*we* have cultivated..."

Miriam's eyes widened as the man's eyes pierced the screen. Green, blue, and brown flecks glowed as he paused while a large crowd roared in the background. An icy shiver ran up Miriam's spine. She folded her arms across her chest in a self-embrace.

"Who...where is this?" Kai said.

"Arshangol. Him..." Nas shook his head and lowered the cuff's volume as a group of wounded marines walked by. "We don't know yet."

On the screen, the white-haired man continued his speech, his hands moving passionately. Kai's eyes grew, then narrowed as she watched and digested her teammate's response. Her voice returned in a whisper. "Wunbies?"

"I don't know," Nas responded.

"Where did you get this?"

"Jace. BigInt. Apparently this is circulating on every feed in alty territories."

Miriam's forehead wrinkled. "This is live?"

"No. It's been playing on repeat along with footage of the… attack here. The original broadcast must've been a couple hours ago."

Kai's hand drifted to her mouth. "Hell…"

But before she could say anything else, Fox gestured for Nas to turn the volume back up.

"The Royals and their cronies have committed hideous acts against their own. They are obsessed with their blood and hoard their science, but all of this, this city, this wealth, was built on our backs. They have forgotten that we are the many, we are the people, and we are their strength. *We* are the power."

Screams and cries rang out in a chorus off-display.

"Your future is in your hands. We are one blood. We are the Promised, and our time is now. Your time is now!"

A soft, stomping rhythm stirred in the background, wrapped in static from Nas's device. Fox clenched his jaw, and Miriam glanced down to see his fists ball up. She realized that she, too, had tightened her own grip on her arms, her fingernails digging into her skin.

"Take back what was promised!"

GLOSSARY

Alterado—Human slang for Altered in the southern region

Alty—Human slang for Altered

Apostates—Also known as The Promised

Arshangol—The capital city of the Altered; where the Royal Court resides and governs

Carbine—A long gun with a shortened barrel

Cardinal Rules of Firearm Safety -

1 Treat every firearm as if it is loaded.

2 Always point your firearm in a safe direction unless defending yourself or others.

3 Always keep your finger off the trigger until you are ready to fire.

4 Always be sure of your target and what is beyond it.

Charonite—Also known as Children of Charon

Children of Charon (COC)—A prominent human-supremacist group

CO—Commanding Officer

Command—UMF's leadership command charged with overseeing the military's operations

Commcuff—A wrist-worn technological device used to communicate and connect to the network

DFAC—Dining Facility; (pronounced dee-fak)

Intel—Intelligence

Legion—A company of Altered soldiers

Legionnaire—An Altered soldier

LOGS—Logistics

Long-range repeater—A device that receives and retransmits a communication signal, extending its range or coverage

LMG—Light Machine Gun

Matam—Large human population center located in the Andes

MED—Medical

MP—Military Police

New Zapala—Southernmost human population center

NVG—Night-Vision Goggles

Praetorian—An elite and special-engineered Altered who reports directly to the Royals

Prowler—A large utility task and terrain vehicle that can carry at least four passengers and cargo

The Promised—A prominent Altered supremacist group

Rabbit—A modular all-terrain vehicle that can carry at least two passengers

Recon—Reconnaissance

Royals/Royal Court—The governing body of the Altered population; legacy of original genetically engineered Altered

SecHut—Security Hut; a SecTeam's office

SecTeam—Security Team; a local security force

SOG—Special Operations Group

Sovereign—The highest authority of the Royal Court

Station—Marine term for UMF headquarters just outside of Station City

Station City—Largest human population center located in a central location

Temunco—UMF's southernmost outpost, which overlooks Matam, New Zapala, and other regional settlements; borders Altered territories

TOC—Tactical Operations Center

UMF—United Military Federation; the unified human military that oversees the defense and security of the entire human population

Ursus—UMF's northernmost outpost, which overlooks Gould and other regional settlements; borders Altered territories

Visor—A head-worn technological device used to communicate and assist with tactics

Wunby—Human slang for The Promised/Apostates based on their mantra, "one blood, one promise"

Yoomy—Slang for UMF

ABOUT THE AUTHOR

S.J. Lee is a foreign service specialist by day, gamer and photographer by night. She has lived and worked in Iraq, Mexico, Chile, India, Brazil, and Guyana, and currently resides in the United States with her spouse and dog. *Of Friction* is her debut novel.

instagram.com/sjleewriter

Printed in Great Britain
by Amazon